William Gilmore Simms

Richard Hurdis

A Tale of Alabama

William Gilmore Simms

Richard Hurdis
A Tale of Alabama

ISBN/EAN: 9783337072186

Printed in Europe, USA, Canada, Australia, Japan

Cover: Foto ©Andreas Hilbeck / pixelio.de

More available books at **www.hansebooks.com**

RICHARD HURDIS:

A

TALE OF ALABAMA.

BY W. GILMORE SIMMS,

AUTHOR OF "THE YEMASSEE," "THE PARTISAN," "MELLICHAMPE," "KATHARINE WALTON," "THE SCOUT," "WOODCRAFT," ETC.

> "I will recall
> Some facts of ancient date.   He must remember
> When, on Citheron, we together fed
> Our several flocks."
>
> SOPHOC, Ædip. Tyran.

New and Revised Edition.

CHICAGO AND NEW YORK:

BELFORD, CLARKE & CO.

1888.

RICHARD HURDIS.

CHAPTER I.

A TRUANT DISPOSITION.

" Enough of garlands, of the Arcadian crook,
  And all that Greece and Italy have sung
  Of swains reposing myrtle graves among!
  Ours couch on naked rocks, will cross a brook,
  Swollen with chill rains, nor ever cast a look
  This way or that, or give it even a thought
  More than by smoothest pathway may be brought
  Into a vacant mind. Can written book
  Teach what to learn?"—WORDSWORTH.

Of the hardihood of the American character there can be no doubts, however many there may exist on the subject of our good manners. We ourselves seem to be sufficiently conscious of our security on the former head, as we forbear insisting upon it; about the latter, however, we are sore and touchy enough. We never trouble ourselves to prove that we are sufficiently able and willing, when occasion serves, to do battle, tooth and nail, for our liberties and possessions; our very existence, as a people, proves this ability and readiness. But let John Bull prate of our manners, and how we fume and fret, and what fierce action and wasteful indignation we expend upon him! We are sure to have the last word in all such controversies.

Our hardihood comes from our necessities, and prompts our enterprise; and the American is bold in adventure to a proverb. Where the silk-shodden and sleek citizen of the European world would pause and deliberate to explore our wilds, we plunge incontinently forward ; and the forest falls before our axe, and the desert blooms under the providence of our cultivator, as if the wand of an enchanter had waved over them with the rising of a sudden moonlight. Yankee necessities, and southern and western curiosity, will probe to the very core of the dusky woods, and palsy, by the exhibition of superior powers, the very souls of their old possessors.

I was true to the temper and the nature of my countrymen. The place in which I was born could not keep me always. With manhood—ay, long before I was a man—came the desire to range. My thoughts craved freedom, my dreams prompted the same desire, and the wandering spirit of our people, perpetually stimulated by the continual opening of new regions and more promising abodes, was working in my heart with all the volume of a volcano. Manhood came and I burst my shackles. I resolved upon the enjoyment for which I had dreamed and prayed. I had no fears, for I was stout of limb, bold of heart, prompt in the use of my weapon, a fearless rider, and a fatal shot. Here are the inevitable possessions of the southern and western man, from Virginia to the gulf, and backward to the Ohio. I had these, with little other heritage, from my Alabama origin, and I was resolved to make the most of them as soon as I could. You may be sure I lost no time in putting my resolves into execution. Our grain-crops in Marengo were ripe in August, and my heart bounded with the unfolding of the sheaves. I was out of my minority in the same fortunate season.

I waited for the coming October only. I felt that my parents had now no claims upon me. The customs of our society, the necessities of our modes of life, the excursive and adventurous habits of our people, all justified a desire, which, in a stationary community, would seem so adverse to the nicer designs of humanity. But the life in the city has very few standards in common with that of the wilderness. We acknowledge few at least. The impulses of the latter, to our minds, are worth any day all the mercantile wealth of the former; and that we are sincere in this opinion may be fairly inferred from the preference which the forester will always show for the one over the other region. Gain is no consideration for those who live in every muscle, and who find enjoyment from the exercise of every limb. The man who lives by measuring tape and pins by the sixpence worth, may make money by his vocation—but, God help him! he is scarce a man. His veins expand not with generous ardor; his muscles wither and vanish, as they are unemployed; and his soul—it has no emotions which prompt him to noble restlessness, and high and generous exertion. Let him keep at his vocation if he will, but he might, morally and physically, do far better if he would.

My resolves were soon known to all around me. They are not yet known to the reader. Well, they are quickly told. The freed youth at twenty-one, for the first time free, and impatient only for the exercise of his freedom, has but few purposes, and his plans are usually single and unsophisticated enough. Remember, I am speaking for the forester and farmer, not for the city youth who is taught the arts of trade from the cradle up, and learns to scheme and connive while yet he clips the coral in his boneless gums. I was literally going abroad, after the fashion of the poorer youth of our neighborhood, to seek my fortune. As yet I had but little of my own. A fine horse, a few hundred dollars in specie, three able-bodied negroes, a good rifle, which carried eighty to the pound, and was the admiration of many who were even better shots than myself—these made pretty much the sum total of my earthly possessions. But I thought not much of this matter. To ramble a while, at least until my money was all gone, and then to take service on shares with some planter who had land and needed the help of one like myself, was all my secret. I had heard of the Chickasaw Bluffs, and of the still more recent Choctaw purchase—at that time a land of promise only, as its acquisition had not been effected—and I was desirous of looking upon these regions. The Choctaw territory was reported to be rich as cream; and I meditated to find out the best spots, in order to secure them by entry, as soon as the government could effect the treaty which should throw them into the market. In this ulterior object I was upheld by some of our neighboring capitalists, who had urged, to some extent, the measure upon me. I was not unwilling to do this for them, particularly as it did not interfere in my own plans to follow up theirs; but my own desire was simply to stretch my limbs in freedom to traverse the prairies, to penetrate the swamps, to behold the climbing hills and lovely hollows of the Choctaw lands, and luxuriate in the eternal solitudes of their spacious forests. To feel my freedom was now my hope. I had been fettered long enough.

But do not think me wanting in natural affection to my parents: far from it. I effected no small achievement when I first resolved to leave my mother. It was no pain to leave my father. He was a man, a strong one too, and could do well enough without me. But, without spoiling me, my mother, of all her children, had made me most a favorite. I was *her Richard* always. She considered me first, though I had an elder brother, and spoke of me in particular when speaking of her sons, and referred to me for counsel in preferenc to all the rest. This may have been because I was soon found to be the most decisive of all my brothers; and folks did me the further courtesy to say, the most thoughtful too. My elder brother, John Hurdis, was too fond of eating to be an adventurous man, and too slow and unready to be a performing one. We often quarrelled, too; and this, perhaps, was another reason why I should desire to leave a place from which he was quite too lazy ever to depart. Had he been bold enough to go forth, I might not have been so ready to do so, for there were motives and ties to keep me at home, which shall have developed as I proceed.

My father, though a phlegmatic and proud man, showed much more emotion at the declaration of my resolve to leave him, than I had ever expected. His emotion arose, not so much from the love he bore me, as from the loss which he was about to sustain by my departure. I had been his best negro, and he confessed it. Night and day, without complaint, my time had been almost entirely devoted to his service, and his crops had never been half so good as when I had directed the labor of his force, and regulated his resources. My brother John had virtually given up to me the entire management, and my father was too well satisfied with the fruits of the change to make any objection. My resolution to leave him now, once more threw the business of the plantation upon John; and his incompetence, the result of his inertness and obesity, rather than of any deficiency of mind, was sorely apprehended by the old man. I felt this to be the strongest argument against my departure. But was I always to be the slave I had been? Was I always to watch peas and potatoes, corn and cotton, without even the poor satisfaction of choosing the spot where it would please me best to watch them? This reflection strengthened me in my resolves, and answered my father. In answer to the expostulation of my mother, I made a promise, which in part consoled her.

" I will go but for a few months, mother — for the winter only; you will see me back in spring; and then if father and myself can come to anything like terms, I will stay and superintend for him, as I have done before."

' Terms, Richard! " were the old lady's words in reply; " what terms would you have, my son, that he will not agree to, so that they be in reason? He will give you one-fifth — I will answer for it, Richard — and that ought to be quite enough to satisfy any one."

" More than enough, mother; more than I ask or expect. But I can not now agree even to that. I must see the world a while; travel about; and if, at the end of the winter, I see no better place — no place, I mean, which I could better like to live in — why then I will come back, as I tell you, and go to work as usual."

There was some little indignation in the old lady's answer:

" Better place! like better to live in! Why, Richard, what has come over you? Are not the place you were born in, and the parents who bred you, and the people whom you have lived with all your life — are they not good enough for you, that you must come to me at this time of day, and talk about better places, and all such stuff? Really, my son, you forget yourself to speak in this manner. As if everything was not good enough for you here!"

" Good enough, mother," I answered gloomily; " good enough; perhaps — I deny it not; and yet not exactly to my liking. I am not pleased to waste my life as I do at present. I am not satisfied that I do myself justice. I feel a want in my mind, and an impatience at my heart; a thirst which I can not explain to you, and which, while here, I can not quench. I must go elsewhere—I must fix my **eyes on other** objects. You forget, too, **that** I have been repulsed, rejected—though you told me I should not be—where I had set **my heart**; and that the boon **has** been given to another, for which **I had** struggled long, and for **a** long season had hoped to attain. Can you wonder that I should seek to go abroad, even were I not moved by a natural desire at my time of life to see some little of the world?"

There were some portions of my reply which were conclusive, and to which my mother did not venture any answer; but my last remark suggested the tenor of a response which she did not pause to make.

"But what **can you see of** the world, my son, among the wild places to which **you** think to **go?** What can you see at the Bluffs, or down by the Yazoo but woods and Indians? Besides, Richard, the Choctaws are said to be troublesome **now in** the nation. Old Mooshoolatubbé and La Fleur are going to **fight, and** it will be dangerous travelling."

"The very thing, mother," was my hasty reply. "**I** will take side with La Fleur, and when we have to fight Mooshoolatubbé, **get** enough land for my reward, to commence business for **myself.** That last speech of yours, mother, is conclusive in my favor. I will be a rich man yet; and then"—in the bitterness of a disappointed spirit I spoke—"and then, mother, we will **see** whether John Hurdis is a better man with thirty negroes than Richard Hurdis with but three.

"Why, who says he is, my son?" demanded my mother with a tenderness of accent which increased while she spoke, and with eyes that filled with tears in the same instant.

My heart told me I was wrong, but I could not **forbear the** reply that rose to my lips.

"Mary Easterby," were the two words which made my only answer.

"Richard, Richard!" exclaimed the old lady, "you envy your brother."

"Envy him! No! I envy him nothing, **not even** his better fortune. Let him wear **what he has** won, whether **he** be worthy of it or **not. If,** knowing **me, she** prefers him, be it so. She is not the woman for **me. I envy not** his **possessions;** neither

his wife, nor his servant, his ox, nor his ass. It vexes me that
I have been mistaken, mother, both in her, and in him; but,
thank Heaven! I envy neither. I am not humble enough for
that."

"My dear Richard, you know that I have always sought to
make you happy. It grieves me that you are not so. What would
you have me do for you?"

"Let me go forth in peace. Say nothing to my father to prevent it. Seem to be satisfied with my departure yourself. I will try
to please you better when I return."

"You ask too much, my son: but I will try. I will do anything
for you, if you will only think and speak less scornfully of your elder
brother."

"And what are my thoughts and words to him, mother? He
feels them not — they do not touch him. Is he not my elder brother?
Has he not all? The favor of our grandmother gave him wealth,
and with his wealth, and from his wealth, comes the favor of
Mary Easterby."

"You do her wrong!" said my mother.

"Do I, indeed?" I answered bitterly. "What! she takes
him then for his better person, his nobler thoughts, his boldness,
his industry, and the thousand other manly qualities, so winning
in a woman's eyes, which I have not, but which he possesses in
such plenty? Is it this that you would say, my mother? Say it
then if you can; but well I know you must be silent. You can
not speak, mother, and speak thus. For what then has Mary
Easterby preferred John Hurdis? God forgive me if I do her
wrong, and Heaven's mercy to her if she wrongs herself and me.
At one time I thought she loved me, and I showed her some like
follies. I will not say that she has not made me suffer; but I rejoice
that I can suffer like a man. Let me go from you in quiet, dear
mother; urge my departure, and believe, as I think, that it will be
for the benefit of all."

My father's entrance interrupted a conversation, which neither of
us was disposed readily to assume.

CHAPTER II.

MARY EASTERBY.

"There was but one
  In whom my heart took pleasure amongst women;
  One in the whole creation; and in her
  You dared to be my rival."—*Second Maiden's Tragedy.*

THE reader has discovered my secret. I had long loved
Mary Easterby, and without knowing it. The knowledge
came to me at the moment when I ceased to hope. My brother
was my rival, and, whatever were the charms he used, my successful rival. This may have given bitterness to the feeling of
contempt with which his own feebleness of character had taught
me to regard him. It certainly took nothing from the barrier,
which circumstances and time had set up as a wall between us.
Mary Easterby had grown up beside me. I had known no
other companion among her sex. We had played together
from infancy, and I had been taught to believe, when I came
to know the situation of my own heart, and to inquire into that
of hers, that she loved me. If she did not, I deceived myself
most wofully; but such self-deception is no uncommon practice
with the young of my age, and sanguine temperament. I
would not dwell upon her charms could I avoid it; yet though
I speak of, I should fail to describe and do not hope to do
them justice. She was younger by three years than myself,
and no less beautiful than young. Her person was tall, but not
slight; it was too finely proportioned to make her seem tall,
and grace was the natural result, not less of her physical sym-
metry, than of her maiden taste, and sweet considerateness of
character. Her eye was large and blue, her cheek not so round
as full, and its rich rosy color almost vied with that which
crimsoned the pulpy outline of her lovely mouth. Her hair

was of a dark brown, and she wore it gathered up simply in volume behind, a few stray tresses only being suffered to escape from bondage at the sides, to attest, as it were, the bountiful luxuriance with which nature had endowed her. See these tresses on her round white neck, and let your eye trace them in their progress to the swelling bosom on which they sometimes rested; and you may conceive something of those charms, which I shall not seek further to describe.

Though a dweller in the woods all her life, her mind and taste had not been left without due cultivation. Her father had been taught in one of the elder states, one of the old thirteen, and he carried many of the refinements of city life with him into the wilderness. Books she had in abundance, and these taught her everything of those old communities, which she had never yet been permitted to see. Her natural quickness of intellect, her prompt appreciation of what she read, enabled her at an early period duly to estimate those conventional and improved forms of social life to which her books perpetually referred, and which belong only to stationary abodes, where wealth brings leisure, and leisure provokes refinement. With such aid, Mary Easterby soon stood alone among the neighboring damsels. Her air, manner, conversation, even dress, were not only different from, but more becoming, than those of her associates. She spoke with the ease and freedom of one bred up in the most assured society; and thought with a mind filled with standards which are not often to be met with in an insulated and unfrequented community. In short she was one of those beings such as lift the class to which they belong; such as represent rather a future than a present generation; and such as, by superior grasp of judgment or of genius, prepare the way for, and guide the aims of all the rest.

It were folly to dwell upon her excellences, but that my narration may depend upon their development. They were powerful enough with me; and my heart felt, ere my mind could analyze them. A boy's heart, particularly one who is the unsophisticated occupant of the forests, having few other teachers, is no sluggish and selfish creation, and mine was soo filled with Mary Easterby, and all its hopes and desires depended upon hers for their fulfilment. It was the thought :

all, that hers was **not less dependent upon mine**; and when **the**
increasing intimacy **of the maiden with my** brother, and **his**
confident **demeanor toward herself and** parents, led us all **to**
regard **him as the possessor of those** affections which everybody had supposed to be **mine, the matter was no** less surprising
to all than it was, for a season, bitter and overwhelming to me.
I could have throttled my more fortunate **brother — brother**
though he was — in the first moment of my rage at this discovery; and all my love for Mary did not save her from sundry
unmanly denunciations which I will not now venture to repeat.
I did **not utter these** denunciations in her ears though I uttered
them aloud.   **They** reached her ears, however, and the medium
of communication was **John** Hurdis.   This last baseness aroused
me to open rage against him.   I told him to his teeth he was a
scoundrel; and he bore with the **imputation, and** spoke of our
blood connection as the reason for **his** forbearance to resent an
indignity which, agreeably to our modes of thinking, could only
be atoned for by blood.

"Brother, indeed!" I exclaimed furiously **in reply.**   "No,
John Hurdis, you are no brother **of mine, though our** father
and mother be the same.   I acknowledge no relationship be-
tween us.   We are of **a** different family — of far-removed and
foreign natures.   **My** kindred shall **never be** found among the
base; and from **this moment I** renounce **all** kindred with you.
Henceforth, we know nothing of each other only so far as it may
be necessary to keep from giving pain and offence to our parents.
But we shall not be **long** under that restraint.   I will shortly
leave you to yourself, to your conquests, and the undisturbed
enjoyment of that happiness which you have toiled for so basely at the expense of mine."

He would have explained and expostulated, but I refused to
hear him.   He proffered me his hand, but with a violent blow
of my **own,** I struck it down, and turned my shoulder upon him.
It was thus, in such relationship, that we stood, when I announced
to my mother my intention to leave the family.   We barely spoke
to **one** another when speech was absolutely unavoidable, and it
was soon known to Mary Easterby, **not less than to** the persons
of my own household, that our hearts were lifted in enmity
against each other.   **She seized an early opportunity and** spoke

to me on the subject. Either she mistook the nature of our quarrel, or the character of my affections. Yet how she could have mistaken the latter, or misunderstood the former, I can not imagine. Yet she did so.

"Richard, they say you have quarrelled with your brother."

"Does *he* say it—does John Hurdis say it, Mary?" was my reply.

She paused and hesitated. I pressed the question with more earnestness as I beheld her hesitation. She strove to speak with calmness, but was not altogether successful. Her voice trembled as she replied :—

"He does not, Richard—not in words; but I have inferred it from what he does say, and from the fact that he has said so little. He seemed unwilling to tell me anything."

"He is wise," I replied bitterly; "he is very wise; but it is late. Better he had been thus taciturn always!"

"Why speak you so, Richard?" she continued; "why are you thus violent against your brother? What has he done to vex you to this pass? Let me hear your complaint."

"Complaint! I have none. You mistake me, Mary—I complain not. I complain of nobody. If I can not right my own wrongs, at least, I will not complain of them."

"Oh, be not so proud, Richard! be not so proud!" she replied earnestly; and her long white fingers rested upon my wrist for an instant, and were as instantly withdrawn. But that one touch was enough to thrill to the bone. It was my turn to tremble. She continued—"There is no wisdom in this pride of yours, Richard; it is unbecoming in such frail beings as we are, and it will be fatal to your happiness."

"Happiness!—my happiness! Ah, Mary, if it be my pride only which is to be fatal to my happiness, then I am secure. But I fear not that. My pride is my hope now, my strength. It protects me—it shields my heart from my own weakness."

She looked in my face with glances of the most earnest inquiry for a little while, and then spoke as follows :—

"Richard, there is something now-a-days about you which I do not exactly understand. You utter yourself in a language which is strange to me, and your manners have become strange! Why is this—what is the matter?"

"Nay, Mary; but that should be my question The change
is in you, not me. I am conscious of no change such as you
speak of. But a truce to this. I see you are troubled. Let us
talk of other things."

"I am not troubled, Richard, except on your account. But
as you desire it, let us talk of other things; and, to return, why
this hostility between yourself and your brother?"

"Let him tell you. Demand it of him, Mary; he will better
tell the story than I, as it will probably sound more to his credit than to mine, in your ears!"

"I know not that," she replied; "and know not why you
should think so, Richard, unless you are conscious of having
done wrong; and, if thus conscious, the cure is in your own
hands."

"What!" I exclaimed impetuously. "You would have me
go on my knees to John Hurdis, and humbly ask his pardon,
for denouncing him as a scoundrel ——"

"You have not done this, Richard?" was her sudden inquiry,
silencing me in the middle of my hurried and thoughtless speech.
The error was committed, and I had only to avow the truth.
Gloomily I did so, and with a sort of sullen ferocity that must
have savored very much of the expression of a wolf goaded to
the verge of his den by the spear of the hunter.

"Ay, but I have, Mary Easterby! I have called John Hurdis a scoundrel, and only wonder that he told you not this along
with the rest of my misdoings which he has been careful to relate to you. Perhaps, he might have done so, had the story
spoken more favorably for his manhood."

We had been sitting together by the window while the conversation proceeded; but at this stage of it, she arose, crossed
the apartment slowly, lingered for a brief space at an opposite
window, then quietly returned to her seat. But her eyes gave
proof of the big tears that had been gathering in them.

"Richard, I fear that you are doing me, and your brother
both injustice. You are too quick, too prompt to imagine
wrong, and too ready to act upon your imaginings. You speak
to me with the tone of one who has cause of complaint— of anger! Your eyes have an expression of rebuke which is painful to me —and I think unjust. Your words are sharp, and

sometimes hostile and unfriendly. You are not what you were, Richard—in truth, you are not."

"Indeed! do you think so, Mary?"

"Ay, I do. Tell me, Richard, in what have I done you wrong? Where is my error? Of what do you complain?"

"Have I not told you, Mary, that I have no cause of complaint—that I hold it unmanly to complain? And wherefore should I complain of you?—I have no right. You are mistress of your own words and actions so far as Richard Hurdis is concerned."

The stubborn pride of my spirit was predominant, and the moment of explanation had gone by. A slight sigh escaped her lips as she replied—

"You are not what you used to be, Richard; but I know not what has changed you."

She had spoken soothly—I was not what I was. A dark change had come upon me—a gloomy shadow had passed over my spirit, chilling its natural warmth and clouding its glory The first freshness of my heart's feelings was rapidly passing from me. I had worshipped fruitlessly, if not unwisely; and, if the deity of my adoration was not unworthy of its tribute, it gave back no response of favor to the prayer of the supplicant.

Such were my thoughts—such the conviction which was driving me into banishment. For banishment it was—utter, irrevocable banishment, which I then meditated. The promise given to my mother was meant to soothe her heart, and silence her entreaties. I meant never to return. In deeper forests —in a wilder home—I had resolved to choose me out an abode, which, if it had fewer attractions, had, at the same time, fewer trials for a bosom vexed like mine. I feared not the silence and the loneliness of the Indian habitations, when those to which I had been accustomed, had become, in some respects, so fearful. I dreaded no loneliness so much as that of my own heart, which, having devoted itself exclusively to another, was denied the communion which it sought.

CHAPTER III.

COMRADE IN EXILE.

' Now go we in content
To liberty, and not to banishment."—*As You Like It.*

" Brothers in exile,
Hath **not old** custom made this life more sweet
Than **that** of painted pomp?"—*Same.*

WAS I right in such a resolution ? Was it proper in me, be
cause one had made me **desolate, to make others**—and not that
one—equally so ? I know not. I inquired not thus at the
time, and the question is unnecessary now. **My** resolution was
taken **at** a leap. It was a resolution **made** by my feelings, in
which my thoughts had little part. And yet I reasoned upon
it, and gave stubborn arguments in its defence to others. It is
strange how earnestly the mind will devote itself to the exactions of the blood, and cog, and connive, and cavil, in compliance with the appetites and impulses of the body. The animal
is no small despot when it begins to sway.

In leaving home, however, and going abroad among strangers
I did not purpose to go alone. My arguments, which had **not**
moved myself, had their influence upon another. A young man
of the neighborhood, about my own age, with whom I had been
long intimate, consented to **go** along with **me.** His situation
and motives were alike different from mine. He was not only
a wealthy man, in the estimation **of the** country, but he was for
tunate—perhaps because he was **wealthy**—in the favor and re
gard of a young damsel to whom **he** had proffered vows which
had proved acceptable. **He** was an accepted man, fortunate or
not; and in this particular of fortune he differed from me as
widely as in his moneyed concerns. His property consisted in
negroes and ready money. He had forty of the former, and

some three thousand dollars, part in specie, but the greater part in United States bank notes, then considered quite as good. He wanted lands, and to supply this want was the chief motive for his resolve to set out with me. The damsel to whom he was betrothed was poor, but she wore none of the deportment of poverty. The neighborhood thought her proud. I can not say that I thought with them. She was more reserved than young women commonly, at her time of life—more dignified, thoughtful, and, perhaps, more prudent. She was rather pensive in her manner; and yet there was a quickness of movement in the flashing of her dark black eye, that bespoke sudden resolve, and a latent character which needed but the stroke of trial and the collision of necessity to give forth unquenchable flame. She said little; but that little, when spoken, was ever to the point and purpose, and seemed unavoidable. Yet, though thus taciturn in language, there was speech in every movement of her eyes—in all the play of her intelligent and remarkable features. She was not beautiful—scarcely pretty, if you examined her face with a design to see its charms. But few ever looked at her with such an object. The character which spoke in her countenance was enough, and you forbore to look for other beauties. Emmeline Walker was a thinking and intelligent creature, and her mind pre-occupied yours at a glance, and satisfied you with her, without suffering you to look farther. You felt not as when gazing on mere beauty—you felt that there was more to be seen than was seen—that she had a resource of wealth beyond wealth, and which, like the gift of the fairy, though worthless in its outward seeming was yet inexhaustible in its supplies.

Her lover, though a youth of good sense, and very fair education, was not a man of mind. He was a man to memorize and repeat, not to reason and originate. He could follow promptly, but he would not do to lead. He lacked the thinking organs, and admired his betrothed the more, as he discovered that she was possessed of a readiness, the want of which he had deplored in himself. It is no unfrequent thing with us to admire a quality rather because of our own lack of it, than because of its intrinsic value.

William Carrington was not without his virtues of mind, as

well as of heart. He was temperate in his deportment, forbearing in his prejudices, modest in correspondence with his want of originality, and earnest in his desire of improvement. His disposition was gentle and playful. He laughed too readily, perhaps; and his confidence was quite as free and unrestrainable as his mirth. While my nature, helped by my experience, perhaps, made me jealous, watchful, and suspicious, his, on the other hand, taught him to believe readily, to trust fearlessly, and to derive but little value even from his own experience of injustice. We were not unfit foils, and consequently not unseemly companions for one another.

Carrington was seeking lands, and his intention was to be at the land-sale in Chocchuma, and to purchase with the first fitting opportunity. Having bought, he proposed to hurry back to Marengo, marry, and set forth in the spring of the ensuing year for his new home. His plans were all marked out, and his happiness almost at hand. Emmeline offered no objection to his arrangements, and showed no womanly weakness at his preparations for departure. She gave my hand a gentle pressure when I bade her farewell, and simply begged us to take care of each other. I did not witness the separation between the lovers, but I am convinced that she exhibited far less, yet felt much more than William, and that, after the parting, he laughed out aloud much the soonest of the two. Not that he did not love her. He loved quite as fervently as it was in his nature to love; but his heart was of lighter make and of less earnest temper than hers. He could be won by new colors to a forgetfulness of the cloud which had darkened his spirits, and the moan of his affliction was soon forgotten in gayer and newer sounds. Not so with her. If she did not moan aloud, she could brood in secret, like the dove upon the blasted bough, over her own heart, and, watching its throbs, forget that the world held it no propriety to weep.

CHAPTER IV.

THE HOSTILE GRAPPLE.

Oliver. Know you before whom, sir!

Orlando. Ay, better than he I am before knows me.   I know you are my elder brother; and, in the gentle condition of blood, you should so know me.   The courtesy of nations allows you my better, in that you are the first born; but the same tradition takes not away my blood were there twenty brothers betwixt us.   I have as much of my father in me as you; albeit, I confess your coming before me is nearer to his reverence.

Oliver. What, boy!

Orlando. Come, come, elder brother, you are too young in this.

Oliver. Wilt thou lay hands on me, villain!

Orlando. I am no villain: wert thou not my brother, I would not take this hand from thy throat, till this other had pulled out thy tongue for saying so!   *As You Like It.*

THE time approached which had been appointed for our departure, and the increased beating of my heart warned me of some trial-scenes yet to be undergone.   I knew that I should have little difficulty at parting with my father, and much less with my more fortunate brother.   The parting from my mother was a different matter, as, knowing well the love which she bore me, I was already prepared for her sorrow, if not agony when bidding me farewell.   Besides, resolving in my secret mind never to return, I had a feeling of compunction for my meditated hypocrisy, which added the annoyance of shame to my own sorrow on the occasion.   I did not think less of the final separation from Mary Easterby, but my pride schooled my heart in reference to her.   I resolved that she should see me go without a change of feature, without the quivering of a single muscle.   I resolved to see her.   A more prudent man would nave gone away in silence and in secrecy.   He would have as resolutely avoided as I sought the interview.   But I was not a

prudent man. My feelings were too impetuous, my pride too
ostentatious, to suffer me to hide it from exhibition. To depart
without seeking and seeing Mary would be a tacit acknowledgment of weakness. It would seem that I feared the interview;
that I questioned my own strength to contend against an influence which all around me suspected, but which it was my pride
not to acknowledge even to myself.

The day came preceding that on which I was to depart; and
the dinner was scarcely over, when, ordering my horse, I set
out to go to Squire Easterby's plantation. The distance was
seven miles, a matter of no importance in a country where,
from childhood, the people are used equally to fine horses and
long distances. I rode slowly, however, for I was meditating
what I should say, and how I should demean myself during the
interview which I sought. While I deliberated, I discovered
that I had overtasked my strength. I felt that I loved too ear
nestly not to be somewhat, if not severely, tried. Could it have
been that at that late moment I could have re-resolved, and
without a depreciation of my self-esteem, have turned back, I
feel that I should have done so. But my pride would not suffer
this, and I resolved to leave it to the same pride to sustain and
succor me throughout. To lose emotions which I found it impossible to subdue, I increased the speed of my horse. Striking the rowel into his flanks, and giving him free rein, I
plunged into the solitary yet crowded woods, over a road which
I had often trodden, and which was now filled at every step in
my progress with staring, obtrusive memories, which chattered
as I went in sweet and bitter yet familiar tongues.

How often had I trodden the same region with her, when I
had no fears, and none but pleasant images rose up before my
contemplation! What harmonies were my unspoken, my un-
challenged hopes on those occasions! What pictures of felicity
rose before the mind on every side! Not that I then thought
of love—not that I proposed to myself any plan or purpose
which regarded our union. No! it was in the death of my
hope that I was first taught to know that it had ever lived. It
was only in the moment that I was taught that I loved in vain,
that my boy-heart discovered that it had ever loved at all.
Memories were all that I had rescued from the wreck of hope,

and they were such as I had been most willing to have lost forever. It was but a sad consolation to know how sweet had been those things which I had once known, but which I was doomed to know no longer.

Bitter were the thoughts which attended me as I rode; yet in their very bitterness my soul gathered its strength. The sweets of life enfeeble us. We struggle among them as a greedy fly in the honey which clogs its wings, and fetters it forever. The grief of the heart is sometimes its best medicine, and though it may not give us back the lost, it arms us against loss, and blunts the sensibility which too frequently finds its fate in its own acuteness. From my bitter thoughts I gathered resolution. I remembered the intimacy which had formerly prevailed between us; how we had mutually confided to each other—how I had entirely confided to her; how joint were our sympathies, how impatient our desires to be together; how clearly she must have seen the feelings which I never spoke; how clearly had like feelings in her been exhibited (so I now thought) to me: and, as I dwelt on these memories, I inly resolved that she had trifled with me. She had won me by her arts, till my secret was in her possession, and then, either unmoved herself, or willing to sacrifice her affections to a baser worship, she had given herself to another whom she could not love, but whose wealth had been too great a temptation to her woman-eyes for her feeble spirit to withstand.

That she was engaged to my brother, I never doubted for an instant. It was as little the subject of doubt among the whole neighborhood. Indeed, it was the conviction of the neighborhood, and the old women thereof which produced mine; and then, the evidence seemed utterly conclusive. John Hurdis spoke of Mary Easterby, as if the right were in him to speak for her; and she—she never denied the imputation. It is true I had never questioned her on the subject, nor indeed, do I know that she had ever been questioned by others; but where was the necessity to inquire when there was seemingly so little occasion for doubt? The neighborhood believed, and it was no hard matter for one, so jealous and suspicious as myself, to leap with even more readiness to a like conclusion.

And yet, riding along that road, all my memories spoke

against so strange a faith. It was impossible that she who had
so freely confided to me the fancies and the feeling of her childhood, to whom I had so readily yielded mine, should have given
herself up to another, with whom no such communion had
existed—to whom no such sympathy had been ever shown.
We had sat or reclined under the same tree—we had sought
the same walks together—the same echoes had caught the
tones of our kindred voices, and chronicled, by their responses
from the hill-side and among the groves, the sentiments of our
unfettered hearts. And how could she love another? Her
hand had rested in mine without a fear—my arm had encircled
her waist without a resistance on her part, or a meditating
wrong on mine. And had we not kissed each other at meeting
and parting, from childhood, and through its pleasant limits,
until—ay, almost until the moment when the right of another
first led me to know what dear privileges had been my own?
Wonder not at the bitterness of my present memories.

It was at the moment when they were bitterest, that a sudden
turn in the road revealed to me the person of John Hurdis. I
recoiled in my saddle, and, under the involuntary impulse of
my hands, bore back my horse until he almost sunk upon his
haunches. The movement of both could not have been more
prompt if we had beheld a vexed and ready adder in our path.
And had he not been the adder in my path? Had he not, by
his sly and sneaking practices, infused his venom into the mind
of her upon whom my hope, which is the life of life, utterly
depended? Had he not struck at my heart with a sting not less
fearful, though more concealed, than that of the adder; and if
he had failed to destroy, was it not rather because of the feebleness of his fang, than either its purpose or its venom. If he
had not, then did I do him grievous wrong. I thought he had,
and my soul recoiled, as I surveyed him, with a hatred, which,
had he been other than my mother's son, would have prompted
me to slay him.

I had rounded a little swamp that lay upon the side of the
road, and gave it the outline of a complete elbow. John
Hurdis was some fifty yards in advance of me. I had not seen
him at dinner, and there was he now on his way to the dwelling
of her to whom I was about to pay my parting visit. The

thought that I should meet him with her, that he might behold these emotions which it shamed me to think I might not be altogether able to conceal, at once brought about a change in my resolve. I determined to give him no such chance of triumph; and was about to turn the head of my horse and return to my father, when he stopped short, wheeled round and beckoned me to advance. My resolution underwent a second change. That he should suppose that I shrunk from an encounter with him of any description was, if possible, even more mortifying than to expose the whole amount of my heart's weakness to Mary Esterby before his eyes. I determined to give him no such cause for exultation, and furiously spurring forward, another instant brought me beside him.

His face was complaisance itself, and his manner was presuming enough; and there was something in the slight smile which played about the corners of his mouth, and in the twinkle of his eye, which I did not relish. It may have been that, in the morbid state of my feelings, I saw through a false medium; but I could not help the thought, that there was exultation in his smile, and my jaundiced spirit put on new forms of jealousy with this conviction. The blood boiled within my veins, as I regarded him, and thought thus; and I trembled like a dry leaf in the gusts of November, while I suppressed, or strove to suppress, the rebellious and unruly impulses to which it prompted me: I struggled to be calm. For my mother's sake, I resolved to say and do nothing which should savor of violence at the moment when I was about to part with her forever.

" I will bear it all — all. I will be patient," I said to my soul; " It is not long, it will soon be over. Another day and I will be free from the chance of contact with the base, dishonest reptile. Let him gain, let him triumph as he may. It may be — the day may come ! But no — I will not think of such a thing; revenge is not for me. He is still, though base, a brother. Let the eternal avenger decree his punishment, and choose his fitting executioner."

These thoughts, and this resolution of forbearance, were all over in the progress of an instant; and we rode by the side of one another, as two belligerents who had lately been warring to the very knife, but who, under the security of a temporary

truce, look on one another, and move together with a mixed air.
half of peace, half of war, and neither altogether assured of the
virtue which is assumed to exist in their mutual pledges.

"Did I not see you turn your horse, Richard, as if to go
back?"

"You did," was my reply; and my face flushed as he thus
compelled me to the acknowledgment.

"And wherefore?"

"Wherefore!" I paused when I had repeated the word. It
would have been too galling to have spoken out the truth. I
continued thus :—

"I saw you proceeding in the same direction, and cared not
to be in the way. Your good fortune is too well-known, to
require that you should have fresh witnesses. · Besides, my
farewell—for it is only to say farewell, that I go now—is no
such important matter."

"You are right, Richard. My good fortune needs no witnesses, though it likes them. But why should you think that
you could be in the way? What do you mean by that?"

"Mean! can you ask," I replied, with something of a sneer
growing on my lips as I proceeded, "when you know it is
proverbial that young lovers, who are apt to be more senti
mental than sensible, usually, need no third persons at their
interviews? Indeed, for that matter, the third person likes it
quite as little as themselves."

"Less, perhaps, Richard, if he himself has been a loser at
the game," was the retort.

"Ay," I rejoined bitterly; "but if the game be played
foully, his dislike is quite as much the result of his scorn, as of
his disappointment. He is reconciled to his loss, when he finds
its worthlessness, and he envies not the victor, whose treachery, rather than his skill, has been the source of his greater
success."

The lips of my brother grew positively livid, as he opened
them, as if in the act to speak. He was prudent in forbearing,
for he kept silent.

"Look you, John Hurdis," I continued, turning full upon
him as I spoke, and putting my hand upon his shoulder. He
shrank from under it. His guilty conscience had put a morbid

nerve under every inch of. flesh in his system. I laughed aloud as I beheld him.

"Why do you shrink?" I demanded, now in turn becoming the questioner.

"Shrink—I shrink—did I shrink?" he answered me confusedly, scarcely conscious what he said.

"Ay—did you," I responded, with a glance intended to go through him. "You shrank as if my finger were fire—as if you feared that I meant to harm you."

His pride came to his relief. He plucked up strength to say, "You mistake, Richard. I did not shrink, and if I did, it was not through fear of you or any other man."

My hand again rested on his shoulder, as I replied—my eye searching through him all the while with a keenness, beneath which, it was a pleasure to me to behold him again shrink and falter.

"You may deceive yourself, John Hurdis, but you can not deceive me. You did shrink from my touch, even as you shrink now beneath mine eye. More than this, John Hurdis, you do fear me whatever may be your ordinary courage in the presence of other men. I see—I feel that you fear me; and I am not less assured on the subject of your fears. You would not fear were you not guilty—nor tremble now while I speak were you less deserving of my punishment. But you need not tremble. You are secure, John Hurdis. That which you have in your bosom of my blood is your protection for the greater quantity which you have that is not mine, and with which my soul scorns all communion."

His face grew black as he gazed upon me. The foam flecked his blanched lips even as it gathers upon the bit of the driven and infuriated horse. His frame quivered—his tongue muttered inaudible sounds, and he gazed on me, laboring, but in vain, to speak. I laughed as I beheld his feeble fury—I laughed in the abundance of my scorn, and he then spoke.

"Boy!" he cried—"boy—but for your mother, I should lay this whip over your shoulders."

He shook it before me as he spoke, and I grappled with him on the instant. With a sudden grasp, and an effort, to oppose which, he had neither strength of soul nor of body, I dragged him from his horse.　Straining feebly and ineffectually to resist his coward tendency, he, at length, after a few struggles, fell heavily upon the ground and almost under the feet of my animal.　His own horse passed away, and at the same moment, I leaped down from mine.　My blood was in a dreadful tumult—my fingers twitched nervously to grapple with him again, but ere I could do so, a sound—a scream—the sudden and repeated shrieks of a woman's voice, arrested me in my angry purpose, and I stood rooted to the spot.　Too well I knew that voice, and the tremor of rage which an instant before had shaken me to the center was now succeeded by a tremor far more powerful.　Unlike the former it was enfeebling, palsying—it took from me the wolfish strength with which the former seemed to have endued me.　The voice of a girl had given me the weakness of a girl, and like a culprit I stood, as if fixed and frozen, until my brother had arisen from the ground where I had thrown him, and Mary Easterby stood between us.

CHAPTER V.

PARTING SCENES.

"I thought to chide thee, but it will not be ;
True love can but awhile look bitterly."
HEYWOOD — *Love's Mistress.*

"You have led me
Into a subtle labyrinth, where I never
Shall have fruition of my former freedom."
The Lady's Privilege.

SHE stood between us like some judge suddenly descended from heaven, and armed with power to punish, and I stood before her like a criminal conscious of my demerits and waiting for the doom. An instant before she came, and I had a thousand arguments, each, to my mind, sufficient to justify me for any violence which I might execute upon John Hurdis. Now I had not one. The enormity of the act of which I had been guilty, seemed to expand and swell with every accumulated thought upon it ; and my tongue, that had been eloquent with indignation but a little while before, was now frozen with silence, and without even the power of evasion or appeal. I did not venture to look her in the face—I did not venture even to look upon my brother. What were his feelings I know not ; but if they partook, at that moment, of any of the intense humility which made up the greater part of mine, then was he almost sufficiently punished for the injuries which he had done me. I certainly felt that he was almost if not quite avenged in my present humility for the unbrotherly anger of which he had been the victim.

" Oh, Richard Hurdis," she exclaimed, " this violence, and upon your brother too."

Why had she not addressed her speech to him ? Was I alone

guilty? Had he not provoked—had he not even threatened me? The thought that she was now again showing the partiality in his favor which had been the source of my unhappiness, changed the tenor of my feelings. My sense of humiliation gave way to offended pride, and I answered with sullen defiance.

"And am I only to blame, Mary Easterby? Can you see fault in no other than me? Methinks this is less than justice, and I may safely deny the authority which so openly affronts justice with an avowal of its partialities."

"I have no partialities, Richard—it is you that are unjust. The violence that I witnessed was only yours. I saw not any other."

"There was indignity and insolence—provocation enough, Mary Easterby," I replied hastily, "if not violence, to justify me in what I did. But I knew not that you beheld us. I would not else have punished John Hurdis. I would have borne with his insolence—I would have spared him his shame—if not on his account, on yours. I regret that you have seen us, though I have no regret for what I have done."

I confronted my brother as I spoke these words, as if to satisfy him that I was ready to give him the only form of atonement which I felt his due. He seemed to understand me, and to do him all justice, his port was as manly as I could desire that of my father's son to be at all times. His eye flashed back a family expression of defiance, and his lips were closed with a resoluteness that showed him to be fully roused. But for the presence of Mary Easterby, we had come to the death struggle in that very hour. But we felt ourselves too greatly wrong not to acknowledge her superiority. Vexed and sullen as I was, I was doubly vexed with the consciousness of error; and when she spoke again in answer to my last words my chagrin found due increase in what she said.

"I know nothing of the provocation, Richard, and need nothing to believe that there was provocation, or that you thought so, which moved you to what you did. I could not suppose, for an instant, that you would proceed to such violence without provocation; but that any provocation short of violence itself, will justify violence—and violence too upon a brother—I can not admit, nor, in your secret heart, Richard, do you admit it yourself. What would your mother say, Richard, were she to hear this story ?"

" She might be less angry, and less pained, Mary Easterby, than you imagine, if she knew *all* the story. If she knew —— but no ! why should I recount his villanies, Mary Easterby, and least of all why recount them to you ?   I will not."

" Nor do I wish—nor would I hear them, Richard," she replied promptly, though gently. I saw the eyes of John Hurdis brighten, and my soul felt full of bitterness.

" What ! you would not believe me, then, Mary Easterby. Can it be that your prejudices go so far as that ?"

The tears gathered in her eyes as they were fixed upon mine and beheld the sarcastic and scornful expression in them, but she replied without hesitation.

" You are unjust, and unkind to me, Richard ;" and her voice trembled : she proceeded :—

" I would be unwilling to believe, and am quite as unwilling to hear anything which could be prejudicial to the good name of any of your family, your brother or yourself. I have loved them all too long and too truly, Richard, to find pleasure in anything which spoke against their worth. I should be not less unwilling, Richard, to think that you could say anything which did not merit and command belief. I might think you guilty of error, never of falsehood."

" Thank you, Mary ; for so much, at least, let me thank you. You do me justice only. When I speak falsely, of man or wo- man, brother or stranger, friend or foe, let my tongue cleave to my mouth in blisters."

John Hurdis mounted his horse at that moment, and an air of dissatisfaction seemed to hang upon his features. He mut- tered something to himself, the words of which were unintelli- gible to us ; then speaking hurriedly to Mary, he declared his intention of riding on to her father's farm, then but a short mile off. She begged him to do so, courteously, but, as I thought coldly ; and giving a bitter glance of enmity towards me, he put spurs to his horse and was soon out of sight.

His absence had a visible effect upon her, and I felt that much of the vexation was passing from my own heart. There

was something in the previous conversation between us which
had softened me, and when the tramp of his horse's heels was
no longer in hearing, it seemed as if a monstrous barrier had
been broken down from between us. All my old thoughts and
fancies returned to me; sweet memories, which I had just before angrily dismissed, now came back confidently to my mind,
and taking her hand in one of mine, while leading my horse
with the other, we took our course through a narrow path
which wound through a pleasant thicket, we had trodden together a thousand times before.

"Mary," I began, as we proceeded, "this is our old walk.
Do you remember? That pine has lain across the path from
the first time we knew it."

"Yes, it looks the same as ever, Richard, with one exception which I have remarked more than once and particularly
this morning. The end of it, upon which we used to sit, is
scarcely to be got at now, the bushes have grown up so thickly
around it."

"It is so long, Mary, since we have used it. It was our
visits that kept the brush down. The weeds grow now without
interruption from us—from me at least; and the time is far
distant when I shall visit it again. Do you know, Mary, I am
come to bid you good-by? I leave Marengo to-morrow."

"To-morrow! so soon?"

"Soon! Do you think it soon, Mary? I have been making
preparations for months. Certainly, I have declared my intention for months."

"Indeed! but not to me. I did hear something of such a
purpose being in your mind; but I hoped, I mean I believed
that it was not true."

"Did you hope that it was not true?" I demanded with some
earnestness. She answered with the ready frankness of childhood.

"Surely I did; and when John Hurdis told me ———"

"John Hurdis is no authority for me," I said gloomily,
breaking off her speech in the middle. The interruption brought
us back to our starting-place, from the contemplation of which,
since my brother's departure, we had both tacitly seemed to
shrink.

"Oh, Richard, this an evil temper!" she exclaimed. "Why do you encourage it? Why this angry spirit toward your brother! It is an evil mood, and can do no good. Besides, I think you do him injustice. He is gentle and good natured; he wants your promptness, it may be, and he lacks something of your enterprise and industry. Perhaps, too, he has not the same zealous warmth of feeling, but truly I believe that his heart is in the right place."

"It is your policy to believe so, Mary; else where is yours?"

"Mine!" she exclaimed; and her eye was fixed upon me with an expression of mixed curiosity and wonder.

"Ay, yours," I continued, giving a construction to the equivocal form of my previous speech, differing from that which I originally intended; "ay, yours, for if it be not, your charity is wasted. But no more of this, Mary, if you please. The subject, for sundry reasons, is an unpleasant one to me. John Hurdis is fortunate in your eulogy, and for your sake, not less than his, I will not seek, by any word of mine, to disturb your impressions. My words might prejudice your opinion of his worth, without impairing its intrinsic value; and it may be, as you think, that I am all wrong about it. He is a fortunate man, that John Hurdis—doubly fortunate, Mary. He has the wealth which men toil for, and fight for, and lie for, and sell themselves to the foul fiend for in a thousand ways: he has the favor of women; a greater temptation, for which they do a thousand times worse. He has those possessions, Mary, some of which I am never to have, but for the rest of which I am even now about to leave the home and perhaps all the happiness of my childhood."

"You surely do not envy your brother, Richard, any of his possessions?"

"Let me know what they are, Mary; let them be enumerated, and then will I answer you. Envy John Hurdis I do not; that is to say, I do not envy him his wealth, or his wisdom, his lands, his negroes, or any of his worldly chattels. Are you satisfied now, Mary, that there is nothing base in my envy, though it may be that he has something yet which provokes it?"

"And what is that, Richard?"

Why did I not answer her in plain language? How often
have I repented that I did not! How much sorrow might have
been spared me else! But I was proud of heart as Lucifer—
proud in my own despite, stubborn to my own sorrow.

"Mary, ask me not," I answered. "What matter is it to
know, when, even were he to lose that which I envy him, it
might be that I would not be esteemed worthy to possess it?"

"Richard, there is something strange to me in your tones,
and mysterious in your language. Why do you not speak to
me as formerly? Why are you changed—why should you be
changed to me? You scarcely speak now without saying something which I do not thoroughly comprehend. There is a hidden meaning in everything you say; and it seems to me that
you are suspicious and distrustful of the honesty of every
body."

"And should I not be, Mary? He is not a wise man who
learns no lessons of caution from the deception of others; who,
wronged once, suffers himself to be wronged a second time from
the same source. I may be distrustful, but I am prudently so,
Mary."

"You prudent, Richard! I fear that even now you deceive
yourself, as it seems to me you must have deceived yourself
before. You have not said, Richard, by whom you have been
wronged—by whose dishonesty you have acquired all these
lessons of prudence and circumspection."

How could I answer this? Whom could I accuse? I could
only answer by replying to another portion of her remarks.

"You think me changed, Mary, and I will not deny it. I
am certainly not so happy as I have been; but my change has
only corresponded with the changed aspects of the world around
me. I know that I have undergone no greater changes than
others that I know—than you, for example. You are changed,
Mary, greatly changed in my sight."

The deepest crimson and the utmost pallor succeeded to each
other in rapid alternations upon her cheek. Her bosom heaved
—her hand trembled within my own. I thought at first that
she would have fainted, and, dropping the bridle of my horse,
I supported her shrinking form with my arm. But she recovered herself almost instantly; and, advancing from the clasp of

my arm, which had encircled her waist, with a sudden composure which astonished me, she replied : —

"I did not think it, Richard; I am not conscious of any
change in me, but it may be even as you say. I could have
wished you had not seen it, if it be so; for, of a truth, I have
not striven for change, and it gives me pain to think that I do
seem so — to my friends at least."

"It is so, Mary. I once thought — but no! wherefore should
I speak of such things now ?—"

She interrupted me by a sudden and hurried effort — seemingly an impulsive one : —

"Oh, speak it, Richard — speak aloud — speak freely as you
used to speak when we were happy children together. Be no
longer estranged — think me not so! Speak your thought, and,
as I hope for kindness from all I love, I will as freely utter
mine."

"No !" I exclaimed coldly, and half-releasing her fingers from
my grasp; "no, Mary, it were but a folly now to say what were
my thoughts once — my feelings — my fancies. I might have
done so in a former day; but now I can not. I acknowledge
the change, and so must you. It is a wise one. Ere long,
Mary, long before I return to Marengo, you will undergo another change, perhaps, which I shall not witness, and shall not
desire to witness."

"What is it that you mean, Richard ?"

"Nothing — no matter what. It will be a happy change to
you, Mary, and that should be enough to make me satisfied with
it. God knows I wish you happiness — all happiness — as complete as it is in man's power to make it to you. I must leave
you now. The sun is gone, and I have to ride over to Carrington's to-night. Good-by, Mary, good-by."

"Are you going, Richard ?" she said, without looking up

"Yes, I have loitered too long already."

"You will write to us — to father ?"

"No; of what use to write ? Wherefore tax your sympathies
by telling the story of my sufferings ?"

"But your successes, Richard ?"

"You will believe them without the writing."

"So cold, Richard ?"

"So prudent, Mary—prudent."

"And you will not go to the house?"

"What! to meet *him* there? No, no! Good-by—God bless you, Mary, whatever be your changes of fortune or condition!" I carried her hand to my lips, flung it from me, and, gathering up the bridle of my steed, was soon upon my way. Was it in truth a sob which I heard behind me? I stole a glance backward—and she sat upon the log, with her face buried in her hands.

CHAPTER VI

EVIL MOODS

' **Why talk we not together hand-in-hand,**
And tell **our griefs in more familiar terms!**
But thou art gone, and **leav'st me here alone,**
To dull the air with my discoursive moan!"

MARLOWE AND NASH.

"SHE sat upon the log, with her face buried in her hands." More than once, as I rode away that evening, did I repeat these words to myself. Wherefore should she exhibit such emotion? wherefore should she sob at my departure? Did she not love —was she not betrothed to another? Of this I had no doubt, and what could I think? Was not such emotion natural enough? Had we not been born as it were together? Had we not been together from the earliest dawn of infancy—at that period when children, like clustering buds upon a rose-bush in early spring, rejoice to intertwine, as if the rude hands of the world were never to pluck them asunder, and place them in different and foreign bosoms? Was it not natural enough that she should show some sign of sorrow at thus parting with a youthful play mate?

I labored to persuade myself that this was all; yet, the more I reflected upon the matter, the more mysterious and contradictory did it seem. If it were that her emotions were natural to her as a long-familiar playmate, why had she been so estranged from me for so many previous and painful months? why did she look always so grave, in later days, whenever we met? why so reserved—so different from the confiding girl who had played with me from infancy? why so slow to meet me as formerly? why so unwilling to wander with me as before, among the secluded paths which our own feet had beaten into confirmed tracks? why, above all, so much more intimate and free with John Hurdis, who had never been her companion in childhood, and who, it was the most surprising thing in the world to me, should be her companion now?—he coarse, listless, unsympathizing; in his taste low, in his deportment unattractive, in his conversation tedious and prosing, in his propensities, if not positively vicious, at least far from virtuous or good!

What had they in common together? how could they mingle, how unite? by what arts had he won her to his wishes? by what baser arts had he estranged her from mine? Of some of these, indeed, I had heard. More than once already had I exposed him. His hints and equivoques had, as I thought, recoiled only upon his own head; and yet the ties grew and increased between them, even as the walls and barriers continued to rise and thicken between herself and me. I degraded him, but disdained any longer to strive for her. The busy neighborhood soon informed me how idle would be such struggles. They declared her betrothed to John Hurdis, and did not stop at this. They went further, and proclaimed her to have been bought by his money to see in him those qualities and that superior worth which, but for this, she had been slow to discover. Should I struggle against his good fortune? should I desire to win one whose market value was so readily understood by all? I turned from the contest in disdain; and, wondering at her baseness as a matter no less surprising than humiliating, I strove to fling her from my thoughts as I would the tainted and offensive weed, which had been, at one time, a pure and chosen flower.

I had not been successful. I could not fling her from my thoughts. Night and day she was before me; at all hours, whatever were my pursuits, my desires, my associates. Her image made the picture in the scene; her intelligence, her mind, the grace of her sentiments, the compass and the truth of her thoughts, were forced upon me for contemplation, by the obtrusive memory, in disparagement of those to which I listened. How perfect had she ever before seemed to me in her thoughts and sentiments! How strange that one so correct in her standards of opinion, should not have strength enough to be the thing which she approved! This is the most mortifying conviction of humanity. We build the temple, but the god does not inhabit it, though we solicit him with incense, and bring our best offerings to his altars.

I reached the dwelling of William Carrington ere I felt that my journey was begun. The velocity of my thoughts had made me unconscious of that of my motion — nay, had prompted me to increase it beyond my ordinary habit. When I alighted, my horse was covered with foam.

"You have ridden hard," said Carrington.

"No; I think not. I but came from 'Squire Easterby's."

He said no more then, for the family was around; but that night, when we retired, our conversation was long, upon various subjects; and, in the course of it, I told him all the particulars of my rencontre with John Hurdis, and of my parting interview with Mary Easterby. He listened with much attention, and then spoke abruptly:—

"You do that girl wrong, Richard. You are quite too harsh to her at times. I have heard and seen you. Your jealousy prompts you to language which is ungenerous, to say the least, and which you have no right to use. You never told her that you loved her — never asked her to love you! What reason can you have to complain, either that she is beloved by, or that she loves another?"

"None! I do not complain."

"You do! Your actions, your looks, your language, are all full of complaint. The show of dissatisfaction — of discontent — is complaint, and that, too, of the least manly description. It savors too much of the sullenness of the whipped school-boy, or one denied his holyday, to be manly. Let us have no more of it, Richard."

"You speak plainly enough."

"I do; and you should thank me for it. I were no friend if I did not. Do not be angry, Richard, that I do so. I have your good at heart, and, I think, you have been fighting seriously against it. You think too bitterly of your brother to do him justice."

"Speak nothing of him, William."

"I will not say much, for you know I like him quite as little as yourself. Still, I do not hate him as you do; and can not agree with you, therefore, as to the propriety of your course toward him. You can not fight him as you would a stranger, and have done with it."

"I could!—you mistake. I feel that I could fight him with even less reluctance than I would a stranger."

"I grant you that your hostility is bitter enough for it, but you have too much sense of propriety left to indulge it. You can not, and should not, were I by, even if you were yourself willing. Have done with him, then; and, as you have already separated, let your thoughts maintain as rigid a distance from him as your person."

"And leave him the field to himself?"

"Have you not already done so? Have you not pronounced the field unworthy fighting for? Pshaw, man! this is but wasting valor."

I listened gloomily, and in utter silence as he went on thus:—

"But," he continued, "I am not so sure, either that the field is in his possession, or that it is unworthy. I tell you, you do Mary Easterby injustice! I do not think that she loves your brother. I doubt that she even likes him. I see no proof of it."

"Ay, but there is proof enough. You see not because your eyes are elsewhere. But say no more, William; let us drop this hateful subject."

"I am afraid your jealous spirit makes it hateful, Richard. That girl, Mary, is a treasure too valuable to be given up so lightly. By my soul, were I not otherwise bound, I should struggle for her myself!"

"You!"

"Yea, even I, William Carrington! Nay, look not so grim and gluttonous! You forget that you renounce the spoil, and that I am sworn elsewhere! I would that all others were as little in your path as I am!"

"And I care not how many crowd my path when I am out of it!" was my sullen answer.

"Ah, Richard! you were born to muddy the spring you drink from. You will pay for this perversity in your nature. Be more hopeful—more confiding, man! Think better of your own nature, and of the nature of those around you. It is the best policy. To look for rascals is to find rascals; and to believe in wrong, is not only to suffer, but to do wrong. For my part, I would rather be deceived than doubt; rather lose, than perpetually fear loss; rather be robbed, than suspect every one I meet of roguery!"

"I answer you through my experience, William, when I tell you that you will pay dearly for your philanthropy. Your faith will be rewarded by faithlessness."

"Stay!" he cried—"no more! You would not impute insincerity to Emmeline Walker?"

"No! surely not."

"Then let the world be false, and play double with me as it pleases! She can not! I know her, Dick—I know her! She will perish for me as freely, I am sure, as I would for her! And shall I doubt, when she is true? Would to heaven, Richard, you would believe but half so confidently in Mary!"

"And what use in that?"

"Why, then, my life on it, she will believe in you! I somehow suspect that you are all wrong in that girl. I doubt that these old women, who have no business but their neighbors' to attend to, and for whose benefit a charitable society should be formed for knocking them all in the head, have been coining and contriving, as usual, to the injury of the poor girl, not to speak of your injury. What the devil can she see in that two-hundred-pounder, John Hurdis, to fall in love with?"

"His money!"

"No! by G—d, Richard, I'll not believe it! The girl is too humble in her wants, and too content in her poverty, and too gentle in her disposition, and too sincere in her nature, to be a thing of barter. If she is engaged to John Hurdis, it is a d———d bad taste, to be sure, of which I should not have suspected her—but it is not money!"

"There is no disputing tastes," I rejoined bitterly; "let us sleep now."

"Ah, Richard, you have an ugly sore on your wrist, which you too much love to chafe. You toil for your own torture, man. You labor for your own defeat. I would you could rid yourself of this self-troubling nature. It will madden you, yet."

"If it is my nature, William," I responded gloomily, "I must even make the most of the evil, and do as well with it as I can."

"Do nothing with it—have done with it! Believe better of yourself and others. Think better of Mary Easterby and your brother."

"I can not! You ask me to think better of them, yet name them together. To have been successful in your wish, you should have put them as far asunder as the poles. But say no more to me now, William. I am already fevered, and can hear nothing, or heed nothing that I hear. I must sleep now."

"Well, as you will, But, look out and tell me what sort of night we have. I would be sure of a pleasant day to-morrow."

He was already in his bed, and I looked out as he desired. The stars were few and gave a faint light. The winds were rising, and a murmur, almost a moan, came from the black forests in the distance. It seemed like the voice of a spirit, and it came to me as if in warning. I turned to my companion, but he was already asleep. I could not then sleep, desire it as I might. I envied him—not his happiness, but what I then misdeemed his insensibility. I confounded the quiet mind, at peace with all the world and in itself secure, with the callous and unfeeling nature. Sleep is only the boon of the mind conscious of its own rectitude, and having no jealous doubts of that of its fellows. I had no such consciousness and could not sleep. I resumed my seat beside the window, and long that night did I watch the scene—lovely beyond comparison—before, in utter exhaustion, I laid my head upon the pillow. The night in the forests of Alabama was never more beautiful than then. There was no speck in the heaven—not even the illuminated shadow of a cloud—and the murmur of the wind swelling in gusts from the close curtaining woods, was a music, rather than a mere murmur. In the vexed condition of my mood, the hurricane had been more soothing to my rest, and more grateful to my senses.

CHAPTER VII.

THE FAREWELL TO HOME.

" My father blessed me fervently,
But did not much complain ;
Yet sorely will my mother sigh,
Till I come home again."—BYRON.

AT the dawn of day I rose, and, without waiting breakfast hurried off to the habitation of my father. I should have slept at home the last night, but that I could not, under my excited state of feeling, have trusted myself to meet John Hurdis. For that matter, however, I might have safely ventured; for he, probably with a like caution, had also slept from home. It was arranged between William Carrington and myself that we were to meet at mid-day, at a spot upon the road equidistant from both plantations, and then proceed together. The time between was devoted to our respective partings—he with Emmeline Walker, and I with my father and mother. Could it have been avoided with propriety, I should have preferred to leave this duty undone. I wished to spare my old mother any unnecessary pain. Besides, to look her in the face, and behold her grief at the time when I meditated to make our separation a final one, would, I well knew, be a trial of my own strength to which I was by no means willing to subject it. My sense of duty forbade its evasion, however, and I prepared for it with as much manful resolve as I could muster.

My mother's reproaches were less painful to me than the cold and sullen forbearance of my father. Since I had resolved to work for him no longer, he did not seem to care very greatly where I slept. Not that he was indifferent; but his annoyance at my resolution to leave him made him less heedful of my other and minor movements; so he said nothing to me on my return. Not so my mother.

"The last night, Richard, and to sleep from home! Ah, my son, you do not think but it may be indeed the very last night! You know not what may happen while you are absent. I may be in my grave before you return."

I was affected; her tears always affected me; and her reproaches were always softened by her tears. From childhood she had given me to see that she sorrowed even when she punished me; that she shared in the pain she felt it her duty to inflict. How many thousand better sons would there be in the world, if their parents punished and rewarded from principle, and never from passion or caprice? I am sure, with a temperament reckless and impatient like mine, I should have grown up to be a demon, had not my mother been to me a saint. I sought to mollify her.

"I did wish to come, mother—I feel the truth of all you say—but there was a circumstance—I had a reason for staying away last night."

"Ay, to be sure," said my father, sullenly; "it would not be Richard Hurdis if he had not a reason for doing what he pleased. And pray what was this good and sufficient reason, Richard?"

"Excuse me, sir, I would rather not mention it."

"Indeed!" was the response; you are too modest by half, Richard. It is something strange that you should at any time distrust the force of your own arguments."

I replied to the sarcasm calmly—

"I do not now, sir—I only do not care to give unnecessary particulars; and I'm sure that my mother will excuse them. I trust that she will believe what I have already said, and not require me to declare what I would be glad to withhold."

"Surely, my son," said the old lady, and my father remained silent. A painful interval ensued, in which no one spoke, though all were busily engaged in thought. My father broke the silence by asking a question which my mother had not dared to ask.

"And at what hour do you go, Richard?"

"By twelve, sir. My horse is at feed now, and I have

nothing but my saddle-bags to see to. You have the biscuit ready, mother, and the venison?"

"Yes, my son; I have put up some cheese also, which you will not find in the way. Your shirts are all done up, and on the bed."

It required some effort on my mother's part to tell me this. I thanked her, and my father proceeded:—

"You will want your money, Richard, and I will get it for you at once. If you desire more than I owe you, say so; I can let you have it."

"I thank you, sir, but I shall not need it; my own money will be quite enough."

He had made the proffer coldly—I replied proudly; and he moved away with a due increase of sullenness. The quick instinct of my mother, when my father had gone, informed her of the matter which I had been desirous to withhold.

"You have seen your brother, Richard?"

"How know you?"

"Ask not a mother how she knows the secret of a son's nature, and how she can read those passions which she has been unable to control. You have seen your brother, Richard—you have quarrelled with him."

I looked down, and my cheeks burned as with fire. She came nigh to me and took my hand.

"Richard, you are about to leave us: why can you not forgive him? Forget your wrongs, if indeed you have had any at his hands, and let me no longer have the sorrow of knowing that the children, who have been suckled at the same breasts, part, and perhaps for ever, as enemies."

"Better, mother, that they should part as enemies, than live together as such. Your maternal instinct divines not all, mother—short of the truth. Hear me speak, and have your answer. I not only quarrelled with John Hurdis, yesterday, but I laid violent hands upon him."

"You did not—you could not!"

"I must speak the truth, mother—I did."

"And struck him?"

"No, but would have done so, had we not been interrupted."

"Thank God for that. It is well for you, Richard. I should

have cursed you with bitterness, had you struck your brother with clinched hands."

"I came nigh it, mother. He shook his whip over my head, and I dragged him from his horse. I would at that moment have trampled him under my very feet, but that the voice of Mary Easterby arrested me. She came between us. She alone—I confess it, mother—she alone kept me from greater violence."

"Heaven bless her! Heaven bless the chance that brought her there! O Richard Hurdis!—my son, my son!—why will you not bear more patiently with John? why will you not labor for my sake, Richard, if not for his and your own?"

She trembled as if palsied, while I related to her the adventure of the preceding day; and though schooled, as women in the new countries of the South and West are very apt to be, against those emotions which overcome the keener sensibilities of the sex in very refined communities, yet I had never seen her exhibit so much mental suffering before. She tottered to a chair, at the conclusion of her speech, refusing my offer to assist her, and, burying her face in her hands, wept without restraint, until suddenly aroused to consciousness by the approaching footsteps of my father. He was a stern man, and gave little heed and no sympathy to such emotions for any cause. He would have been more ready to rebuke than to relieve them; and that feeling of shame which forbids us to show our sorrows to the unsympathizing, made her hasten to clear up her countenance, and remove the traces of her suffering, as he re-entered the apartment.

"Well, Richard," he said, throwing down a handkerchief of silver dollars—a more profuse collection than is readily to be met with in the same region now—"here is your money; half in specie, half in paper. It is all your own; count it for yourself, and tell me if it's right."

"I'm satisfied if you have counted it, sir; there's no use in counting it again."

"That's as you think proper, my son; yet I shall be better satisfied if you will count it."

I did so to please him, declared myself content, and put the money aside. This done, I proceeded to put up my clothes, and get myself in readiness. Such matters took but little time, however ; the last words form the chief and most serious business in every departure. The fewer of them the better.

So my father thought. His farewell and benediction were equally and almost mortifyingly brief : —

"Well, Richard, since it must be so—if you will be obstinate—if you will go from where your bread has been so long buttered—why, God send you to a land where you won't feel the want of those you leave. I trust, however, to see you return before long, and go back to the old business."

"Return I may, father, but not to the old business," was my prompt reply; "I have had enough of that. If I am able to be nothing better than an overseer, and to look after the slaves of others, the sooner I am nothing the better."

"You speak bravely now, boy," said my father; "but the best bird that ever crowed in the morning has had his tail-feathers plucked before evening. Look to yourself my son ; be prudent—keep a bright eye about you as you travel, and learn from me what your own fortunes have not taught you yet, but what they may soon enough teach you unless you take counsel from experience—that there is no chicken so scant of flesh, for which there is not some half-starved hawk to whom his lean legs yield good picking. You have not much money, but enough to lose, and quite enough for a sharper to win. Take care of it. Should you find it easily lost, come back, I say, and you can always find employment on the old terms."

"I doubt it not, father—I doubt not to find the same terms anywhere on my route from Marengo to Yalo-busha. There is no lack of employment when the pay is moderate and the work plenty."

"I can get hundreds who will take your place, Richard, for the same price," said my father, hastily, and with no little disquiet.

"And do what I have done, sir?"

He did not answer the question, but walked to and fro for several moments in silence, while I spoke with my mother.

"And what about your own negroes, Richard ?" he again abruptly addressed me.

"Why, sir, you must work them as usual if you have no objections. I shall have no need of them for the present."

"Yes, but you may want them when the next year's crop is to be put into the ground."

"Hardly, sir—but if I should, I will then charge you nothing for their time. It shall be my loss."

"No, that it shall not be, Richard; you shall have what is right since you leave it altogether to me. And now, good-by, I'll leave you with your mother and go into the woods: you can always talk more freely with her than you are willing to talk with me; I don't know why, unless it is that I have some d———d surly ways about me. Tell her if you want anything from me, or if I can do anything for you, don't spare your speech—let her know it, and if it's to be done at all, I'll do it. I won't palaver with you about my love and all that soft stuff, but I do love you Richard, as a man and no sneak. Good-by, boy—good-by and take care of yourself."

Thus, after his own rough fashion, my father spoke his parting. A fountain of good feeling was warm and playing at his heart, though it seemed stolid and impenetrable as the rocky surface that shut it in. He was cold, and phlegmatic in his manner only. One hurried embrace was taken, and seizing his staff, he disappeared in another instant from my sight. The soul of my mother seemed to expand at his departure. His presence restrained her; and with more than woman's strength, she kept down, while under the inspection of his stern and piercing eye, all of the warmth and tenderness of woman—of a mother.

"My son, my son, you leave me, you leave me doubly unhappy—unhappy as you leave me and perhaps for ever— unhappy as you leave me with a deadly enmity raging in your breast against your brother. Could you forget this enmity—could you forgive him before you go, I should be half-reconciled to your departure. I could bear to look for you daily and to find you not—to call for you hourly, and to have no answer—to dream of your coming, and to wake only to desire to dream again. Can you not forgive him, Richard ? Tell me that you will. I pray you, my son, to grant me this, as a gift and a blessing to myself. I will pray Heaven for all gifts upon you in return. Think, my son, should death come among us—should one of us be taken during the time you think to be gone—how dreadful to think of the final separation without peace being made between us. Let there be peace, my son. Dismiss your enmity to John. You know not that he has wronged you—you know not that he has used any improper arts with Mary—but if he has, my son—admitting that he has, still I pray you to forgive him. Wherefore should you not forgive him? Of what use to cherish anger? You can not contend with him in violence; you must not, you dare not, as you value a mother's blessing, as you dread a mother's curse. Such violence would not avail to do you justice; it could not give you what you have lost. To maintain wrath is to maintain a curse that will devour all your substance and lastly devour yourself. Bless your poor mother, Richard, and take her blessing in return. Grant her prayer, and all her prayers will go along with you for ever."

"Mother, bless me, for I do forgive him."

Such were my spontaneous words. They came from my uninstructed, untutored, impulse, and at the moment when I uttered them, I believed fervently, that they came from the bottom of my heart. I fear that I deceived myself. I felt afterward, as if I had not forgiven, and could not forgive him. But when I spoke, I thought I had, and could not have spoken otherwise. Her own voluminous and passionate appeal, had overcome me, and her impulse bore mine along with it. I may have deceived her, but I as certainly deceived myself. Be it so. The error was a pious one, and made her happy; as happy, at least, as, at that moment, she could well be.

I need not dwell upon our parting. It was one of mixed pain and pleasure. It grieved me to see how much she suffered, yet it gratified my pride to find how greatly I was beloved. Once taught how delicious was the one feeling of pleasure which such a trial brought with it, I feel—I fear—that I could freely have inflicted the pain a second time, if sure to enjoy the pleasure. Such is our selfishness. Our vanity still subdues our sufferings, and our pride derives its most grateful aliment from that which is, or should be, our grief.

In an hour I was on the road with my companion, and far out of hearing of my mother's voice. And yet—I heard it,

CHAPTER VIII.

ROADSIDE PROGRESS.

> " But with the word, the time will bring on summer,
> When briars shall have leaves as well as thorns,
> And be as sweet as sharp. We must away ;
> Our wagon is prepared, and time revives us."—SHAKSPERE.

I HEARD it then—in long **days after, when she** was speech-less, I heard it—I still **hear it—I shall never lose its** lingering memories. They cling to **me** with a **mother's love; the purest,** the least selfish of all human affections. **The love of woman is** a wondrous thing, but the love of a mother is yet more **wonder-ful.** What is there like **it** in nature? What tie is there **so** close, so warm, so uncalculating in its compliances, so unmeas-ured in its sacrifices, so enduring **in** its tenacious tenderness? It may accompany the feeble intellect, the coarse form, the equivocal virtue; but, in itself, it is neither feeble, nor coarse, nor equivocal. It refines vulgarity, **it** softens violence, **it qualifies and chastens,** even when it may not redeem, all other vices. **I am convinced** that, of all human affections, **it is endowed with the greatest** longevity; **it is the most** hardy, if not the **most acute in its vi-tality.** Talk of the love of young people **for one another; it is** not to be spoken of in the same breath; nothing can **be more** inferior. Such love is of the earth, earthy—a passion **born of** tumults, wild and fearful as the storm, and yet more **capricious.** An idol of clay—a miserable pottery, the work, which **in a fit of** frenzied devotion we make with our own **hands, and** in another, and not more mad fit of brutality, we trample **to pieces with our** feet. Appetite is the fiend that degrades **every passion, and the** flame, of which **it is a** part, **must always end in** smoke and ashes.

Thus I mused when I encountered my **friend and companion.**

He was in fine spirits; overjoyed with the novelty of the situation in which he found himself. For the first time in his life, he was a traveller, and his nature was one of those that correspond with the generous season, and keep happy in spite of the cloudy. His soul began to expand with the momentarily increasing consciousness of its freedom; and when he described to me the sweet hour which had just terminated, and which he had employed for his parting with Emmeline Walker, he absolutely shouted. His separation from his former home, his relatives, and the woman whom he loved, was very different from mine; and his detail of his own feelings, and his joys and hopes, only added bitterness to mine. Going and coming, the world smiled upon him. Backward and forward, an inviting prospect met his eyes. He saw no sun go down in night. He was conscious of no evening not hallowed by a moon. Happy world, where the blessed and blessing heart moves the otherwise disobedient and froward elements as it pleases, banishes the clouds, suspends the storm, and lighting up the sky without, from the heaven within, casts for ever more upon it, the smile of a satisfied and indulgent Deity. The disappointed demon in my soul actually chafed to hear the self-gratulations of the delighted God in his.

And yet what had been my reflections but a moment before! To what conclusion had I come? In what—supposing me to have been right in that conclusion—in what respect was his fortune better than mine? In what respect was it half so good? The love of the sexes I had proclaimed worthless and vulnerable; that of a mother beyond all price. I had a mother, a fond, unselfish mother, and Carrington was an orphan. He had only that love, which I professed to think so valueless. But did I seriously think so? What an absurdity. The love of the young for each other is a property of the coming time, and it is the coming time for which the young must live. That of a mother is a love of the past, or, at the best, of the present only. It can not, in the ordinary term of human allotment, last us while we live. It is not meant that it should, and the Providence that beneficently cares for us always, even when we are least careful of ourself, has wisely prompted us to seek and desire that love which may. It was an instinct that made me envy my companion, in spite of my own philosophy. I would have given up the love of a thousand mothers to be secure of that of Mary Easterby.

I strove to banish thought, by referring to the most ordinary matters of conversation; matters, indeed, about which I did not care a straw. In this way, I strove, not only to dispel my own topics of grief, but to silence those of triumph in my companion. What did I care to hear of Emmeline Walker, and how she loved him, and how she cheered him, with a manly spirit, on a journey from which other and perhaps finer damsels would have sought to discourage their lovers; and how she bade him return as soon as he had bought the lands on which they were to settle all their future lives? This was talk no less provoking than unnecessary; and it was not without some difficulty that I could divert him from it. And even then my success was only partial. He was forever getting back to it again.

"And what 'route are we to take, William?" I demanded, when we had reached a point of fork in the road. "You spoke yesterday of going up by way of Tuscaloosa. But if you can do without taking that route, it will be the better; it is forty miles out of our road to Columbus, and unless you have some business there, I see no reason to go that way. The town is new, and has nothing worth seeing in it."

"It is not that I go for, Richard. I have some money owing me in that neighborhood. There is one Matthew Webber, who lives a few miles on the road from Tuscaloosa to Columbus, who owes me a hundred and thirty dollars for a mule I sold him last spring was a year. I have his note. The money was due five months ago, and it needs looking after. I don't know much of Webber, and think very little of him. The sooner I get the money out of his hands, the better, and the better chance then of his paying me. I'm afraid, if he stands off much longer, he'll stand off for ever, and I may then whistle for my money."

"You are wise; and forty miles is no great difference to those who have good horses. So speed on to the right. It's a rascally road, let me tell you. I have ridden it before."

"I know nothing about it; but, thank the stars, I care as little. When a man's heart is in the right place, sound and satisfied, it matters not much what is the condition of the road

he travels. One bright smile, one press of the hand from Emmeline, makes all smooth, however rough before."

I struck the spurs into my horse's flanks impatiently. He
saw the movement, and, possibly, the expression of my countenance, and laughed aloud.

"Ah, Dick, you take things to heart too seriously. What if
you are unfortunate, man? You are not the first—you will not
be the last. You are in a good and godly company. Console
yourself, man, by taking it for granted that Mary has been less
wise than you thought her, and that you have made a more fortunate escape that you can well appreciate at present."

"Pshaw! I think not of it," was my peevish reply. "Let us
talk of other matters."

"Agreed. But what other matters to talk of that shall please
you, Richard, is beyond my knowledge now. My happiness,
at this moment, will be sure to enter into everything I say; as
I certainly can think of no more agreeable subject. I shall
speak of Emmeline, and that will remind you of Mary, however
different may be their respective treatment of us. If I talk of
the land I am looking for, and resolve to settle on, you will be
gin to brood over the solitary life in store for you; unless, as I
think very likely, it will not be long before you console yourself with some Mississippi maiden, who will save you the trouble
of looking for lands, and the cost of paying for them, by bringing you a comfortable portion."

"I am not mercenary, William," was my answer, somewhat
more temperately spoken than usual. I had discovered the
weakness of which I had been guilty, and at once resolved that,
though I was not successful, I would not be surly. Indeed, a
playful commentary, which Carrington uttered about my savage
demeanor, brought me back to my senses. It was in reply to
some uncivil sarcasm of mine.

"Hush, man! hush! Because you have been buffeted, you
need not be a bear! Let the blows profit you as they do a
beefsteak, and though I would not have your tenderness increased by the process, Heaven keep you from any increase of
toughness! Forgive me, my dear fellow, for being so happy!
I know well enough that, to the miserable, the good humor of
one's neighbors is sheer impertinence. But I am more than a

neighbor to **you, Dick** Hurdis!   I am a friend; and you must forgive mine!"

"Ay, that **I** do, William!" I answered frankly, and 'aking his hand while I spoke.   "**I** will **not only** forgive, but to'erate **your** happiness.   You **shall see that I will; and to** prove 't to you, I beg that you **will** talk **on, and only talk of that.   W** 'at were Emmeline's last words?"

"Come back soon."

"And she smiled when she said **them**?"

"Ay; that was **the** strangest thing of all, Richard.   **She did** smile when we parted, and neither then nor at any time since I **have known** her, have **I** ever seen her shed a tear.   I almost bleated like **a calf.**"

"She is a strong woman, high-spirited, firm, and full of character.   She does not feel the less for not **showing her feelings** Still water runs deep."

"A suspicious proverb, **Richard!**   One that has too many meanings to be complimentary.   Nevertheless, **you** are quite right.   Emmeline **is** a still girl—thinks **more** than she says —feels more than she will acknowledge; and loves the more earnestly that she does **not** proclaim it from the pine-tops Your professing women, like your professing men, are all puff **and** plaster.   They know their **own** deficiencies, and in the in ventory which they make of their virtues, take good **care to** set them down as the very chattels in possession.   Like church-builders and church-goers, they seek to make up for the substantials, which they have not, by the shows and symbols which belong to them; and, truth to **say, such** is the universality of this habit, that, now-a-days, **no one looks further** than the surplice, and the color of the cloth.   Forms are virtues, **and** names things. **You** remember the German story, where the devil bought the **man's** shadow in preference to his soul.   Heaven help mankind, were the devil disposed to pursue his **trade!**   What universal bankruptcy among men would follow the loss of their shadows! How the church would groan—the pillars crumble and fall— the surplice and the black coat shrivel and stink!   What a loss would there be of demure looks and saintly faces—of groaning and psalm-singing tradesmen—men who seek to make a brotherhood **and** sisterhood in order to **carry their** calicoes to a good market! Well, thank heaven! the country to which we are now bending our steps, Richard, is not yet overrun by these saintly hypocrites. Time will come, I doubt not, when we shall have them where the Choctaws now hunt and pow-wow, making long prayers, and longer sermons, and concluding, as usual, with a collection."

"It may be that the country is quite as full of rascals, William, though it may lack hypocrites. We have bold villains in place of cunning ones, and whether we fare better or worse than the city in having them, is a question not easily decided. We shall have need of all our caution in our travelling. I have no fear of the Indians while they are sober; and it will not be hard to avoid them when they are drunk; but we have heard too many stories of outlaws and robbery on the borders of the nation and within it, where the villains were not savages, to render necessary any particular counsel to either of us now."

"I don't believe the half of what I hear of these squatters. No doubt, they are a rough enough set of people; but what of that? Let them but give us fair play, and, man to man, I think, we need not fear them. I know that you can fling a stout fellow with a single flirt, and I have a bit of muscle here that has not often met its match. I fear not your bold boys—let them come. It is your city sneaks, Richard, that I don't like; your saintly, demure, sly rogues, that pray for you at the supper-table, and pick your pocket when you sleep."

Carrington extended his brawny and well-shaped arm as he spoke, giving it a glance of unconcealed admiration. He did not overrate his own powers; but, in speaking of rogues, and referring to their practices, it was no part of my notion that they would ever give us fair play. I told him that, and by a natural transition, passed to another topic of no little importance on the subject.

"I don't fear anything from open violence, William," was my reply. "You know enough of me for that; but men who aim to rob, will always prefer to prosecute their schemes by art rather than boldness. Valor does not often enter into the composition of a rogue. Now, I have enough money about me to tempt a rascal, and more than I am willing to surrender to one. You have, probably, brought a large sum with you also,"

"All I have; three thousand dollars, more or less, in United States bank bills, some few Alabama, and Georgia, all passable at the land-office," was his reply.

"The greater need of caution. There are land-pirates on the Black Warrior, and Alabama, who are said to be worse by far than the pirates of the gulf. Look to it, William, and keep your money out of sight. The more poor your pretensions, the more certain your safety. Show no more money than you wish to spend."

"I will not, Richard; and yet I should have no objection to put my money down upon the butt-end of a log, and take a hug with any pirate of them all who should have it."

"More brave than wise," was my reply. "But let us have no more of this; there are travellers before and behind us. Let our circumspection begin from this moment. We have both need of it, being at greater risk, as we bring, like a terrapin, our homes and all that is in them, on our backs. You have too much money about you. In that, William, you were anything but wise. I wish I had counselled you. You could have entered the lands with one fourth of it. But it is too late now to repent. You must be watchful only. I am not at so great a risk as you, but I have quite enough to tempt a Red river gambler to his own ruin and mine."

"I shall heed you," replied my companion, buttoning his coat, and turning the butt of a pistol in his bosom, making it more convenient to his grasp. "But who are these travellers? Settlers from North Carolina, I reckon. Poor devils from Tar river as usual, going, they know not where, to get, they know not what."

"They can not go to a poorer region, nor fare much worse than they have done, if your guess be right."

"I'll lay a picayune upon it. They look sleepy and poor enough to have lived at Tar river a thousand years But, we shall see."

CHAPTER IX

THE EMIGRANTS.

An aged man whose head some seventy years
Had snowed on freely, led the caravan ;—
His sons and sons' sons, and their families,
Tall youths and sunny maidens — a glad group
That glowed in generous blood, and had no care,
And little thought of the future, followed him :—
Some perched on gallant steeds — others more slow,
The infants and the matrons of the flock,
In coach and jersey — but all moving on
To the new land of promise, full of dreams
Of western riches, Mississippi mad !"

By this time we had overtaken the cavalcade, and sure enough, it turned out as my companion had conjectured. The wanderers were from one of the poorest parts of North Carolina, bent to better their condition in the western valleys, "full of dreams," and as one of our southern poets, whom I quote above, energetically expresses it, "Mississippi mad." They consisted of several families, three or four in number, all from the same neighborhood, who were thus making a colonizing expedition of it; and as they had all along formed a little world to themselves before, now resolving with a spirit not less wise than amiable, to preserve the same social and domestic relations in the new regions to which they bent their steps. They thus carry with them the morals and the manners to which they have been accustomed, and find a natural home accordingly wherever they go. But even this arrangement does not supply their loss, and the social moralist may well apprehend the deterioration of the graces of society in every desertion by a people of their ancient homes. Though men may lose nothing of their fecundity by wandering, and in emigration to the

west from a sterile region like North Carolina, most commonly,
gain in their worldly goods, their losses are yet incomputable.
The delicacies of society are most usually thrust from the sight
of the pioneers; the nicer harmonies of the moral world become
impaired; the sweeter cords of affection are undone or rudely
snapped asunder, and a rude indifference to the claims of one's
fellow, must follow every breaking up of the old and stationary abodes. The wandering habits of our people are the great
obstacles to their perfect civilization. These habits are encouraged by the cheapness of our public lands, and their constant
exposure for sale. The morals not less than the manners of
our people are diseased by the license of the wilderness; and the
remoteness of the white settler from his former associates approxi-
mate him to the savage feebleness of the Indian, who has been
subjugated and expelled simply because of his inferior morality.

We joined the wayfarers, and accommodating our pace to the
slow and weary movement of their cavalcade, kept with them
long enough to answer and to ask a hundred questions. They
were a simple and hardy people, looking poor, but proud; and
though evidently neither enterprising nor adventurous, yet,
once abroad and in the tempest, sufficiently strong and bold to
endure and to defy its buffeting. There was a venerable grand-
father of the flock, one of the finest heads I ever looked upon,
who mingled the smiling elasticity of youth, with the garrulity
of age. He spoke as sanguinely of his future prospects in Mississippi, as if he were only now about to commence the world;
and while he spoke, his eyes danced and twinkled with delight,
and his laugh rang through the forests, with such fervor and
life, that an irrepressible sympathy made me laugh with him,
and forget, for a moment, my own dull misgivings, and heavy
thoughts. His mirth was infectious, and old and young shared
in it, as most probably they had done from childhood. We
rode off, leaving them in a perfect gale of delighted merriment,
having their best wishes, and giving them ours in return.

To one ignorant of the great West; to the dweller in the
Eastern cities—accustomed only to the dull, unbroken routine
of a life of trade, which is at best only disturbed by some splen-
did forgery, or a methodical and fortunate bankruptcy, which
makes the bankrupt rich at the expense of a cloud of confiding

creditors—the variety, and the vicissitudes of forest life, form a series of interesting romances. The very love of change, which is the marked characteristic of our people in reference to their habitations, is productive of constant adventures, to hear which, the ears tingle, and the pulses bound. The mere movement of the self-expatriated wanderer, with his motley caravan, large or small, as it winds its way through the circuitous forests, or along the buffalo tracks, in the level prairies, is picturesque in the last degree. And this picturesqueness is not a whit diminished by the something of melancholy, which a knowledge of the facts provokes necessarily in the mind of the observer. Not that they who compose the cavalcade, whether masters or men, women or children, are troubled with any of this feeling. On the contrary, they are usually joyful and light spirited enough. It is in the thoughts and fancies of the spec tator only that gloom hangs over the path, and clouds the fortune of the wayfarer. He thinks of the deserted country which they have left—of the cottage overgrown with weeds—of the young children carried into wildernesses, where no sabbath bell invites them to a decorous service—where the schoolmas ter is never seen, or is of little value—and where, if fortune deigns to smile upon the desires of the cultivator, the wealth which he gains, descends to a race, uninformed in any of its duties, and, therefore, wholly ignorant of its proper uses. Wealth, under such circumstances, becomes a curse, and the miserable possessor a victim to the saddest error that ever tempted the weak mind, and derided it in its overthrow.

These thoughts force themselves upon you as you behold the patient industry of the travellers while they slowly make their way through the tedious forests. Their equipage, their arrangements, the evidence of the wear and tear inevitable in a loi journey, and conspicuous in shattered vehicles and bandaged harness, the string of wagons of all shapes, sorts, and sizes, the mud-bespattered carriages, once finely varnished, in which the lady and the children ride, the fiery horse of the son in his teens, the chunky poney of the no less daring boy, the wriggling jersey—the go-cart with the little negro children; and the noisy whoop of blacks of both sexes, mounted and afoot, and taking it by turns to ride or walk—however cheering all these may **seem at a first sight,** as **a** novelty, removing the sense of loneliness **which you** may have felt before, can not but impress **upon you a sentiment of gloom, which** will not **be** lessened **as you watch their progress.** **Their very** light-heartedness — so full of hope and confidence **as** it denotes them to be, is a subject of doubtful reflection. **Will their hopes** be confirmed? Will the dreams so seducing **to** them now, be realized? Will they find the fortune which tempted them to new homes and new dangers? Will they even be secure of health, without which wealth is a woful mockery. These are doubts **which** may well make the thoughtful sad, and the doubtful despondent.

And yet the wayfarers themselves feel but little of this. Their daily progress, **and** the new objects of interest that now and then present themselves, divert them from troublous thoughts **The lands, the woods,** the waters, that attract the eye **of the** planter **on** every side, serve to fix his attention and keep it in constant exercise and **play.** **They** travel slowly, but twelve or fifteen miles a day, and by night **they encamp** upon the roadside, hew down a tree, clear the brush, and **build up** fires that illuminate the woods for miles round. Strange, **fantastic** forms dance in the mazes which the light makes among the receding **trees;** and the boisterous song of the woodman, and the unmeasured laugh of the negro, as he rends the bacon with his **teeth** and fingers, and hearkens **to the ready** joke of his companion **the** while, convey no faint idea of those German stories of the wild **men, or** demons of the Hartz Mountains or the Black Forest, which **we can** not but admire, however uncouth, grotesque, and disproportioned, for their felicitous and playful ingenuity. **The watch-dog** takes his place under the wagon by night, sometimes he sleeps within it, and upon the baggage. The men crouch by the **fire, while rude** and temporary couches of bush and blanket are made for the women and the children of the party. These arrangements necessarily undergo changes according to circumstances. The summer tempests compel **a** more compact disposition of their force; the sudden storm by night drives the more weak and timid to the deserted house, **or if** there be none in the neighborhood, to the bottom of the wagon, where they are sheltered by skins or blankets, with both of which the accustomed traveller is usually well provided

Before the dawn of day they are prepared to renew their journey with such thoughts as their dreams or their slumbers of
the night have rendered most active in their imaginations. The
old are usually thoughtful when they rise, the young hopeful.
Some few of both are sad, as an obtrusive memory haunts them
with threatening or imploring shadows. Others again, and not
the smaller number, cheerily set forth singing, the first day being safely passed—singing some country ditty; and when
they meet with travellers like themselves—an event, which,
in our western woods, may be likened to a "sail" at sea—
cracking with them some hearty joke upon their prospects,
trim and caparison, with a glee that would startle the nerves
and astound the measured sensibilities of the quiet occupant of
more civilized abodes.

The negroes are particularly famous for the light-heartedness
of their habit while journeying in this manner. You will sometimes see ten or twenty of them surrounding a jersey wagon,
listening to the rude harmony of some cracked violin in the
hands of the driver, and dancing and singing as they keep time
with his instrument, and pace with his horse. The grin of
their mouths, the white teeth shining through the glossy black
of their faces, is absolutely irresistible; while he, perched, as I
have often seen him, upon the fore-seat, the reins loosely flung
over his left arm, in the hand of which is grasped the soiled and
shattered instrument, the seams and cracks of which are carefully stopped with tar or pine-gum; while the bow in his right
hand scrapes away unmercifully until it extorts from the reluctant strings the quantity of melody necessary to satisfy the ama-
teur who performs, or the self-taught connoiseurs who hearken
to and depend upon him.

Sometimes the whites hover nigh, not less delighted than
their slaves, and partaking, though with a less ostentatious show
of interest, in the pleasure and excitement which such an exhibition, under such circumstances, is so well calculated to inspire.
Sometimes the grinning Momus of the group is something more
than a mere mechanician, and adds the interest of improvisation
to the doubtful music of his violin. I have heard one of these
performers sing, as he went, verses suited to the scene around
him, in very tolerable rhythm, which were evidently flung off

as he went. The verses were full of a rough humor which is characteristic of all inferior people. In these he satarized his companions without mercy; ridiculed the country which he left, no less than that to which he was going; and did not spare his own master, whom he compared to a squirrel that had lived upon good corn so long, that he now hungered for bad, in his desire of change. This was a native figure, by which his fruitless and unprofitable discontent with what was good in his previous condition was clearly bodied forth. The worthy owner heard the satire, with which he was not less pleased than the other hearers, who were so much less interested in it. Enough of episode. We will now resume our progress.

CHAPTER X.

GOOD AND EVIL SPIRITS.

Ulysses. Had she no lover there
　　　That wails her absence?
Troilus. O, sir, to such as, boasting, show their scars,
　　　A mock is due.　Will you walk on, my lord?
　　　She was beloved — she loved — she is, and doth —
　　　But still, sweet love is food for fortune's tooth.
　　　　　　　　　　　　　Troilus and Cressida.

THAT night we slept at a miserable hovel, consisting of but one apartment, into which the whole family, husband, wife, three children, and ourselves, were oddly clustered together. The house was of logs, and the rain, which fell in torrents before we sought shelter in so foul a sty, came through upon the trundle-bed in which we strove to sleep.　Still we had no occasion for discontent.　The poor wretches who kept the hovel gave us the best they had.　A supper of bacon, eggs, and hoecake, somewhat consoled us for the doubtful prospect in our eyes; and our consolation was complete, when, at rising in the morning, we found that the storm had passed over, and we were in safety to depart.　We had not been so sure that such would be the case at retiring for the night.　Our host had quite a cutthroat and hang-dog expression, and we lay with dirk and pistol at hand, ready for the last emergencies.　Fortunately, we had no need to use them; and, bestowing a couple of dollars upon the children, for their parents refused all pay, we sallied forth upon our journey.　That night we arrived at Tuscaloosa, a town now of considerable size, of increasing prosperity and population, but, at the time of our visit, but little more than opened in the woods.　Here we took lodgings at the only hotel in the place, and were assigned a room in common with two other persons. To this arrangement we objected in vain. The chambers were too few and the crowd too great to permit a tavern-keeper to tolerate any unnecessary fastidiousness on the part of his guests.

Here let me pause in the narrative of my own progress, and retrace for a brief period my steps. Let me unfold the doings of others, necessarily connected with my own, which are proper to be made known to the reader in this place, though only known to me long after their occurrence. The parting with my brother will be remembered. It will be recollected, that, when Mary Easterby came between us after I had dragged him from his horse, and prevented strife, and possibly bloodshed, that he left us together, and proceeded to the habitation of her parents. There, with a heart full of bitterness toward me, and a mind crowded with conflicting and angry emotions, he yet contrived effectually to conceal from observation both the struggle and the bitterness. His words were free, easy, well arranged, and good-natured, as usual, to all around; and, when Mary Easterby returned to the cottage after I had left her, she started with surprise to see how effectually he could hide the traces of that fierce and unnatural strife in which, but a little while before, he had been so earnestly engaged. The unlooked-for ease with which this was done, effectually startled and pained her. By what mastery of his emotions had this been done, and what was the nature of that spirit which could so hermetically seal its anger, its hate, its human and perhaps holiest passions? She saw him in a new light. Heretofore she had regarded him but in one aspect—as a man more solicitous of his ease than of his reputation, good-natured in the extreme, too slothful to be irritable, too fond of repose and good living to harbor secret hostilities. If her opinion on this subject did not suffer change, it at least called for prompt revision and re-examination under the new light in which it appeared, and which now served only to dazzle and confound her. The wonder increased as the evening advanced. He was even humorous and witty in his easy volubility; and, but for the annoyance which she naturally felt at what seemed to her his unnatural low of spirits, she would have been constrained to confess that ever before had he seemed so positively agreeable. All his resources of reading and observation were brought into requisition, and he placed them before the company with so much order, clearness, and facility, that she was disposed to give him credit for much more capacity of nature and acquisition than she had ever esteemed him to possess before. He was acting a part, and, had she not been troubled with misgivings to this effect, he might have acted it successfully. But he overshot his mark. He had not the art, the result only of frequer.' practice, to conceal the art which he employed. His purpose was to seem amiable—to be above the passions which governed me—and to possess the forbearance which could forgive them, even where he himself had been in a measure their victim. He erred in seeming, not only above their control, but free from their annoyance. Had he been slightly grave during the evening, had he seemed to strive at cheerfulness, and at a forgetfulness of that which could not but be unpleasant to any brother, he had been far more successful with Mary Easterby. Her natural good sense revolted at the perfect mastery which he possessed over his emotions. Such a man might well become an Iago, having a power, such as he certainly exhibited, "to smile and smile, and be," if not a villain, one at least wholly insensible to those proper sentiments and sorrows which belonged to his situation under existing circumstances. Little did my brother conjecture the thoughts passing through her mind as he thus played his part. What would I have given to know them! how many pangs, doubts, and sorrows, would have been spared me! what time had I not saved—what affections had I not spared and sheltered! But this is idle.

John Hurdis lingered late that night for an opportunity which was at length given him. Mary and himself were left alone together; and he proceeded to do that which, with the precipitate apprehensions of a jealous lover, I had long before supposed to have been over. Either emboldened by the belief that my rash conduct had sufficiently offended the maiden, and that he had properly prepared the way for his declaration—or, possibly, somewhat anxious lest, in my parting interview, I had poured out desperately those emotions which I had with undue timidity hopelessly and long locked up, and anxious to know the result he resolved to close a pursuit which he had hitherto conducted with no less art than perseverance. John Hurdis was a vain man, and confident of his position; and yet he did not approach that calm and high-minded girl without some trepidation. His first overture began with a reference to the conflict which she had so happily interrupted: —

"Mary, you have this day witnessed that which I should willingly have kept for ever from your knowledge. You have seen the strife of brother with brother; you have beheld a violence shocking to humanity, and, if not ending like that of the first murderer, one which, but for your timely coming, might have had, for one or both of us, a no less fatal termination. I hope, Mary, you do me the justice to believe that I was not to blame in this quarrel."

He drew his chair nigher to hers, as he thus spoke, and waited for her answer with no little solicitude. She hesitated. How could she else than hesitate, when an assenting answer sanctioned the address, the sincerity of which she seriously questioned?

"I know not what to say, Mr. Hurdis," was her reply. "I saw not enough of the strife of which you speak to pass judgment upon it. I will not pretend to say who began it; I would rather not speak on the subject at all."

"Yet he—Richard Hurdis—*he* spoke of it to *you?*" he replied suspiciously.

"No, I spoke of it to him, rather," was the fearless answer. "In the first moment of my surprise and terror, Mr. Hurdis, I spoke to Richard—to your brother—about his rashness; and yet, though I spoke, I know not truly what I said. I was anxious—I was alarmed."

"Yet you know that it was his rashness, Mary, that provoked the affair," he said quickly.

"I know that Richard is rash, constitutionally rash, John," she replied gravely. "Yet I will not pretend to say, nor am I willing to think, that the provocation came entirely from him."

"But you saw *his* violence only, Mary."

"Yes, that is true; but did his violence come of itself, John? Said you nothing? did you nothing to provoke him to that violence? was there no vexing word? was there no cause of strife well known before, between you? I am sure that there must

have seen, John, and I leave it to your candor to say if they
were not. I have known Richard long—we were children together—and I can not think that in sheer wantonness, and
without provocation, he could do what I this day beheld."

A faint yet bitter smile passed over his lips as he replied :—

"And do you think, Mary—is it possible that you, a lady,
one brought up to regard violence with terror, and brutality
with disgust—is it possible that you can justify a resort to
blows for a provocation given in words ?"

The cheek of the maiden crimsoned beneath the tacit reproach ; but she replied without shame :—

"God forbid! I do not; blows *are* brutal, and violence de
grading to humanity i. my eyes! But though I find no sanc
tion for the error of Richard, I am not so sure that you have
your justification in his violence for every provocation of which
you may have been guilty. Your brother is full of impulse,
quick, and irritable. You know his nature well. Did you
scruple to offend it ? Did you not offend it ? I ask you in
honor, John Hurdis, since you have invited me to speak, was
there not some previous cause of strife between you which provoked, if it did not justify, your brother in his violence ?"

"It may be—nay, there was, Mary! I confess it. And
would you know the cause, Mary ? Nay, you must; it is of
that I would speak! Will you hear me ?"

"Freely, John!" was the ready and more indulgent reply.
"If the cause be known, the remedy can not be far off, John,
if we have the will to apply it."

He smiled at what he considered the aptness of the reply.
He drew his chair still nigher to her own ; and his voice fell
and trembled as he spoke

"You are the cause, Mary!"

"I—I the cause!" She paused and looked at him with unreserved astonishment.

"Yes, you, and you only Mary! Richard Hurdis hates me,
simply because I love you! Not that he loves you himself,
Mary!" he spoke quickly—"no, he would control you for his
own pride! he would rule you and me, and everything alike!
But that he shall not! No, Mary! hear me—I have been
slow to speak, as I was fearful to offend! I would not be pre-

cipitate. I sought to **win your regard before I** ventured to **proffer** mine. The affair **this day** prompts me to **speak sooner** than **I** might have done. **Hear me,** then, Mary; **I love you! I** proffer you my heart, my life! **I will live for you! I implore** you, then— be **mine!**"

The head **of** Mary **Easterby sank as she** heard **this language.** Her cheek assumed a deeper flush; there was **a sorrowful expres-** sion in her eye which did not encourage the pleader; and **when** she spoke, which, after a little pause, she did, it annoyed him to perceive that she was composed and dignified in **her** manner, and that all trace **of** emotion had departed from **her** voice.

"I thank you, John—I thank you for your favorable opin- ion; but I am not satisfied that I should **be the** occasion of strife between you and your brother. **You tell me** that I am— that he is unwilling **that you should love me, or that I** should love you in return!"

"It is—it is that, Mary!" **he exclaimed hastily, interrupting** her speech, which was uttered composedly, and **even slow.**

"I am sorry that **it is—sorry** that you **think so, John;** for I am sure you must be mistaken."

"Mistaken!" he exclaimed.

"**Yes,** John, mistaken! You are—you must be mistaken! **It** can not be as you imagine. Supposing that Richard was unwilling **that** you should regard **me with** favor, and that I should **respond** favorably to your regard—for which I see no reason—"

He interrupted her again, **and** with some show **of** impatience.

'There is reason—reason enough—though **you may not see** it! I tell you that **he** would rule us both! **His nature is des** potical. A younger brother, he has yet the **management of** everything at home; and, having been brought up as **your com-** panion from childhood, he claims to have some right to manage your concerns also. He would rule in all things, **and over** everybody, and would **not have** me love **you, Mary,** or you **me,** for that very reason. **Not** that he loves **you** himself, **Mary;** **no,** no!—that might alter the case, were it **so—but I am sure,** I know, that he **loves another! It is a sort of** dog-in-the-man- ger spirit that **possesses** him, **and which** brought about our quar- rel."

Here was a batch of lies; and yet there was truth in much that he said. Without doubt, I had much of that despotic nature which he ascribed to me, and which, more or less, affected my deportment in all my associations; but the whole tissue of his speech was woven in falsehood, and one difficulty in which he had involved himself by a previous remark led even to a greater number yet. He had ascribed to her the occasion of our quarrel, without reflecting that he had already persuaded her that my regards were given to another. It was difficult now for him to account for my hostility to his success with Mary, unless by supposing in me a nature unnaturally froward and contradictory. And such a nature, whatever were my other faults, could not fairly be laid to my charge. To have suffered Mary to suppose that I really loved her, was no part of his subtle policy. For months it had been his grateful labor to impress upon her mind a different belief.

After hearing him patiently through his hurried tirade, Mary resumed:

."I think you do your brother much injustice, John, when you ascribe to him a temper so unreasonable. I have known him for many years, and, while I have often found him jealous and passionate, I must defend him from any charge of mere wilful and cold perversity. He is too irritable, too quick and impetuous, for such a temper. He does not sufficiently deliberate to be perverse; and as for the base malignity of desiring to keep one, and that one a brother, from the possession of that which he did not himself desire to possess, I can not think it. No, John, that can not be the true reason, I have no doubt that you think so, but as little is my doubt that you think unjustly."

"I know no other reason, Mary," was the somewhat cold answer.

"Nay, John, I speak not so much of the general cause of the difference between you, as of the particular provocation of the strife to-day. Let it be as you say, that Richard is thus perverse with little or no reason, yet it could not be that without immediate and rude cause of anger he should rush upon you in the high road and assault you with blows. Such violence is that of the robber who seeks for money, or the blood-thirsty assassin who would revenge, by sudden blow, the wrong for which

he dared not crave open and manly atonement. Now, I know
that Richard is no robber; and we both know him too well to
think that he would assassinate, without warning, the enemy
whom he had not the courage to fight. Cowardice is not his
character any more than dishonesty; and yet it were base cowardice if he assaulted you this day without due warning."

The cool, deliberate survey which Mary Easterby took of the
subject, utterly confounded her companion. He was unprepared
for this form of the discussion. To dwell longer upon it was
not his policy; yet, to turn from it in anger and impatience was
to prejudice his own cause and temper, in the estimation of one
so considerate and acute as Mary had shown herself to be.
Passing his hand over his face, he rose from his seat, paced the
room slowly twice or thrice, and then returned to his place with
a countenance once more calm and unruffled, and with a smile
upon his lips as gently winning as if they had never worn any
other expression. The readiness of this transition was again
unfavorable to his object. Mary Easterby was a woman of
earnest character — not liable to hasty changes of mood herself, and still less capable of those sudden turns of look and
manner which denote strong transitions of it. She looked dis-
trustfully upon them accordingly, when they were visible in
others.

"You are right, Mary!" said the tempter, approaching her,
and speaking in tones in which an amiable and self accusing
spirit seemed to mingle with one of wooing solicitation. "You
are right, Mary; there was an immediate provocation of which
I had not spoken, and which I remember occasioned Richard's
violence. He spoke to me in a manner which I thought in-
solently free, and I replied to him in sarcastic language. He
retorted in terms which led me to utter a threat which it did not
become me to utter, and which, I doubt not, was quite too provoking for him to bear with composure. Thence came his
violence. You were right, I think, in supposing his violence
without design. I do not think it myself; and, though, as I
have said, I regard Richard's conduct toward me as ungracious
and inexcusable, I am yet but too conscious of unkind feelings
toward him to desire to prolong this conversation. There is
another topic, Mary, which is far more grateful to me —

you suffer me to speak on that? You have heard my declaration. I love you, Mary! I have long loved you! I feel that I can not cease to love, and can not be happy without you! Turn not from me, Mary! hear me, I pray you! be indulgent, and hear me!"

"I should not do justice to your good regards, John, nor to our long intimacy, if I desired to hear you farther on this subject! Forgive me—leave me now—let me retire!"

She arose as if to depart. He caught her hand and led her back to the seat from which she had arisen. It was now that he trembled—trembled more than ever, as he beheld her so little moved.

"You are cold, Mary! you dislike—you hate me!" he stammered forth, almost convulsively.

"No, John, you are wrong. I neither hate nor dislike you; and you know it. On the contrary, I have much respect for you, as well on your own account as on that of your family."

"Family! respect! Oh, Mary, choose some other words! Can not you hear me speak of warmer feelings—closer ties? Will you not heed me when I say that I love?—when I pray you to accept—to love me in return?"

"It must not be, John! To love you as a husband should be loved—as a wife should love—wholly, singly, exclusively, so that one should leave father, mother, and all other ties only for that one—I can not! I should speak a base untruth, John, were I to say so! It gives me pain to tell you this, sir! it gives pain—but better that both of us should suffer the present and momentary anguish which comes from defrauded expectations, than risk the permanent sorrow of a long life, passed in the exercise of falsehood! I am grateful for your love, John! for the favor with which you distinguish me; but I can not give you mine. I can not reply as you would wish me."

"Mary, you love another!"

"I know not, John! I would not know! I pray that you would not strive to force the reflection upon me!"

"You mistake Richard Hurdis, if you think that he loves you, Mary. He does not; you can have no hope of him."

The coarse, base speech of the selfish man was well answered by the calm and quiet tone of the maiden.

"And if I had hopes of him, or of any man, John Hurdis, they should be entombed in the bosom, where they had their birth, before my lips or looks should declare them to other bosoms than my own. I have no hopes, such as you speak of; and, so truly as I stand before you, I tell you that I know not, that I have in my heart a solitary sentiment with reference to your brother, which, according to my present thought, I would not you should hear. That I have always regarded him with favor, is true; that I deem him to be possessed of some very noble qualities, is no less true. More; I tell you, it is with pain, anxious and deep pain, that I have beheld his coldness, when we have met of late, and his estrangement from me, for so long a period. I would give much to know why it is. I would do much that it should be otherwise."

"And yet you know not, Mary, that you love him?"

"I know not, John; and if the knowledge may be now obtained, I would infinitely prefer not to know. It would avail me nothing, and might — might become known to him."

There is no need to dwell longer upon this interview, though the vexing spirit of my brother, clothing what he spoke still in the language of dissimulation, protracted it for some time longer, in vain assaults upon her firmness, and, failing in that, in mean sarcasms, which were doubly mean as they were disguised alternately in the language of humiliation and of love. When he left her, she hurried to her chamber, utterly exhausted with a struggle in which all the strength of her mind had been employed in the double duty of contending with his and of keeping her own feelings, upon which it was his purpose to play, in quiet and subjection. Her tears came to her relief, when she found herself alone, but they could not banish from her mind a new consciousness, which, from the moment when she parted with my brother, kept forcing itself upon her. "Did she, in truth, love Richard Hurdis?" was her question to herself. How gladly, that moment would I have listened to her answer!

CHAPTER XI.

GUILTY PRACTICE.

Macbeth. ———— Know
That it was he, in the times past, which held you
So under fortune   which, you thought, had been
Our innocent self· this I made good to you
In our last conference ; passed in probation with you
How you were borne in hand; how crossed.
     *   *   *   *   *   *
Now, if you have a station in the file,
And not in the worst rank of manhood, say it;
And I will put that business in your bosoms,
Whose execution takes your enemy off ;
Grapples you to the heart and love of us,
Who wear our health but sickly in his life,
Which in his death were perfect.
  Murderer. I am one, my liege,
Whom the vile blows and buffets of the world
Have so incensed, that I am reckless what
I do to spite the world.—SHAKSPERE.

THE interview had barely terminated when my brother left the habitation of the maiden. He had preserved his composure, at least he had concealed the passion which his disappointment had aroused within him, until fairly out of sight. It was then that he gave vent to feelings which I had not supposed him to possess. Base I thought him, envious it may be ; but of malignity and viperous hate, I had never once suspected him. He had always seemed to me, as he seemed to others, too fat for bitterness, too fond of ease and quiet to suffer any disappointment to disturb him greatly. We were all mistaken. When he reached the cover of the woods he raved like a madman. The fit of fury did not last very long, it is true; but while it lasted, it was terrible, and in the end exhausting. He threw himself from his horse, and, casting the bridle over a shrub, flung himself indifferently upon the grass, and gave way to the bitterest meditations. He had toiled long, without cessation, and his toils had all been taken in vain. It did not offer any qualification to his mortified feelings to reflect that he had also toiled dishonorably.

But on a sudden he rose, and resumed his seat in the saddle. His meditations had taken a new course. His hopes had revived; and he now planned projects, the character of which, even worse than those already known to the reader, will soon be developed. He put spurs to his steed, and rode furiously through the wood. It was deep, dark and tangled; but he knew the country, with which, it was fortunate for him, his horse was also familiar. Through by-paths which were made by the cattle, or by scouting negroes, he hurried through the forest, and in a couple of hours' space, emerged from it into a more beaten path. A ride of an hour more carried him beyond the plantation of my father, which the circuit through the forest had enabled him to avoid, and in the immediate neighborhood of a miserable cabin that stood in a secluded and wild spot, and was seen with difficulty through the crowding darkness. A faint light shone through the irregular logs of which it was built, and served, while indicating the dwelling, to convey to the observer an increased idea of its cheerlessness.

It was before this habitation, if such it might be called, that John Hurdis drew up his horse. He alighted, and, having first led the animal into shadow behind the house, he returned to the door in front, and tapping, obtained immediate entrance. The room into which he was admitted was a small one, and so filled with smoke that objects were scarce discernible. Some light wood thrown into the fire on his entrance served to illumine, if not to disperse it, and John spoke to the inmates with a degree of familiarity which showed him to have been an old acquaintance. They were old acquaintance, not only of him but of myself. The man was a villain whom I had caught stealing corn from our fields, and whom, but for John, I should have punished accordingly. I little knew what was the true motive which prompted his interference, and gave him credit for a greater degree of humanity than was consistent either with his character. He was a burly ruffian, a black

. .ed. black-faced fellow, rarely clean, seldom visible by
day, a sullen, sour, bad-minded wretch, who had no mode of
livelihood of which the neighbors knew except by inveigling
the negroes into thefts of property which, in his wanderings,
he disposed of. He was a constant wanderer to the towns
around, and it was said, sometimes extended his rambles to
others out of the state. His rifle and a mangy cur that slept in
the fireplace, and like his master was never visible by day,
were his sole companions when abroad. At home he had a
wife and one child. The wife, like himself, seemed sour and
dissatisfied. Her looks, when not vacant, were dark and threatening. She spoke little but rarely idly, and however much her
outward deportment might resemble that of her husband, it
must be said in her favor, that her nature was decidedly gentler,
and her character as far superior as it well could be, living in
such contact, and having no sympathies save those which she
found in her child and husband. Perhaps, too, her mind was
something stronger, as it was more direct and less flexible, than
his. She was a woman of deliberate and composed manner,
rarely passionate, and careful to accommodate her conduct and
appearance to the well-known humility of condition in which
she lived. In this lay her wisdom. The people around com
miserated her as she was neither presumptuous nor offensive,
and tolerated many offences in him, in consideration of herself
and child, which would have brought any other person to the
whipping post. The child, an unhappy creature, a girl of fifteen, was an idiot-born. She was pretty, very pretty, and
sometimes, when a sudden spark of intelligence lighted up her
eye, she seemed really beautiful. But the mind was utterly
lacking. The temple was graceful, erect, and inviting, but the
god had never taken possession of his shrine.

Enough! It was to this unpromising family and mean abode
that John Hurdis came late at night. The inmates were watch
ful and the man ready to answer to the summons. The woman,
too, was a watcher, probably after an accustomed habit, but the
idiot girl slept on a pallet in one corner of the apartment.
When John Hurdis entered, she raised her head, and regarded
him with a show of interest which he did not appear to see

He looked with some curiosity at her couch, however; but for an instant only. His regards that night were for her father only.

"Ah, Pickett," said he with an air of jocularity on entering, "how goes it? How does the world use you now-a-days? How d'ye do, Mrs. Pickett? And Jane—how is Jane?"

"I'm well, sir, I'm quite well, Mr. John," was the quick response of the poor innocent in the corner, whom everybody thought asleep. The answers of Pickett and his wife were not so prompt. That of the former was somewhat surly, that of the wife slow. A brief formal dialogue passed between the party, in which John Hurdis spoke with infinite good humor. He did not seem to heed the coldness of his host and hostess; and all traces of his late anger had passed effectually from his voice and visage. His only concern seemed now to conciliate those whom he sought, and it does not take long for the rich man to make the poor and the inferior unbend. In a little time John Hurdis had the satisfaction to see the hostess smile, and to hear a broken and surly chuckle of returning good-nature from the lips of Pickett. The preliminary difficulty was over; and making a sign to Pickett, while his wife's back was turned, the guest led the way to the door bidding the latter good-night. The idiot girl half raised herself in the bed and answered for the mother.

"Good-night, Mr. John, good-night, Mr. John."

Pickett followed Hurdis to the door, and the two went forth together.

They soon buried themselves in the thick cover of the neighboring wood, when John Hurdis, who had led the way, turned and confronted his companion.

"Well, 'squire," said Pickett with abrupt familiarity, "I see you have work for me. What's the mischief to-night?"

"You are right. I have work for you, and mischief. Will you do it?"

"If it suits me. You know I'm not very nice. Let's hear the kind of work, and then the pay that I'm to get for doing it, 'fore I answer."

"Richard Hurdis goes for the 'Nation' to-morrow," said John in a lower tone of voice.

"Well, you're glad to get rid of him, I suppose. He's out

of your way now. I wish I could be certain that he was out of mine."

"You can make it certain."

"How?"

" 'Tis that I came about. He goes to the 'Nation,' on some wild goose chase; not that he wishes to go, but because he thinks that Mary Easterby is fond of me."

"So; the thing works, does it?"

"Ay, but does not work for me, though it may work against him. I have succeeded in making them misunderstand each other but I have not yet been successful in convincing her that I am the only proper person for her. You know my feeling on that subject, it is enough that she declines my offer."

" Well, what then are you to do?"

" That troubles me. She declines me simply because she prefers him."

" But you say she has no hope of him. She thinks he loves another."

" Yes! But that does not altogether make her hopeless. Hope is a thing not killed so easily; and when woman love, they cling to their object even when they behold it in the arms of another. The love lives, in spite of them, though, in most cases, they have the cunning to conceal it. Mary Easterby would not give up the hope of having Richard Hurdis, so long as she could lay eyes on him, and they are both single."

" Perhaps you're right; and yet, if Richard drives for the 'Nation' she'll lose sight of him, and then——"

" Will he not return?" replied the other sternly and gloomily. " Who shall keep him away? The discontent that drives him now will bring him back. He goes because he believes that she is engaged to me. He will come back because he doubts it. He will not sleep until he finds out our deception. They will have an explanation—had he not been blinded by his own passions he would have found it out before—and then all my labors will have been in vain. It will be my turn to go among the Choctaws."

" Well—but, 'squire, while he's off and out of sight, can't you get her to marry you and have done with it?" said Pickett.

" Not easily; and if I could, what would it avail? Loving

him as she does, I should but marry her for him. His hand
would be in my dish, and I should but fence in a crop for his
benefit No, no, that would not do either. I tell you, where
these women once love a man, to see him, to have opportunity
with him, is fatal, though they be lawfully bound to another. I
should not sleep secure in her arms, as I should not be able to
think that I only was their occupant."

"Now, that is what I call being of a mighty jealous sort of
disposition, 'squire. I'm sure that you're wrong in your notion
of Miss Mary. I don't think she'd be the woman to do wrong
in that way. She's a mighty nice girl, is so modest and well
behaved, and so much of a lady; I'm always afraid to look at
her when I speak to her; and she carries herself so high, that
I'm sure if a man had anything wrong to say to her, he could
not say it if he looked at her and saw her look."

"Ay, that is her look to you, Pickett, and to me, perhaps,
whom she does not love," said John bitterly; "but let her look
on Richard Hurdis, and meet his eye, and the face changes
fast enough. She has no dignified look for him; no cold, composed, commanding voice. Oh, no! It is then her turn to
tremble, and to speak brokenly and with downcast eyes; it is
then her turn to feel the power of another, and to forget her
own; to be awed, rather than to awe; to fear herself, rather
than to inspire that fear in him which she may in both of us."

"I reckon he feels it too, 'squire, quite as much, if not more,
than you; for, say what you please, there's no saying Richard
Hurdis don't love her. I've watched him often when he's been
with her, and when he has not thought that anybody was looking at him — and that was at a time, too, when I had no reason
to like any bone in his skin — and I saw enough to feel certain
that he felt a real, earnest love for her."

"Let us say no more of that now," said John Hurdis coldly,
as if not altogether pleased with the tone of his companion's
speech. "Do you like him any better now, Ben Pickett? is
he not the same man to you now that he has ever been? would
he not drive you out of the country if he could? has he not
tried to do it? And who was it stood between you and the
whipping-post, when, at the head of the county regulators, he
would have dragged you to it, for robbing the courthouse, and

buying cotton from the negroes? Have you forgotten all this
Ben Pickett? and do you like Richard Hurdis any better when
you remember that, to this moment, he has not relaxed against
you, and, to my knowledge, only a month ago threatened you
with the horsewhip, if he found you prowling about the plantation?"

"Ay, I hear you," said the man, while the thick sweat actually stood upon his forehead, as he listened to an enumeration
of events from which his peril had been great—"I hear you,
John Hurdis: all is true that you say, but you say not all the
truth. Did you hear what I said to Richard Hurdis when he
threatened me with the horsewhip? do you know what I said
to myself, and swore in my own heart, when he would have
hauled me to the whipping-post from which you saved me?"

"No; what said you? what did you swear?"

"To put my bullet through his head, if he laid the weight of
his finger upon me; and but that you saved him in saving me,
so surely would I have shot him, had the regulators tied me to
the tree and used one hickory upon me."

"I was a fool for saving you, then, Pickett—that's all. Had
I known that you could so well have fought your own battles,
I had let him go on. I am not sorry, Ben, that I saved you
from the whip; but, by G—d, I am sorry to the soul that I saved
him from the shot!"

"I'm not sorry," said the other. "Let Richard Hurdis live;
I wish him no harm.. I could even like him; for, blast me, but
he has something about him that I'm always glad to see in a
man, and if he would only let me alone—"

"He will not let you alone, Ben Pickett. He can not let you
alone, if you would look at the matter. He comes back from
the 'nation,' and Mary Easterby is still unmarried. What then
—an explanation takes place between them. They find out
the truth: they find, perhaps, that you put the letter in the way
of Mary that told her about Richard's doings at Coosauda; that
you have been my agent in breeding the difference between
them. More than this, they marry, and Richard brings his
wife home to live with him at the old man's, where, if he does
that, he will have full authority. Do you suppose, when that
time comes I will stay in the neighborhood? Impossible. It

will be as impossible for me to stay here as it will be for you The moment I go, who will protect you? Richard will rout you out of the neighborhood; he has sworn to do it; and we both know him too well not to know that, if he once gets the power to do what he swears, he will not hesitate to use it. He will drive you to Red river as sure as you're a living man."

"Let the time come," said the other gloomily, "let the time come. Why do you tell me of this matter now, 'squire?"

"You are cold and dull, Ben Pickett—you are getting old," said John Hurdis, with something like asperity. "Do I not tell you other things? do you not hear that Richard Hurdis sets off to-morrow for the 'nation'? I have shown you that his absence is of benefit to both of us, that is return is to our mutual injury. Why should he return. The gamblers may cut his throat and the fighting Choctaws may shoot him down among their forests, and nobody will be the wiser, and both of us the better for it."

"Why, let them, it will be happy riddance," said Pickett.

"To be sure, let them," said the other impatiently; "but suppose they do not, Ben? should we not send them a message, telling them that they will serve and please us much by doing so? that they will rid us of a very troublesome enemy, and that they have full permission to put him to death as soon as they please."

"Well, to say the truth, 'Squire John," said Pickett, "I don't see what you're driving at."

"You mean that you won't see, Ben," responded the other quickly; "listen awhile. You are agreed that it will do us no small service if the gamblers or the Choctaws put a bullet through the ribs of Richard Hurdis; it will be a benefit rather than a harm to us."

"Well."

"But suppose they think it will not benefit *them*, are we to forgo our benefits because they show themselves selfish? Shall Richard Hurdis survive the Choctaws, and come home to trouble us? Think of it, Ben Pickett; what folly it would be to suffer it! Why not speed some one after the traveler, who will apprize the gamblers, or the Choctaws, of our enemy—who will show them how troublesome he is—how he carries a good sum of money in his saddle-bags? how easy it will be for them to stop a troublesome traveller who has money in his saddle-bags? It may be that such a messenger might do the business himself in consideration of the benefit and the money; but how should we or anybody know that it was done by him? The Choctaws, Ben—the Choctaws will get the blame, we the benefit, and our messenger, if he pleases, the money."

"I understand you now, 'squire," said Pickett.

"I knew you would," replied John Hurdis, "and only wonder that you did not readily comprehend before. Hear me, Ben: I have a couple of hundred dollars to spare—they are at your service. Take horse to-morrow, and track Richard Hurdis into the 'nation;' he is your enemy and mine. He is gone there to look for land. Give him as much as he needs. Six feet will answer all his purposes, if your rifle carries as truly now as it did a year ago."

The man looked about him with apprehension ere he replied. When he did so, his voice had sunk into a hoarse breathing, the syllables of which were scarce distinguishable.

"I will do it," he said, grasping the hand of his cold and cowardly tempter, "I will do it—it shall be done; but, by G—d, 'squire, I would much rather do it with his whip warm upon my back, and his angry curses loud in my ears."

"Do it as you will, Ben; but let it be done. The Choctaws are a cruel and treacherous people, and these gamblers of the Mississippi are quite as bad. Their murders are very common. It was very imprudent for Richard to travel at this season; but if he dies, he has nobody but himself to blame."

They separated. The infernal compact was made and chronicled in their mutual memories, and witnessed only by the fiends that prompted the hellish purpose.

CHAPTER XII.

A POOR MAN'S WIFE.

> "Thou **trust'st a villain**; he will take thy **hand**
> And **use it for his own**; yet when the brand
> **Hews** the dishonored member—not his loss—
> Thou art **the victim!**"—*The Flight.*

WHEN Pickett returned to his hovel, on leaving John Hurdis, his wife abruptly addressed him thus:—

"Look you, Ben, John Hurdis comes after no good to-night. I see it in that smile he has. I know there's mischief in his eye. He laughs, but he does not look on you while he laughs: it isn't an honest laugh, as if the heart was in it, and as if he wasn't afraid to have everything known in his heart. He's a bad man, Ben, whatever other people may think; and, though he has helped you once or twice, I don't think him any more certain your friend for all that. He only wants to make use of you; and if you let him go too far, Ben, mark my words, he'll leave you one day in a worse hobble than ever he helped you out of."

"Pshaw, Betsy, how you talk! you've a spite against John Hurdis, and that's against reason too. You forget how he saved me from his brother."

"No, I do nor forget it, Ben. He did no more than any man should have done who saw a dozen about to trample upon one. He saved you, it is true, but he has made you pay him for it. He has made you work for him long enough for it, high and low, playing a dirty sort of a game; carrying letters to throw in people's paths, there's no knowing for what; and telling you what to say in people's ears, when you haven't always been certain that you've been speaking truth when you did so. I don't forget that he served you, Ben, but I also know that you are serving him day and night in return. Besides, Ben, what he did for you is what one gentleman might readily do for another: I'm not sure that what he makes you do for him isn't rascal-work."

"Hush!" said Pickett, in a whisper, "you talk too loud. Is Jane asleep?"

The watchful idiot, with the cunning of imbecility which still has its object, closed her eyes, and put on the appearance of one lost to all consciousness.

"Yes, she's asleep; but what if she does hear us? She's our own child, though not a wise one, and it will be hard if we can't trust ourselves to speak before her," said the mother.

"But there's something, Betsy, that we shouldn't speak at all before anybody."

"I hope the business of John Hurdis ain't of that character, Ben Pickett," she retorted quickly.

"And what if it is?" he replied.

"Why then, Ben, you should have nothing to do with it, if you'll mind what I'm telling you. John Hurdis will get you into trouble. He's a bad man."

"What, for helping me out of trouble?"

"No, but for hating his own brother as he does, his own flesh and blood as I may say, the child that has suckled at the same nipple with himself; and, what's worse, for fearing the man he hates. Now, I say that the hate is bad enough, and must lead to harm; but when he's a coward that hates, then nothing's too bad for him to do, provided he can keep from danger when he does it. That's the man to light the match, and run away from the explosion. He'll make you the match, and he'll take your fingers to light it, and then take to his own heels and leave you all the danger."

"Pshaw, Betsy, you talk like a woman and a child," said Pickett, with an air of composure and indifference, which he was far from feeling.

"And so I do, Ben; and if you'll listen to a woman's talk, it will be wise. It would have saved you many times before, and it may do much to save you now. Why should you do any business that you're afraid to lay out to me. There must be something wrong in it, I'm sure; and it can't be no small wrong neither, Ben, that you're afraid to tell me. What should the rich 'Squire Hurdis want of Ben Pickett the squatter? Why should he come palavering you, and me, and that poor child with fine words; and what can we, poor and mean and hated as we are by everybody, what can we do for so great a man as him? I tell you, Ben Pickett, he wants you to do dirty work, that he's ashamed and afraid to do himself. That's it, Ben; and there's no denying it. Now, why should you do his dirty work? He's better able to do it himself, he's rich enough to do almost what he pleases; and you, Ben, you're too poor to do even what is proper. These rich men ask what right a poor man has to be good and honest; they expect him to be a rascal."

"Well," said the other sulkily, "we ought to be so, then, if it's only to oblige them."

"No, Ben-Pickett, we ought hardly to oblige them in anything; but, whether we would oblige them or not, my notion is, we ought to keep different tracks from them altogether. If we are too mean and poor, to be seen by them without turning up their noses, let us take care not to see them at any time, or if we do see them, let us make use of our eyes to take different tracks from them. There's always two paths in the world, the one's a big path for big people; let them have it to themselves, and let us keep off it; the other's a little path for the little, let them stick to it and no jostling. It's the misfortune of poor people that they're always poking into the wrong path, trying to swell up to the size of the big, and making themselves mean by doing so. No wonder the rich despise such people. I despise them myself, though God knows I'm one of the poorest."

"I'm not one to poke in big paths," said Pickett.

"No! But why do big folks come out of their road into yours, Ben Pickett? I'll tell you. Because they think they can buy you to go into any path, whether big or little, high or low, clean or dirty. John Hurdis says in his heart, I'm rich; Pickett's poor; my riches can buy his poverty to clean the road for me where it's dirty. Isn't that it, Ben Pickett?"

The keen gray eyes of the woman were fixed on him with a glance of penetration, as she spoke these words, that seemed to search his very soul. The eyes of Pickett shrank from beneath their stare,

"Betsy, you're half a witch," he exclaimed with an effort at jocularity which was not successful.

"I knew it was something like that, Ben Pickett. John Hurdis would never seek you, except when he had dirty work on hand. Now, what's the work, Ben Pickett?"

"That's his secret, Betsy: and you know I can't tell you what concerns only another and not us."

"It concerns you; it is your secret too; Ben Pickett — it is my secret — it is the secret of that poor child."

The speaker little knew that the idiot was keenly listening. She continued :—

"If it's to do this work, and if it's work done in his name, work that you won't be ashamed of, and he won't be ashamed of when it's done, Ben Pickett, then it's all right enough. You may keep his secret and welcome ; I would not turn on my heel to know it. But if it's dirty work that you'll both be ashamed of, such as carrying stories to Mary Easterby, who is a good girl, and deserves the best; then it's but too much of that sort of work you've done already."

"It's nothing like that," said Pickett quickly. "But don't bother me any more about it, Betsy; for if you were to guess a hundred times, and guess right, I shouldn't tell you. So have done and go to bed."

"Ben Pickett, I warn you, take care what you do. This man, John Hurdis, is too strong for you. He's winning you fast, he'll wrong you soon. You're working for him too cheaply; he'll laugh at you when you come for pay; and may be put to your own account the work you do on his. Beware, look what you're about, keep your eyes open; for I see clear as daylight, that you're in a bad way. The work must be worse than dirty you're going upon now, when you are so afraid to speak of it to me."

"I tell you, Betsy, shut up. It's his business, not mine, and I'm not free to talk of it even to you. Enough that I don't work for nothing. The worst that you shall know of it will be the money it will bring."

"The devil's money blisters the fingers. And what's money to me, Ben Pickett, or what is money to you? What can money do for us? Can it make men love us and seek us?

Can it bring us pride and character? Can it make me forget the scorn that I've been fed on from the time I was a simpler child than that poor idiot in the corner? Can it bring sense into her mind, and make us proud of her? Can it make you forget or others forget, Ben Pickett, that you have been hauled to the whipping-post, and saved from it only to be the slave of a base coward, such as John Hurdis has ever been, and ever will be?"

"No more of that, Betsy, if you please. You are quite too fond of bringing up that whipping-post."

"And if I do, it has its uses. I wish you would think of it half as frequently, Ben Pickett; you would less frequently stand in danger of it. But I speak of it, because it is one of the black spots in my memory—like the lack of that child— like the scorn of those around us—like everything that belongs to us, as we are living now. Why will you not go, as I wish you, away from this neighborhood? Let us go to the Red river where we know nobody; where nobody knows us. Let us go among the savages, if you please, Ben Pickett, where I may see none of the faces that remind me of our shame."

"Why, so we will. Just as you say, Betsy, I will but do some business that I'm bound for, that will give us money to go up and then———"

"No, don't wait for that. Let the money stay; we have enough to carry us to the Red river, and we shall want but little of it there. When you talk to me of money you vex me. We have no use for it. We want hommony only and homespun. These are enough to keep from cold and hunger. To use more money, Ben Pickett, we must be good and conscious of good. We must not stand in fear and shame, to meet other than our own eyes. I have that fear and shame, Ben Pickett: and this dirty business of John Hurdis—it must be dirty since it must be a secret—makes me feel new fear of what is to come; and I feel even shame to sickness as I think upon it. Hear me, Ben; hear me while it is in time for me to speak. There may not be time tomorrow, and if you do not listen to me now, you might listen another day in vain. Drop this business of John Hurdis———"

"I've promised him,"

"Break your promise."

"No! d——d if I do that!"

"And why not? There's no shame in breaking a bad promise. There shame and cowardice in keeping it."

" I'm no coward, Betsy."

"You are! You are afraid to speak the truth to me, to your wife and child. I dare you to wake up that poor idiot and say to her, weak and foolish as she is, the business you are going on for John Hurdis. You'd fear that, in her very ignorance, she would tell you that your intention was crime!"

" Crime?"

" Ay, crime—lies, perhaps, in a poor girl's ear—theft; perhaps the robbery of some traveler on the highway; perhaps—perhaps—Oh, Ben Pickett, my husband, I pray to God it be not murder!"

" Damnation, woman! will you talk all night?" cried the pale and quivering felon in a voice of thunder. " To bed, I say, and shut up. Let us have no more of this."

The idiot girl started in terror from her mattress.

" Lie down, child; what do you rise for?"

The stern manner of her father frightened her into obedience, and she resumed her couch, wrapping the coverlet over her head, and thus, hiding her face and hushing her sobs at the same moment. The wife concluded the dialogue by a repetition of her exhortation in brief.

"Once more, Ben, I warn you. You are in danger. You will tell me nothing; but you have told me all. I know you well enough to know that you have sold yourself to do wrong—that John Hurdis has bought you to do that which he has not the courage to do himself—"

" Yet you say I am a coward."

"I say so still. I wish you were brave enough to want no more money than you can honestly get; and when a richer man than yourself comes to buy you to do that which he is too base to do himself, to take him by the shoulders and tumble him from the door. Unfortunately you have courage enough to do wrong—there's a greater courage than that, Ben Pickett, that strengthens even a starving man to do right."

Pickett felt that he had not this courage, and his wife had before

this discovered that the power **was not in her to endow him with it.**
Both parties, were compelled when **they discovered the idiot girl to**
be awake **and** watchful, to forego their **discussion of the subject for**
the night; and when the woman did resume it, which **she did with a**
tenacity of purpose, worthy of **a** more **ostentatious virtue, she was**
only succesful in arousing that sort of anger in her companion, **which**
is but **too** much the resort of the wilful when **the** argument **goes**
against them.   It was more easy for Pickett, **with the** sort of courage
which he **possessed, to do wrong than right, and having once resolved**
to sin, the exhortations of virtue **were only so many suggestions to**
obstinacy.   **With a** warmth **and** propriety **infinitely** beyond her situation did the wife plead; but her earnestness, **though great, was not**
equal to the doggedness **of his resolve.   She was compelled to give**
up the cause in despair.

CHAPTER XIII.

THE BLOODHOUND ON THE SCENT.

> " His was the fault ; be his the punishment.
> 'Tis not own their crimes only men commit ;
> They harrow them into another's breast,
> And they shall reap the bitter growth with pain."
>
> LANDES.

THE messenger of blood departed the next day upon his fearful mission. His calculation was to keep due pace with his victim; to watch his progress; command his person at all times, and to avail himself of the first fitting opportunity, to execute the cruel trust which he had undertaken. Such a purpose required the utmost precaution and some little time. To do the deed might be often easy; to do it secretly and successfully, but seldom. He was to watch the single moment in a thousand, and be ready to use it before it was gone forever.

" You will not be gone long, Ben ?" said the wife, as he busied himself in preparation.

" I know not—a day, a week, a month !—I know not. It matters little ; you can do without me."

" Yes, your wife can do without you—I wish that John Hurdis could do without you also. I do not like this business, Ben, upon which he sends you now."

" What business ? what know you of it ?" he demanded hastily. " Why should you dislike the business which you know nothing about ?"

" That's the very reason that makes me dislike it. Why should I know nothing about it ? Why should a man keep his business from his wife's knowledge ?"

" Good reason enough, to keep it from the knowledge of everybody else. You might as well print it in the Montgomery paper, as to tell it to a woman. There won't be a Methodist preacher that don't hear of it the first week, and not a meeting in the country that won't talk of it in the second. They have quite enough of other folks' affairs to blab, Betsey; we needn't give them any of mine."

"You well enough know, Ben Pickett, that this sort of talk means nothing. You know I am not the woman to make her own or her husband's concerns the business of the country. I go not often to the church. I do not often see the preachers, and there is very little to say between us. It might be much better if there were more: and you know well enough that I see few women and have no neighbors. We are not the people to have neighbors—what would tempt them? It is enough for me, Ben, to stay at home, and keep as much out of sight as I can, as well on your own account as on account of that poor ignorant creature."

"Pshaw! you talk too much of Jane, and think too much of her folly. She is no more a fool than most other girls of her age, and talks far less nonsense. She's quite as good as any of them, and a devilish sight handsomer than most of them. There's hardly one that wouldn't be glad to have her face."

"You mean me, father Ben, don't you!" said the witless one, perking up her face with a smile, and raising it under the chin of Pickett.

"Go, Jane, go and put things to rights on the table, and don't mind what we're a saying."

The girl obeyed reluctantly, and the father, tapping her on the head kindly, the only parting which he gave her, left the house, and proceeded to his horse which was fastened to the fence. There he arranged the saddle, and while thus employed his wife came to him.

"Ben Pickett," she said, resuming the subject of her apprehensions, "I hear that Richard Hurdis is going to the 'nation' to-day."

"Well! what of that!" said Pickett gruffly.

"Nothing but this, Ben; I'm afraid that his going to the 'nation' has something to do with your journey. Now, I don't know what it is that troubles me, but I am troubled, and have been so ever since I heard that Richard was going to-day."

"And how did you hear it?"

"From Jane."

"Jane, the fool! and how did she hear it?"

"She's a fool, but there's no need for you to call her so always, Ben. It's not right; it's not like a father. As for where she heard it, I can't say; I didn't ask her; perhaps from some of the negroes; old Billy, from 'Squire Easteby's was over here, last night."

"Last night! old Billy! at what hour was he here?"

"Nay I don't know exactly. He went away just before John Hurdis came."

Pickett appeared annoyed by the intelligence, but was silent and concealed his annoyance, whatever may have occasioned it, by strapping his saddle and busying himself with the bridle of his horse.

"You say nothing, Ben; but tell me, I beg you, and ease my mind, only tell me that the business you're going upon don't concern Richard Hurdis. Say, only say, you don't go the same road with Richard Hurdis, that you didn't know that he was going, that you won't follow him."

"And how should I say such a thing, Betsy," replied the now obdurate ruffian, "when I don't know which road he's going? How can I follow him, if I don't know the track he takes?"

"That's not it — not it. Tell me that you won't try to find it, that you don't mean to follow him, that — oh! my God, that I should ask such a thing of my husband — that you are not going after Richard Hurdis to kill him?"

"Betsy, you're a worse fool than Jane," was the reply of Pickett. "What the devil put such nonsense into your head? What makes you think I would do such a thing? It's true, I hate Dick Hurdis, but I don't hate him bad enough to kill him unless in fair fight. If he'll give me fair fight at long shot, by G—d, I'd like nothing better than to crack at him; but I'm not thinking of him. If I had wanted to kill him, don't you think I'd a done it long before, when he was kicking me about like a foot-ball. You may be sure I won't try to do it now, when he's let me alone, and when, as you say yourself, he's going out of the country. Damn him, let him go in peace, say I."

"Amen," exclaimed the woman, "amen; yet look you, Ben Pickett. What you mightn't feel wicked enough to do for yourself, you may be weak enough to do for one who is more wicked than you are. That's the misfortune of a great many people; and the devil gets them to do a great deal of work which they wouldn't be willing to do on their own account. Oh, Ben, take care of that John Hurdis. If you didn't hate Richard Hurdis bad enough to kill him on your own score, don't let that cowardly John tempt you to do it for him. I know he hates his brother and wants to get him out of the way; for he wants to marry Mary Easterby; but don't let him make use of you in any of his wickedness. He stands no chance of Mary with all his trying, for I know she won't have him; and so if you work for him, you'll work against the wind, as you have done long enough both for yourself and him. But whether you work for him or not, hear me, Ben Pickett, do nothing that you'll be ashamed or afraid to hear of again. My mind misgives me about Dick Hurdis. I wish you were not a-going—I wish you were not a-going the same day with him."

"Don't I tell you, Betsy, I'm not on his trail. I shan't look after him, and don't care to see him."

"Yes; but should you meet?"

"Well, what then? Would you have me cut and run like a nigger's dog?

"No; but I would not have you go to-day. I would rather you shouldn't meet."

"We won't, be sure of that. I promise you, we won't meet; and, if we do, be sure we shan't quarrel."

"You'll promise that, Ben?—you'll swear it?" said the woman eagerly.

"Ay, to be sure I will; I swear, Betsy, I won't meet him, and we shan't quarrel if I can help it."

"That's enough, Ben; and now go in peace, and come back soon. It's off my mind now, Ben, since you promise me; but it's been a trouble and a fear to me, this going of yours to-day, ever since I heard that Richard Hurdis was to be on the road."

"Pshaw! you're a fool all over about Dick Hurdis!" said Pickett, with a burly air of good humor; "I believe now, Betsy, that you like him better than me."

"Like him!" exclaimed the woman, relapsing into the phlegmatic and chilling sternness of expression and countenance which were her wonted characteristics in ordinary moods. "Like him! .... neither like nor dislike, Ben Pickett, out of this paling. These old logs, and this worm fence, contain all that I can expend feeling upon, and when you talk to me of likes and dislikes, you only laugh at your own condition and mine."

The man said no more and they separated. She returned to the house, and in a few moments he leaped upon his horse, which was light-made and fast-going, though small, animal, and was soon out of sight even of the idiot-girl, who laughed and beckoned to him, without being heeded, until his person was no longer visible in the dull gray of the forest which enveloped him.

"Fool!" he exclaimed, as he rode out of hearing; "fool, to think to make me swear what she pleases, and then to take the oath just as I think proper! I will not meet him, and still less will I quarrel with him, if I can help it; but I will try and put a bullet through him for all that! It's an old score, and may as well be wiped out now as never. This year is just as good for settlement as the next. Indeed, for that matter, it's best now. It's much the safest. He breaks off from one neighborhood, and they know nothing of him in any other. 'Well,' as John Hurdis said, 'the Choctaws have done it, or the gamblers. Ben Pickett has been too long quiet, and lives too far from the nation, to lay it at his door. And yet, by G—d! it's true what Betsy says, that John Hurdis is a poor coward after all!"

It was in thoughts and musings such as these—sometimes muttered audibly, but most frequently entertained in secret—that Ben Pickett commenced his pursuit of me, a few hours only after I had begun my journey. Circumstances, however, and probably an error in the directions given him by my brother, misled him from the path, into which he did not fall until late the ensuing day. This gave me a start of him which he woud not have made up, had I not come to a full stop at Tuscaloosa. But of this afterward.

CHAPTER XIV.

THE SILLY JANE.

" She dwelt among the untrodden ways,
    Besides the springs of Dove,
A maid, whom there were none to praise,
    And very few to love,
A violet by a mossy stone,
    Half hidden from the eye,
Fair as a star when only one
    Is shining in the sky."—WORDSWORTH.

"And yet lack!"—SHAKSPERE

THE afternoon of the day following that of Pickett's departure was one the loveliest among the lovely days so frequent
in the Alabama November. The glances of the oblique sun
rested with benignant smile, like that of some venerable and
single-hearted sire, upon the groves of the forest, which, by this
time, had put on all the colors of the rainbow. The cold airs
of coming winter had been just severe enough to put a flush-like
glow into the cheeks of the leaf, and to envelop the the green, here
and there, with a coating of purple and yellow, which served it
as some rich and becoming border, and made the brief remains
of the gaudy garb of summer seem doubly rich, and far more
valuable in such decorations. Dark brown and blooded berries
hung wantonly from bending branches, and trailing vines, that
were smitten and torn asunder by premature storms of cold, lay
upon the path and depended from overhead, with life enough
in them still, even when severed from the parent-stem, to nour-
ish and maintain the warm and grape-like clusters which they
bore. Thousands of flowers, of all varieties of shape and color,
came out upon the side of the path, and, as it were, threw themselves along the thoroughfare only to be trodden upon; while

hidden in the deeper recesses of the woodland, millions beside appeared to keep themselves in store only to supply the places of those which were momently doomed to suffer the consequences of exposure and to perish beneath the sudden gusts of the equally unheeding footsteps of the wayfarer. Hidden from sight only by the winter bloom that absorbed all space, and seemed resolute to exclude from all sight, thousands of trees, of more delicate nature already stripped of their foliage, stood like mourning ghosts or withered relics of the past — the melancholy spider, the only living decoration of their gaunt and stretching arms, her web now completely exposed in the absence of the leaves, under whose sheltering volume, it had been begun in secret. At moments the breeze would gather itself up from the dead leaves that strewed the paths of the forest, and ruffle lightly, in rising, the pleasant bed where it had lain. A kindred ruffler of leaves and branches, was the nimble squirrel, who skipped along the forests, making all objects subservient to his forward motion; and now and then the rabbit timidly stealing out from the long yellow grass beside the bay, would bound and crouch alternately; the sounds that shake the lighter leaves and broken branches, stirring her heart with more keen and lasting sensations, and compelling her to pause in her progress, in constant dread of the pursuer.

A fitting dweller in a scene of such innocence and simplicity was the thoughtless and unendowed creature that now enters it; her hand filled with bush and berry and leaf, sought with care, pursued with avidity, gathered with fatigue, and thrown away without regard. A thousand half-formed plans in her mind — if the idiot child of Ben Pickett may be said to possess one — a thousand crowding, yet incomplete, conceits, hurrying her forward in a pursuit only begun to be discarded for others more bright, yet not more enduring; and from her lips a heartfelt laugh or cry of triumph poured fourth in the merriest tones of childhood, while the tears gather in her eyes, and she sits upon the grass, murmuring and laughing and weeping all by turns, and never long. From the roadside she has gathered the pale blue and yellow flowers, and these adorn her head and peep out from her bosom. Now she bounds away to hidden bushes after flaunting berries, and now she throws herself upon a bank and tears to pieces the flowers and shrubs which have cost her so much pains to gather. She sings and talks by turns as she thus employs herself, and prating in idiot soliloquy at fits, she speaks to the flowers that she rends, and has some idle history of each.

"There's more of blue than of the others, and sure there should be, for the skies are blue, and they take their color from the skies. But I don't want so much of the blue; I won't have so much; I must have more yellow; and there's a little pink flower that Mr. John showed me long time ago, if I could get only one of them; one would do me to put in the middle. There's a meaning in that little flower, and Mr. John read it like a printed book. It has drops of yellow in the bottom, and it looks like a little cup for the birds to drink from, I must look for that. If I can only get one now, I would keep it for Mr. John to read, and I would remember what he tells me of it. But Mr. John don't love flowers, he does not wear them in his button-hole as I see Mr. Richard; and Miss Mary loves flowers too; I always see her with a bunch of them in her hand, and she gathers great bunches for the fireplace at home. She reads them, too, like a book; but I will not get her to read my little pink flower for me. I will get Mr. John; for he laughs when he reads it, and Miss Mary looks almost like she would cry; and she looks at me, and she does not look at the flower, and she carries me home with her; but Mr. John takes me a long walk with him in the woods, and we gather more flowers together, and we sit down upon the log, and pull them to pieces. I wish he would come now. If he were with me, I could go deeper into the woods; but they look too black when I am by myself, and I will not go alone. There's more than twenty bears in those black woods, so mother tells me; and yet, when I go there with Mr. John, I don't see any, and I don't even hear them growl; they must be afraid of him, and run when know he's coming. I wish he were coming to read my flower. I have one — I have two — if he would but come. Oh, me, mother! — what's that?"

The girl started from the bank in fear, dashing down the flowers in the same instant, and preparing herself for flight. The voice of the intruder reassured her: —

"Ah, Jane, my pretty, is it you?"

"Dear me, Mr. John, I'm so glad you're come! I thought it was the black bears. Mother says there's more than twenty in these woods, and tells me that I musn't go into them; that they'll eat me up, and won't even leave my bones. But when you're with me, Mr. John, I'm not afraid of the bears."

"Humph!" was the muttered thought of the new-comer; "not the less danger perhaps, but of this no matter."

"So you're afraid of the bears, my pretty Jane?" he said aloud.

"Ah, no, not when you're with me, Mr. John; they're afraid of you. But when I'm by myself, the woods look so black, I'm afraid to go into them."

"Pretty idiot!" exclaimed John Hurdis, for it was he; "but you're not afraid now, Jane: let us take a walk, and laugh at these bears. They will not stop to look at us; and if they do, all we have to do is to laugh at them aloud, and they'll be sure to run. There's no danger in looking at them when they run, you know."

"No, to be sure; but, Mr. John — stop. I don't know whether I ought to go with you any longer; for do you know——" Here she lowered her voice to a whisper, and looked cautiously around her as she spoke — "do you know mother's been talking to dad about you, and she says — but I won't tell you."

And, with a playful manner, she turned from him as she finished the sentence, and proceeded to gather up the flowers, which, in her first alarm, she had scattered all around her. He stooped to assist her, and, putting his arm about her waist, they walk forward into the wood, the silly creature all the while refusing to go, yet seeming perfectly unconscious that she was even then complying with his demand. When they were somewhat concealed within its recesses, he stopped, and with some little anxiety demanded to know what it was that her mother had said.

"I won't tell you, Mr. John, I won't."

He knew very well how to effect his purpose, and replied calmly —

"Well, if you won't tell me, Jane, I will call the bears—"

"No, don't!" she screamed aloud; "don't, Mr. John! I'll

tell you everything. **Did you** think **I** wouldn't **tell you, Mr. John?**—I was only **in play.** Wait, **now, till I pick up this** little pink flower, **Mr. John, that's got the yellow drops in the** bottom, and I'll **tell you all. This is the flower that you read** to me, Mr. John: **do, now—that's a good dear—do read it to** me now."

"Not now, Jane—after you tell **me** about your **mother.**"

"Yes—but, Mr. John, would you set the bears on me for **true?**"

"To be sure, if you wouldn't tell me. Come, Jane, be quick, **or** I'll call **them.**"

"No, don't—don't, I beg you! I'm sure it's nothing so great to tell you; but I tell you, Mr. John, you see, because mother didn't **want** you to know. **Dad** and she talked **out,** but when they thought **I was** awake, **Ob, then** there **was no more talk for a while;** but I heard them all."

"All what, **Jane?**"

"Oh, **don't you know?** All **about you and dad, and Mr.** Richard, and **how you hate Mr. Richard, and how dad is to** shoot him—"

"The d—l! you didn't **hear** that, **Jane!" was the exclama-** tion of the thunderstruck criminal; his **voice thick with appre-** hension, his limbs trembling, his **flesh shrinking and shivering, and** his eyes, full of wonder **and affright,** absolutely **starting from the** **sockets.** So sudden had been **the** revelation, **it might well have** **startled or** stunned a much bolder spirit than **was his.** He led, almost dragged **her,** still deeper into the woods, as **if he dreaded the** heedful ears of any passing traveler.

"What have you heard, Jane? what more **did your mother** say? She surely said not what you tell me; **how could she** know—how could she say it? She did **not say it, Jane—she** could not."

"Oh, **yes, but** she did : she said a great deal more, **but it's no use** telling you."

"How no **use?** Tell me all, **Jane.** Come, **my pretty, tell me all** that your mother said, and how she came to **say it. Did your father** **say it** to her first?"

"Who, dad? Lord bless **you,** Mr. John, no! **Dad never** tells **mother** nothing, and what she knows she **knows by herself** without **him.**"

"Indeed! But this about Richard and your father—you don't mean that your mother knew any such thing. Your father told her; you heard him talking to her about it."

"No, I tell you. Father wouldn't talk at all; it was mother that talked the whole. She asked dad, and dad wouldn't tell her, and so she told him."

"Told him what? did she hear?"

"Yes, she told him as how you loved Miss Mary; but, Mr. John, it isn't true you love Miss Mary, is it?"

"Pshaw! Jane, what nonsense! Go on, tell me about your mother."

"Well, I knew it couldn't be that you loved Miss Mary. I don't wan't you to love her. She's a fine lady, and a sweet, good lady, but I don't like you to love her; it don't seem right; and—"

The impatient, anxious spirit of John Hurdis could no longer brook the trifling of the idiot, which, at another period, and with a mind less excited and apprehensive, he would rather have encouraged than rebuked; but now, chafing with excited feelings and roused fears, he did not scruple to interrupt her.

"Nonsense, Jane—nonsense! Say no more of Mary, but tell me of your mother. Tell me how she began to speak to your father—what she said—what she knows—and we'll talk of Miss Mary and other matters afterward. What did she say of Richard? what of me, and this shooting of your father?"

"Oh, she didn't say about shooting dad; no, no, it was Mr. Richard that he was to shoot."

"Well, well—tell me that—that!"

"Oh, dear me, Mr. John, what a flurry you're in! I'm sure I can't tell you anything when you look so. You frighten me too much; don't look so, Mr. John, if you please."

The criminal tried to subdue the appearance of anxiety and terror which the girl's countenance and manner sufficiently assured him must be evident in his own. He turned from her for an instant, moved twice or thrice around a tree—she meanwhile watching his proceedings with a degree of curiosity that made her forget her fears—then returning, with a brow somewhat smoothed, and a half-smile upon his lips, he succeeded in persuading her to resume a narrative which her natural imbecility of mind, at no period, would have enabled her to give consecutively. By questions carefully put, and at the proper moment, he at length got from her the whole amount of her knowledge, and learned enough to conclude, as was the truth, that what had been said by the mother of the girl had been said conjecturally. His fear had been that she had stolen forth on the previous night, and, secreting herself near the place of conference between Pickett and himself, had witnessed the interview, and comprehended all its terms. However relieved from his fear by the revelation of the idiot, he was still not a little annoyed by the close guessing of the woman. A mind so acute, so penetrating, so able to search into the bosom, and watch its secret desires without the help of words, was able to effect yet more; and he dreaded its increased activity in the present business. Vague apprehensions still floated in his soul, though he strove to dissipate them, and he felt a degree of insecurity which made him half-forgetful of his simple and scarcely conscious companion. She, meanwhile, dwelt upon the affair which she had narrated, with a tenacity as strange as had been her former reluctance or indifference, until, at length, she repeated her mother's unfavorable opinion of himself, his disquiet got the better of his courtesy, for he exclaimed aloud : —

"No more of this nonsense, Jane! Your mother's a fool, and the best thing she can do hereafter is to keep her tongue."

"No, no, Mr. John!" replied the girl, earnestly, "mother's no fool, Mr. John; it's Jane that's a fool. Everybody calls Jane a fool, but nobody calls mother so."

"I don't call you so, Jane," said Hurdis kindly, sitting beside her as he spoke, and putting his arm about her waist.

"No, Mr. John, I know you don't, and "— in a whisper — "I'd like you to tell me, Mr. John, why other people call me so. I'm a big girl, and I can run, and walk, and ride like other people. I can spin and I can sew. I help mother plant potatoes, I can break the corn, hull it and measure it, and can do a hundred things besides. I talk like other people; and did you ever see a body pick flowers, and such pretty ones, faster than me, Mr. John?"

"No, Jane, I never did."

"And such pretty ones, too, Mr. John! Look at this little

pink one, with the yellow drops. Come, read it to me now, Mr. John, and show me how to read it like you."

"Not now, Jane—some other time. Give me a kiss, now—a sweet kiss!"

"Well, there, nobody asks me to kiss but you and Miss Mary sometimes Mr. John. Sometimes I kiss mother, but she don't seem to like. I wonder why, Mr. John—it must be because I'm a fool."

"No, no, Jane, you're not a fool."

"I wish I wasn't, Mr. John—I don't think I am; for, you know, I told you how many things I can do just like other people,"

"Yes, Jane, and you have a sweeter little mouth than anybody. You kiss like a little angel, and your cheeks are as rosy—"

"Oh, don't, Mr. John,! that's enough. Lord, if mother was only to see us now, what would she say? Tell me, Mr. John, why don't I want mother to see me when you're so good to me? And when you kiss me so, what makes me afraid and tremble? It is strange, Mr. John!"

"It's because your mother's cross to you, and cold, and gets vexed with you so often, Jane."

"Do you think so, Mr. John? But, it can't be; mother isn't cross to me, Mr. John, and she hasn't whipped me I don't know the day when. She don't know that you walked with me into the woods, Mr. John: why don't I want to tell her—it's so very strange? She would be mighty vexed if she was to see me now."

Hurdis answered her with a kiss; and in the next instant the tread of a sudden footstep behind them, and the utterance of a single word by the intruder, caused the simple girl to scream out, and to leap like an affrighted deer from the arms that embraced her.

CHAPTER XV.

THE STRONG MOTHER.

Medea. I thought as much when first from thickest 'es**
I saw you trudging in such posting pace.
But to the purpose, what may be the cause
Of this most strange and sudden banishment?
  Fausta. The cause, ask you? a simple cause, God **wot**
'Twas neither treason, nor yet felony,
But for because I blamed his foolishness.
  Medea. I hear you **say** so, but **I greatly fear**,
Ere that your tale be brought **unto an end**,
You'll prove yourself **the author of the same.**
But pray, be brief; **what folly did your spouse,**
And how will you revenge **your wrong on him!**

ROBERT GREENE.

Her fear seemed to possess **the** power **of a spell** to produce the very person whose presence she most dreaded. **As if in** compliance with its **summons, her** mother stood before **her.** Her tall, majestic form, **raised** to its fullest height by the **fever** of indignation in her mind, stood between her idiot daughter and the astounded John Hurdis. He had sprung **to** his feet **on** the instant when Jane, in terror, had started **from his embrace,** and, without daring to face the woman, he stood **fixed to the** spot where she first confronted him. Her meager, **usually pale** and severe features, were now crimsoned with **indignation; her** eyes flashed a fire of feeling and of character which **lifted her,** however poor and lowly had been her birth **and was her station,** immeasurably above the base **creature whose superior** wealth had furnished the facilities, **and, too frequently** in the minds of men, provide a sanction, for **the vilest abuses of** the dependence and inferiority of the poor. **The consciousness** of wrong in his mind totally deprived him at that instant of those resources of audacity with which he who meditates villany should always be well supplied; and, woman as she was—poor, old, and without character and command, as was the wife of the worthless Pickett—the sound of her voice went through the frame of Hurdis with a keenness that made him quiver. And yet the tones were gentle; they were studiously subdued, and from this cause, indeed. their influence was most probably increased upon both Hurdis and the daughter:—

"Jane, my child, go home—go home!"

These were words not to be disobeyed by the trembling and weeping idiot. Yet she looked and lingered; she fain would have disobeyed them for the first time; but the bony and long finger of the mother was uplifted, and simply pointed in the direction of their cottage, which was not visible from the point on which they stood. Slowly at first—then, after she had advanced a few paces, bounding off with the rapidity of fear—the girl hurried away, and was soon lost to the sight of the two remaining persons.

When satisfied that she was no longer within sound of their voices, for her keen eye had followed all the while the retreating footsteps of the maiden, she turned the entire force of its now-voluminous expression upon the man before her. Her gray eyebrows, which were thick, were brought down, by the muscular compression of the skin of the forehead, into a complete penthouse above her eyes, and served to concentrate their rays, which shot forth like summer lightning from the sable cloud! The lips were compressed with a smiling scorn, her whole face partaking of the same contemptuous and withering expression. John Hurdis stole but a single glance at the features which were also full of accusation, and, without looking a second time, turned uneasily away. But the woman did not suffer him to escape. She drew nigher—she called him by name; and, though she spoke in low and quiet tones, they were yet such that he did not venture to persist in his movement, which seemed to threaten as prompt and rapid a departure as that of the idiot. Her words began, abruptly enough, with one of the subjects nearest to her heart. She was not a woman to trifle. The woods in which she had lived, and their obscurity. had taught lessons of taciturnity; and 't was, therefore, in the fullness of her heart only that she suffered her lips to speak.

"And wherefore is it," she demanded, "that Mr. Hurdis takes such pains to bring the idiot daughter of Ben Pickett into these secret places? Why do these woods, which are so wild—so little beautiful and attractive—so inferior to his own—why do they tempt him to these long walks? And this poor child, is it that he so pities her infirmity—which everybody should pity—that he seeks her for a constant companion in these woods, where no eye may watch over his steps, and no ear hear the language which is uttered in her own? Explain to me this, I pray you, Mr. Hurdis. Why is it that these woods are so much more agreeable to you than your father's or 'Squire Easterby's? and why a gentleman, who makes bold to love Mary Easterby, and who values her sense and smartness, can be content with the idle talk of an unhappy child like mine? Tell me what it means, I entreat you, Mr. Hurdis; for in truth—supposing that you mean rightly—it is all a mystery to me."

The very meekness of the woman's manner helped to increase the annoyance of Hurdis. It was too little offensive to find fault with; and yet the measured tones of her voice had in them so much that was bitter, that he could not entirely conceal from her that he felt it. His reply was such as might have been ex pected:—

"Why, Mrs. Pickett, I meant no harm, to be sure. As for the woods, they are quiet and pretty enough for me; and though it is true that my own or Mr. Easterby's are quite as pretty, yet that's no reason one should be confined only to them. I like to ramble elsewhere, by way of change; and to-day, you see, happening to see your daughter as I rambled, I only joined her, and we walked together; that's all."

"And do you mean to say, Mr. Hurdis, that you have never before joined Jane Pickett in these walks?"

"To be sure not—no—"

"Ha!"

"Yes—that's to say, I don't make a practice of it. I may have walked with her here once or it may be twice before, Mrs. Pickett—"

"Ay, sir, twice, thrice, and a half-dozen times if the truth is to be told!" exclaimed the woman vehemently. "I have seen you, sir, thrice myself, and watched your footsteps, and heard your words—words cunningly devised, sir, to work upon the simple feelings of that poor ignorant, whose very feebleness should commend her to the protection, not the abuse, of a noble-minded man. Deny it, sir, if you dare! I tell you here, in the presence of the eternal God, that I have heard and seen you walk secretly in this wood with Jane Pickett more than three several times—nay, more, sir, you have enticed her into it by various arts; and have abused her ignorance by speaking to her in language unbecoming in a gentleman to speak, and still more unbecoming in a female to hear. I have seen you, and heard you, sir, with my own eyes and ears; and that you have not done worse, sir, is perhaps only owing to her ignorance of your meaning."

"You, at least, would have known better, Mrs. Pickett," replied Hurdis with a sneer—the discovery of the woman being too obviously complete to leave him any hope from evasion.

"Your sneer falls harmlessly upon my mind, Mr. Hurdis. I am too poor, and too much of a mother, sir, to be provoked by that. It only shows you to me in a somewhat bolder point of view than I had been accustomed to regard you. I knew well enough your character, when I watched you in your walks with my child, and heard the language which you used in her ears—"

"Certainly a very commendable and honorable employment, Mrs. Pickett! I give you credit for it."

"Ay, sir, both proper and commendable when employed as a precaution against those whose designs are known to be improper, and whose character is without honor. I well enough understand your meaning. It was scarcely honorable, you would say, that I should place myself as a spy upon your conduct, and become an eavesdropper to possess myself of your counsels. These are fashions of opinion, sir, which have no effect upon me. I am a mother, and I was watching over the safety of a frail and feeble child, who—God help her that made her so!—was too little able to take care of herself not to render it needful that I should do so. It was a mother's eye that watched—not you, sir, but her child; it was a mother's ear that sought to know—not the words which were spoken by John Hurdis, but all words, no matter of whom, which were poured into the ears of her child. I watched not you, but her; and learn from me now, sir, that you never whistled her from our cabin that my ears caught not the signal as readily as hers—she never stole forth at your summons, but my feet as promptly followed hers. Do you wonder now that I should know you as I do? Ah, Mr. Hurdis, does it not shame you to the heart to think that you have schemed so long, with all the arts of a cunning man, for the ruin of a feeble idiot scarcely sixteen years of age?"

"'Tis false!" exclaimed John Hurdis, hoarse with passion; "I tell you, woman, 'tis false, what you say! I had no such design."

"'Tis true, before Heaven that hears us, Mr. Hurdis; I say it is true," replied the woman in moderate tones. "You may deny it as you please, sir, but you can neither deceive Heaven nor me, and to us your denial must be unavailing. I could not mistake nor misunderstand your arts and language. You have striven to teach Jane Pickett an idea of sin, and perhaps you have not succeeded in doing so only because nobody yet has been able to teach her any idea—even one of virtue. But it was not only her mind that you strove to inform. You have appealed to the blood and to the passion of the child, and, but for the mother that watched over her, you might have succeeded at last in your bad purposes. O John Hurdis, if Ben Pickett could only know, what, for the sake of peace, and to avoid bloodshed, I have kept to myself, he would have thrust his knife into your throat long before this! I could have stopped you in your pursuit of my child, by a word to her father; for, low and poor as he is, and base as you may think you have made him, he has pride enough to yet avenge our dishonor. I have kept back what I had to say to this moment; and now I tell you, and you only, what I do know—it will be for yourself to say whether Ben Pickett shall ever know it."

"Pshaw, woman! you talk nonsense; and, but that you are a woman, I could be very angry with you. As for doing anything improper with Jane Pickett, I swear—"

"No, do not swear; for if you do, John Hurdis—if you dare swear that you had no such design—I will swear that you belie yourself—that your oath is false before Heaven—and that you are as black-hearted and perjured as I hold you base and cowardly! And if you did swear, of what use would be your oath? Could you hope to make me believe you after my own oath? could you hope to deceive Heaven? Who else is here to listen? Keep your false oath for other witnesses, John Hurdis, who are more blind and deaf than I am and more easily deceived than the God who alone sees us now."

"Mrs. Pickett, you are a very singular woman. I don't know what to make of you."

The manner of the woman had absolutely quelled the base spirit of the man. When he spoke thus, he literally knew not what he said.

"You shall know more of me, Mr. Hurdis, before I have done," was her reply. "My feelings on the subject of my child have almost made me forget some other matters upon which I have sought to speak with you. You questioned my child upon the subject of a conversation between her father and myself. She told you that we spoke of you."

"Yes, I think I remember," he said breathlessly, and with feeble utterance.

"You do remember—you must," said the woman. "You were very anxious to get the truth from my child: you shall hear it all from me. You have sent Ben Pickett upon your business."

"He will not tell you that," said Hurdis.

"Perhaps not; but I know it."

"Well, what is it?"

"Dare you tell? No! and he dare not. The husband may not show to his own wife the business upon which he goes. There is something wrong in it, and it is your business."

"It is not; he goes, if he goes at all, upon his own, not mine. I do not employ him."

"You do. Beware, John Hurdis! you are not half so secure as you pretend, and perhaps think yourself. The eyes that watch the footsteps of a weak and idiot child, will not be the less heedful of those of a weak and erring husband. If Ben Pickett goes to do wrong, he goes upon your business. If wrong is done, and is traced to him, believe me—for I swear it—I will perish in the attempt, but I will trace it home to its projector and proprietor! You are not, and you shall not be, safe. I have my suspicions."

"What suspicions? I defy you to say I have anything to do with your husband."

The boldness of John Hurdis was all assumed, and the veil was readily seen through by the keen-sighted woman.

"I will confirm to your own ears the intelligence which you procured from my child. It was base in me to follow and to watch over her safety : it was not base in you to pick from her thoughtless lips the secrets of her parents, and the private conversation of her household! I will not ask you to define the distinction between the two. She told you the truth. I suspected that you were using Ben Pickett to do the villany which you had the soul to conceive, but not to execute. I know some villanies on which you have before employed him."

"What villanies mean you?" he demanded anxiously.

"No matter now — I may find them of more use to me some future day than now. I will tell you now what were my fears — my suspicions — when you came to our cabin the last night, and carried Ben Pickett with you into the woods—"

"You followed us? You heard—you listened to what was said between us?" was the hurried speech of Hurdis, his apprehensions denoted in his tremulous and broken utterance, in the startling glare of his eyes, and the universal pallor of his whole countenance. A smile of scorn played upon the lips of the woman—she felt her superiority. She spoke, after a moment's pause, during which the scorn of her face changed into sorrow :

"Your cheek betrays you, John Hurdis, and confirms my worst fears. I would that you had been more bold. I would have given much to have seen you more indifferent to my answer. Could you defy me now, as you did but a little while ago, I should sleep much easier to-night. But now I tremble quite as much as you. I feel that all my doubts are true. I would have forgiven you your meditated wrong to my child could you have looked and spoken differently."

"God of heaven, woman!" exclaimed John Hurdis, with a feeling of desperation in his voice and manner, "what is that you mean? Speak out and tell me all — say the worst — what is it that you know? what is it you believe? Did you or did you not follow us last night? did you hear my conference with your husband?"

"I did not!"

Hurdis was relieved by the answer. He breathed freely once more, as he replied—

"Ha! say no more, then; I do not care to hear you now. I have had wind and fury enough."

"You must hear me. I will tell you now what I believe."

"I will not hear you. Let me go! I have heard enough What is your belief to me?"

He would have passed her, but she caught his arm.

"You shall—but for one moment."

He paused, and, like an impatient steed beneath a curb which chafes him, and from which he can not break away, John Hurdis turned in her grasp, revolving on the same ground while she spoke, and striving not to hear the language which yet forced itself upon his senses.

'I believe, John Hurdis, that you have sent my husband to do some violence. He denies it, and have striven to believe him, but I can not. Since he has left me, I find my suspicions return; and they take a certain shape to my mind, the more I think of them. I believe that you have sent him against your own brother, whom you both hate and fear—"

"Woman—you lie!"

He broke away from her grasp, but lingered.

"I will not call you man, John Hurdis; but I will not think ankindly of you, if it be, as you say, that I lie. God grant that my fears be false! But, believing what I say—that you have despatched my husband to do a crime which you dare not do yourself— I tell you that if it be done—"

"He will be the criminal!" said Hurdis, in low but emphatic tones, as he turned from her; "he will be the criminal, and, if detected — if, as you think, he has gone to commit crime, and such a crime — the gallows, woman, will be the penalty, and it may be that your hand will guide him to it."

The woman shrank back, and shivered; but only for an instant. Recovering, she advanced :—

"Not my hand, John Hurdis, but yours, if any. But let that day come no matter whose hand shall guide Ben Pickett to such a doom, I tell you, **John** Hurdis, he shall have company You are rich, John Hurdis, **and I am poor;** but **know from me** that there is energy **and resolution enough** in this withered bosom to follow you **in all your secret machinations, to trace** your steps in any forests, **and to bring you to the same punish** ment, or **a worse,** than **that which you bring on him!** I am poor and old: men **scorn me, and my own sex turns away, and,** sickening at my poverty, forget **for a while** that **they are human,** in ceasing to believe **me so.** But **the very** scorn of mankind **will** strengthen me; and when **I** am alone—when the weak **man** whom you entice with your money **to do** the deed from which you shrink, becomes your victim—beware **of me;** for so surely as there is a God in heaven, he will **help me to find the** evidence which shall bring you to punishment **on earth!"**

"The **woman** is a fiend—a very **devil!"** cried Hurdis, as he rushed from **the strong and resolute spirit before him.** Her tall form was lifted beyond **her ordinary height as she spoke, and** he shrank from the intense fire **that shot through her long, gray** eyebrows. "I would sooner face **the devil!"** he muttered, as he fled. "There's something speaks **in her that I fear.** Curse the chance, but it is terrible to have **such an enemy, and to feel** that one is doing **wrong!"**

He **looked back** but once **ere he left the forest, and her** eyes were still fixed upon him. **He ventured** no second glance; but, annoyed with a thousand apprehensions, to which the interview had given existence, he **hurried** homeward like one pursued— starting **at** every sound **in the woods, though** it **were only the** falling of **a** leaf in the sudden **gust of November.**

CHAPTER XVI.

THE TRAVELLERS FALL AMONG THIEVES.

> "You must eat men. Yet thanks, I must you con,
>   That you are thieves professed; that you work not
>   In holier shapes; for there is boundless theft
>   In limited professions. Rascal thieves,
>   Here's gold."—*Timon of Athens.*

> "So I leave you
>   To the protection of the prosperous gods,
>   As thieves to keepers."—*Ibid.*

In the meanwhile, Ben Pickett, moved with no such consid-erations as those which touched his wife, set forth in pursuit of his destined victim. His footsteps I may not pursue at present. It will be enough that I detail my own progress. The reader has already seen that I arrived safely at Tuscaloosa. How I came to escape him so far, I can not say; since, allowing that he pursued me with even moderate avidity, he must have over-taken me if he had so purposed it. But, it is believed, that he mistook my route. He believed that I had struck directly for the river, on my nearest path to Chochuma. He had no knowl-edge of my companion's business in Tuscaloosa; and John Hur-dis, being equally ignorant on that subject, could . not counsel him. Whatever may have been the cause of my escape so far, from a foe whose aim was certain, and who had overcome all scruples of policy or conscience — if, indeed he ever held them —I had reason for congratulating myself upon my own good fortune, which had availed for my protection against his murder-ous purpose. But, conscious of no evil then, and wholly ignorant of the danger I had thus escaped, I gave myself no concern against the future; and with all the buoyant recklessness of youth, pleased with novelty, and with faces turned for a new my companion and myself entered our strange lodgings in Tuscaloosa, with feelings of satisfaction amounting to enthusiasm.

The town was little more than hewn out of the woods. Piles of brick and timber crowded the main, indeed the only street of the place, and denoted the rawness and poverty of the region in all things which could please the eye, and minister to the taste of the traveller. But it had other resources in my sight. The very incompleteness, and rude want of finish, indicated the fermenting character of life. The stagnation of the forests was disturbed. The green and sluggish waters of its inactivity were drained off into new channels of enterprise and effort. Life had opened upon it; its veins were filling fast with the life-blood of human greatness; active and sleepless endeavors and a warm sun, seemed pouring down its rays for the first time upon the cold and covered bosom of its swamps and caverns. -

To the young, it matters not the roughness and the storm. Enthusiasm loves the encounter with biting winds, and active opposition; but there is death in inaction—death in the sluggish torpor of the old community, where ancient drones, like the old man of the sea on the shoulders of Sinbad, keep down the choice spirit of a country, and chill and palsy all its energies. There was more meaning in the vote of the countryman who ostracised Aristides, because he hated to hear him continually called "the Just," than is altogether visible to the understanding. The customary names of a country are very apt to become its tyrants.

Our lodging-house was poor enough, but by no means wanting in pretension. You would vainly look for it now in Tuscaloosa. It has given way to more spacious and better conducted establishments. When we arrived it was filled to overflowing, and, much against our will, we were assigned a chamber in common with two other persons, who were strangers to us. To this arrangement we vainly opposed all manner of objections. We were compelled to submit. Our landlord was a turbulent sort of savage, who bore down all opposition, and held to his laws, which were not often consistent with one another, with as hardy a tenacity as did the Medes and Persians. The long and short of it was that we must share our chamber with two other men.

or seek lodgings elsewhere.   This, in a strange town where no other tavern was yet dreamed of, was little else than a downright declaration, that we might "go to the d—l and shake ourselves;" and with whatever grace given, we were compelled to take the accommodations as they were accorded to us.   We insisted on separate beds, however, and here we gained our point.

"Ay, you may have two a-piece," was the cold and ready answer; "one for each leg."

Our objections to a chamber in connection with strangers, did us no service in that wild community; and the rough adventurers about, seemed to hold us in no fair esteem on the strength of them.   But they saw that we were able to hold our own, and that, in our controversy with the landlord, though we had been compelled to yield our point, we had yet given him quite as good as he sent; and so they suffered their contempt to escape in winks to each other, and muttered sentences, which, as we only saw and heard them indistinctly, we were wise enough to take no heed of.   Not that we did not feel in the humor to do so.   My comrade fidgetted more than once with his heavy-headed whip-handle, and my own hand felt monstrously disposed to tap the landlord on his crown; but it was too obviously our policy to forbear, and we took ourselves off to our chamber as soon as we could beat a retreat gracefully.

Well might our landlord have given us two or four beds each. There were no less than twelve in the one apartment which had been assigned us.   We chose our two, getting them as nigh each other as possible; and having put our saddle-bags in a corner behind them, and got our dirks and pistols in readiness, some on the table and some under our pillows, we prepared to get to bed as fast as possible.   Before we had entirely undressed, however, our two other occupants of the chamber appeared, one of whom we remembered to have seen in the bar-room below, at the time of our discussion with the landlord.   They were, neither of them, calculated to impress me favorably. They were evidently too fond of their personal appearance to please one who was rather apt to be studiless of his.   They were dandies—a sort of New York dandies—men with long coats and steeple-crowned hats, great breast-pins, thick gold chains, and a big bunch of seals hanging at their hips.   "What the deuce," thought I, to myself, "brings such people into this country? Such gewgaws are not only in bad taste anywhere, but nowhere in such bad taste as in a wild and poor country such us ours. Of course, they can not be gentlemen; that sort of ostentation is totally incompatible with gentility." Their first overtures did not impress me more favorably toward them. They were disposed to be familiar at the start. There was an assumed composure, a laborious ease about them, which showed them to be practising a part. There is no difficulty in discovering whether a man has been bred a gentleman or not. There is no acquiring gentility at a late day; and but few, not habituated to it from the first, can ever, by any art, study, or endeavor, acquire, in a subsequent day, those nice details of manners, that exquisite consideration of the claims and peculiarities of those in their neighborhood, which early education alone can certainly give. Our chamber companions evidently strove at self-complacency. There was a desperate ostentation of *sang-froid*, a most lavish freedom of air about them, which made their familiarity obtrusiveness, and their ease swagger. A glance told me what they were, so far as manners went; and I never believed in the sympathy between bad manners and morals. They may exist together. There's some such possibility; yet I never saw them united. A man with bad manners may not steal, nor lie, but he can not be amiable; he can not often be just; he will be tyrannical if you suffer him; and the cloven hoof of the beast must appear, though it makes its exhibition on a Brussels carpeting.

These fellows had a good many questions to ask us, and a good many remarks to make, before we got to sleep that night. Nor was this very much amiss. The custom of the country is to ask questions, and to ask them with directness. There the southwest differs from the eastern country. The Yankee obtains his knowledge by circumlocution; and his modes of getting it, are as ingeniously indirect as the cow-paths of Boston. He proceeds as if he thought it impertinent to gratify his desire, or — and, perhaps, this is the better reason — as if he were conscious of motives for his curiosity, other than those which he acknowledges. The southwestern man, living remotely from the great cities, and anxious for intelligence of regions of which he has little personal acquaintance, taxes, in plain terms, the resources of every stranger whom he meets. He is quite as willing to answer, as to ask, and this readiness acquits him, or should acquit him, of any charge of rudeness. We found no fault with the curiosity of our companions, but I so little relished their manners, as to forbear questioning them in return. Carrington was less scrupulous, however; he made sundry inquiries to which he received unsatisfactory replies, and toward midnight, I was pleased to find that the chattering was fairly over.

We slept without interruption, and awakened before the strangers. It was broad daylight, and, hastening our toilets, we descended to the breakfast-room. There we were soon followed by the two, and my observation by day, rather confirmed my impressions of the preceding night. They were quite too nice in their deportment to be wise; they found fault with the arrangements of the table—their breakfast did not suit them—the eggs were too much or too little done, and they turned up their noses at the coffee with exquisite distaste. The landlord reddened, but bore it with tolerable patience for a republican, and the matter passed off without a squall, though I momently looked for one. Little things are apt to annoy little people and I have usually found those persons most apt to be dissatisfied with the world, whose beginnings in it have been most mean and contemptible. The whole conduct of the strangers increased my reserve toward them.

To us, however, they were civil enough. Their policy was in it. They spoke to us as if we were not merely friends, but bed-fellows; and in a style of gentility exceedingly new to us, one of them put his arm about the neck of my friend. I almost expected to see him knocked down; for, with all his gentleness of mood, Carrington was a very devil when his blood was up, and hated every sort of impertinence; but whether he thought it wiser to forbear in a strange place, or was curious to see how far the fellow would go, he said nothing, but smiled patiently till the speech which accompanied the embrace was fairly over and then quietly withdrew from its affectionate control.

The day was rainy and squally—to such a degree that we could not go out. How to amuse ourselves was a question not so easily answered in a strange country-tavern where we had no books, and no society. After breakfast we returned to our apartment, and threw ourselves upon the beds. To talk of home, and the two maidens, whom we had left under such differing circumstances, was our only alternative; and thus employed our two stranger companions came in. Their excuse for the intrusion was the weather, and as their rights to the chamber were equal to ours, we had nothing to say against it. Still I was disquieted and almost angry. I spoke very distantly and coldly in reply to their speeches, and they quickly saw that I was disposed to keep them at arm's length. But my desire, with such persons, was not of so easy attainment. The reserve of a gentleman is not apt to be respected, even if seen by those who have never yet learned the first lessons of gentility; and do what I would, I still found that they were uttering propositions in my ears which I was necessarily obliged to answer, or acknowledge. In this, they were tacitly assisted by my friend.

Carrington, whose disposition was far more accessible than mine, chatted with them freely, and, what was worse, told them very nearly all of his purposes and projects. They, too, were seeking land; they were speculators from New York — agents for great land-companies — such as spring up daily in that city, and flood the country with a nominal capital, that changes like magic gold into worthless paper every five years or less. They talked of thousands, and hundreds of thousands, with the glibness of men who had handled nothing else from infancy; and never was imagination more thoroughly taken prisoner than was that of Carrington. He fairly gasped while listening to them. Their marvellous resources confounded him. With three thousand dollars, and thirty negroes, he had considered himself no small capitalist; but now he began to feel really humble, and I laughed aloud as I beheld the effects of his consternation upon him. Conversation lagged at length; even those wondrous details of the agents of the great New York company tired the hearers, and, it would seem, the speakers too; for they came to a pause. The mind can not bear too much glitter any more than the eye. They now talked together, and one of them, at length, produced cards from his trunk

"Will you play, gentlemen?" they asked civilly.

"I am obliged to you," was my reply, in freezing tones, "but I would rather not.'

I was answered, greatly to my mortification, by Carrington —

"And why not, Dick? You play well, and I know you like it."

This was forcing upon me an avowal of my dislike to our would-be acquaintance which I would have preferred to avoid. But, as it was, I resolved upon my course.

"You know I never like to play among strangers, William!"

"Pshaw! my dear fellow, what of that? Come, take a hand —we're here in a place we know nothing about, and where nobody knows us. It's monstrous dull, and if we don't play, we may as well drown."

"Excuse me, William."

"Can't, Dick—can't think of it," was his reply.

"You must take a hand, or we can't play. Whist is my only game, you know, and there's but three of us without you."

"Take dummy," was my answer.

"What! without knowing how to value him? Oh, no! Besides, I can't play that game well."

You may fight, or eat, or speak, or travel with a man, without making yourself his companion—but you can't play with him without incurring his intimacy. Now, I was somewhat prejudiced against these strangers, and had so far studiously avoided their familiarity. To play with them was to make my former labor in vain, as well as to invite the consequences which I had been so desirous to avert. But to utter these reasons aloud was to challenge them to the bull-ring, and there was no wisdom in that. My thoughtless friend urged the matter with a zeal no less imprudent in his place than it was irksome in mine. He would hear no excuses, and appealed to my courtesy against my principle, alleging the utter impossibility of their being able to find the desired amusement without my help.

Not to seem churlish, I at length gave way. Bitterly do I reproach myself that I did so. But how was I then—in my boyhood, as it were—to anticipate such consequences from so seemingly small a source. But, in morals, no departure from principles is small. All principles are significant—are essential—in the formation of truth; and the neglect or omission of the smallest among them is not one evil merely, or one error—but a thousand—it is the parent of a thousand, each, in its turn, endowed with a frightful fecundity more productive than the plagues of Egypt—more enduring, and not less hideous and frightful. Take care of small principles, if you would preserve great truths sacred.

As I have said, I suffered myself—it matters not with what motives or feeling—to be persuaded by my friend to play with him and the strangers. I took my seat opposite to Carrington. The strangers played together. Whist was the game—a game we both delighted in, and which we both played with tolerable skill. The cards were thrown upon the table, and we drew for the deal.

"What do you bet?" said one of the strangers addressing me. At the same moment, his companion addressed a like inquiry to my partner.

"Nothing; I never bet," was my reply.

"A Mexican!" said Carrington, throwing the coin upon the table. My opponent expressed his disappointment at my refusal.

"There's no fun in playing unless you bet!"

"You mistake," was my reply. "I find an interest in the game which no risk of money could stimulate. I do not bet; it is a resolution."

My manner was such as to forbid any further prosecution of his object. He was compelled to content himself as he might; and drawing for the deal, it fell to him. He took the cards, and, to my surprise, proceeded to shuffle them after a fashion which I had been always taught to regard as dishonorable. He would draw single cards alternately from top and bottom, and bring them together; and, in this way, as I well knew, would throw all the trump-cards into the hands of himself and partner. I did not scruple to oppose this mode of shuffling.

"The effect will be," I told him, "to bring the trumps into your own and partner's hands. I have seen the trick before. It is a trick, and that is enough to make it objectionable. I have no pleasure in playing a game with all the cards against me."

He denied the certainty of the result which I predicted, and persisted in finishing as he had begun. I would have arisen from the table but my friend's eyes appealed to me to stay. He was anxious to play, and quite too fond of the game, and, perhaps, too dull where he was, to heed or insist upon any little improprieties. The result was as I predicted. There was but a single trump between myself and partner.

"You see," I exclaimed, as the hand was finished, "such dealing is unfair."

"No! I see not. It so happens, it is true; but it is not unfair," was the reply of the dealer.

"Fair or not," I answered, "it matters not. If this mode of shuffling has the effect of throwing the good cards invariably into one hand, it produces such a disparity between the parties as takes entirely from the pleasure in the game. There is no game, indeed, when the force is purely on the one side."

"But such is not invariably the result."

Words were wasted upon them. I saw then what they were. Gentlemen disdain the advantage, even when fairly obtained, which renders intelligence, skill, memory, and reflection—indeed, all qualities of mind—entirely useless. As players, our opponents had no skill; like gamblers usually they relied on trick for success, and strove to obtain, by miserable stratagem, what other men seek from thought and honest endeavor. I would have risen from the table as these thoughts passed through my mind. We had lost the game, and I had had enough of them and it. But my friend entreated me.

"What matters one game?" he said. "It is our turn now. We shall do better."

The stake was removed by his opponent, and, while I shuffled the cards, he was required to renew his bet. In doing so, by a singular lapse of thought, he drew from a side-pocket in his bosom, the large roll of money with which he travelled, forgetting the small purse which he had prepared for his travelling expenses. He was conscious, when too late, of his error. He hurried it back to its place of concealment, and drew forth the purse; but in the one moment which he employed in doing so I could see that the eyes of our companions had caught sight of the treasure. It may have been fancy in me, the result of my suspicious disposition, but I thought that their eyes sparkled as they beheld it, and there was an instant interchange of glances between them.

Hurriedly I shuffled through, and with an agitation which I could not well conceal, I dealt out the cards. There was a general and somewhat unwonted silence around the table. We all seemed to be conscious of thoughts and feelings, which needed to be concealed. The cheeks of my companion were red; but he laughed and played. His first play was an error. I fixed my eye upon one of the strangers and his glance fell beneath it. There was a guilty thought busy in his bosom. Scarcely a word was spoken — none unnecessarily — while that hand lasted. But when it came to the turn of one of our opponents to deal, and when I found him shuffling as before, I grew indignant. I protested. He insisted upon his right to shuffle as he pleased — a right which I denied. He would not yield the point, and I left the table. The fellow would have put on airs, and actually thought to bully me. He used some big words, and, rising at the same time, approached me.

"Sir, your conduct—"

I stopped him half way, and in his speech —

"Is insulting you would say."

"I do, sir; very insulting, sir, very."

"Be it so. I can not help it. I will play with no man who employs a mode of shuffling which puts all the trump cards into his own and partner's hands. I do not wish to play with you, anyhow, sir; and very much regret that the persuasions of my friend made me yield against my better judgment. My rule is never to play with strangers, and your game has confirmed me in my opinion of its propriety. I shall take care never to depart from it in future."

"Sir, you don't mean to impute anything to my honor. If you do, sir ——"

My reply to this swagger was anticipated by William, who had not before spoken, but now stood between us.

"And what if he did, eh?"

"Why, sir — but I was not speaking to you, sir," said the fellow.

"Ay, I know that, but I'm speaking to you. What if he did doubt your honor, and what if I doubt it, eh!"

"Why then, sir, if you did—" The fellow paused. He was a mere bully and looked round to his companion, who still kept a quiet seat at the table.

"Pshaw!" exclaimed William, in a most contemptuous manner.

"You are mistaken in your men, my good fellow. Take up your Mexican, and thank your stars you have got it so easily. Shut up now and be quiet. It lies upon the table." The fellow obeyed.

"You won't play any longer?" he demanded.

"No," was my reply. "To play with you, is to make you and declare you, our friends. We will fight with you, if you please, but not play with you!"

To this proposition the answer was slow. We were, at least, possessors of the ground. But our triumph was a monstrous small one, and we paid for it. The annoyance of the whole scene was excessive to me. Carrington did not so much feel it. He was a careless, buoyant, good sort of creature, having none of my suspicion, and little of that morbid pride which boiled in me. He laughed at the fellows and the whole affair, when I was most disposed to groan over it, and to curse them. I could only bring his countenance to a grave expression, when I reminded him of his imprudence in taking out his roll of money.

"Ay, that was cursed careless," he replied; "but there's no helping it now—I must only keep my wits about me next time; and if harm comes from it, keep a stiff lip and a stout heart, and be ready to meet it."

William Carrington was too brave a fellow to think long of danger, and he went to bed that night with as light a heart as if he had not a sixpence in the world.

CHAPTER XVII.

AMONG PITS AND TRAPFALLS.

"I heard myself proclaim'd;
And, by the happy hollow of a tree,
Escaped the hunt. No port is free; no place.
That guard and most unusual vigilance
Does not **attend my taking.** While I may 'scape,
I will preserve myself."

King Lear.

THE next day opened **bright and beautiful, and** we prepared to resume our journey. **Our fellow-chamberers had not shown** themselves to us since **our rupture; they had not slept that** night at the tavern. **Their absence gave us but little concern** at the time, though **we discovered afterward that it had no little** influence upon **our movements. I have already said that** my companion held a **claim upon a man in the neighborhood of** Tuscaloosa, for some hundred **and thirty dollars, the price of a** mule which he had **sold to him during** the previous **season.** To collect this debt **had been the only motive** for carrying **us** so far from our direct **route, which had** been to Chochuma. The man's name was Matthew **Webber; of his** character **and** condition we knew nothing, save **that he was a** small farmer supposed to be doing well. **That he had not paid the money** before, when **due,** was rather **an** unfavorable **symptom; but of** the ultimate payment of it William **had not the** slightest doubt. He was secured by the indorsed **promise of a** Colonel Grafton, a gentleman of some wealth, **who** planted **about fourteen miles** from Tuscaloosa, in the direction **of Columbus, but fully eleven** miles from the road. There **was a short cut to his house, and** we proposed to ride thither **and obtain directions for finding** the debtor. He had once **been Grafton's** overseer **and the lat-** ter knew all about him. **Our landlord, who had grown civil** enough to us, and who was really a very good sort of body when taken in the grain, freely gave us proper instructions for finding our road by the short cut. Of Grafton he spoke with kindness and respect, but I could not help observing, when we inquired after Webber, that he evaded inquiry, and when repeated, shook his head and turned away to other customers. He evidently knew enough to think unfavorably, and his glance when he spoke of the man was uneasy and suspicious. Finding other questions unproductive, we had our horses brought forth, paid our charges, and prepared to mount. Our feet were already in the stirrups, when the landlord followed us, saying abruptly, but in a low tone, as he reached the spot where we stood:—

"Gentlemen, I don't know much of the people whom you seek, but I know but little that is very favorable of the country into which you're going. Take a hint before starting. If you have anything to lose, it's easy losing it on the road to Chochuma, and the less company you keep as you travel, the better for your saddle-bags. Perhaps, too, it wouldn't be amiss, if you look at your pistols before you start."

He did not wait for our answer, but returned to his bar-room and other avocations as if his duty was ended. We were both surprised, but I did not care to reject his warnings. William laughed at the gravity of the advice given us, but I saw it with other eyes. If I was too suspicious of evil, I well knew that my companion was apt to err in the opposite extreme—he was imprudent and thoughtless; and, in recklessness of courage only, prevented a thousand evil consequences which had otherwise occurred from his too confiding nature.

"Say nothing now," I observed to him—"but let us ride till we get into the woods, then see to your pistols."

"Pshaw, Dick," was his reply, "what do you suspect now? The pistols have been scarcely out of sight since we left home."

"They have been out of sight. We left them always in the chamber when we went to meals.'

"True, but for a few moments only, and then all about the house were at meals also."

"No; at breakfast yesterday those gamblers came in after us, and I think then they came from our chamber. Besides, though

they did not sleep with us last night, I am persuaded that one
or both of them were in the room. I heard a light step at midnight, or fancied it; and found my overcoat turned this morning upon the chair."

"The chambermaid, or Cuffy for the boots. You are the
most suspicious fellow, Dick, and, somehow, you hated these
two poor devils from the very first moment you laid eyes on
them. Now, d—n 'em. for my part, I never gave 'em a second
thought. I could have licked either, or both, and when that
chap with the hook-nose began to swagger about, I felt monstrous like doing it. But he was a poor shote, and the less said
and thought of him the better. I should not care much to meet
him if he had carried the pistols quite off, and presented them
to me, muzzle-stuffed, at the next turning."

"He may yet do so," was my calm reply. "At least it will
do us no harm to prepare for all events. Let us clear the town,
and when we once get well hidden in the woods, we'll take
counsel of our landlord, and see to our priming."

"Why not do it now?"

"For the best of reasons—there are eyes on us, and some of
them may be unfriendly. Better that they should suppose us
ignorant and unprepared, if they meditate evil."

"As you please, but I would not be as jealous and suspicious
as you are, Dick, not for all I'm worth."

"It may be worth that to you to become so. But ride on;
the ferryman halloos, and beckons us to hasten. There are
other travellers to cross. I'm sorry for it. We want no more
company."

"Ay, but we do, Dick. The more the merrier, say I. If
there's a dozen, no harm, so they be not in our way in entering
land. I like good company. A hearty joke, or a good story,
sets me laughing all the day. None of your travellers that need
to be bawled at to ride up, and open their ovens; none of your
sober-sided, drawling, croaking methodists, for me—your fellows that preach against good living, yet eat of the fat of the
land whenever they can get it, and never refuse a collection,
however small the amount. If I hate any two-legged creature
that calls himself human, it is your canting fellow, that preaches
pennyworths of morality, and practises pounds of sin; that says

long grace at supper, till the meat grows cold, and that same night inveigles your chambermaid into the blankets beside him. I wouldn't think so much of the sin if it wasn't for the hypocrisy. It's bad enough to love the meal; but to preach over it, before eating, is a shame as well as a sin. None but your sneaks do it; fellows whom you might safer trust with your soul than with your purse. They could do little harm to the one, but they'd make off with the other. None of those chaps for me, Dick; yet give me as many travellers as you please. Here seem to be several going to cross; all wagoners but one, and he seems just one of the scamps I've been talking of—a short, chunky, black-coated little body: ten to one his nose turns up like a pug-puppy's, and he talks through it."

It was in such careless mood and with such loose speech that my companion beguiled the time between our leaving the hotel and reaching the flat which was to convey us across the river. William was in the very best of spirits, and these prompted him to a freedom of speech which might be supposed to denote some laxity of morals; and yet his morals were unquestionable. Indeed, it is not unfrequently the case that a looseness of speech is associated with a rigid practice of propriety. A consciousness of purity is very apt to prompt a license of speech in him who possesses it; while he, on the other hand, who is most apt to indulge in vice, will most usually prove himself most circumspect in speech. Vice, to be successful, calls for continual circumspection; and in no respect does it exhibit this quality more strikingly than in the utterance of its sentiments. The family of Joe Surface is a singularly numerous one. My companion was no Joe Surface. He carried his character in his looks, in his speech, and in his actions. When you saw the looks, heard the speech, and witnessed the actions, you had him before you, without possibility or prospect of change, for good and for evil, and, to elevate still more highly the character which I admired, and the man I could not but love, I will add that he was only too apt to extenuate the motives of others by a reference to his own. He had no doubts of the integrity of his fellow—no fears of wrong at his hand; was born with a nature as clear as the sunlight, as confiding as the winds, and had seen too little of the world, at the period of which I speak, to have had experi-

once unteach the sweeter lessons of his unsophisticated humanity. Let not the reader chide me as lavish in my eulogy : before he does so, let me pray him to suppose it written upon his tombstone.

We soon reached the flat, and were on our way across the river in a few minutes after. The little man in the black coat had, in truth, as my companion had predicted, a little pug-puppy nose, but in his other guesses he was quite out. We soon discovered that he was no sermonizer — there was anything but hypocrisy in his character. On the contrary, he swore like a trooper whenever occasion offered ; and I was heartily rejoiced, for the decency of the thing, if for no other reason, to discover, as I soon did, that the fellow was about to take another road from ourselves. The other men, three in number, were farmers in the neighborhood, who had been in to supply the Tuscaloosa market. Like the people of all countries who live in remote interior situations and see few strangers who can teach them anything, these people had each a hundred questions to ask, and as many remarks to make upon the answers. They were a hearty, frank, plain-spoken, unequivocal set, who would share with you their hoe-cake and bacon, or take a fling or dash of fisti-cuffs with you, according to the several positions, as friend or foe, which you might think proper to take. Among all the people of this soil, good humor is almost the only rule which will enable the stranger to get along safely.

We were soon over the river, which is broad and not so rapid at this spot as at many others. The Tuscaloosa or Black Warrior river is a branch of the Tombeckbe.

The site of the town which bears its name, and which is now the capital town of Alabama, was that of the Black Warrior's best village. There is no remnant, no vestige, no miserable cabin, to testify to what he and his people were. The memorials of this tribe, like that of all the American tribes, are few, and yet the poverty of the relics but speak the more emphatically for the mournfulness of their fate. Who will succeed to their successors, and what better memorials will they leave to the future ? It is the boast of civilization only that it can build its monument — leave its memorial ; and yet Cheops, could he now look upon his mausoleum, might be seen to smile over the boast. Enough of this.

Ve naa no sooner separated from our companions of the boat and got fairly into the shelter of the woods, than I reminded William of the inspection of our firearms, which I proposed to make after the cautionary hint of my landlord. We rode aside, accordingly, into a thick copse that lay to the right, and covered a group of hills, and drew out our weapons. To the utter astonishment of my companion, and to my own exasperation, we found, not only no priming in the pans of our pistols, but the flints knocked out, and wooden ones, begrimed with gunpowder, substituted in their place! Whom could we suspect of this but our two shuffling companions of the chamber? The discovery was full of warning. We were in a bad neighborhood, and it behooved us to keep our wits about us. We were neither of us men to be terrified into inactivity by the prospect of danger; and, though aroused and apprehensive, we proceeded to prepare against the events which seemed to threaten us, and we know not on which hand. Fortunately, we had other flints, and other weapons, and we put all of them in readiness for instant requisition. We had scarcely done so, and remounted, when we heard a horseman riding down the main track toward the river We did not look to see who the traveller might be, but, taking our own course, entered upon the left-hand trail of a fork, which took us out of the main, into a neighboring road, by which we proposed to reach the plantation of Mr. Grafton in the rear, avoiding the front or main road, as it was some little distance longer. To our own surprise, we reached the desired place in safety, and without the smallest interruption of any kind. Yet our minds had been wrought up and excited to the very highest pitch of expectation, and I felt that something like disappointment was predominant in my bosom, for the very security we then enjoyed. A scuffle had been a relief to that anxiety which was not diminished very greatly by the knowledge that, for a brief season, we were free from danger. The trial, we believed, was yet to come; and the suspense of waiting was a greater source of annoyance than any doubts or apprehension which we might have had of the final issue.

CHAPTER XVIII.

A FOREST HOME.

"This night at least . . . .
The hospitable hearth shall flame
And . . . .
Find for the wanderer rest and fire." — WALTER SCOTT.

COLONEL GRAFTON—for we are all colonels at least, in the southern and southwestern states—received us at the doorsteps of his mansion, and gave us that cordial kind of reception which makes the stranger instantly at home. Our horses were taken, and, in defiance of all our pleading, were hurried off to the stables; while we were ushered into the house by our host, and made acquainted with his family. This consisted of his wife, a fine, portly dame of forty-five, and some five children, in the several stages from seven to seventeen—the eldest, a lovely damsel, with bright blue eyes and dark-brown hair, fair as a city lily; the youngest an ambitious urchin, the cracking of whose knotted whip filled the room with noises, which it required an occasional finger-shake of the indulgent mother finally to subdue. Hospitality was a presiding virtue, not an ostentatious pretender, in that pleasant household; and, in the space of half an hour, we felt as comfortably at home with its inmates as if we had been associates all our lives. Colonel Grafton would not listen to our leaving him that night. When William pleaded his business, he had a sufficient answer. The man whom he sought lived full twelve miles off; and, through a tedious region of country, it would take us till dark, good riding, to reach and find the spot, even if we started before dinner—a violation of good breeding not to be thought of in Alabama. We were forced to stay, and, indeed, needed no great persuasion. The *air* of the whole establishment took us both at first

sight. There is a household as well as individual manner,
which moves us almost with as great an influence; and that of
Colonel Grafton's was irresistible. A something of complete life
—calm, methodical, symmetrical life—life in repose—seemed
to mark his parlor, his hall, the arrangements of his grounds
and gardens, the very grouping of the trees. All testified to
the continual presence of a governing mind, whose whole feeling of enjoyment was derived from order—a method as rigor-
ous as it was simple and easy of attainment. Yet there was no
trim formality in either his own or his wife's deportment; and,
as for the arrangement of things about his house, you could impute to neither of them a fastidious nicety and marked disposition to set chairs and tables, books and pictures, over and against
each other of equal size and like color. To mark what I mean
more distinctly, I will say that he never seemed to insist on
having things *in their places,* but he was always resolute to have
them *never in the way.* There is no citizen of the world who
will not readily conceive the distinction.

We had a good dinner, and, after dinner, taking his wife and
all his children along, he escorted us over a part of his grounds,
pointed out his improvements, and gave us the domestic history
of his settlement. Miss Grafton afterward, at her father's suggestion, conducted us to a pleasant promenade of her own finding, which, in the indulgence of a very natural sentimentality,
she had entitled "The Grove of Coronatte," after a lovesick
Indian maiden of that name, who, it is said by tradition, preferred leaving her tribe when it emigrated to the Mississippi,
to an exile from a region in which she had lived from infancy
and which she loved better than her people. She afterward
became the wife of a white man named Johnson, and there the
tradition ends. The true story—as Colonel Grafton more than
hinted—was, that Coronatte was tempted by Johnson to be
come his wife long before the departure of the tribe, and she
in obedience to natural not less than scriptural laws, preferred
cleaving to her husband to going with less-endearing relations
into foreign lands. The colonel also intimated his doubts as to
the formality of the ceremony by which the two were united
but this latter suggestion was made to us in a whisper—Julia
Grafton wholly denying, and with some earnestness I thought,

even such portions of her father's version of the romance as he
had permitted to reach her ears.

That night we rejoiced in a warm supper, and, when it was
ended, I had reason to remark with delight the effect upon the
whole household of that governing character on the part of its
head which had impressed me at first entering it. The supper-
things seemed removed by magic. We had scarcely left the
table, Mrs. Grafton leading the way, and taken our places around
the fire, when Julia took her mother's place at the waiter; and
without noise, bustle, or confusion, the plates and cups and sau-
cers were washed and despatched to their proper places. A
single servant only attended, and this servant seemed endowed
with ubiquity. She seemed to have imbibed the general habits
of her superiors, and did quite as much, if not more, than would
have been done by a dozen servants, and with infinitely less
confusion. Such was the result of method in the principal:
there is a moral atmosphere, and we become acclimated, when
under its action, precisely as in the physical world. The slave
had tacitly fallen into the habits and moods of those above her
—as inferiors are very apt to do—and, without a lesson prescribed or a reason spoken, she had heeded all lessons, and felt,
though she might not have expressed, the reasons for all. The
whole economy of the household was admirable : not an order
was given; no hesitation or ignorance of what was needed,
shown; but each seemed to know by instinct, and to perform
with satisfaction, his or her several duties. Our repasts are seldom conducted anywhere in the Southwest with a strict attention to order. A stupid slave puts everything into confusion,
and we do not help the matter much by bringing in a dozen to
her aid. The fewer servants about houses the better: they
learn to do, the more they are required to do, and acquire a
habit of promptness without which a servant might be always
utterly worthless.

When the table was removed, Julia joined us, and we all
chatted pleasantly together for the space of an hour. As soon
as the conversation seemed to flag, at a signal from Colonel
Grafton, which his daughter instantly recognised and obeyed,
she rose, and, bringing a little stand to the fireside, on which
lay several books, she prepared to read to us, in compliance

with one of the fireside laws of her father—one which he had insisted upon, and which she had followed, from the first moment of her being able to read tolerably. She now read well—sweetly, unaffectedly, yet impressively. A passage from "The Deserted Village" interested us for half an hour; and the book made way for conversation among the men, and needlework among the women. But the whole scene impressed me with delight—it was so natural, yet so uncommon in its aspect—done with so much ease, with so little effort, yet so completely. Speaking of it in compliment to our host when the ladies had retired, we received a reply which struck me as embodying the advantages of a whole host of moral principles, such as are laid down in books, but without any of their cold and freezing dry-nesses. "Sir," said Colonel Grafton, "I ascribe the happiness of my family to a very simple origin. It has always been a leading endeavor with me to make my children love the family fireside. If the virtues should dwell anywhere in a household, it is there. There I have always and only found them."

And there they did dwell of a truth. I felt their force, and so did my companion. William, indeed, was so absolutely charmed with Julia Grafton, that I began to apprehend that he would not only forget his betrothed, but his journey also—a journey which, I doubt not, the reader, agreeing with myself, would have us instantly resume. But we had consented to stay with our friendly host that night; and before we retired we made all necessary inquiries touching his debtor. Colonel Grafton gave my friend little encouragement on the subject of his claim.

"I am almost sorry," he said, "that I endorsed that man's note. I fear I shall have to pay it; not that I regard the loss, but that it will make me the more reluctant hereafter to assist other poor men in the same manner. The dishonesty of one beginner in this way affects the fortunes of a thousand others, who are possibly free from his or any failings of the kind. When I signed the note for Webber, he was my overseer, but disposed to set up for himself. I had found him honest—or, rather, I had never found him dishonest. If he was, he had rogue's cunning enough to conceal it. Since he left me, how-ever he has become an object of suspicion to the whole neigh-

borhood, and many are the tales which I hear of his miscon
duct. It is not known how he lives. A miserable patch of
corn and one of potatoes form his only pretence as a farmer,
and to these he pays so little attention, that his apology is
openly laughed at. The cattle are commonly in the cornfield,
and the hogs do what they please with the potato-patch. He
does not see, or does not care to see. He is seldom at home,
and you may have to return to-morrow without finding him.
If so, scruple not to make my house your home so long as it
may serve your purpose and prove agreeable."

We thanked him with due frankness, and he proceeded:—

"This man has no known resources whatsoever, yet he is sel
dom without money. He is lavish of it, and must get it easily.
It is commonly thought that he gambles, and is connected with
a vast association of gamblers that live upon the steamboats,
and harass the country from Georgia to Louisiana, assessing the
unwary traveller wherever they meet with him; and you know
how many thoughtless, confident youth we have, who lose their
money from an unwillingness to believe that they can be out-
witted by their neighbor."

"My eye, as these words were spoken, caught that of William, which turned away in confusion from my glance. I felt
mischievous enough to relate our adventure at the Tuscaloosa
tavern, but Colonel Grafton talked too well, and we were both
too much interested in what he said, to desire to interrupt him.
He proceeded:—

"It is even said and supposed by some that he does worse—
that he robs where he can not win, and seizes where he can not
cheat. I am not of this opinion. Rogues as well as honest
men find it easy enough to get along in our country without
walking the highway; and, though I know him to be bold
enough to be a ruffian, I doubt whether such would be his policy. My notion is that he is a successful gambler, and, as such,
if you find him at home, I doubt not that you will get your
money. At least, such is my hope, for your sake, as well as
my own. If you do, Mr. Carrington, you will trust again, and
I—yes—I will endorse again the poor man's promise to pay."

"And how far from you is the residence of this man?" was
my question.

"From twelve to fourteen miles, and through a miserably wild country. I do not envy you the ride; you will have an up-hill journey of it full two-thirds of the route, and a cheerless one throughout. I trust you may not take it in vain; but, whether you do or not, you must return this way. It is your nearest route to Columbus, and I can put you on your way by a short cut which you could not find yourself. I shall, of course, expect you."

Such was the amount of our conference with this excellent man that night. We separated at twelve o'clock—a late hour in the country, but the evening had passed too pleasantly to permit us to feel it so. A cheerful breakfast in the morning, and a renewal of all those pleasant thoughts and images which had fascinated us the night before, made us hesitate to leave this charming family; and slow were the first movements which carried us from the happy territory. Well provided with directions for finding the way, and cautious to be circumspect and watchful, we set out for the dwelling of our suspicious debtor.

CHAPTER XIX.

MAT WEBBER.

"Old Giaffar sat in his divan,
    Deep thought was in his agéd eye;
And though the face of mussulman
    Not oft betrays to standers-by
The mind within — well skilled to hide
All but unconquerable pride —
His pensive cheek **and** pondering **brow**
Did more than he was wont avow."— *Bride of Abydos.*

OUR host had in no respect exaggerated the tediousness **of** our journey. Perhaps **it became doubly so** to us from the **pleas**ant consciousness, fresh in our minds, **of the few** preceding hours which had been so unqualifiedly delightful. **The hills rose be**fore us, and we felt it to **be** indeed toilsome **to ascend them,** when we knew that by such ascent we **only threw them as bar**riers between us and the spot to which **we both felt every dis**position to return. It is strange how **susceptible to** passing **and** casual influences are the **strongest among us. Let our pride not** rise in our path **as a** dogged **opponent, and what flexibility is** ours — what may **we** not become — **what not achieve! How** lovely will seem place and person, **if,** when **they commend them**selves to our affections, they **forbear** to **assail or offend our pride!** I could tear myself from **the** dwelling **of my childhood — from** the embrace of the fondest of mothers — from **all the** sympathies and ties to which **I** had been accustomed — **yea, from the** sight of her to whom **all** my **hopes** had been **addressed — in** obedience to this arbitrary influence; **and,** failing **to** derive **even** the coldest satisfaction from friends, and family, **and** birthplace, could **yet** be sensible of pleasure derived **from the** contemplation of a strange home, and a passing intercourse **with** strangers. Perhaps it may be safe to assert that the greatest enemy to our affections is our mind. The understanding, even among the weakest—as if conscious of its superior destiny—will assert its sway, and sacrifice the heart which depends on it for life, in deference to that miserable vanity which lives only on its diseases. I have always been conscious of this sort of warfare going on with me. I have spoken the sarcasm to the loved one, even when my own bosom felt the injustice, and when my heart, with the keenest sympathy, quivered also with the pang.

We had ridden, perhaps, an hour, and were winding our way down from gorge to gorge among a pile of hills of which there seemed to be no end, when we came suddenly upon three men sitting among the bushes at a little distance from the road-side. Two of them we knew at the first glance to be our chamber companions at Tuscaloosa. The third we had neither of us seen before. He was a short, thick-set person of black hair and unimposing features, presenting in his dress, a singular contrast to the trim and gaudy caparison of his comrades. They were sitting around a log, and may have been eating for aught we knew. They had something between them which called for their close scrutiny, and seemed so well to receive it that we completely surprised them. When they heard us, there was a visible start, and one of the two gamblers started to his feet. I rode on without giving them the least notice; but, thoughtless as ever, William half advanced to them, and in a good-humored, dare-devil style of expression, cried out to them aloud :—

"Halloo, my good fellows, do you feel like another game to-day ?"

What their answer was, and whether they sufficiently heard to understand his words or not, I can not say — they stood motionless and watched our progress; and I conceived it fortunate that I was able to persuade my companion to ride on without farther notice. He did not relish the indifference with which they seemed to regard us, and a little pause and provocation might have brought us into a regular fight. Perhaps — the issue of our journey considered — such would have been a fortunate event. We might not have suffered half so much as in the end we did.

"Now could I take either or both of those fellows by the neck, and rattle their pates together, for the fun **of it," was the speech of** my companion, as we rode off.

There was a needless display of valor in this, **and** my answer exhibited a more cautious temper. Rash **enough myself at times, I** yet felt the necessity of temperateness when in **company with one so** very thoughtless as my friend.

" Ay, and soil your fingers **and** bruise your knuckles **for your** pains. If they are merely dirty dogs, you would surely soil your fingers, and if they were at all insolent, you would run some risk of getting them broken. The least we have to do with all such people, the better for all parties — I, at least, have no ambition to couple with them either in love or hostility. Enough to meet **them** in their own way when they cross the path, and prevent our progress."

" Which these chaps will **never do,** I warrant you."

" We have less need to cross theirs — the way is broad enough for both of us. But let us on, **since** our **road** grows more level, though not less wild. I am tired of this jade **pace** — our nags will **sleep at** last, and stop at the next turning."

We quickened our pace, and, in another hour we approached the confines of our debtor's habitation. We knew it by the generally sterile and unprepossessing aspect of everything around it. **The** description which Colonel Grafton had given us was so felicitous that **we** could have no doubts ; and, riding up to the **miserable** cabin we were fortunate enough to meet in proper person the man we sought.

He stood at the entrance, leaning sluggishly against one **of** the doorposts — a slightly-built person, **of** slovenly habits, **an** air coarse, inferior, unprepossessing, and dark lowering features. His dress was shabby, his hat mashed down on **one side of his** head — his arms thrust **to** the elbows **in the pockets of his** breeches, and he wore the moccasins of an Indian. Still, there was something in the keen, lively glances of his small **black** eye, that denoted a restless and **quick** character, and his **thin,** closely-pressed lips were full of promptness and decision. **His** skin was tanned almost yellow, and his long, uncombed but flowing hair, black as **a** coal, falling down upon **his** neck which was bare, suited well, while contrasting **strongly with his** swarthy lineaments. He **received** us with **civility — advanced** from his tottering doorsteps on our approach, and held our horses while we dismounted.

"You remember me, Mr. Webber?" said my companion calling him by name.

"Mr. Carrington, I believe," was the reply; "I don't forget easily. Let me take your horses, gentlemen?"

There was a composure in the fellow's manners that almost amounted to dignity. Perhaps, this too was against him. Where should he learn such habits—such an air? Whence could come the assurance—the thorough ease and self-complacency of his deportment? Such confidence can spring from two sources only—the breeding of blood—the systematic habits of an unmingled family, admitting of no connection with strange races, and becoming aristocratic from concentration—or the recklessness of one indifferent to social claims, and obeying no other master than his own capricious mood.

We were conducted into his cabin and provided with seats. Wretched and miserable as everything seemed about the premises, our host showed no feeling of disquiet or concern on this account. He made no apology; drew forth the rude chairs covered with bull's hides; and proceeded to get the whiskey and sugar, the usual beverage presented in that region to the guest.

"You have ridden far, and a sup of whiskey will do you good, gentlemen. From Tuscaloosa this morning—you've ridden well."

William corrected his error by telling where we had stayed last night. A frown insensibly gathered above the brow of the man as he heard the name of Colonel Grafton.

"The colonel and myself don't set horses now altogether," was the quick remark, "he's a rich—I'm a poor man."

"And yet I should scarce think him the person to find cause of disagreement between himself and any man from a difference of condition," was the reply of William to this remark.

"You don't know him, Mr. Carrington, I reckon. For a long time I didn't know him myself—I was his overseer, you know, and it was then he put his name to that little bit of paper, that I s'pose you come about now."

Carrington nodded.

7

"Well," continued the debtor, "so long as I was his overseer, things went on smoothly; but the colonel don't like to see men setting up for themselves, and tried to keep me from it, but he couldn't; and since I've left him, he doesn't look once in the year over to my side of the country. He don't like me now, I know. Did you hear him say nothing about me?"

I could detect the keen black eye of the speaker, as he finished, watching the countenance of Carrington as he waited for the reply. I feared that the perfect frankness of William might have betrayed him into a partial revelation of Colonel Grafton's information; but he evaded the inquiry with some address.

"Yes; he gave us full directions how to find your place, and warned us that we might not find you at home. He said you travelled a great deal about the country, and didn't plant much. You deal in merchandise, perhaps?"

The fellow looked somewhat disappointed as he replied in the negative. But dismissing everything like expression from his face, in the next instant he asked if we had met with any travellers on the road. I replied quickly by stating with the utmost brevity, the fact that we had met three, whose appearance I briefly described without giving any particulars, and studiously suppressed the previous knowledge which we had of the gamblers at Tuscaloosa; but I had scarcely finished when William, with his wonted thoughtlessness, took up the tale where I had left it incomplete and omitted nothing. The man looked grave, and when he was ended, contented himself with remarking that he knew no person like those described, and inquired if we had not met with others. But, with my wonted suspiciousness of habit, I fancied that there was a something in his countenance that told a different story, and whether there were reason for this fancy or not, I was inly persuaded that our debtor and the two gamblers were birds of a feather. It will be seen in the sequel that I was not mistaken. There was an awkward pause in the conversation, for Carrington, like a man not accustomed to business seemed loth to ask about his money. He was relieved by the debtor.

"Well, Mr. Carrington," he said, "you come, I s'pose, about that little paper of mine. You want your money, and, to say truth, you ought to have had it some time ago. I would have sent it to you, but I couldn't get any safe hand going down into your parts."

Carrington interrupted him.

"That's no matter, Mr. Webber, I didn't want the money, to say truth, till just now; but if you can let me have it now, it will be as good to me as if you had sent it to me six months ago. I'm thinking to buy a little land in Mississippi, if I can get it moderate, and can get a long credit for the best part of it, but it will be necessary to put down something, you know, to clinch the bargain, and I thought I might as well look to you for that."

"To be sure — certain — it's only reasonable; but if you think to go into Mississippi to get land now on a long credit, and hardly any cash, Mr. Carrington, you'll find yourself mightily mistaken. You must put down the real grit, if you want to do anything in the land-market."

"Oh, yes, I expect to put down some—"

The acute glance of my eye arrested the speech of my thoughtless companion. In two minutes more he would probably have declared the very amount he had in possession, and all the purposes he had in view. I do not know, however, but that the abrupt pause and silence which followed my interposition, revealed quite as much to the cunning debtor as the words of my companion would have done. The bungling succession of half-formed and incoherent sentences which William uttered to hide the truth, and conceal that which by this time, was sufficiently told, perhaps contributed to impress him with an idea of much greater wealth in our possession than was even the case. But, whatever may have been his thoughts, his countenance was too inflexibly indifferent to convey to us their character. He was stolid and seemingly unobservant to the last degree, scarcely giving the slightest heed to the answers which his own remarks and inquiries demanded. At length, abruptly returning to the business in hand, he spoke thus:—

"Well, now, Mr. Carrington, I'll have to give you a little disappointment. I can't pay you to-day, much as I would like to do it; for, you see, my money is owing to me, and is scattered all about the neighborhood. If you could take a bed with me to-night, and be satisfied to put off travelling for a day, I could you, I think, for certain, to give you the whole of your money by to-morrow night. I can get it, for that matter, from a friend, but I should have to ride about fifteen or twenty miles for it, and that couldn't be done to-day."

"Nor would I wish it, Mr. Webber," was the reply of William. "To-morrow will answer, and though we are obliged to you for your offer of a bed to-night, yet we have a previous promise to return and spend the night with Colonel Grafton."

The brows of the man again blackened, but he spoke in cool, deliberate accents, though his language was that of enmity and dissatisfaction.

"Ay, I supposed as much. Colonel Grafton has a mighty fine house, and everything in good fix — he can better accommodate fine gentlemen than a poor man like me. You can do what you like about that, Mr. Carrington — stay with me to-night, or come at mid-day to-morrow — all the same to me — you shall still have your money. I'll get it for you, at all hazards, if it's only to get rid of all further obligation to that man. I've been obligated to him too long already, and I'll wipe out the score to-morrow, or I'm no man myself."

On the subject of Webber's motive for paying his debt, the creditor, of course, had but little to say. But the pertinacity of the fellow on another topic annoyed me.

"You speak," said I, "of the greater wealth and better accommodations of Colonel Grafton, as prompting us to prefer his hospitality to yours. My good sir, why should you do us this wrong? What do you see in either of us to think such things? We are both poor men — poorer, perhaps, than yourself — I know I am, and believe that such, too, is the case with my companion."

"Do you though?" said the fellow, coolly interrupting me. I felt that my blood was warming; he, perhaps, saw it, for he instantly went on :—

"I don't mean any offence to you, gentlemen — very far from it — but we all very well know what temptations are in a rich man's house more than those in a poor man's. I'm a little jealous, you see, that's all; for I look upon myself as just as good as Colonel Grafton any day, and to find people go from my door to look for his, is a sort of slight, you see, that I can't always stomach. But I suppose you are another guess sort of people; and I should be sorry if you found anything amiss in what I say. I'm a poor man, it's true, but, by God! I'm an honest one, and come when you will, Mr. Carrington, I'll take up that bit of paper almost as soon as you bring it."

We drank with the fellow at parting, and left him on tolerably civil terms; but there was something about him which troubled and made me apprehensive and suspicious. His habits of life—as we saw them—but ill compared with the measured and deliberate manners and tone of voice which he habitually employed. The calmness and dignity of one, conscious of power and practised in authority, were conspicuous in everything he said and did. Such characteristics never mark the habitually unemployed man. What, then, were his occupations? Time will show. Enough, for the present, to know that he was even then meditating as dark a piece of villany, as the domestic historian of the frontier was ever called upon to record

CHAPTER XX.

THE OUTLAWS.

"—— They are a lawless brood,
　But rough in form nor mild in mood;
　And every creed and every race,
　With them hath found—may find a place."—*Byron.*

WE had not well departed from the dwelling of the debtor before it was occupied by the two gamblers, whose merits we had discovered in Tuscaloosa, and the third person whom we had seen with them on the road-side. They had watched and followed our steps; and by a better knowledge of the roads than we possessed, they had been enabled to arrive at the same spot without being seen, and to lurk in waiting for the moment of our departure before they made their appearance. No sooner were we gone, however, than they emerged from their place of concealment, and made for the house. A few words sufficed to tell their story to their associate, for such he was.

"Do you know the men that have left you? What was their business with you?"

They were answered; and they then revealed what they knew. They dwelt upon the large sum in bills which William had incautiously displayed to their eyes; and, exaggerating its amount, they insisted not the less upon the greater amount which they assumed, nay, asserted, to be in my possession—a prize, both sums being considered, which they coolly enough contended, would be sufficient to reward them for the most extreme and summary efforts to obtain it.

"We must pursue them instantly," said the scoundrel, who had sought to bully us at the tavern. "There are four of us, and we can soon overhaul them."

"They are armed to the teeth, George," said our debtor.

"We have seen to that," was the reply. "Ben had an opportunity to inspect their pistols, which they wisely left in their chamber when they went down to eat; and with his usual desire to keep his neighbors from doing harm, he knocked out the priming, and for the old flints, he put in fine new ones, fashioned out of wood. These will do no mischief, I warrant you, to anybody, and so let us set on. If my figures do not fail me, these chaps have money enough about them to pay our way, for the next three months, from Tennessee to New Orleans and back."

His proposal was seconded by his immediate companions, but the debtor, with more deliberateness and effectual judgment, restrained them.

"I'm against riding after them now, though all be true, as you say, about the money in their hands."

"What! will you let them escape us? Are you growing chicken, Mat, in your old days? You refuse to be a *striker*, do you? It's beneath your wisdom and dignity, I suppose?" said our bullying gambler, who went by the name of George.

"Shut up, George, and don't be foolish," was the cool response. "You ought to know me by this time, and one thing is certain, I know enough of you! You talk of being a *striker!* Why, man, you mistake! You're a chap for a trick—for making a pitfall—but not for shoving the stranger into it! Be quiet, and I'll put you at your best business. These men come back here at mid-day to-morrow."

"Ha!—the devil they do!"

"Ay; they dine with me, and then return to Colonel Grafton's. To one of them, as I told you—the younger of the two, a full-faced, good-natured looking fellow—I owe a hundred or two dollars. He hopes to get it by coming. Now, it's for you to say if he will or not. I leave it to you. I can get the money easily enough; and if you've got any better from that camp-meeting that you went to, on the 'Bigby, you will probably say I ought to pay him, but if not—"

"Pshaw!" was the universal answer. "What nonsense! Pay the devil! The very impudence of the fellow in coming here to make collections, should be enough to make us cut his throat."

"Shall we do that, men ?" was the calm inquiry of the debtor.

"It's best!" was the bloody answer of the gambler, George. Cowards of bad morals are usually the most sanguinary people when passion prompts and opportunity occurs. "I'm clear," continued the same fellow, "for making hash of these chaps. There is one of them—the slenderer fellow with the long nose, (meaning me)—his d—d insolence to me in Tuscaloosa is enough to convict him. The sooner we fix him the better."

"George seems unwilling to give that chap a chance. I rather think it would be better to let him go in order that the two might fight out their quarrel. Eh, George ! what say you ?"

The host proposed a cutting question, but in his own cool and measured manner. It did not seem to fall harmlessly upon the person to whom it was addressed. His features grew darkly red with the ferocity of his soul, but his reply was framed with a just knowledge of the fearless nature of the man who had provoked him.

"You know, Mat, I can fight well enough when it pleases me to do so."

"True," was the answer; "nobody denies that. I only meant to say that you don't often find pleasure in it ; nor, indeed, George, do I ; and that's one reason which I have for disagreeing with you about these stranger-chaps."

"What !" said one of the companions, "you won't *lift?*"

"Who says I won't ? To be sure I will. We'll lift what we can, and empty the sack ; but I'm not for slitting any more pipes if I can help it—not in this neighborhood, at least."

"Mat's going to join the methodists. He'll eat devil's broth, but dip no meat," said George.

"No—if it's needful, I'll eat both ; but one I don't like so much as the other, and, when I can get the one without the other, I'll always prefer to do so."

"But they'll blab."

"So they may ; but what care we about that, when we're going where they can't find us ? Let us keep them quiet till to-morrow midnight, and then they may use their pipes quite as much as they please. By that time we shall all be safe in the 'nation,' and the sheriff may whistle for us."

" Well, as to that part of the plan," said George, " I'm opposed to it now, and have always been against it. I see no reason to leave a country where we've done, and where we're still doing, so excellent a business."

"What business?—no *striking* for a week or more!" said one of the party.

" But what's the chance to-morrow? These very chaps show us the goodness of the business we may do by holding on a time longer. Here's hundreds going for the ' nation ' and there-abouts every week, and most of them have the real stuff. They sell out in the old states, raise all the cash they can, and give us plenty of picking if we'll look out and wait for it. But we mustn't be so milk-hearted. There's no getting on in safety if we only crop the beast's tail and let it run. We can stay here six months longer, if we stop the mouth of the sack when we empty it."

" Ah, George, you are quite too brave in council, and too full of counsel in the field," was the almost indifferent reply of the debtor ; " to stay here six weeks, would be to hang us all. The people are getting too thick and too sober between this and 'Bigby. They'll cut us off from running after a while. Now, you are too brave to run ; you'd rather fight and die any day than that. Not so with me ; I'm for *lifting and striking* anywhere, so long as the back door's open ; but the moment you shut up that, I'm for other lodgings. But enough of this. We've made the law for going already, and it's a mere waste of breath to talk over that matter now. There's other business before us, and, if you'll let me, we'll talk about that."

" Crack away !" was the answer.

" These lads come here to-morrow—they dine with me. The old trick is the easiest ; we'll rope them to their chairs, and then search their pockets. They carry their bills in their bo soms, I reckon ; and if they've got specie, it's in the saddle bags. We can rope them, rob them, and leave them at table. All the expense is a good dinner, and we'll leave them that too, as it will be some hours, I reckon, before anybody will come along to help them out of their hobble, and they'll be hungry when their first trouble's fairly over. By that time, we'll be mighty nigh Columbus ; and if the lads have the money you

say they have, it will help us handsomely through the 'nation.'
It will be a good finishing stroke to our business in this quarter."

The plan thus briefly stated was one well understood by the
fraternity, as it had been practiced in their robberies more than once
before; and it received the general approbation. The bully,
George, was opposed to leaving us alive, but he was compelled to
yield his bloody wishes in compliance with the more humane resolution of the rest.

"I am against cutting more throats than I can help, George,"
said the calculating host; "it's a dirty practice, and I don't like it,
as it's always so hard for me to clean my hands and take the spots
out of my breeches. Besides, I hate to see a man dropped
like a bullock, never to get up again. There's only one chap in the
world that I have such a grudge against that I should like
to shed his blood, and even him I should forgive if he was only willing to bend his neck when a body meets him, and say 'How d'ye
do?' with civility."

"Who's that, Bill?" demanded George.

"No matter about the name. If I have to cut his throat, I don't
care to trouble you to help me."

"I am willing."

"Ay, if I hold him for the knife. Enough, George—we'll
try you to-morrow. You shall have the pleasure of dropping
the slip over that fellow with the long nose. See that you do
it bravely. If you don't pinion his arms, you may feel his elbow,
and he looks very much like a chap that had bone and muscle to
spare."

"I'll see to that—but suppose they refuse to dine?" was the
suggestion of the bully.

"Why, then, we must take them when at the drink, or as they go
through the passage. You must watch your chance, and choose the
moment you like best; but you who are the *strikers* must be careful
to move together. If you miss a minute, you may have trouble, for
one will certainly come to help the other, and it may compel us to use
the knife at last."

"It's a shorter way to use it at first," said George.

"Perhaps so—but let me tell you it lasts much longer. The
business is not dead with the man; and when you have done

:hat sort of thing once or twice, you'll find that it calls for you to do a great deal more business of different kinds which will be not only troublesome but disagreeable. I tell you, as I told you before, it is the very devil to wash out the stains."

This affair settled, others of like nature, but of less immediate performance, came up for consideration; but these need not be related now. One fact, however, may be stated. When they had resolved upon our robbery, they set themselves down to play for the results; and, having made a supposed estimate of our effects, they staked their several shares in moderate sums and won and lost the moneys which they were yet to steal! It may be added that my former opponent, the bully George, was one of the most fortunate; and, having won the right from his comrades to the spoils which they were yet to win, he was the most impatient for the approach of the hour when his winnings were to be realized. Let us now relate our own progress.

CHAPTER XXI.

THE HAPPY FAMILY.

"So thy fair hand, enamored fancy gleans
　The treasured pictures of a thousand scenes;
Thy pencil traces on the lover's thought
Some cottage home, from towns and toil remote.
Where love and peace may claim alternate hours
With peace embosom'd in Idalian **bowers!**
Remote from busy life's bewildered **way**
O'er all his heart shall taste **and beauty sway—**
Free on the sunny slope, **or winding shore,**
With hermit steps to wonder and **adore."—CAMPBELL.**

ON our return to Colonel **Grafton's, we were received with a**
welcome due rather **to a long and tried intimacy, than to our**
new acquaintance. **There we met a Mr. Clifton — a young**
man about twenty-five years **of age — of slight, but elegant**
figure, **and** a face decidedly **one of the most** handsome I had
ever seen among men. **It was evident to me** after a little
space that such also **was the opinion of Julia** Grafton. **Her**
eyes, when an opportunity **offered, watched him** narrowly; **and**
I was soon enabled **to see that the gentleman** himself **was as-**
siduous in those attentions **which are apt enough to occasion**
love, and to yield **it** opportunity. **I** learned **casually in the**
course of the evening, and after the young man **had retired, what**
I had readily inferred from my previous observation — **namely**
that they had been **for some** time known to each **other. Mr.**
Clifton's manners were **good — artless** exceedingly, **and frank,**
and he seemed **in** all respects, **a perfect and** pleasing gentleman.
He left us before **night, alleging a necessity to ride some miles**
on business which admitted **of no delay. I could see the dis-**
appointment in the cheek **of** Julia, and **the quivering of** her
lovely lips **was** not entirely concealed. **That night she** sang

as a plaintive ditty, to the music of an ancient, but nobly-toned harpsichord, and trembling but anticipative love was the burden of her song. The obvious interest of these two in each other, had the effect of carrying me back to Marengo—but the vision which encountered me there drove me again into the wilderness and left me no refuge but among strangers. I fancied that I beheld the triumphant joy of John Hurdis; and the active and morbid imagination completed the cruel torture by showing me Mary Easterby locked in his arms. My soul shrank from the portraiture of my fancy, and I lapsed away into gloom and silence in defiance of all the friendly solicitings of our host and his sweet family.

But my companion had no such suffering as mine, and he gave a free rein to his tongue. He related to Colonel Grafton the circumstances attending our interview with the debtor, not omitting the remarks of the latter in reference to the colonel himself.

"It matters not much," said the colonel, "what he thinks of me, but the truth is, he has not told you the precise reason of his hostility. The pride of the more wealthy is always insisted upon by the poorer sort of people, to account for any differences between themselves and their neighbors. It is idle to answer them on this head. They themselves know better. If they confessed that the possession of greater wealth was an occasion for their constant hate or dislike they would speak more to the purpose, and with far more justice. Not that I think that Webber hates me because I am wealthy. He spends daily quite as much money as I do—but he can not so well convince his neighbors that he gets it as honestly; and still less can he convince me of the fact. In his own consciousness lies my sufficient justification for the distance at which I keep him, and for that studied austerity of deportment on my part of which he so bitterly complains. I am sorry for my own sake, not less than his, that I am forced to the adoption of a habit which is not natural to me and far from agreeable. It gives me no less pain to avoid any of my neighbors than it must give them offence. But I act from a calm conviction of duty, and this fellow knows it. Let us say no more about him. It is enough that he promises to pay you your money—he can do it if he will; and I doubt not that he will keep his promise, simply because my name is on his paper. It will be a matter of pride with him to relieve himself of an obligation to one who offends his self-esteem so greatly as to provoke him to complaint."

About ten o'clock the next day we left Colonel Grafton's for the dwelling of the debtor. He rode a mile or two with us, and on leaving us renewed his desire that we should return and spend the night with him. His residence lay in our road, and we readily made the promise.

"Could I live as Grafton lives," said William, after our friend had left us—"could I have such an establishment, and such a family, and be such a man, it seems to me I should be most happy. He wants for nothing that he has not, he is beloved by his family, and has acquired so happily the arts of the household—and there is a great deal in that—that he can not but be happy. Everything is snug, and everything seems to fit about him. Nothing is out of place; and wife, children, servants—all, not only seem to know their several places, but to delight in them. There is no discontent in that family; and that dear girl, Julia, how much she reminds me of Emmeline—what a gentle being, yet how full of spirit—how graceful and light in her thoughts and movements, yet how true, how firm."

I let my friend run on in his eulogy without interruption. The things and persons which had produced a sensation of so much pleasure in his heart, had brought but sorrow and dissatisfaction to mine. His fancy described his own household, in similarly bright colors to his mind and eye—whilst my thoughts, taking their complexion from my own denied and defeated fortunes, indulged in gloomy comparisons of what I saw in the possession of others, and the cold, cheerless fate—the isolation and the solitude—of all my future life. How could I appreciate the enthusiasm of my friend—how share in his raptures? Every picture of bliss to the eye of the sufferer is provocation and bitterness. I felt it such and replied querulously:—

"Your raptures may be out of place, William, for aught you know. What folly to judge of surfaces! But your young traveller always does so. Who shall say what discontent reigns in that family, in the absence of the stranger? There may be bitterness and curses, for aught you know, in many a bosom the possessor of which meets you with a smile and cheers you with a song—and that girl Julia—she is beautiful you say—but is she blest? She loves—you see that!--Is it certain that she loves wisely, worthily—that she wins the object of her love—that he does not deceive her—or that she does not jilt him in some moment of bitter perversity and chafing passion? Well did the ancient declare, that the happiness of man could never be estimated till the grave had closed over him."

"The fellow was a fool to say that, as if the man could be happy then. But I can declare him false from my own bosom. I am happy now, and am resolved to be more so, Look you. Dick—in two weeks more I will be in Marengo. I shall have entered my lands, and made my preparations. In four weeks Emmeline will be mine; and then, hey for an establishment like Grafton's. All shall be peace and sweetness about my dwelling as about his. I will lay out my grounds in the same manner—I will bring Emmeline to see his—"

I ventured to interrupt the dreamer: "Suppose she does not like them as much as you do? Women have their own modes of thinking and planning these matters. Will you not give her her own way?"

He replied good-naturedly but quickly: "Oh, surely; but she will like them—I know she will. They are entirely to her taste; and, whether they be or not, she shall have her own way in that. You do not suppose I would insist upon so small a matter?"

"But it was anything but a small matter while you were dwelling upon the charms of Colonel Grafton's establishment. The grounds make no small part of its charms in both our eyes, and I wonder that you should give them up so readily."

"I do not give them up, Richard. I will let Emmeline know how much I like them, and will insist upon them as long as I can in reason. But, however lovely I think them, do not sup-pose that I count them as anything in comparison of the family beauty—the harmony that makes the circle a complete system, in which the lights are all clear and lovely, and the sounds all sweet and touching."

"I will sooner admit your capacity to lay out your grounds as tastefully as Colonel Grafton, than to bring about such results

in your family, whatever it may be. You are not Colonel Grafton, William: you lack his prudence, his method, his experience, his years. The harmony of one's household depends
greatly upon the discretion and resolve of its master. Heaven
knows I wish you happy, William; but, if you promise yourself
a home like that of this gentleman, you must become a cooler-
headed and far more prudent personage than any of your friends
esteem you now. You are amiable enough, and therefore worthy to have such a family; but you are not grave enough to
create its character, and so to decree and impel as to make the
lights revolve harmoniously in your circle, and call forth the
music in its place. Your lights will sometimes annoy you by
their glare, or go out when you most need their assistance; and
your music will ring in your ears at times when your evening nap
seems to you the most desirable enjoyment in nature. Joy itself is
known to surfeit, and you, unhappily, are not a man to feed in
moderation."

He received my croakings with good nature, and laughed heartily
at my predictions.

"You are a sad boy, Richard; you are quite too philosoph-
ical ever to be happy," was his good-natured reply. "You
analyze matters too closely. You must not subject the things
which give you pleasure to a too close inspection of your mind,
or ten to one you despise them. The mind has but little to do
with the affections—the less the better. I would rather not
think, but only believe, where I have set my heart. It is so
sweet to confide—it is so worrying to doubt! It appears to
me, now, for example, that the fruit plucked by Eve, producing all
the quarrel between herself and daddy Adam, was from the tree of
jealousy."

"What a transition!" was my reply. "You have brought down
your generalization to a narrow and very selfish point. But give
your horse the spur, I pray you—when your theme becomes domestic, I feel like a gallop."

He pricked his steed, in compliance with my wish; but the
increased pace of our horses offered no interruption to his discourse
on a subject so near his heart. He continued to speak in the same
fashion:—

"Once fairly married, Dicky, you will see how grave I can

me. I will then become a public man. You will hear of me as a commissioner of the poor, of roads, bridges, and ferries. I will get up a project for an orphan-asylum in Marengo, and make a speech or two at the muster-ground in favor of an institute for coupling veteran old maids and inveterate old bachelors together. The women will name all their first children after me, and in five years I will be godfather to half Marengo. You smile—you will see! And then, Dick, when Emmeline gives me a dear little brat of our own—ah, Dick!—"

He struck the spur into his steed, and the animal bounded up the hill, as if a wing, like that in the soul of his master, was lifting him forward and upward without his own exertions. I smiled, with a sad smile, at the enthusiast-lover; and bitterly did his dream of delight force me to brood over my own experience of disappointment. The brightness of his hope was like some glowing and breathing flower cast upon the grave of mine I could almost have quarrelled with him for his joy on such subject. Little did he or I think, poor fellow, that his joy was but a dream—that the doom of denial, nor of denial merely was already written by the fates against him! Terrible indeed with a sudden terribleness—when I afterward reflected upon his boyish ardor—appeared to me the sad fate which lay, as it were, in the very path over which he was bounding with delight! Could he or I have lifted the thick veil at that moment, how idle would have appeared all his hopes—how much more idle my despondency!

CHAPTER XXII

SAVAGE PASSIONS

I hate him for he is a Christian —
But more, for that, in low simplicity,
He lends out money gratis, and brings down
The rate of usance here with us in Venice.
If I can catch him once upon the hip,
I will feed fat the ancient grudge I bear him!"

Merchant of Venice.

WE at length reached the dwelling of our debtor. He re
ceived us as before, with a plain, rude indifference of manner,
mingled with good nature nevertheless, that seemed willing to
give pleasure, however unwilling to make any great exertion
for it. There was nothing to startle our apprehension, or make
us suspicious. Nobody appeared, save the host, who played
his part to admiration. He would have carried our horses to
the stable, but we refused to suffer him to do so, alleging our
intention to ride back to Colonel Grafton's as soon as possible.

"What! not before dinner?—you will surely stay and dine
with me. I have prepared for you."

The rascal spoke truly. He had prepared for us with a vengeance. I would have declined, for I did not like (though, to
confess a truth, I did not distrust) appearances. But finding us
hesitate, and fearing probably to lose his prey, he resorted to a
suggestion which at once determined us.

"I'm afraid, if you can't stop for dinner, I can't let you have
the money to-day. A neighbor of mine, to whom I lent it a
month ago, promised to bring it by meal-time ; and, as he lives
a good bit off, I don't look for him before."

This, uttered with an air of indifference, settled our irresolu-
tion. The idea of coming back again to such a place, and so

wasting another day, was anything but agreeable, and we resolved to stay by all means, if by so doing we could effect our
object. Still, as we were bent to ride, as soon as we had got
the money, we insisted that he should not take our horses, which
were fastened to the swinging limbs of a shady tree before the
entrance, in instant readiness for use. This preparatory conference took place at the door. We then entered the hovel,
which it will be necessary, in order to detail following events,
briefly to describe. In this particular, our task is easy—the
arts of architecture, in the southwestern country, being of no
very complicated character. The house, as I have said before,
was built of logs—unhewn, unsquared, rude, ill-adjointed—the
mere hovel of a squatter, who cuts down fine trees, spoils a
good site, and establishes what he impudently styles his improvements! It consisted of a single story, raised upon blocks
four feet from the ground, having an entrance running through
the centre of the building, with apartments on either hand. To
the left-hand apartment, which was used as a hall, was attached
at each end a little *lean-to*, or shed, the doors to which opened
at once upon the hall. These rooms were possibly meant as
sleeping-apartments, nothing being more common in the Southwest than such additions for such purposes. In this instance,
however, all regard to appearances seemed to have been neg-
lected, since, in attaching the shed to each end of the hall, one
of these ugly excrescences was necessarily thrown upon the
front of the building, which, without such an incumbrance, was
already sufficiently uncouth and uninviting. If the exterior of
this fabric was thus unpromising, what could be said of it within? It was a mere shell. There was no ceiling to the hall,
and the roof which covered it was filled with openings that let
in the generous sunlight, and with undiscriminating liberality
would have let in any quantity of rain. The furniture consisted
of an old sideboard, garnished with a couple of common decan-
ters, a pitcher with the mouth broken off, and some three or
four cracked tumblers. A rickety table was stationary in the
centre of the room, which held, besides, some half-dozen high-
backed and low-bottomed chairs, the seats of which were covered with untanned deerskins.

Into these we squatted with little ceremony. Our host placed

before us a bundle of cigars. I did not smoke, and declined to
partake; but my companion joined him, and the two puffed
away cosily together, to my great annoyance. Meanwhile an
old negro wench made her appearance, spread a cloth which
might have been clean in some earlier period of the world's
history, but which was inconceivably dirty now, and proceeded
to make other shows, of a like satisfactory nature, of the promised dinner. The cloth was soon laid—plates, dishes, knives
and forks, produced from the capacious sideboard; and, this
done, she proceeded to fill the decanter from a jug which she
brought from the apartment opposite. She then retired to make
her final preparations for the feast.

To join with him in a glass of whiskey was the next proceeding, and, setting us a hearty example by half filling his own
glass, he would have insisted upon our drinking with equal liberality. Fortunately for me, at least, I was stubborn in my
moderation. I was not moderate from prudence, but from fastidiousness. In the society and house of one whom I esteemed
more than I did the vulgar creature who sought to persuade
me, I feel and confess I should have been more self-indulgent.
But I could not stomach well the whiskey of the person whose
frequent contact I found it so difficult to endure. I should not
have drunk with him at all, but that I was unwilling to give
offence. Such might have been the case in the event of my
refusal, had it been his cue to quarrel.

We drank, however, and resumed our seats; our host with a
sang-froid which seemed habitual, if not natural, dashing into
speech without any provocation.

"So you're going back to Colonel Grafton's, are you? He's
a mighty great man now-a-days, and it's no wonder you young
men like him. It's natural enough for young men to like great
men, particularly when they're well off, and have handsome
daughters. You've looked hard upon Miss Julia, I reckon?"

I said nothing, but Carrington replied in a jocular manner,
which I thought rather too great a concession of civility to such
a creature. He continued:—

"Once, to tell you a *dog-truth*, I rather did like him myself.
He was a gentleman, to say the littlest for him; and, dang it!
he made me feel it always when I stood before him. It was

that very thing that made me come to dislike him. I stood it well enough while I worked for him, but after I left him the case was different—I didn't care to have such a feeling when I set up business for myself. And then he took it upon him to give me advice, and to talk to me about reports going through the neighborhood, and people's opinions of me, and all that d——d sort of stuff, just as if he was my godfather. I kicked at that, and broke loose mighty soon. I told him my mind, and then he pretty much told me his—for Grafton's no coward—and so we concluded to say as little to one another as we well could spare."

"The wisest and safest course for both of you, I doubt not," was Carrington's remark.

"As for the safety now, Mr. Carrington," replied the debtor, "that's neither here nor there. I would not give this stump of tobacco for any better security than my eyes and fingers against Grafton, or any other man in the land. I don't ask for any protection from the laws—I won't be sued, and I don't sue. Catch me going to the 'squire to bind my neighbor's fist or fingers. Let him use them as he pleases; all I ask is good notice beforehand, a fair field, and no favor. Let him hold to it then, and see who first comes bottom upward."

"You are confident of your strength," was my remark, "yet I should not think you able to match with Colonel Grafton. He seems to me too much for you. He has a better frame, and noble muscle."

Not displeased at what might look like personal disparagement, the fellow replied with cool good nature

"Ah, you're but a young beginner, stranger, though it may be a bold one! For a first tug or two, Grafton might do well enough; but his breath wouldn't hold him long. His fat is too thick about his ribs to stand it out. I'd be willing to run the risk of three tugs with him to have a chance at the fourth. By my grinders, but I would gripe him then. You should then see a death-hug, stranger, if you never saw it before."

The fellow's teeth gnashed as he spoke, and his mouth was distorted, and his eyes glared with an expression absolutely fiendish. At the same moment, dropping the end of the segar from his hand, he stuck forth his half-contracted fingers, as if in

the effort to grasp his opponent's throat; and I almost fancied
I beheld the wolf upon his leap. The nails of his fingers had
not been cut for a month, and looked rather like the claws of a
wild beast than the proper appendages of a man.

"You seem to hate him very much," was my unnecessary remark. I uttered it almost unconsciously. It prompted him to
further speech.

"I do hate him," was the reply, "more than I hate anything
besides in nature. I don't hate a bear, for I can shoot him;
nor a dog, for I can scourge him; nor a horse, for I can manage
him; nor a wild bull, for I have taken him by the horns when
he was maddest. But I hate that man, Grafton, by the eternal!
and I hate him more because I can't manage him in any way.
He's neither bear, nor bull, nor dog—not so dangerous, yet
more difficult than all. I'd give all I'm worth, and that's something, though you don't see it, perhaps, only to meet him as a
bear, as a bull, as a dog—ay, by the hokies, as all three together!—and let us all show after our own fashion, what we
are good for. I'd lick his blood that day, or he should lick
mine."

"It seems to me," I replied, and my looks and language must
both have partaken largely of the unmitigated disgust within my
soul—"It seems to me strange, indeed, how any man, having
the spirit of manhood, should keep such a hatred as that fester-
ing in his heart, without seeking to work it out! Why, if you
hate him, do you not fight him?"

"That's well enough said, young master!" he cried, without
hearing me to the end—"but it's easier to say that, and to desire it, than to get it! Fight it out, indeed!—and how am I
to make him fight? send him a challenge? Ha! ha! ha!
Why, he'd laugh at it, and so would you, young sir, if he
showed you the challenge, while you happened to be in the
house. His wife would laugh, and his daughter would laugh,
and even nigger Tom would laugh. You'd have lots of fun
over it. Ha! ha! a challenge from Mat. Webber to Colonel
John Grafton, Grafton Lodge! What a joke for my neighbor
democrats! Every rascal among them—each of whom would
fight you to-morrow, sir, if you ventured to say they were not
perfectly your equal—would yet laugh to split their sides to

think of the impudence of that poor devil, Webber, in challenging Colonel John Grafton, 'Squire Grafton, tl e great
planter cf Grafton Lodge! Oh, no, sir! that's all my eye
There's no getting a fight out of my enemy in that way. You
must think of some other fashion for righting poor men in this
country."

There was certainly some truth in what the fellow said. He
felt it, but he seemed no longer angry. Bating a sarcastic grin,
and a slight and seemingly nervous motion of his fingers, which
accompanied the words, they were spoken with a coolness almost amounting to good nature. I had, meanwhile, got some
what warmed by the viperous malignity which he had indicated
toward a gentleman, who, as you have seen, had won greatly
upon my good regards; and, without paying much attention to
the recovered ease and quiet of the fellow—so entirely different
from the fierce and wolfish demeanor which had marked him but
a few moments before—I proceeded, in the same spirit in which
I had begun, to reply to him :—

" Had you heard me out, sir, you would, perhaps, have spared
your speech. I grant you that it might be a difficult, if not an
impossible thing to bring Mr. Grafton to a meeting; but this
difficulty would not arise, I imagine, from any difference be ·
tween you of wealth or station. No mere inequalities of fortune would deprive any man of his claim to justice in any field,
or my own affairs would frequently subject me to such deprivation. There must be something besides this, which makes a
man incur a forfeiture of this sort."

" Yes, yes," he replied instantly, with surprising quickness;
" I understand what you would say. The world must esteem
me a gentleman."

" Precisely," was my careless reply. The fellow looked
gravely upon me for an instant, but smoothing down his brow,
which began to grow wrinkled, he proceeded in tones as indif·
ferent as before.

" I confess to you, I'm no gentleman—I don't pretend to it
—I wasn't born one and can't afford to take up the business.
It costs too much in clothes, in trinkets, in fine linen, in book-
learning, and other matters."

I was about to waste a few sentences upon him to show that

these were not the requisites of gentility, but he spared me any such foolish labor by going on thus:—

"That's neither here nor there. You were going to tell me of some way by which I could get my revenge out of Grafton. Let's hear your ideas about that. That's the hitch."

"Not your revenge; I spoke of redress for wrong."

"Well, well," he replied, shaking his head, "names for the same things, pretty much, but, as you please. Only tell me how, if you are no gentleman—mark that! I don't want the revenge—the redress, I mean, of a gentleman—I want the redress of a man—tell me how I am to get it, when the person who has wronged me, thinks me too much beneath him to meet me on a fair ground! What's my remedy? Tell me that, and I'll give you my thanks, and call you a mighty clever fellow in the bargain!"

His insolence annoyed me, and he saw it in my quick reply—"I thank you, sir, I can spare the compliment—"

He grinned good-naturedly: "You a poor man!" he exclaimed, interrupting me. "By the hokies, you ought to be rich; and your mother must have had some mighty high notions when she carried you! But go on. I ask your pardon. Go on."

I should not have complied with the fellow's wish, but that I felt a secret desire which I could not repress, to goad him for his insolence: "Well, sir, I say that I see no difficulty, if the person injured has the commonest spirit of manhood in him, in getting redress from a man who has injured him, whatever be his station. I am convinced, if you seriously wish for it, you could get yours from Grafton. There is such a thing, you know, as taking the road of an enemy."

"Ha! ha! ha! and what would that come to, or rather what do you think it would bring me to, here in Tuscaloosa county? I'll tell you in double quick time—the gallows. It wouldn't bring you to the gallows, or any man passing for a gentleman, but democrats can't bear to see democrats taking upon themselves the airs of gentlemen. They'd hang me, my good friend, if they didn't burn me beforehand; and that would be the upshot of following your counsel. But your talk isn't new to me; I have thought of it long since. Do you think—but to talk about what you didn't do, is mighty little business To put a good deal in a small calabash, let me tell you, then, that Mat Webber isn't the man to sit down and suck his thumbs when his neighbor troubles him, if so be he can help himself in a quicker way. I've turned over all this matter in my mind, and I've come to this conclusion, that I must wait for some odd hour when good luck is willing to do what she has never done yet, and gives me a chance at my enemy. Be certain when that hour comes, stranger, my teeth shall meet in the flesh!"

He filled his glass and drank freely as he concluded. His face had in it an air of resolve as he spoke which left little doubt in my mind that he was the ruffian to do what he threatened, and involuntarily I shuddered when I thought how many opportunities must necessarily arise to him for the execution of any villany from the near neighborhood in which he lived with the enemy whom he so deeply hated. I was not suffered to meditate long upon this or any subject. The negro woman appeared bringing in dinner. Some fried bacon and eggs formed the chief items in our repast; and with an extra hospitality, which had its object, our host placed our chairs, which were both on the one side of the table, he, alone, occupying the seat opposite. Without a solitary thought of evil we sat down to the repast, which might well be compared to the bait which is placed by the cunning fowler for the better entrapping of the unwary bird.

8

CHAPTER XXIII.

IN THE SNARE

Titius Sabinus.—Am I then catched!
Rufus.—How think you, sir! you are.

BEN JONSON.

THOUGH neither William Carrington nor myself sat entirely
at ease at the table of our host, neither of us had any suspicion
of his purposes. Regarding the fellow as essentially low in
his character, and totally unworthy the esteem of honorable
men, we were only solicitous to get our money and avoid collision with him. And, so far, we had but little reason to complain. Though indulging freely in remarks upon persons—
Colonel Grafton for example—which were not altogether inof-
fensive, his language in reference to ourselves was sufficiently
civil; and bating a too frequent approach which he made to an
undue familiarity, and which, when it concerned me particularly, I was always prompt to check, there was nothing in his
manner calculated to offend the most irritable. On the contrary, the fellow played the part of humility in sundry instances
to admiration; when we resisted him on any subject, he shrank
from pursuing it, and throughout the interview exhibited a disposition to forbear all annoyance, except probably on the one
subject of Colonel Grafton. On that point even his present
policy did not suffer him to give way—his self-esteem had
been evidently wounded to the quick by his former employer,
and, with a forbearance like his own, which, under any other
circumstances, would have been wisdom, we avoided controversy on a topic in which we must evidently disagree. But
not so Webber. He seemed desirous to gain aliment for his
anger by a frequent recurrence to the matter which provoked

it, and throughout the whole of our interview until the occurrence of those circumstances which served, by their personal importance, to supersede all other matters in our thoughts, he continued, in spite of all our discouragements, to bring Grafton before us in various lights and anecdotes, throughout the whole of which, his own relation to the subject of remark was that of one who hated with the bitterest hate, and whom fear, or some less obvious policy, alone, restrained from an attempt to wreak upon his enemy the full extent of that malice which he yet had not the wisdom to repress.

It was while he indulged in this very vein that we heard the approaching tramp of horses. Webber stopped instantly in his discourse.

"Ah, there he comes," he remarked, "the debtor is punctual enough, though he should have been here an hour sooner. And now, 'Squire Carrington, I hope we shall be able to do your business."

Sincerely did I hope so too. There was an odd sort of smile upon the fellow's lips as he said these words which did not please me. It was strange and sinister. It was not good-humored certainly, and yet it did not signify any sort of dissatisfaction. Perhaps it simply denoted insincerity, and for this I did not like it. Carrington made some reply; and by this time we heard a bustling among our horses which were fastened to the branches of a tree at the entrance. I was about to rise, for I recollected that we had money in the saddle-bags, when I was prevented by the appearance of the stranger who entered in the same moment. One glance at the fellow was enough. His features were those of the undisguised ruffian; and even then I began to feel some little apprehension though I could not to my own mind define the form of the danger which might impend. I could not think it possible that these two ruffians, bold however they might be, would undertake to grapple with us face to face, and in broad daylight. They could not mistake our strength of body; and, body and soul, we felt ourselves more than a match for them, and a third to help them. And yet, when I reflected upon the large amount of money which William had in his possession, I could not but feel that nothing but a like knowledge of the fact, was wanting to prompt, not only these but a dozen other desperates like them, to an attempt, however unfavorable **the aspect, to possess themselves of it.** Besides, **we had surely heard the** trampling of more horses than one when the newcomer was **approaching.** Had he companions? Where were they? These thoughts began to **annoy** and make me suspicious, **and I turned to** William. **Never was** anquestioning confidence so clearly **depicted in any** countenance as in his. He looked on the stranger with, perhaps, no less disgust than myself, but suspicion of foul play he had none. I determined that he should be awakened, and was about to rise and suggest the conclusion of our business, in such a manner as to make it absolutely impossible that he should not see that I **was** placing myself against the wall, **when** Webber of himself proposed the adjustment **of the** debt. Everything seemed to be unequivocal and **above board.** The stranger pulled forth his wallet, and sitting down to **the table, on** the side next to Carrington, proceeded **to count out the money** before him. The amount was in small bills, and having completed **his count,** which took him an uneasy time, he pushed the **bundle toward** Webber, who slowly proceeded to go through a like examination. I grew impatient at the delay, but concluded that it would be better to say nothing. To show temper at **such** a moment might have been to defeat the purpose which we had in view ; and send us off with a satisfaction, essentially different from that for which we came. Webber's face grew more grave than usual as he counted the money, and I could observe that his eyes were frequently lifted from the bills, and **seemed to wander** about the room as if his thoughts were elsewhere. But he finished at length, and handing the required **sum** over to William, he begged him to see that all was right. The latter was about **to do so — had actu-**ally taken the bills in his hands, when I heard **a** slight footstep behind me — before **I** could turn, under the **influence of the** natural curiosity which prompted me to do so, I heard a sudden exclamation from my companion, and in the very same instant, felt something falling over **my face.** Suspicious of foul play before, I leaped, as if **under a natural instinct to** my feet, but was as instantly jerked down, and falling **over the** chair behind, dragged it with me upon **the floor. All this was the work of** a moment. Striving to rise, I soon **discovered** the full extent of my predicament, and the way in which we were taken. My arms were bound to my side—almost drawn behind my back— by a noose formed in a common plough-line, which was cutting into the flesh at every movement which I made.

That I struggled furiously for release need not be said. I was not the man to submit quietly to martyrdom. But I soon found my exertions were in vain. The cords were not only tightly drawn, but securely fastened behind me to one of the sleepers of the cabin—a vacant board from the floor enabling my assailants to effect this arrangement with little difficulty. Added to this, my struggles brought upon me the entire weight of the two fellows who had effected my captivity. One sat upon my body as indifferently as a Turk upon his cushions; while the other, at every movement which I made, thrust his sharp knees into my breast, and almost deprived me of the power of breathing. Rage, for the moment, added to my strength, which surprised even myself as it surprised my enemies. More than once, without any use of my arms, by the mere writhings of my body, did I throw them from it; but exhaustion did for them what their own strength could not, and I lay quiet at length, and at their mercy. The performance of this affair took far less time than the telling of it, and was over, I may say, in an instant.

With William Carrington the case was different. He was more fortunate : I thought so at the time, at least. He effected his escape. By what chance it was, I know not; but they failed to noose him so completely as they had done me. The slip was caught by his hand in descending over his shoulders, and he threw it from him; and, in the same moment, with a blow of his fist that might have felled an ox, he prostrated the ruffian who had brought the money, and who stood most convenient to his hand. Without stopping to look at the enemy behind, with that prompt impulse which so frequently commands success, he sprang directly over the table, and aimed a second blow at Webber, who had risen from his seat and stood directly in the way. With a fortunate alacrity the fellow avoided the blow, and, darting on one side, drew his dirk, and prepared to await the second.

By this time, however, I was enabled, though prostrated and

overcome, to behold the combat in which **I could bear no** part. **I saw** that the only chance of my **companion was** in flight. Our enemies, as if by magic, had sprung up **around us** like the teeth of the dragon. There were no less than seven persons in **the** room besides ourselves. With my utmost voice **I commanded** William **to** fly. He saw, in the same instant with myself, the utter inability of any efforts which he might make, and the click of a pistol-cock in the hands of a fellow behind me was a warning too significant to be trifled **with.** With a single look at me, which fully convinced me of the pang which he felt at being compelled to leave me in such a situation, he sprang through the entrance, and in another **moment had** disappeared from sight Webber and three others immediately rushed off **in** pursuit, leaving me in the custody and at the mercy of the three remaining.

CHAPTER XXIV.

THE RUFFIAN CONFERENCE.

"How stubbornly this fellow answered me!"

BEAUMONT AND FLETCHER.

WHEN, more complacently, I looked around, and into the faces of my captors, what was my surprise to behold in the most turbulent the bullying gambler with whom I had refused to play at the tavern in Tuscaloosa! The countenance of the rascal plainly showed that he remembered the transaction. There was a complacent and triumphant grin upon his lips, which, as I could not then punish him, added to the bitterness of my situation. I tried to turn away from regarding him, but the relative situation in which we were now placed was but too grateful to his mean and malicious soul, and, changing his position to correspond with mine, he continued to face me with a degree of coldness which could only be ascribed to his perfect consciousness of my inability to strive with him. I felt that my anger would be not only vain to restrain him in his impudence, but, must, from its impotence, only provoke him to an increased indulgence of it, besides giving him a degree of satisfaction which I was too little his friend to desire. I accordingly fixed my eyes upon him with as much cool indifference as I could of a sudden put into them, and, schooling my lips to a sort of utterance which fell far short of the feverish wrath in my bosom, I thus addressed him : —

"If you are the same person who would have cheated me at cards in Tuscaloosa a few days ago, I congratulate you upon a sudden increase of valor. You have improved amazingly in a very short space of time, and, though I can not say that your courage is even now of the right kind, yet there's no saying

how fast one may acquire it who has commenced so happily
Perhaps—as I doubt not that you desire still further to im-
prove—you would be pleased to give me some little opportu
nity to try you, and test your progress. If you would but free
an arm or so, and let us try it with fist or hickory—ay, or with
other weapons with which I see you are well enough provided
—I should very much alter the opinion I had formed of you
at our first meeting."

The fellow chafed to hear these words, and let fly a volley
of oaths, which only served to increase the coolness of my temper. I felt that I had a decided advantage over him, and a
speech so little expected from one in my situation, and so contemptuous at the same time, provoked the unmitigated laughter
of the fellow's companions, who had assumed with him the custody of my person.

"And what the h—ll is there to grin about?" he said to them,
as soon as their subsiding merriment enabled him to be heard;
"do you mind, or do you think I mind, the crowings of this
cock-sparrow, when I can clip his wings at any moment? Let
him talk while he may—who cares? It will be for me to
wind up with him when I get tired of his nonsense."

"But won't you let the chap loose, Bully George?" cried one
of the companions; "let him loose, as he asks you, and try a
hickory. I know you're famous at a stick-fight: I saw you
once at the Sipsy, when you undertook to lather Jim Cudworth.
You didn't know Jim before that time, George, or you wouldn't
ha' chose that weapon. But this lark, now—he, I reckon's,
much easier to manage than Jim: let him try it, George."

This speech turned the fury of the bully from me to his comrades; but it was the fury of foul language only, and would not
bear repetition. The fellow, whom they seemed pleased to
chafe, foamed like a madman in striving to reply. The jest
was taken up by the two, who bandied it to and fro. as two
expert ball-players do their ball without suffering it once to
fall to the ground, until they tired of the game; and they repeated and referred to a number of little circumstances in the
history of their vexed associate, all calculated at once to provoke him into additional fury, and to convince me that the fellow was, as I had esteemed him at the very first glance, a poor

and pitiable coward. In due proportion as they found merriment in annoying him, did they seem to grow good natured toward myself—perhaps, because I had set the ball in motion which they had found it so pleasant to keep up; but their sport had like to have been death to me. The ruffian, driven almost to madness by the sarcasms of those whom he did not dare to attack, turned suddenly upon me, and with a most murderous determination aimed his dagger at my throat. I had no way to ward the weapon, and must have perished but for the promptitude of one of the fellows, who seemed to have watched the bully closely, and who caught his arm ere it descended, and wrested the weapon from him. The joke had ceased. The man who stayed his arm now spoke to him in the fierce language of a superior:—

"Look you, Bully George, had you bloodied the boy, I should ha' put my cold steel into your ribs for certain!"

"Why, what is he to you, Geoffrey, that you should take up for him?" was the subdued answer.

"Nothing much, and for that matter you're nothing much to me either; but I don't see the profit of killing the chap, and Mat Webber ordered that we shouldn't hurt him."

"Mat Webber's a milk-and-water fool," replied the other.

"Let him hear you say so," said Geoffrey, "and see the end of it! It's a pretty thing, indeed, that you should talk of Mat being a milk-and-water fool—a man that will fight through a thicket of men, when you'd be for sneaking round it! Shut up, Bully George, and give way to your betters. The less you say the wiser. Don't we know that the chap's right? If you were only half the man that he seems to be, you wouldn't be half so bloody-minded with a prisoner; you wouldn't cut more throats than Mat Webber, and perhaps you'd get a larger share of the plunder. I've always seen that it's such chaps as you, that don't love fight when it's going, that's always most ready to cut and stab when there's no danger, and when there's no use for it. Keep your knife till it's wanted. It may be that you may soon have better use for it, since, if that other lark get off, he'll bring Grafton and all the constables of the district upon us."

"It's a bad job, that chap's getting off," said the other ruffian. "How did you happen to miss, Geoffrey?"

"The devil knows! I had the rope fair enough, I thought; but somehow he twisted round, or raised his hand just when I dropped it over him, and threw it off a bit quicker than I threw it on. He's a stout fellow that, and went over the table like a ball. I'm dubious he'll get off. Look out, John, and say what you see."

The fellow complied, and returned after a few moments with an unsatisfactory answer. Some further conference ensued between them touching the probable chances of Carrington's escape, and my heart grew painfully interested, as I heard their cold and cruel calculations as to the wisest course of action among the pursuers. Their mode of disposing of the difficulty, summary and reckless as it showed them to be, was enough to inspire me with the most anxious fear. If they, unvexed by flight, and unexcited by the pursuit, could yet deliberately resolve that the fugitive should be shot down rather than suffered to escape, the event was surely not improbable. I could listen no longer in silence.

"I hear you, sir," I said, interrupting the fellow who was styled Geoffrey, and who seemed the most humane among them; "you coolly resolve that my friend should be murdered. You can not mean that Webber will do such a deed? I will not believe you. If you only think to annoy and frighten me, you are mistaken. I am in your power, it is true, and you may put me to death, as your companion, who thinks to make up in cruelty what he lacks in courage, appeared just now to desire— but is this your policy? What good can come of it? It will neither help you in present flight nor in future safety. As for my money, if it is that which you want, it is quite as easy for you to take that as my life. All that I have is in your possession. My horse, my clothes, my cash—they are all together; and, having these, the mere shedding of my blood can give you no pleasure, unless you have been schooled among the savages As for your men overtaking my friend, I doubt it, unless their horses are the best blood in the country. That which he rides I know to be so, and can not easily be caught."

"A bullet will make up the difference," said Geoffrey; "and, sure as you lie there, Webber will shoot if he finds he can't catch. He can't help doing so, if he hopes to get off safely himself. If the chap escapes, he brings down old Grafton upon us, and Webber very well knows the danger of falling into his clutches. We must tie you both up for to-night if we can. As for killing you or scaring you, we want to do neither one nor t'other, if we can tie up your hands and shut up your mouths for the next twenty-four hours If we can't—"

He left the rest of the sentence unuttered—meaning, I suppose, to be merciful in his forbearance; and nothing mo.e was said by either of us for some time, particularly affecting the matter in hand. A full hour had elapsed, and yet we heard nothing of the pursuit. My anxiety began to be fully shared among my keepers. They went out to the road alternately at different periods, to make inquiries, but without success. Geoffrey at length, after going forth with my gambling acquaintance of the Tuscaloosa tavern for about fifteen minutes, returned, bringing in with them, to my great surprise, the saddle-bags of William Carrington. In my first fear, I demanded if he was taken, and my surprise was great when they told me he was not.

"How, then, came you by those saddle-bags?" was my question.

"What! are they his?" replied Geoffrey.

"Yes."

"Then he's taken your horse, and not his own," was the answer; "for we found these on one of the nags that you brought with you."

They were not at all dissatisfied with the exchange, when they discovered the contents, which they soon got at, in spite of the lock, by slashing the leather open with their knives in various places. The silver dollars rolled from the handkerchief in which they had been wrapped, in every direction about the floor, and were scrambled after by two of the fellows with the avidity of urchins gathering nuts. But I observed that they put carefully together all that they took from the saddle-bags, as if with reference to a common division of the spoil. The few clothes which the bags contained were thrown out without any heed upon the floor, but not till they had been closely examined in every part for concealed money. They got a small roll of bills along with the silver, but I was glad when I recol

lected that William had the greater sum in his bosom. **Poor**
fellow!—at that moment I envied him his escape. I thought
him fortunate; and regarded myself as the luckless wretch
whom fate had frowned upon only. Alas for him I envied!—
my short-sightedness was pitiable. Little **did** I dream, or he
apprehend, the dreadful fate that lay in his path.

CHAPTER XXV.

THE SUDDEN BOLT.

Hub. Behold, sir,
A san-writ tragedy, so feelingly
Languaged and cast; with such a crafty cruelty
Contrived and acted, that wild savages
Would weep to lay their ears to!—ROBERT DAVENPORT.

IT may be just as well that the knowledge of the reader should anticipate my own, and that I should narrate in this place those events of which I knew nothing till some time after. I will therefore proceed to state what happened to William Carrington after leaving me at the hovel where I had fallen into such miserable captivity. Having, by a promptness of execution and a degree of physical energy and power which had always distinguished him, gained the entrance, he seized upon the first horse which presented itself to his hand, and which happened to be mine. It was a moment when, perhaps, he could not discriminate, or, if he could, when it might have been fatal for him to attempt to do so. The bloodhounds were close in pursuit behind him. He heard their cries and following footsteps, and in an instant tore away the bridle from the swinging bough to which it was fastened, tearing a part of the branch with it. He did not stop to throw the bridle over the animal's neck. To a rider of such excellent skill, the reins were hardly necessary. He leaped instantly upon his back, making his rowels answer all purposes in giving the direction which he desired him to take.

His foes were only less capable and energetic than himself; they were no less prompt and determined. With a greater delay, but at the same time better preparedness, they mounted in pursuit. Their safety, perhaps, depended upon arresting his flight and preventing him from bringing down upon them a

competent force for their arrest, which certainly would be the
case if they suffered him to convey the intelligence to such an
active magistrate as Colonel Grafton. Their desire was further
stimulated by the knowledge which they had of the large
amount of money which William carried with him.

If their motives were sufficient to quicken their movements to
the utmost point within their endeavors, his were not less so.
His life, he must have known, depended upon his present
escape. Nor was it merely necessary to keep ahead of them;
he must keep out of bullet-reach also to be safe. But I will not
do him the injustice to suppose, for an instant, that his considerations were purely selfish. I knew better. I feel assured
that my safety was no less the matter in his thoughts than his
own. I feel sure he would never have been content with his
own escape, did he not believe that mine now depended upon it.
These were all considerations to move him to the fullest exertion; and never did good steed promise to serve at need his
rider better than did mine in that perilous flight. An animal
only inferior to his own, my horse had the blood of a racer that
was worthy of his rider's noble nature. He answered the expectations of Carrington without making necessary the frequent
application of the spur. He left the enemy behind him. He
gained at every jump; and the distance between them at the
first, which was not inconsiderable, for the movement of William had been so unexpected as to have taken Webber and the
rest by surprise, was increased in ten minutes nearly double.
At moments they entirely lost sight of him, until very long
stretches of a direct road again made him visible; but he was
already far beyond the reach of their weapons. These, with
but one exception, were pistols of large size, which in a practised hand might carry truly a distance of thirty yards. Webber, however, had a short double-barrelled ducking-gun, which
he had caught up the moment his horse was ready. This was
loaded with buck-shot, and would have told at eighty yards in
the hands of the ruffian who bore it.

But the object was beyond its reach, and the hope of the pursuers was now in some casualty, which seemed not improbable
in the desperate and headlong manner of Carrington's flight.
But the latter had not lost any of his coolness in his impetuosi-

ty. He readily comprehended the nature of that hope in his enemies which prompted them to continue the pursuit; and, perhaps, less confident than he might have been, in his own horsemanship, he determined to baffle them in it.

Looking round, as he did repeatedly, he availed himself of a particular moment when he saw that he might secure his bridle and discard the fragment of the bough which was still attached to it, before they could materially diminish the space between them; and drawing up his horse with the most perfect coolness, he proceeded to unloose the branch and draw the reins fairly over the head of the animal. The pursuers beheld this, and it invigorated the pursuit.

If the reader knows anything of the region of country in which these events took place, he will probably recognise the scene over which I now conduct him. The *neighborhood* road, leading by Grafton's and Webber's, was still a distinct trace, though but little used, a few years ago. It was a narrow track at best and been a frontier road for military purposes before the Chickasaws left that region. The path was intricate and winding, turning continually to right and left, in avoiding sundry little creeks and difficult hills which sprinkled the whole face of the country. But the spot where William halted to arrange his bridle was more than usually straight, and, for the space of half a mile, objects might be discerned in a line nearly direct. Still the spot was an obscure and gloomy one. The road in one place ran between two rising grounds, the elevations of which were greater and more steep than usual. On one side there was an abrupt precipice, from which the trees almost entirely overhung the path. This was called at that period, the "day-blind," in a taste kindred with that which named a corresponding region, only a few miles off, "the shades of death." For a space of forty yards or more, this "blind" was sufficiently close and dense, almost to exclude the day—certainly the sunlight.

William had entered upon this passage, and the pursuers were urging their steeds with a last and despairing effort, almost hopeless of overtaking him, and, perhaps, only continuing the chase under the first impulse of their start, and from the excitement which rapid motion always provokes. He now felt his security, and laughed at the pursuit. The path, though dim and dusky, was yet distinct before him. At the outlet the sun shine lay, like a protecting spirit, in waiting to receive him; and the sight so cheered him, that he half turned about upon his horse, and while he stayed not his progress, he shook his unemployed arm in triumph at his enemies. Another bound brought him out of the dim valley through which he had ridden; and when he was most sure of his escape, and when his pursuers began to meditate their return from the hopeless chase, a sudden shot was heard from the woods above, and in the same instant, Webber, who was in the advance, saw the unhappy youth bound completely out of his saddle, and fall helplessly, like a stone, upon the ground, while his horse passed from under him, and, under the impulse of sudden fright, continued on his course with a more headlong speed than ever

The event which arrested for ever the progress of the fugitive, at once stopped the pursuit as suddenly. Webber called one of his companions to his side: a sallow and small person, with a keen black eye, and a visage distinguished by dogged resolution, and practised cunning.

"Barret," said the one ruffian to the other, "we must see who it is that volunteers to be our *striker*. He has a ready hand, and should be one of us, if he be not so already. It may be Eberly. It is high time he should have left Grafton's, where the wonder is he should have trifled so long. There's something wrong about that business; but no matter now. We must see to this. Should the fellow that tumbled the chap not be one of us, you must make him one. We have him on our own terms. Pursue him though he takes you into Georgia. Away, now; sweep clean round the *blind*, and come on his back—he will keep close when he sees us two coming out in front—and when you have got his trail, come back for an instant to get your instructions. Be off, now; we will see to the carrion."

When Webber and his remaining companion reached the body, it was already stiff. In the warm morning of youth—in the flush of hope—with a heart as true, and a form as noble, as ever bounded with love and courage—my friend, my almost brother, was shot down by a concealed ruffian, to whom he had never offered wrong! What a finish to his day! What a sudden night for so fair a morning!

CHAPTER XXVI.

NARROW ESCAPE.

'Villain, I know thou com'st to murder me."
MARLOWE.—*Edward the Second*

MATTHEW WEBBER was no trifler. Though represented by his comrades, as we have seen in a previous dialogue, as unwilling to shed blood, it may be added that his unwillingness did not arise from any scruples of humanity, which are always unnecessary to the profession of the outlaw. He was governed entirely by a selfish policy, which calmly deliberated upon its work of evil, and chose that course which seemed to promise the greatest return of profit with the greatest security. To avoid bloodshed was simply to avoid one great agent of detection. Hence his forbearance. To the moral of the matter, none could have been more thoroughly indifferent. We beheld him giving instructions to an associate the moment that William Carrington fell by an unknown hand, to pursue the murderer, not with a view to his punishment, but with a desire to secure a prompt associate. It was not the wish of the fraternity of robbers, herding on the Choctaw frontier, that anybody should take up the trade in that region, of which they desired the monopoly. When the fellow, thus instructed, had gone, Webber, with his remaining associates, at once proceeded to examine the body, which was lifeless when they reached it. They wasted no time in idle wonder, and gave but a single glance at the wound, which they saw was inflicted by a rifle-bullet; then lifting the inanimate form into the wood, they rifled it of the large sum of money which Carrington had concealed in his bosom, and taking it into a little crevice in the hill-side, which could not hide it, they threw it down indifferently, trusting to the wolves, of which that neighborhood had numerous herds, to remove it in due season. Poor youth! with such a heart—so noble, so brave—with affections so warm, and hopes so full of promise—to be shot down in the sun-light—in the bloom of manhood—by an obscure ruffian, and be denied a grave!

When they had possessed themselves of the money, the amount of which gave them no small pleasure, they put spurs to their horses and rode back with as great speed as they had used in the pursuit. It was necessary that they should do so, and hasten their flight from the spot where their evil-doings had been begun. My horse had continued on his course with a speed which had been increased by his alarm and unrestraint after the fall of his rider; and Webber saw, with no small anxiety, that he was in the direct road to Colonel Grafton's, to which place he did not doubt that he would return, having been so lately lodged there. The scoundrels, who were guarding me, had, in the meantime, become greatly disquieted by their apprehensions at the delay of the pursuers, and not small was their relief when they saw them safe, and felt themselves once more secure in their united strength. They consulted together apart, and frequently pointed to me where I lay, on my back, and bound rigidly to an exposed joist of the floor. What had taken place in the pursuit, they did not reveal in my hearing; and bitter, indeed, were my feelings as I lay in this doubly evil state of incapacity and suspense. The doubtfulness of my own, was not less a subject of concern in my mind than was his fate—for my strongest impression with regard to Carrington was, that he had escaped in safety to Grafton's. All then that I had to fear might be the present rage of my captors. They might sacrifice me before relief could come. I strove not to think of this; still less was I willing that the villains should see I feared them; yet, to confess a truth, it required no small effort to conceal the apprehensions which I could not subdue, and my success, with all my efforts, was partial only. They must have beheld the struggle of my bosom in my face. But of this they seemed to take no heed. They were too much interested in their own situation and apprehensions, to give much regard to mine. They consulted together, earnestly with the air of men who had need of haste in their resolutions. "We must be off at once," I heard Webber say at one time; "there will be no help for us now, if he gets to Grafton's." This last sentence brought warmth and assurance to my heart, I did not doubt of my friend's safety. "But this lark?" said Geoffrey; and I saw from the quick, malignant glance which my gambler acquaintance bestowed upon me when these words were uttered, that it was of me they spoke. The latter bent forward to hear the resolve of Webber—whose word here seemed to be law—with an air of anxiety not less great than that which I might have shown myself. The answer of Webber did not seem to satisfy him.

"What of him?" said the latter. "Shall we stretch him?" was the further inquiry of Geoffrey; an equivocal phrase which I suppose coolly meant "shall we cut his throat?"

"Pshaw, no!" replied the other. "What's the good of it?—let the fellow lie where he is and cool himself. By to-morrow, somebody will cut his strings, and help him turn over. He will get hungry in the meantime, for he didn't eat a hearty dinner—all his own fault. Come, let us jog."

Ten minutes had not elapsed when they were all ready, and I saw them prepare to depart, leaving me as I lay, bound to the floor by my body and arms, and capable of moving my legs only. Webber took leave of me with the composure of one who has nothing with which to reproach himself.

"Grafton will be here after a while," said he, "and set you free. You may tell him I'm sorry, but it don't suit me to wait for him now. He will see me, however, at his daughter's marriage. Good by."

The man called Geoffrey said something to me in a similar spirit; the gambler grinned only upon me as he passed, but with such an expression of malice in his visage, that, though I did not fear the reptile, it yet made me shudder to behold him. In a few moments more I was left alone to muse over my disconsolate condition. I heard the trampling of their horses die away in the distance, and such was the cheerlessness of my situation, that I positively seemed to be chilled by their departure. This, however, was but the feeling of the moment, and I was allowed a brief time for its indulgence. To my surprise the gambler reappeared, when I had thought him with the rest of his companions full a half mile off; and the increased malignity embodied and looking green in his visage, left me little doubts as to the motive which had made him lag behind. If I had doubts at the beginning, he did not suffer me to entertain them long. His words removed them.

"And now," he said, "my brave fellow, the time is come for your quittance. You have had the word of me long enough You are in my power. What have you to say for yourself?"

"What should I say?" was my ready and indignant reply. Truly and miserably did I feel at the conviction, that I was indeed in the power and at the mercy of this vile wretch; but if worlds had depended upon it, I could not have answered him other than in language of the most unadulterated scorn.

"Ha! do you not understand me?" he cried. "Your life, I tell you, is in my power! The only man in the world who could have kept me from taking it, is Mat Webber, and he's out of reach and hearing. It is but a blow, and with all your pride and insolence I let your blood out upon this floor! What do you say that I should not?—what prayer will you make to me that I should spare your life?"

The fellow leaned upon the table which, occupying the middle of the floor, stood between him and the place where I lay. My feet were half under it. He leaned over it, and shook at me a long knife, bared ready for the stroke, in sundry savage movements. I gave him look for look, and a full defiance for all his threatenings.

"Prayer to you!" I exclaimed; "that were putting myself, indeed, within your power! You may stab!—I can not help myself—but you shall only murder!—wretch! you shall have no triumph!" and, grown utterly reckless, as I believed there was no hope of escape, and that I must die, I lifted my feet, and thrusting them with all my might against the table, I sent it forward with such force as to hurl it upon him, when both came to the floor together. The fellow was not much hurt, and a few moments sufficed for his extrication. With accumulated fury, that foamed but did not speak, he was about to rush upon me, when a sudden footstep behind him drew all his attention to the new-comer. Never could I have believed, till then, that fear could so suddenly succeed to rage in any bosom. The villain grew white as a sheet the moment that he heard the sound and saw the person. It was Webber who looked upon him with the eye of a master.

"You're a pretty fellow! ain't you? So you kept behind for this? Geoffrey warned me to expect it, as soon as I found you missing; and it's well I got back in time. You are a fool, bully boy, and you'll be stretched for it. Mount before me, and if you're wise, forget you've ever seen this chap. Come—begone, I say! no word—not one—Grafton's under way already!"

The assassin was actually incapable of answer. Certainly he made none. The main villain of this precious set must have seen a various life of service. The whole train of proceedings which he had this day witnessed—the first assault upon William and myself—the pursuit of the former—his death—and the subsequent attempt of my enemy upon my person—all seemed to awaken in him but little emotion. There was but one subject upon which he could not preserve his temper, and that was his old employer, Colonel Grafton—but with regard to all others, his selfishness had schooled him successfully to suffer no feeling or passion to interfere in the slightest degree with what might be his prevailing policy. With the inflexibility of a superior, suspicious of his slave, he waited until he saw my enemy mount and set forth, then nodding to me with the freedom of an old friend, he left the entrance, and I was once more left alone.

CHAPTER XXVII.

JOY—SORROW.

'When Lycabas his Athis thus beheld,
  How was his friendly heart with sorrow filled!
  A youth so noble, to his soul so dear,
  To see his shapeless look—his dying groans to hear!"
                              OVID — *Metamorphoses*, B. V.

Hour after hour rolled on, night was approaching, and yet
no aid came. What could this mean? What had become of
my friend? Had he grown indifferent to my fate? did he fear
to encounter a second time with the wretches **who** had pursued
him for his life? I dismissed **this** doubt as soon as it was suggested to my mind; but I conceived any but the true occasion
for his delay. I knew William too well to fear that he would
desert me. I knew that he had no pusillanimous fears to deter
him from a proper risk. He had probably not been able to get
assistance readily, and **to** come without an adequate force was
to commit a rashness and incur **a** danger without any corresponding advantage. I tried **to** solace myself with the **conviction** that he would not **be** much longer absent, but how cheerless
did I feel the while! The very inability under which **I** labored **to** do anything for myself, **was, to a mind and** body like
mine—accustomed **to** do for themselves **always**—enough to
discourage the hope of being effectually relieved by **others.**
The approach of night did not diminish my apprehensions.
The sun had now set, and there was a brief interval of dusk
and silence between its disappearance and the rising of the
moon, which was particularly gloomy. How dreadfully active
my imagination grew in that interval, and what effect it had
upon my nerves, I almost shame to say; but I felt **a** degree of
fear in that brief space of time which I had never suffered be-

fore, and trust that, in no situation, I shall ever be compelled to endure again.

A state of conscious helplessness suggests a thousand fears and fancies that could not be forced upon the mind under other circumstances. Forms of danger that would seem impossible even in our dreams, become, at such a period, unquestionable foes; and the mind, losing its balance after a brief contest, foregoes all examination of the danger, and yields up the contest in utter imbecility. But now the moon rose to cheer me. Light is always cheerful. I could not see her orb where I lay, but her smiles, like those of some benign and blessed spirit, streamed through the thousand cracks and openings of the log-hovel which was now a prison as secure to keep me as the donjon of the feudal baron. Her beams fell around me in little spots that dimpled the whole apartment with shining and bright glances.

Yet even this cheering spectacle impressed me with added disquiet when I found myself so securely fastened to the floor as not to be able with all my writhings to avoid the occasional rays that fell upon my face and eyes. How bitterly did this make me feel my incapacity!—and when, at moments, I heard the faint but protracted bay of the wolf in his leafy den not far off, which I did as soon as the night set in, I could not doubt that he would soon make his appearance in the deserted hovel: and I, who could not shelter my face from the light of the moon, had still fewer hopes of being able to protect myself from him. With every sound in the neighboring thickets I imagined him approaching, under the instinct of a scent as keen as that of the vulture, to his bloody feast; and I vainly asked myself what I should do in my defence, when his gaunt and shaggy body was stretched out upon my own, and his slobbering snout was thrust into my face! I strove, but could not lift an arm— I could only shout, in the hope to scare him from his prey, and, such was my conscious impotence, that it struck me as not impossible but that I might have lost the use of my voice also. Such was the vivid force of this childish apprehension in my mind, that I actually shouted aloud, to convince myself that it was groundless: I shouted aloud, and, to my great joy—without any such hope or expectation—I heard my shouts returned. Another and another! Never were there sweeter echoes to the ery for relief. In a few minutes more I was surrounded by a troop.—a half-dozen at least—all friends—yet where was William Carrington, the dearest friend of all—where? where? My demand was quickly answered.

Colonel Grafton, who led the company, told his story, which was painfully unsatisfactory. My horse, freed from his rider, had brought the only intelligence which Colonel Grafton had received. He had seen nothing of my friend. He was not at home when the horse came to his gate, and the animal was taken in by a servant. When he did return, he immediately proceeded to my assistance; though not before calling up a patrol of such of his neighbors as he could rely upon, to assist him in an inquiry in which he not only feared foul play, but apprehended an issue with more than the one villain into whose clutches we had fallen. I was soon freed from my bonds, but how much more unhappy than I was before! How puerile had been my selfish apprehensions, compared to those which now filled my heart when I thought of Carrington! What had been his fate? where was he? How icy cold in my bosom did my blood run as I meditated these doubts, and dreaded the increase of knowledge which I was yet compelled to seek!

Let me pass over this dreadful interval of doubt, and hurry on the palsying conviction of the truth which followed. Our search that night was unavailing, but the next morning the woods were scoured, and it was my fortune to be the first to fall upon traces which led me to the body of my friend. I saw where he had fallen—where the horse had evidently *shyed* as the shot was given and the rider fell. The earth was still smooth where he had lain, for Webber was too much hurried, or too indifferent, to endeavor to remove the marks of the event. It was not now difficult to find the body. They had not carried it far; and I removed a clump of bushes which grew over the hollow in which they had thrown it, and started with a convulsion of horror to find it lying at my feet. Cold, silent, stiff— there he lay, the friend of my heart, battered and bruised—his noble face covered with blood and dust, one of his eyes protruding from its socket, and the limbs, once so symmetrical and straight, now contracted and fixed in deformity by the sudden spasms of death!

All my strength left me as this dreadful spectacle met my eyes. I sunk down beside it, incapable of speech or action. My knees were weakened—my very soul dead within me. I could only sob and moan, and my choking utterance might well have moved the wonder and pity of those about me, to behold one who seemed otherwise so strong and bold, now sunk into such a state of womanlike infirmity. Colonel Grafton condoled with me like a father; but what could he, or any one, say to me in the way of consolation? Who could declare the amount of my loss? and yet what was my loss to hers—the poor girl who waited for his return? From me she was to hear that he never could return!—that he lay cold in his gore—his voice silent, his body mangled, his noble figure stiffened into deformity! I shivered as with an ague-fit when I remembered that it was from my lips she was to hear all this.

An examination of the body proved two things which struck me with surprise. It was found that the fatal wound had been received in front, and that it had been inflicted by a rifle-bullet. How to account for this I knew not. I had seen no rifle among the weapons carried by any of the outlaws; and even if there had been, how should the shot have taken effect in front, he flying from them—evidently in rapid flight when shot, and they some distance behind him? There was only one way at that moment to account for this, and that was to suppose that some associate of the pursuers had either been stationed in front, or had, opportunely for them, appeared there as he approached the point where he had fallen. Though still unsatisfactory to me, and perhaps to all, we were yet compelled, in the absence of all better knowledge, to content ourselves with a conjecture, which, though plausible enough, did not satisfy us. I felt that there was some mystery still in the transaction, and that William had not been slain willingly by the pursuers. Webber had headed them, and why should he have been so prompt to murder one, and spare another—ay, even protect him from harm —who was so completely in his power? There was as little personal hostility toward William in the mind of Webber as toward me—and yet the blood, warmed by pursuit, might have grown too rash for the deliberate resolve even if one so habitually cool as the master-villain on this occasion.

Doubts thickened in my mind with every added moment of conjecture, and at length I strove to think no more upon it. I resolved to do so, though I soon found my resolution idle. How could I forbear the thought, when I found it had made my hair gray in that single night! Either that or my fears had done so, and I fain would believe it was not the latter. I could think now of nothing else. That mangled body lay before me whichever way I turned. I saw the ghastly glaze upon the starting eye that bulged half way from its socket. I saw that mouth, whose smile it had been a pleasure to see, distorted from its natural shape, and smeared with dust and mire. There, too was the narrow orifice through which life had rushed, prayerless perhaps, and oh, with such terrific abruptness! I thought then of all his ways—his frank, hearty laugh, his generous spirit, his free, bold character, his love of truth, his friendship, and the sweet heart-ties which had bound him to life and earth, and warmed him with promising hopes, never to be fulfilled. That last thought was the pang above all. Poor William—poor Emmeline! Little, in the gushing fullness of their united hopes, did their hearts dream of a destiny like this!

CHAPTER XXVIII

PAUSE — BUT NOT REPOSE.

" Well ! he is dead——
Murdered perhaps ! and I am faint, and feel
As if it were no painful thing to die !" — COLERIDGE.

WITH a stunned mind and most miserable feelings, I was almost led away by Colonel Grafton to his dwelling. For three days I could resolve on nothing. In that time we committed William to the earth. A quiet spot under a clump of venerable oaks, which the colonel had chosen for his own final resting-place, afforded one to my friend. The heavy moss depended from the trees above him, and the warm sun came to his turf in subdued glances through the withered leaves. Birds had built their nests from time immemorial in their boughs, and the constant rabbit might be seen leaping in the long, yellow grasses beneath them, when the dusky shadows of evening were about to fall. The hunter never crept to this spot to pursue his game of death. The cruel instrument of his sport was forbidden to sound therein. The place was hallowed to solemn sleep and to the brooding watchfulness of happy spirits; and in its quiet round we left the inanimate form of one whose heart had been as lovely in its performances as to the eye were the serene shadows of the spot where we laid him. I envied him the peace which I was sure his spirit knew, when we put his body out of sight. God help me, for truly there was little that felt like peace in mine !

For three days, as I said before, I was like one stunned and deafened. I had no quickness to perceive, nor ability to examine. My thoughts were a perfect chaos, and continual and crowding images of death were passing before my eyes. The kind friends with whom I lingered during this brief but most

painful period, did all in their power to console me. They
spared no attentions, they withheld no consideration, that might
have been gratifying to the bruised and broken spirit. And yet
no ministerings could have been more judicious than were theirs.
The word of kindness was never out of place. There was nothing intrusive in their 'tendance, but a general fitness of speech
and gesture, so far as I perceived them, extended through the
movements of the whole family. Colonel Grafton, with a proper
considerateness, entirely forebore the subject of my loss; his
words were few and well timed; and, though they were not
directly addressed to my griefs, their tendency was to administer to them. If his good sense made him avoid a rude tenting
of the wound, he did not fall into the opposite error of seeking
to make light of it. His countenance had a subdued gravity
upon it, which softened into sweetness a face in which benig-
nity and manliness were evenly mingled, elevating and qualify-
ing one another, and his language was given to subjects belonging to the general interests of humanity which the mourner
might very well apply to his affliction without being curiously
seen to do so. Mrs. Grafton's cares were no less considerate
than his. My mother could not so keenly have studied my
feelings, nor so kindly have administered to them. Julia, too,
seemed to grow less shy than usual, and sat down like a confiding child beside me, bringing me her work to look at, and unfolding to me the most valued stores of her little library. Sorrow has no sex, and woman becomes courageous to serve in
affliction the man whom she would tremble in prosperity barely
to encounter. Her lover made his appearance but once during
my stay, and remained but a short time, so that I had her company in several of my sad rambles. Somehow, I felt my greatest source of consolation in her. It is probable that we derive
strength from the contemplation of a weakness which is greater
than our own. I felt it so with me. The confiding dependence
of this lovely girl—her appeals to my superior information—
taught me at moments to lose sight of my cares: and, perhaps,
as she saw this, with the natural arts of her sex, she became
more confiding—more a child.

At length, I started from my stupor. I grew ashamed of my
weakness. To feel our losses is becoming enough—to yield

to them and sink under their pressure is base and unmanly I was vexed to think that Colonel Grafton should have so long beheld me in the feeble attitude of grief. I was determined to resume my character.

"I must go," I exclaimed; "I must leave you to-morrow colonel."

It was thus I addressed him on the evening of the third day after the family had retired for the night.

"Where will you go?" he asked. The question staggered me. Where was I to go? Should I return to Marengo? Should I be the one to carry suffering to the poor girl whom fate had defrauded of her lover? Could I have strength to speak the words of doom and misery? Impossible! On my own account I had no reason to return. I had nothing to seek in that quarter—no hopes to invite my steps—no duty (so I fancied then) to impel me to retrace a journey begun with so much boldness, and, so far, pursued with so much ill fortune.

"I will not return," my heart said within me. "I dare not. I can not look on Emmeline again. It was my pleadings and persuasions, that made her lover my companion in this fatal adventure, and how can I meet her eye of reproach? How can I hear her ask—'Where is he?—why have you not brought him back to me?' Well did I remember her parting directions—'Take care of one another.' Had I taken care of him? I was the more prudent, the more thoughtful and suspicious. I knew him to be careless, frank, free, confiding. Had I taken due care of him? Had I been as watchful as I should have been? Had I not suffered him heedlessly to plunge into the toils when a resolute word of mine would have kept him from them?"

I could not satisfy myself by my answer to these self-proposed questions, and I resolved to go forward.

"In the wilds of Mississippi I will bury myself. The bosom of the 'nation' shall receive me. I will not look on Marengo again. I will write to Emmeline — I will tell her in a letter, what I dare not look her in the face and speak."

Such was my resolve; a resolve made in my weakness, and unworthy of a noble mind. When I declared it to Colonel Grafton, with the affectionate interest and freedom of a father, he opposed it.

"Pardon me, my young friend, but are you right in this resolution ? Is it not your duty to go back and declare the circumstances to all those who are interested in the fate of your friend ? It will be expected of you. To take any other course will seem to show a consciousness of error with which you can not reproach yourself. Suspicion will become active, and your reluctance, which springs from a natural dislike to give pain, will be set down to other and far less honorable motives. Go back, Mr. Hurdis — seek the friends of Mr. Carrington and your own. Though it wring your heart to tell the cruel story, and rend theirs to hear it, yet withhold nothing. Take the counsel of one who has seen too much of the world not to speak with due precaution, and avoid concealment in all matters of this sort. Suppress nothing—let nothing that is at all equivocal be coupled with your conduct where it affects the interests of others. I have never yet known an instance of departure from duty in which the person did not suffer from such departure. And it is your duty to relate this matter at large to those who were connected with your friend." ·

"But I will write, Colonel Grafton—I will write all, and withhold nothing. My duty to the friends and relatives of William Carrington can not call for more."

"Your duty to yourself does. It requires that you should not shrink from meeting them. Your letter would tell them nothing but bald facts. They must see you when you give your testimony. They must see that you feel the pain that your duty calls upon you to inflict. When you show them that, you give them the only consolation which grief ever demands; you give them sympathy, and their sorrows become lessened as they look on yours. To this poor maiden, in particular, you owe it."

"Ah ! Colonel Grafton, you can not know the torture which must follow such an interview. It was I who persuaded him to go on this hapless journey. She heard me plead with him to go—my arguments convinced him. She will look on me as the cause of all—she will call me his murderer."

"You must bear it all, and bear it with humility, and without reply. If she loved this youth, what is your torture to that which your words will inflict on her ? You have the selfish strength and resources of the man to uphold you—what has she? Nothing—nothing but the past. Phantoms of memory are all that are left to her, and these torture as often as they soothe. Do not speak, then, of your sufferings in comparison with hers. She must of necessity, be the greatest sufferer, and you must submit to see her griefs, and, it may be, to listen to her reproaches. These will fall lightly on your ears when you can reproach yourself with nothing. If you did not submit to them—if you fled from the task before you—in place of her reproaches you would have her suspicions, and your own self-rebuke in all future time."

He had put the matter before me in a new light, and, with a sigh, I changed my purpose, resolving to start for Marengo in the morning. Meanwhile, let me relate the progress of other parties to this narrative.

CHAPTER XIX.

THE ASSASSIN AND HIS EMPLOYER

"I've done the deed."—Macbeth.

THE murderer of William lay close in the thicket after he had done the deed. That murderer was Ben Pickett, and. as the reader may have divined already, his victim had perished through mistake. The fatal cause of this was in his employment of my horse, a circumstance forced upon him by the necessities of his flight. Pickett knew the horse, and looked no further. It was a long shot, from a rising-ground above, where the umbrage was thick, and at such a distance that features were not clearly distinguishable. The dress of William unfortunately helped the delusion. It was almost entirely like mine. We had been so completely associated together for years, that our habits and tastes in many respects had become assimilated. The murderer, having satisfied himself—which he did at a glance—that the horse was mine, it was the prompt conclusion of his mind that I was the rider. Crime is seldom deliberate—the mere act, I mean—the determination may be deliberately enough made; but the blow is most usually given in haste, as if the criminal dreaded that he might shrink from an act already resolved upon. Pickett did not trust himself to look a second time before pulling trigger. Had he suffered the rider to advance ten paces more, he would have withdrawn the sight. The courage of man is never certain but when he is doing what he feels to be right. The wrong-doer may be desperate and furious, but he has no composed bearing. Pickett was of this sort. He shot almost instantly after seeing the horse. He was about to come forward when he saw the rider tumble; but the sudden approach of the pursuers, whose forms had been concealed by the narrow and enclosed "blind" through which they passed, compelled him to resume his position, and remain quiet. He saw them take charge of the body, but had little idea that their aim, like his own, had been vulturous. He saw them busy about the prey which his blow had struck down, but concluded that they were friends seeking to succor and to save. Under any circumstances, his hope of plunder was now cut off, and he silently withdrew into the forest, where his horse had been hidden, and, hurriedly remounting, commenced his return to Marengo. But an eye was upon him that never lost sight of him. The keen hunter that Matthew Webber had set upon his path had found his track, and pursued it with the unerring scent of the bloodhound. More than once the pursuer could have shot down the fugitive' with a weapon as little anticipated, and as unerring, as that which he himself had employed; but he had no purpose of this sort in view. He silently followed on, keeping close watch upon every movement, yet never suffering himself to be seen. When the murderer paused by the wayside, he halted also; when he sped toward evening, he too relaxed his reins; and he drew them up finally, only when he beheld the former, with an audacity which he never showed while I dwelt in Marengo, present himself at the entrance of my father's plantation, and request to see my brother. The pursuer paused also at this moment, and entering a little but dense wood on one side of the road, quietly dismounted from his horse, which he fastened in the deepest thicket, and, under cover of the under-brush, crept forward as nearly as he could, to the place where Pickett waited, without incurring any risk of detection.

It was not long before John Hurdis came to the gate, and his coward soul made its appearance in his face, the moment that he saw his confederate. His lips grew livid and quivered, his cheeks were whiter than his shirt, and his voice so feeble, when he attempted to speak, that he could only articulate at all by uttering himself with vehemency and haste.

"Ah, Pickett, that you?—well! what?"

The murderer had not alighted from his horse, and he now simply bent forward to the other, as he half whispered—

"It's all fixed, 'squire! The nail's clinched! You can

take the road now when you please, and find nothing to trip
you."

"Ha! but you do not mean it, Ben? It is not as you say!
You have not done it! Are you sure?—Did you see?"

"It's done!—I tell you, as sure's a gun!"

"He's dead, then?" said John Hurdis in a husky whisper—
"Richard Hurdis is dead, you say?" and he tottered forward
to the rider, with a countenance in which fear and eagerness
were so mingled as to produce an unquiet shrinking even in the
bosom of his confederate.

"I've said it, 'squire, and I'll say it again to please you! I
had dead aim on his button—just here [he laid his hand on his
breast]—and I saw him tumble and come down all in a heap
like a bag of feathers. There's no doctors can do him good
now, I tell you. He's laid up so that they won't take him
down again—nobody. You can go to sleep now when you
please."

The greater felon of the two shrank back as he heard these
words, and covered his face with his hands. He seemed scarce
able to stand, and leaned against the posts of the gate for his
support. A sudden shivering came over him, and when that
passed off, he laughed brokenly as if with a slight convulsion,
and the corners of his mouth were twitched until the tears started in his eyes. To what particular feeling, whether of remorse
or satisfaction, he owed these emotions, it would be difficult for
me to say, as it was certainly impossible for his comrade to conceive. Pickett looked on with wondering, and was half inclined
to doubt whether his proprietor was not out of his wits. But a
few moments reassured him as John Hurdis again came forward.
His tones were more composed, though still unsubdued, when he
addressed him, and, perhaps, something more of human apprehension dwelt upon his countenance.

"You have told me, Ben Pickett, but I am not certain.
Richard Hurdis was a strong man—he wouldn't die easily!
He would fight—he would strike to the last! How could you
stand against him? Why, Ben, he would crush you with a
blow of his fist! He was monstrous strong!"

"Why, 'squire, what are you talking about? Dick Hurdis
was strong, I know and stout-hearted. He would hold on till

his teeth met, for there was no scare in him. But that's nothing to the matter now, for, you see, there was no fight at all. The rifle did the business — long shot and steady aim ; so, you see, all his strength went for nothing."

"But how could he let you trap him, Ben Pickett ? Richard was suspicious and always on the watch. He wouldn't fall easily into a trap. There must be some mistake, Ben — some mistake. You're only joking with me, Ben; you have not found him ? He was too much ahead of you, and got off. Well, it's just as well you let him go. I don't care. Indeed, I'm almost glad you didn't reach him. He's in the 'nation,' I suppose, by this time ?"

"But I did reach him, 'squire," replied the other, not exactly knowing how to account for the purposeless tenor of John Hurdis's speech, and wondering much at the unlooked-for relenting of purpose which it implied. There was something in this last sentence which annoyed Pickett as much as it surprised him. It seemed to imply that his employer might not be altogether satisfied with him when he became persuaded of the truth of what he said. He hastened, therefore, to reiterate his story.

"He'll never get nearer to the 'nation' than he is now. I tell you, 'squire, I come upon him on a by-road leading out from Tusca-loosa, that run along among a range of hills where I kept. There was a double hill close by, and the road run through it ; it was a dark road. I tracked him and Bill Carrington twice over the ground. They had business farther down with a man named Webber, and they stopped all night with a Colonel Grafton. I got from one of his negroes all about it. Well, I watched when he was to come back. When I heard them making tracks, I put myself in the bush, clear ahead, in a place where they couldn't come upon me till I was clean out of reach. Soon he came running like mad, then I give it to him, and down he come, I tell you, like a miller's bag struck all in a heap."

"But that didn't kill him ? He was only hurt. You're not sure, Ben, that he's dead ? You didn't look at him closely ?"

"No ; dickens ! they were too hard upon me for that. But I saw where I must hit him, and I saw him tumble."

"Who were upon you ?" demanded Hurdis.

"Why, Bill Carrington, and the man he went to see, I suppose. I didn't stop to look ; for, just as I sprawled him out they came from the road behind him, and I saw no more. You didn't tell me that Bill Carrington was going with him."

"No ; I wasn't certain. I didn't know. But didn't Carrington come after you, when you shot Richard ?"

"I reckon he was too much frightened ; he jumped down beside the body, and that was all I stopped to see. I made off, and fetched a compass through the woods that brought me out with dry feet into another road. Then I kept on without stopping, and that's all I can tell you."

"It was strange Bill Carrington didn't take after you ; he's not a man to be frightened easily."

"He didn't, though."

"But you're not sure, Ben, after all. Perhaps you've only hurt him. You have not killed him, I think. It's a hard thing to shoot certain at a great distance. You were far off, you say ?"

"A hundred yards, or so, and that's nothing, being down hill too."

"Richard was a tough fellow."

"Tough or not, I tell you, 'squire, he'll never trouble you again ! It's all over with him ! They've got him under ground before this time. I know by the sort of fall he gave that he hadn't any life left. He didn't know what hurt him."

John Hurdis seemed convinced at last.

"And yet to think, Ben, that a man so strong as Richard should die so sudden ! It was only a week ago that he had his hand on my throat — he had me down upon the ground — he shook me like a feather. And he spoke with a voice that went through me. I was like an infant in his hands; I felt that he could have torn me in two. And now, you say, he can not lift an arm to help himself !"

"No, not to wave off a buzzard from his carrion !" was the reply.

The arm of John Hurdis fell on the neck of Pickett's horse at these words, and his eyes, with a vacant stare, were fixed upon the rider. After a brief pause, he thus proceeded, in a muttered soliloquy, rather than an address to his hearer :—

"If Richard would have gone off quietly, and let me alone ; if — but what's the use to talk of that now ?" He paused, but again began, in similar tones and like a spirit : " He was too rash — too tyrannical ! Flesh and blood could not bear with him, Ben ! He would have mastered all around him if he could — trampled upon all — suffered no life to any — spared no feelings ! He was cruel — cruel to you, and to me, and to all ; and then to drag me from my horse, and take me, his own brother, by the throat ! But, it's all over now. He has paid for it, Ben ! I wish he hadn't done it, though ; for then — but, no matter, this talk's all very useless now."

Here he recovered himself, and in more direct and calmer language, thus continued, while giving his agent a part of the money which he had promised him : —

"Go, now, Pickett — to your own home. Let us not be seen together much. Take this money — 'tisn't all I mean to give you. I will bring you more."

The willing fellow pocketed the price of blood, and made his acknowledgments. Thanks, too, were given by the murderer, as if the balance of credit lay with him who paid in money for the life of his fellow-creature.

"I will come to you to-night," continued Hurdis, "I would hear all of this business. I would know more — stay ! What is that ? Some one comes — hear you nothing, Ben ?"

Guilt had made my wretched brother doubly a coward. The big sweat came out and stood upon his forehead, and his eyes wore the irresolute expression of one about to fly. The composure with which his companion looked round, half reassured him.

"No — there's nobody," said the other, " a squirrel jumped in the wood, perhaps."

"Well — I'll come to-night, Ben — I'll meet you at the Willows."

"Won't you come to the house, 'Squire ?"

"No !" was the abrupt reply. The speaker recollected his late interview with the stern wife of his colleague, and had no desire to encounter her again : "No, Ben ; I'll be at the Willows."

"What time, 'Squire ?"

"I can't say, now — but you'll hear my signal. Three hoots, and a long bark."

"Very good — I'll be sure."

John Hurdis remained at the gate a long time after Pickett rode away. He watched his retreating form while it continued in sight, then seated himself on the ground where he had been standing, and unconsciously, with a little stick, began to draw characters in the sand. To the labors of his fingers, his mind seemed to be utterly heedless, until, aroused to a sense of what he was doing and where he sat, by the approach of some of the field negroes returning from the labors of the day. He started to his feet as he heard their voices, but how did his guilty heart tremble, when his eye took in the letters that he had unwittingly traced upon the sand. The word "murderer" was distinctly written in large characters, before his eyes. With a desperate, but trembling haste, as if he dreaded lest other eyes should behold it too, he dashed his feet over the letters, nor stayed his efforts even when they were perfectly obliterated. Fool that he was—of what avail was all his toil? He might erase the guilty letters from the sand, but they were written upon his soul in characters that no hand could reach, and no labors, obliterate. The fiend was there in full possession, and his tortures were only now begun.

CHAPTER XXX.

THE SPECTRE.

"Let the earth hide thee."—SHAKSPERE.

THE murderer hurried homeward when this dark conference was ended. The affair in which he had acted so principal, yet secondary a part, had exercised a less obvious influence upon him than upon the yet baser person who had egged him on to the deed. There was no such revulsion of feeling in his bosom, as in that of John Hurdis. Endowed with greater nerve at first, and rendered obtuse from habit and education, the nicer sensibilities— the keener apprehensions of the mind—were not sufficiently active in him to warm at any recital, when the deed itself, which it narrated, had failed to impress him with terror or repentance. If he did not tremble to do, still less was he disposed to tremble at the bare story of his misdoings; and he rode away with a due increase of scorn for the base spirit and cowardly heart of his employer. And yet, perhaps, Pickett had never beheld John Hurdis in any situation in which his better feelings had been more prominent. The weaknesses, which the one despised, were the only shows of virtue in the other. The cowardly wretch, when he supposed the deed to have been done on which he had sent his unhesitating messenger—felt, for the first time, that it would not only have been wiser but better, to have borne patiently with his wrong, rather than so foully to have revenged it. He felt that it would have been easier to sleep under the operation of injustice than to become one's self a criminal. Bitterly indeed did this solemn truth grow upon him in the end, when sleep, at length, utterly refused to come at his bidding.

But, though the obvious fears and compunctious visitings of

his employer had provoked the scorn of the murderer, it was
decreed that he himself should not be altogether free from similar weaknesses. They developed themselves before he reached
his home. It was nearly dusk when he entered the narrow by-
road which led to his habitation—night was fast coming on,
yet the twilight was sufficiently clear to enable him to distinguish objects. Without a thought, perhaps, of the crime of
which he had been guilty, or rather, without a regretful thought,
he pursued his way until the road opened upon his dwelling.
The habitation of his wife and child stood before him. He
could now see the smoke rising from the leaning clay chimney,
and his heart rose with the prospect—for the very basest of
mankind have hearts for their homes—but, all on a sudden, he
jerked his bridle with a violence that whirled the animal out
from his path; and then his grasp became relaxed. He had
strength for no more—he had neither power to advance nor
fly. In an instant the avenues to all his fears were in possession of a governing instinct. Guilt and terror spoke in all his
features. His glazed eyes seemed starting from their sockets
—his jaws relaxed—his mouth opened—his hair started up,
and the cold dews gathered at its roots! What sees he?—
what is in his path to make him fear? Why does the bold
ruffian, ready at all times to stab or shoot—why does he lift
no weapon now? He is sinewless, aimless, strengthless. There
rose before him, even at the gate of his hovel, a fearful image
of the man he supposed himself to have murdered. It stood
between him and the narrow gateway so that he could not go
forward in his progress. The gaze of the spectre was earnestly
bent upon him with such a freezing glance of death and doom
as the victim might well be supposed to wear in confronting
his murderer. The bloody hole in his bosom was awfully distinct to the eyes of the now trembling criminal, who could see
little or nothing else. His knees knocked together convulsively
—his wiry hair lifted the cap upon his brow. Cold as the
mildewed marble, yet shivering like an autumn branch waving
in the sudden winds, he was frozen to the spot where it encountered him—he could neither speak nor move. Vainly did he
attempt to lift the weapon in his grasp—his arms were stiffened
to his side—his will was not powerful enough to compel its

natural agents to their duty. He strove to thrust the rowel into his horse's flanks, but even to this effort he found himself unequal. Twice did he strive to cry aloud to the threatening aspect before him, in words of entreaty or defiance, but his tongue refused its office. The words froze in his throat, and it was only able in a third and desperate effort to articulate words which denoted idiocy rather than resolve.

"Stand aside, Richard Hurdis—stand aside, or I'll run over you. You would tie me to the tree—you would try hickories upon me, would you? Go—go to John Hurdis now, and he'll tell you I'm not afraid of you. No, d———n my eyes if I am, though he is! I'm not afraid of your bloody finger—shake it away—shake it away! There's a hole in your jacket wants mending, man; you'd better see to it 'fore it gets worse. I see the red stuff coming out of it now. Go—stand off, or I'll hurt you!—ptsho—ptsho—ptsho!"

And, as he uttered this wandering and incoherent language, his limbs strengthened sufficiently to enable him, to employ with one hand, the action of a person hallooing hogs out of his enclosure. The sound of his own voice seemed to unfix the spell upon him. The ghostly figure sank down before his mazed eyes and advancing footsteps, in a heap, like one suddenly slain, and as he had seen his victim fall. It lay directly before him: he pressed his horse upon it, but it disapeared before he reached the spot. A brief space yet lay between the gate and the hovel, and, passing through the former, he was about to plunge with a like speed toward the latter, when another figure, and one, too, much more terrific to the fears of the ruffian than the first, took its place, and the person of William Carrington emerged at that moment from the dwelling itself, and stood before him in the doorway! If Pickett himself trembled before under his superstitious imaginings, he trembled now with apprehensions of a more human description. It was the vulgar fear of the fugitive that possessed him now. He felt that he was pursued. He saw before him the friend of the man he had murdered, speeding in hot haste to wreak vengeance on his murderer. In the dread of cord or shot, he lost in a single instant all his former and paralyzing terror arising from the blighting visitation of the world of spirits. He was no longer frozen by fear. He was strengthened and stimulated for flight by the appearance of Carrington. He turned the head of his horse, and, with the movement, the avenger advanced upon him. He felt that there was no escape. There was no hope in flight. In desparation, he threw himself from the animal — lifted his rifle, and, in taking deadly aim upon the figure, was surprised to see it move away with rapid footsteps and sink into the neighboring woods, in the shadow of which it was soon lost from sight. The conduct of Carrington was more mysterious to the criminal than was the appearance of the spectre just before. If he came as the avenger of his friend, how strange that he should fly! And how could such timidity be believed of one so notoriously brave as the man in question? The wonder grew in his mind the more he reviewed it, and he found it easier to continue in his wonderment than to seek by any reference to his past experience and present thoughts for any solution of the mystery.

Pale and cold with fright, he at last entered his hovel without further interruption. The anxious and searching eyes of his wife beheld in an instant the disordered emotion so prominent in his, and her fears were renewed.

" What is it, Ben — what disturbs you ? why do you look around so ?" she demanded.

"How long has he been here ? when did he come ? what does he want ?" were the rapid questions which the criminal uttered in reply.

"Who — who has been here ? of whom do you ask ?" was the response of the astonished wife.

"Why, Bill Carrington, to be sure — who else ? I saw him come out of the door just this minute, and take to the woods. What did he want ? where's he gone ?— who's he looking for — eh ?"

" You're sick, Ben," said the wife ; "your head's disordered. You'd better lie down."

"Can't you answer me a plain question ?" was his peremptory answer to her suggestion ; "I ask you what Bill Carrington wanted with me or with you ?"

"He ?—nothing that I know of. He hasn't been here, Ben."

"The devil you say? Better tell me I'm drunk — when I saw him, with my own eyes, come out just a moment ago, and take to the woods!"

"You may have seen him in the woods, but I'm sure you didn't see him come out of this house. I've been in this room for the last hour — never once out of it — and nobody but myself and Jane in it — and nobody's been here that either of us has seen."

The man turned to Jane, and, reading in her eyes a confirmation of her mother's speech, he looked vacantly around him for a few moments; then lifting his rifle, which he had leaned up within the entrance, rushed out of the house, and hurried to the woods in search of the person whom he had seen disappear there. He was gone for an hour, when he returned exhausted. In that time his search had been close and thorough for a circuit of several miles, in all those recesses which he had been accustomed to regard as hiding-places, and which, it may be added, he had repeatedly used as such. The exhaustion that followed his disappointment was an exhaustion of mind rather than of body. The vagueness and mystery which attended all these incidents had utterly confounded him, and when he returned to the presence of his wife he almost seemed to lack the facilities of speech and hearing. He spoke but little, and, observing his fatigue, and probably ascribing his strange conduct to a sudden excess of drink, his wife prudently forebore all unnecessary remarks and questions.

Night hurried on; darkness had covered the face of the earth, and in silence the wife and idiot child of the criminal had commenced their evening meal, Pickett keeping his place at the fireside without heeding the call to supper. A stupor weighed down all his faculties, and he almost seemed to sleep; but a slight tap at the entrance — a single tap; gentle as if made by a woman-hand soliciting admission — awakened in an instant all the guilty consciousness that could not sleep in the bosom of the criminal. He started to his feet in terror. The keen and searching glance of his wife was fixed upon his face, and heedful of every movement of his person. She said nothing; but her looks were so full of inquiry, that it needed no words to make Pickett aware that her soul was alarmed and apprehensive. She looked as if feeling that all her previous fears were realized. The knock at the entrance was repeated.

"Shall I open it, Ben?" was her question, and her eyes motioned him to a window in the rear. But he did not heed the obvious suggestion. Gathering courage as he beheld her glance, and saw her suspicions, he crossed the floor to the entrance, boldly lifting the bar which secured it, and in firm tones bade the unknown visitor "Come in."

CHAPTER XXXI.

THE MYSTIC BROTHERHOOD.

—— —— "Our coming
Is not for salutation — we have business." — *Catiline.*

THE stranger boldly stepped into the light as the door was opened for him. The heart of Pickett sank within him on the instant, for guilt is a thing of continual terrors; but his glance was fixed on the person without recognition, and there was nothing in the air or visage of the intruder to excite alarm. His dark, swarthy features and sinister eye were, it is true, sufficiently unprepossessing; but these were evidently the habitual features of the man, and, being in repose, gave no occult expression to his countenance. His guise was common enough, consisting of the common blue-and-white homespun of the country, and this bespattered with mud as if he had been long a traveller. He demanded traveller's fare, and begged to be accommodated for the night. There was no denial of so small a boon, even in the humblest cottage of Alabama; and though Pickett would rather have had no company, he could not yet refuse.

"Well," said Pickett, "we are not in the habit of taking in travellers; but if you can make out with a blanket by the chimney, you can have it — it's all I can give you."

"Good enough," said the stranger "I'm not particular. Room by the chimney, and light wood enough for a blaze, and I'm satisfied."

"Have you had supper?" demanded Mrs. Pickett; "we can give you some hoe-cake and bacon."

"Thank you, ma'am, but I took a bite from my bag about an hour ago, as I crossed a branch coming on, which baited my hunger. I won't trouble you to get anything more."

"You're from below?" asked Pickett, with some show of curiosity.

"No — from above."

"Do you go much farther?"

"I think not; I've got business in these parts, and shall return when it's over."

"You've a horse to see to?"

"No, I foot it — I'm a very poor man."

The lie was uttered with habitual readiness. The emissary had hidden and hoppled his horse in the neighboring woods. He was too well practiced in his art to forego every precaution. Pickett had no other questions, and but little more was said for the time by either of the parties, all of whom seemed equally taciturn. The wife of Pickett alone continued anxious. The searching glance of the stranger did not please her, though it appeared to have its impulse in curiosity alone. Perhaps, suspecting her husband's guilt, all circumstances removed from those of ordinary occurrence provoked her apprehensions. With a just presentiment, she had trembled on the stranger's knock and entrance, and every added moment of his stay increased her fears. She had as yet had no conference with Pickett, touching the business which carried him abroad; and the presence of their guest denied her all opportunity for the satisfaction of her doubts. Her evident disquiet did not escape the notice of her husband, but he ascribed it in his own mind to her desire to go to bed, which, as they all slept in the same apartment, was rendered somewhat difficult by the presence of the new-comer. His coarse mind, however, soon made this difficulty light.

"Go to bed, Betsy — don't mind us; or, to make the matter easy, what say you, stranger, to a bit of a walk — the night's clear, and not cold neither? We'll just step out till the old woman lies down, if you please."

"To be sure," said the other; "I was about to propose the same thing to you."

The fears of Pickett were newly roused by this seemingly innocent declaration of the stranger — a declaration which, at another time, would not have tasked a thought.

"Why should he wish to take me out to walk with him at

night — why should he propose such a thing ?" was his inward inquiry ; and with hesitating steps he conducted the suspicious guest from the hovel into the open ground before it.

"I was just going to propose the same thing to you," said the stranger the moment they had got there, "for, do you see, it isn't to lodge with you only that I come. I have business with you, my friend — business of great importance."

If Pickett was alarmed before, he was utterly confounded now.

"Business with me !" he cried, in undisguised astonishment ; "what business — what business can you have with me ?" and he stopped full and confronted the stranger as he spoke.

"Well, that's what I'm going to tell you now, but not here ; walk farther from the house, if you please — let's go into this thicket."

"Into the thicket ! No, I'm d——d if I do !" cried the now thoroughly-alarmed Pickett. "I'll go into the thicket with no stranger that I don't know. I don't see what business you can have with me at all ; and if you have any, you can just as well out with it here as anywhere else."

"Oh, that's just as you please," said the other coolly ; "it was for your sake only that I proposed to go into the thicket, for the business is not exactly proper for everybody to hear ; and there's no use in calling the high-road to counsel."

"For my sake ? What the d—l do you mean, my friend ? It's your business, not mine : why is it for my sake that you would have me go into the thicket ? "

"Because it might bring you into trouble, if any ears besides our own were to hear me," replied the stranger with indifference. "For my part, I don't care much where it is said, only to save you from any trouble."

"Me from trouble — me from trouble ! I don't know what you can mean ; but if you're serious, where would you have me go ?'

"There — that thicket will do. It looks dark enough for our business."

The stranger pointed to a dense grove in the neighborhood, but on the opposite side of the road — a part of the same forest in which the reader will remember to have witnessed an interview between John Hurdis and Jane, the idiot girl. Not knowing what to fear, yet fearing everything, the murderer followed the stranger, whom he now regarded as his evil genius. The other was passing more deeply into the woods, after having entered them, than Pickett seemed to think necessary for his object, and the voice of the latter arrested him.

"Dark enough for your business, it may be, but quite too dark for mine. I'll go no further. You can say here all you've got to say, no matter what it is. I'm not afraid, and I think it something strange that you should want me to go into the bush in a dark night with a person I don't know. I don't somehow like it altogether. I'm not sure that it's safe. I mean no harm, but it's not the best sense in the world to trust people one don't know."

"Lord love you," said the other, with a quiet tone of contempt, "you're more scarry than I thought you. There's nothing to be frightened at in me; my business is peaceable, and I'm a peaceable man. I don't carry a rifle, and I never tumbled a fellow from his horse at a hundred yards, in all my life, so far as I can recollect now."

These words were uttered with the utmost coolness, and as if they were entirely without peculiar signification. The effect upon the hearer was almost paralyzing, as it was instantaneous. He started, as if he had been himself shot — for a moment was silent, under the obvious imputation contained in the last sentence of his companion's speech — then recovering himself, with the blustering manner of a bully, he addressed the other, who saw, in the dim light which surrounded them, that Pickett's hand was thrust into the bosom of his vest, as if in search of some concealed weapon.

"How! you do not mean to say that I ever did such a thing ? If you do —"

"Put up your knife, brother, and keep your hand and voice down. Lift either too high, and I have that about me which would drive you into the middle of next summer, if you only looked at me to strike."

Such was the stern reply of the stranger, whose tones changed promptly with the circumstances. Pickett felt himself in the presence of a master. He was cowed. He released his hold upon the weapon, which he had grasped in his bosom, and lowering the sounds of his voice in obedience to the stranger's requisition, he replied in more conciliatory language.

"What mean you, my friend? What is the business that brings you here? What would you have with me, and why do you threaten me?"

"Your hand!" said the other deliberately, while extending his own.

"There it is; and now, what?" Pickett reluctantly complied.

"Only that you are one of us now — that's all."

"One of us — how! who are you? — what mean you?"

"Everything. You are a made man — your fortunes are made. You've become one of a family that can do everything for you, and will do it, if you'll let them."

The silence of Pickett expressed more wonder than his words could have done. The other went on without heeding a feeble attempt which he made at reply.

"You've volunteered to do some of our business, and have, therefore, joined our fraternity."

"Your business! what business — what fraternity? I don't know, my friend, what you possibly can mean."

"I'll tell you, then, and put you out of suspense. You're just from Tuscaloosa, where you've taken some trouble off our hands. I've come to thank you for it, and to do you some kindness in return. One good turn deserves another, you know, and this that you have done for us, deserves a dozen."

The wonder of Pickett was increased. He almost gasped in uttering another request to hear all that the other had to say.

"Why, it's soon said," he replied. "You shot a lad two days ago, near the 'shade,' up beyond Tuscaloosa —"

"Who says — who saw — it is a lie — a d—d lie!" cried the criminal, in husky and feeble accents, while quivering at the same time with mingled rage and fear.

"Oh, pshaw!" said the other, "what's the use of beating about the bush. I saw you tumble the lad myself, and I've followed upon your trail ever since —"

"But you shall follow me no more! One of us must give

way to the other!" cried the criminal in screaming accents, and while drawing his knife with one hand, he aimed to grasp the throat of the stranger with the other. But the latter was too wily a scout to become an easy victim. He had watched his man, even as the cat watches the destined prey—to whom she suffers a seeming freedom and sacrifices at the very moment of its greatest apparent security. With the movement of Pickett to strike, was that of the stranger to defend himself—nor to defend himself only. The strength of the former was far inferior to that of the man whom he assailed, and instead of taking him by the throat, he found his grasp eluded, and, at the same moment, the arm which held the weapon, was secured in a grip which effectually baffled all his efforts at release.

"Don't be rash!" said the stranger, with a laugh in which there was no sign of anger. "Don't be rash—it's of no use! You're only fighting against your own good, and your powder's wasted on me. I'm too much for you, and that's enough to make you quiet. But there's another and a better reason than that to keep you quiet. I'm your friend, I tell you—your best friend—and I can bring you many friends. I'm come all this distance to befriend you; and, if you'll have patience and be civil, you'll soon see how."

"Let go my arm!" said Pickett, chafing furiously, but still ineffectually, as far as his own efforts to release himself were concerned.

"Well, I'll do that," said the stranger, releasing him at the same instant; "but. mind me, if you try to use it again, as you did just now, it will be worse for you! I never suffer a dog to worry me twice. I'm sure to draw his teeth, so that he will bite no other; and, if you lift that knife at me again, I'll put a plug into your bosom that will go quite as deep, if not deeper, than your bullet did in the bosom of that young fellow!"

"You know not what you say—you saw not that!" was the faint answer of Pickett.

"It's a true bill, man, and I'll swear to it! How should I know it, if I did not see it? I saw the lad tumble—saw you scud from the place, rifle in hand, and take to your creature, which was fastened to a dwarf poplar, in a little wood of poplars. What say you to that? Is it not true?

Pickett leaned against a tree, silent and exhausted. He had no answer. The fates had tracked him to his den.

"Nay! fear nothing, though I know your secret," said the other, approaching him. "You are in no sort of danger—not from me, at least; on the contrary, you have done our friends a service—have saved them from the trouble of doing the very thing that we would have had to do for ourselves. Three of us pursued the man that you shot; and, if he had got away, which he must have done, but for your bullet, it would have been an ugly and losing matter for us. You did us good service then, I tell you—you volunteered to be one of our *strikers*, and we have got the game. The search of the body gave us a rich booty, and his death a degree of safety, which we might not else have enjoyed."

"Well; wasn't that enough for you? Why did you come after me?" demanded Pickett, bitterly. "Why follow me with you infernal secret?"

"Lord love you! to give you your share of the spoil, to be sure—what else? Do you think us so mean as to keep all for ourselves, and give none to a man who did, I may say, the dirtiest part of the business? Oh, no, brother! no! I've brought you your share of the booty. Here it is. You will see when you come to look at it, that we are quite as liberal as we should be. You have, here, a larger amount, than is usually given to a *striker*." And, as the stranger spoke these words, he pulled out something from his pocket, which he presented to his astonished auditor. Pickett thrust away the extended hand, as he replied:—

"I want none of it! I will have no share—I am not one of you!"

"But that's all nonsense, my brother. You must take it. You must be one of us. When a *striker* refuses his share, we suspect that something's going wrong, and he takes his share, or he pays for it, by our law," was the reply of the stranger, who continued to press the money upon him.

"Your laws!—of what laws—of whom do you speak?"

"Of our fraternity, to be sure!—of the Mystic Brotherhood. Perhaps, you have never heard of the Mystic Brotherhood?"

"Never."

"You are unfortunate to have lived long enough to be wise. Let me enlighten you. The Mystic Brotherhood consists of a parcel of bold fellows, who don't like the laws of the state exactly, and of other societies, and who have accordingly associated together, for the purpose of making their own, and doing business under them. As we have no money of our own, and as we must have money, we make it legal to take it from other people. When they will not shut their eyes and suffer us to take it without trouble, we shut them up ourselves; a task for the proper doing of which we have a thousand different modes. One of these, the task of a *striker*, you employed in our behalf, and very effectually shut up for us, the eyes of that foolish young fellow, who had already given us some trouble, and, but for you, might have given us a great deal more. Having done so well, we resolved to do you honor—to make you one of us, and give you all the benefits of our institution, as they are enjoyed by every other member. We have our brethren in all the states, from Virginia to Louisiana, and beyond into the territories. Some of our friends keep agencies for us, even so far as the Sabine, and we send negroes to them daily."

"Negroes! what negroes—have you negroes?"

"Yes! when we take them. We get the negroes to run away from their owners, then sell them to others, get them to run away again, and, in this way, we probably sell the same negro half a dozen times. This is one branch of our business, and might suit you. . When the affair gets too tangled, and we apprehend detection, we tumble the negro into a river, and thus rid ourselves of a possession that has paid good interest already, and which it might not be any longer safe to keep."

"What! you kill the negro."

"Yes; you may say so. We dispose of him."

"And how many persons have you in the brotherhood?"

"Well, I reckon we stretch very nigh on to fifteen hundred?"

"Fifteen hundred! is it possible!—so many?"

"Yes; and we are increasing daily. Let me give you the first sign, brother—the sign of a striker."

"No!" cried Pickett, shrinking back. "I will not join you! I do not know the truth of what you say! I never heard the like before! I will have nothing to do in this business!"

" You must!" was the cool rejoinder—"you must! Nobody shall strike for us, without becoming one of us."

"And suppose I refuse?" said Pickett.

" Then I denounce you as a murderer, to the grand jury," was the cool reply. " I will prove you to have murdered this youth, and bring half a dozen beside myself to prove it."

" What, if I tell all that you have told me, of your brotherhood?"

" Pshaw! brother, you are dreaming. What, if you do tell; who will you get to believe you — where's your proofs? But I will prove all that I charge you with, by a dozen witnesses. Even if it were not true, yet could I prove it."

The discomfited murderer perspired in his agony. The net was completely drawn around him.

" Don't be foolish, brother," said the emissary of a fraternity, upon the borders of the new states, the history of which, already in part given to the public, is a dreadful chronicle of desperate crime, and insolent incendiarism. " Don't be foolish! you can't help yourself — you must be one of us, whether you will or not! We can't do without you — we have bought you out! If you take our business from us; you must join partnership, or we must shut up your shop! We can't have any opposition going on. The thing's impossible — insufferable! Here — take your share of the money. It will help you to believe in us, and that's a great step toward making you comply with my demand. Nay! don't hold back, I tell you, brother, you must go with us, now, body and soul, or you hang, by the Eternal!"

Base and wretched as was the miserable Pickett, in morals and in condition, he was not yet so utterly abandoned as to feel easy, under the necessity so imperatively presented to him. The character or his wife, noble amid poverty and all its consequent forms of wretchedness, if it had not lifted his own standards of feeling and of thought beyond his own nature, had the effect, at least, of making him conceal, as much as he could, his deficiencies from her. Here was something more to conceal, and this necessity was, of itself, a pang to one, having but the one persone to confide in, and feeling so great a dependence upon that one. This step estranged him still further from her, and while he passionately took the proffered money, and looked upon

the uncouth and mystic sign which the other **made before him, in**
conferring his first degree of membership, the cold sweat stood upon
his face in heavy drops, and an icy weight seemed contracting about
his heart.   **He** felt as if had bound himself, hand and foot, and was
about **to be delivered over to the executioner.**

CHAPTER XXXII.

MORE SNARES.

—— "We should know each other:
As to my character for what men call crime,
Seeing I please my senses as I list,
And vindicate that right with force or guile,
It is a public matter, and I care not
If I discuss it with you."—*The Cenci.*

THE emissary of the Mystic Brotherhood, which had just con-
ferred the honors of its membership on one who so richly de-
served them, though pursuing his labors with the rigid directness of an ordinary business habit, and confining himself thereto
with a degree of strictness and method not common to the wicked,
was yet by no means a niggard in his communications. He
unfolded much of the history of that dangerous confederacy,
which it is not thought necessary to deliver here ; and his hearer
became gradually and fully informed of the extent of its resources and ramifications. Yet these gave him but little satisfaction. He found himself one of a clan numbering many hundred persons, having the means of procuring wealth, which had
been limited to him heretofore simply because of his singleness,
and not because of any better principle which he possessed ;
and yet he shuddered to find himself in such a connection. The
very extensiveness of the association confounded his judgment,
and filled him with terrors. He was one of those petty villains
who rely upon cunning and trick, rather than audacity and
strength, to prosecute their purposes; and while the greater
number of the clan found their chief security in a unity of purpose and a concentration of numbers, which in the end enabled
them for a season to defy and almost overthrow the laws of
society, he regarded this very circumstance as that which, above

all others, must greatly **contribute to the risk and dangers of** detection. The glowing **accounts of his companions, which de-** scribed their successes — their profitable murders, fearless burglaries, and a thousand minor **offences, such as negro, horse stealing and** petty thefts — only served to **enlarge the vision with which he beheld** his fears; and, dull **and wretched, he returned with his guest to the** miserable hovel, now become **doubly so since his most** humiliating enlightenment, **and** the formation **of his new ties.** His wife and daughter, meanwhile, **had** retired **for the night; but the** woman **did** not sleep. She was filled with apprehensions for husband scarcely less imposing than those which troubled him for **himself; yet little** did she dream how completely he was in the thrall of **that power from** which her own severe and fruitless virtues had been **utterly unable at all times to restrain him.** Her wildest fears never imagined **a bond so** terrible **as that which had been** imposed upon him in the last half-hour.

"Whenever **you want to lie down,** stranger, you **can do so.** There's your blanket. **I'm sorry there's no** better for you." **It was** with difficulty **that Pickett brought himself to** utter these common words of courtesy.

"Good enough," **said the other —** "I'll take it a little closer by the fire; and, if you have no **objection, I'll throw a stick or** two on. **I've** slept in a better bed, **it's true, but I'll be satisfied if** I never sleep in a worse.

The hesitating utterance **of her** husband, and the cool and ready reply of their guest, **did not escape the** keen hearing of the woman. Pickett muttered **something** in answer **to** this speech, and then threw himself, **without** undressing, **upon the** bed. The other followed **the** example, **and in a few moments** his form, stretched at length **before** the **fireplace, lay** as quietly as if he were already wrapped **in the deepest** slumbers. This appearance was, however, deceptive. **The** emissary had **not** yet fulfilled all **his duties;** and **he** studiously maintained **him-** self in watchfulness, **the** better **to** effect **his objects.** Believing him to be a sleep, **however, the anxieties of** Pickett's wife prompted her, after **a** while, **to** speak **to her** miserable husband, with whom, as yet, she **had had no opportunity** of private speech; but her whispered accents were **checked by** the appre- hensive criminal on the first instant of their utterance. With quick and nervous gripe he grasped her arm in silence, and, in this manner, without a word, put a stop to her inquiries. In silence, thus, and yet with equal watchfulness, did the three remain, for the space of two goodly hours. The night was advancing, and Pickett began to hope that John Hurdis would fail to keep his promise; but the hope had not been well formed in his mind, before he heard the signal agreed upon between them—three hoots and a bark—and, in a cold agony that found in every movement a pitfall, and an enemy in every bush, he prepared to rise and go forth to his employer.

"Where would you go?" demanded the woman in a hurried whisper, which would not be repressed, and she grasped his arm as she spoke. She, too, had heard the signal, and readily divined its import when she saw her husband preparing to leave her.

"Nowhere—what's the matter?—lie still, and don't be foolish!" was his reply, uttered also in a whisper, while with some violence he disengaged his arm from her grasp. She would have still detained him.

"Oh, Ben!" was all she said, and the still, whispered accents went through him with a warning emphasis that well reminded him of that good counsel which he had before rejected, and which he bitterly cursed himself for not having followed.

"She was right," he muttered to his own heart—"she was right: had I listened to what she said, and let John Hurdis do his own dirty work, I would have had no such trouble. But it's too late now—too late! I must get through it as I may."

He rose, and, silently opening the door, disappeared in the night. He had scarcely done so, when the emissary prepared to follow him. The wife saw the movement with terror, and, coughing aloud, endeavored in this way to convince the stranger that she was wakeful like himself; but her effort to discourage him from going forth proved fruitless: he gave her no heed, and she beheld him, with fear and trembling, depart almost instantly after her husband. She could lie in bed no longer; but rising, hurried to the door, which she again opened, and gazed anxiously out upon the dim and speechless trees of the neighboring forests with eyes that seemed to penetrate into the very dimmest of their recesses. She looked without profit. She saw nothing. The forms of both her husband and his guest were nowhere visible. Should she pursue them? This was at once her thought, but she dismissed it as idle a moment after. Shivering with cold, and under the nameless terrors in her apprehension, she re-entered the hovel, and closed the entrance.

"God be with me," she cried, sinking on her knees beside the miserable pallet where she had passed so many sleepless nights; "God be with me, and with him! We have need of thee, O God—both of us have need of thee. Strengthen me, O God, and save him from his enemies! The hand of the tempter is upon him—is upon him even now. I have striven with him, and I plead with him in vain. Thou only, blessed Father—thou only, who art in heaven, and art all-merciful on earth—thou only canst save him! He is weak and yielding where he should be strong, timid when he should be bold, and bold only where it is virtue to be fearful. Strengthen him when he is weak, and let him be weak where he would be wicked. Cut him not off in thy wrath, but spare him to me—to this poor child—to himself! He is not fit to perish: protect him! He's——What is this—who? Is it you, Jane? Is it you, my poor child?"

The idiot girl had crawled to her unseen, during her brief but energetic apostrophe to the Eternal, and, with a simpering, half-sobbing accent, testified her surprise at the unwonted vehemence and seeming unseasonableness of her mother's prayers. With increasing energy of action, the woman clasped the girl around the waist, and dragged her down upon the floor beside her.

"Put up your hands, Jane!" was her exclamation; "put up your hands with me! pray—pray with me. Pray to God, to deliver us from evil—your father from evil—from his own, and the evil deeds of other men! Speak out, child, speak fast, and pray—pray!"

"Our Father who art in heaven"—The child went on with the usual adjuration which had been a possession of mere memory from her infancy: while the mother, with uplifted hands, but silent thoughts, concluded her own heartfelt invocation to the God of bounty and protection. She felt that she could do no more; yet much rather would she have followed her husband into the woods, and dragged him away from the grasp of the tempter, than knelt that moment in prayer.

Pickett meanwhile, little dreaming that he was watched, hurried to the place assigned for meeting John Hurdis, among the willows. The emissary followed close behind him. It was no part of his plan to leave the former ignorant of his proper quality; and the first intelligence which he had of his approach was the sound of his voice, which sank into the heart of Pickett like an ice-bolt. He shivered and stopped when he heard it, as if by an instinct. His will would have prompted him to fly, and leave it behind for ever, but his feet were fastened to the earth. "What's the matter? why do you come after me?" he asked.

"I'll go along with you, brother," said the stranger, coolly in reply.

"As you will, but why? You don't think I'm running off from you, do you?"

"No!—that you can't do, brother, even if you would. We have eyes all around us, that suffer no movement by any of us to be made unseen; and, if you do run, such are our laws, that I should have to follow you. But I know your business, and wish for an introduction to your friend."

"My friend!" exclaimed Pickett in profound astonishment! "what friend?—I know of no friend."

"Indeed! but you must surely be mistaken; your memory is confused, I see. The friend you're going to meet; is he not your friend?"

"I'm going to meet no friend—"

"Surely you are! Brother, you wouldn't deceive me, would you? Didn't I hear the owl's hoot, and the dog's bark? I wasn't asleep, I tell you. I heard the signal as well as you."

"Owl's hoot and dog's bark? why, that's no signal in these parts," said Pickett, with a feeble attempt at laughter which failed utterly; "you may hear owls and dogs all night, if you listen to them. We are wiser than to do that."

The other replied in graver accents than usual:—

"I'm afraid, brother, you are not yet convinced of the powers of the Mystic Brotherhood, or you wouldn't suppose me to have been neglectful of the duties they sent me upon. I tell you, they gave it to me in charge to follow you, and to find out who and what you were; to learn your motives for killing the youth that we were in pursuit of; and to take all steps for making so good a shot and ready a hand one of our own. Do you think I lost sight of you for a single instant from that time to this? Be sure I did not. No!—I saw you from the moment you took your nag from the stunted poplar, where you fastened him. I marked every footstep you have taken since. When you stopped at that plantation, and told your friend of your success—"

"Great God! you didn't hear what we said?"

"Every syllable. That was a most important part of my service: I wouldn't have missed a word or look of that conference."

Pickett turned full upon the inflexible emissary, and gazed upon him with eyes of unmixed astonishment and terror. When he spoke at length, it was in accents of mingled despair and curiosity;—

"And wherefore was this important? Of what use will it be to you to know that I was working for another man in this business!"

"It helps us to another member of the Mystic Brotherhood, my brother. It strengthens our arm; it increases our resources; it ripens our strength, and hastens our plans. He, too, must be one of us! It is for this I seek to know him."

"But there's no need with him," said Pickett.

"How—no need?"

"He's rich; he's not in want of money, as we are. Why should he be one of us?"

"To keep what he's got," said the other coolly.

"But, suppose he won't join you!"

"We'll hang him, then, my brother! You shall prove that he was the murderer!"

"The devil you say!—but I'll do no such thing."

"Then, brother, we must hang you both!"

The eyes of Pickett looked the terror that his lips could not speak; and, without further words, he led the way to the place of meeting, urging no further opposition to a will before which his own quailed in subjection.

CHAPTER XXXIII.

DOMINO!—THE GAME BLOCKED.

———" Now we are alone, sir;
And thou hast liberty to unload the burden
Which thou groan'st under."—MASSINGER.

THERE is no fascination in the snake, true or fabled, of more tenacious hold upon the nature of the victim, than was that of the emissary of the Mystic Brotherhood upon the miserable creature Pickett. A wretch born in degradation, living as it were by stealth, and in constant dread of penal atonement, life was torture enough of itself, when it came coupled with the constant fear of justice. But when to this danger was added that of an accountability to a power no less arbitrary than the laws, and wholly illegitimate, the misery of the wretch was complete. But if such was the influence of such a condition over Pickett's mind, what must it be over the no less dishonorable and far more base offender who employed him? Though a murderer—a cold-blooded, calculating murderer, who could skulk behind a bush, and shoot down his victim from a covert, without warning made, or time given for preparation— he was yet hardy enough, if he had the sensibility for hate, to avenge his wrong by his own hand, and not by that of an agent.

John Hurdis had proved himself deficient even in this doubtful sort of courage. He could smile, and be the villain—could desire and devise the murder of his enemy—but wanted even the poor valor of the murderer. What must be the feeling, the fear, of his leprous heart, when he is taught his true condition —when he finds his secret known—when he feels himself in the power of a clan having a thousand tongues, and hourly exposing themselves to a thousand risks of general detection? It would have been a sight for study, to behold those three vil-

lains gathered together in that nocturnal interview : Hurdis
his soul divided between triumph and horror—eager to learn
the particulars of the horrid crime which his agent had horribly
executed, yet dreading the very recital to which he gave all
ears; Pickett—burdened with the consciousness of unprofitable
guilt, and of its exposure to the dogging bloodhoun . at his
heels; and he, the emissary, like a keen hunter, hanging upon
the flanks of both, pricking them forward when they faltered,
and now by sarcasm, and now by threats, quelling their spirit*
and commanding all their secrets. Secure of his game, he
smiled in his security at the feeble efforts which he beheld them
make, and the futile hopes which he saw they entertained of
being able to baffle his pursuit, and throw out his unerring nos-
tril from the scent which he had so fortunately followed. The
struggle was, indeed, no less pitiful than painful, and well might
the utter villain .smile with contempt at the partial character
which the two brought to bear upon their designs of evil.
Without virtue, and radically vicious, they were alike deficient
in that bold and daring insolence which can defy the laws
which it offends, and by a courage, of however doubtful merit
at least elevate its offences above the level of sneaking and in
sidious vice. His game was that of the cunning angler, who
knows that his hook is keenly fixed in the jaws of his prey,
and who plays with his hopes only to make his fears more
oppressive, and his compliance the more unreserved and un-
qualified.

Hurdis was awaiting his companion in the place appointed.

"What have we here?—who is this?" he exclaimed in surprise, as he beheld the stranger with Pickett.

"It is a friend," replied the latter, with a subdued and dis-
couraging voice.

"A friend!" said Hurdis. "What friend?—who?—we
want no friend; why have you brought him?"

"You mistake," said the stranger, boldly. "You do want a
friend, though you may not think so; and I am the very man
for you. But go aside with Pickett; he'll tell you all about it."

Having thus spoken, the emissary coolly seated himself upon
a log, and John Hurdis, completely confounded by his impu
dence, turned, as he was bidden, for explanation to his agent

They went aside together, and in a confused and awkward manner, Pickett went through the bitter narration, which it almost paralyzed the other to hear.

"Great God! Ben Pickett, what have you done? We are ruined—lost for ever!"

The cold sweat rolled from the forehead of Hurdis, and his knees trembled beneath him. His companion tried to console him.

"No; there's no sort of danger. Hear his story of his business, and we know much more against him, than he knows against us."

"And what is that to us? What is it to me that I can prove him a villain or a murderer, Ben Pickett? Will it help our defence to prove another as worthy of punishment, as ourselves? Will it give us security?"

"We must make the best of it now. It's too late to grieve about it," said the other.

"Ay, we must make the best of it," said Hurdis, becoming suddenly bold, yet speaking in tones that were suppressed to a whisper—"and there is but one way. Hear me, Ben Pickett; does this fellow come alone?"

"He does."

"Ha! that is fortunate; then we have him. His companions are—where, did you say?"

"All about—on the high roads—everywhere—from Augusta to Montgomery, to Mobile, to Tuscaloosa—from the Muscle Shoals to Jackson—from Tuscaloosa to Chochuma. Everywhere, according to his account of it."

"Which is probably exaggerated. They may be everywhere, but they certainly are not here—not in this neighborhood."

"We don't know that, 'squire. God! there's no telling. To think that the fellow should track me so, makes me afraid of everything."

"You were careless, Pickett—frightened, perhaps—"

"No, I wasn't. I was just as cool as I wished to be, and I cleared every step in the road afore I jumped it."

"It needs not to talk of this. We must be more careful in future. We must match his cunning with greater cunning, or

we are undone for ever. We are in his power, and who knows
that he is one of a gang such as you describe? Who knew
that he is not an officer of justice—one who suspects us, and is
come to find out our secrets?"

"No, no, 'squire; how should he be able to tell me all tha
he did? How should he know that I shot Dick Hurdis from
the hill that hangs over the road?"

"You remember you told me that yourself, Ben Pickett; and
you say he overheard our conversation?" cried Hurdis, eagerly

"Yes, 'squire; but how should he know that I hid my nag in
a thicket of poplars?—how should he be able to tell me the
very sort of stump I fastened him to?"

"And did he do that, Ben?"

"That he did—every bit of it. No, no, 'squire, he saw all
that he says he saw, or he got it from somebody that did see
it."

"Great heavens! what are we to do?" exclaimed Hurdis, as
he folded his hands together, and looked with eyes of supplica
tion upward. But his answer and the counsel which it conveyed, came from an entirely opposite region.

"Do! well that's the question," replied Pickett, "and I don't
know what to tell you, 'squire."

"We must do something—we can not remain thus at the
mercy of this fellow! The thought is horrible! The rope is
round our necks, Ben, and he has the end in his hands!"

"It's too true."

"Hear me!" said Hurdis in a whisper, and drawing his companion still farther from the spot where the emissary had been
left in waiting—"there is but one way. He comes alone.
We must silence him. You must do it, Ben."

"Do what, 'squire?"

"Do what!" exclaimed the other impatiently, though still in
a whisper. "Would you have me utter every word? Do with
him as you have done with Dick Hurdis!"

"I've thought of that, 'squire, but—"

"But what?"

"There's a mighty risk."

"There's risk in everything. But there's no risk greater
than that of being at the mercy of such a bloodhound;"

"That's true enough, 'squire; but he's too much for me single-handed. You must help me."

"What's the need? You don't think to do it now?' demanded Hurdis, in some alarm.

"If it's to be done at all, why not now? The sooner, the better, 'squire. This is the very time. He has poked his nose into our pot, and he can't complain, if he gets it scorched Together, we could put it to him, so that there could be no mistake."

But this counsel did not suit the less courageous nature of John Hurdis.

"No, Ben, that would be a risk, indeed. We might tumble him, but a chance shot, from a desperate man, might also tumble one or both of us."

"That's true."

"We must think of something else — some safer course, which will be equally certain. He sleeps at your house."

"Yes," said the other quickly; "but I will do nothing of that sort within smell of Betsy. It's bad enough to draw blood on the high road, but it must not run on one's own hearth."

"Pshaw! where's the difference? Murder is murder wherever it is done!"

"That's true, 'squire; but there's a feeling in it, that makes the difference. Besides, I won't have the old woman worried with any of this business. I've kept everything of this sort from her that I could; and the thing that I most hated Dick Hurdis for, was his making such a blaze of that whipping business, as to bring it to her sight. There's Jane, too. No, 'squire, my wife and child must not know all the dirty matters that stick to my fingers."

"Well, as you please, on that score. But something must be done. You must fix a trap for him. When does he leave you?'

"There's no knowing. He wants to fix you as he's fixed me; to make us both members of his clan — Mystic Brotherhood — as he calls it; and when that's done, I suppose, he'll be off."

"But why should he desire this? What motive can he have in it? Why a society so extensive?"

"There's no telling; only you'll have to consent"

"What! to this accursed brotherhood? Never!"

"How can you help it, 'squire? If you don't, he'll expose you! He swears to hang you, if you do not!"

"But he can not! How can he prove his charge? Besides, I struck no blow — I never left my home!"

"You forget, 'squire; he heard our talk together."

"But who'll believe him, Ben? You can swear him down that you never had such a conversation."

"No! I dare not; for then he'd prove me to be the man that shot the shot. We must submit, 'squire, I'm afraid, or he'd convict us both; and, to save myself, I'd swear against you! I'd have to do it, 'squire!"

This declaration completed the misery of Hurdis, as it showed him how insecure was the tenure by which the slaves of vice are held together. The bitterness of fear — the very worst bitterness of human passion — was in his heart, in all its force and fulness, and he had to drink deeper draughts of its humiliating waters even than this.

"What! Ben Pickett, can it be that you would give evidence against me, after all I have done for you? You do not tell me so?"

"To save life only, 'squire! To save life only — for no other necessity. But life is sweet, 'squire — too sweet for us to stand on any friendship, when we can save it by giving everything up beside. It wouldn't be at the first jump, neither, 'squire, that I would let out the secrets of an old friend. It is only when I see there's no other hope to save myself, and, then, I should be mighty sorry."

"Sorry!" exclaimed Hurdis, bitterly. "Thus it is," he thought, "to use base instruments for unworthy ends. The slave becomes the arbiter — the master — and to silence and to subdue our fears, we add to our secret consciousness of shame."

In anxiousness, but without expression, he mused thus with his own thoughts.

"Well, Ben, since it can be no better," he spoke to his companion "we must even hold together, and do as well as we can to work ourselves out of this difficulty. You are resolved to do nothing with the fellow at your own house?"

Pickett replied in words and a tone, which made his negative conclusive.

"We must see his hand, then, and know the game he intends to play," continued Hurdis. "You are agreed that we must get him out of the way for our own safety. To say when and how is all the difficulty. Am I right?"

"That's it, 'squire; though, somehow, if we could clinch him now, it seems to me it would be better than leaving it over for another day."

"That's not to be thought on, Ben. It's too great a risk."

"I don't know, 'squire. I could give him a dig while you are talking with him; and if, when I made the motion, you could take him by the throat, or only dash your hat in his face to confuse him, I think it might be done easily enough."

Pickett showed his bowie-knife as he spoke, which he had carefully hidden in his bosom, unperceived by his guest, before he went abroad. But this plan, though, perhaps, the best, met with no encouragement from his more politic, or, to speak plainly, more timid companion. He shook his head, and the voice of the emissary at a little distance, was heard, as he sang some rude ditty to cheer the solitude of his situation, or perhaps to notify the twain that he was becoming impatient.

"Hark! he approaches us," said Hurdis. "Let us say no more now. Enough that we understand each other. We must watch his game, in order to determine upon our own; and, though, I would not we should do anything to-night; yet, what we do, must not only be done without risk, but must be done quickly. Let us go to him now."

CHAPTER XXXIV.

"Your oaths are past, and now subscribe your name,
That his own hand, may strike his honor down,
That violates the smallest branch herein."
— *Love's Labor's Lost.*

" **Unto bad causes, swear
Such creatures as men doubt.**—*Julius Cæsar.*

THE **emissary** had **awaited the end of their long conference** with exemplary patience.

"I could have told you **all in fewer words,"** he said bluntly to John Hurdis the moment they came in sight.　"The story is soon **told by** one who is accustomed **to it. I am compelled** to talk it over **to so many,** that I go through **it now almost as a matter of** memory, with a **certain set** of words which **I seldom have occasion to** change.　I trust **that my brother, here, has done no discredit to my skill,** by halving **it in** repeating."

"I fear not," replied **Hurdis.** "He has certainly told enough to startle one less confidently **assured** in his own innocence, **than** myself. He **has** unfolded a strange **history** in my ears.　Can it be **true ?"**

"As gospel !"

"And you really have the large number of persons leagued together which he **mentions ?"**

"Full fifteen hundred."

"And for such purposes ?"

"Ay !"

"And what is your **object here ?**　What do you seek from us ?"

"To increase the number.　We seek friends."

"Wherefore ?　Why should you increase your number, when such an increase must only diminish **your resources ?"**

"I don't know that such will be its effect, and it increases our power. We gain in strength, when we gain in number."

"But why desire an increase of strength, when even now you have enough for all your purposes?"

"Indeed! but who shall know—who declare—our purposes? I, even I, know nothing of them all. I may suspect—I may conjecture—but I know them not. They are kept from us till the proper moment."

"Indeed—who should then if you do not? Who keeps them from you?"

"The grand council. They determine for us, and we execute."

"Who are they?"

"That must be a secret from you, yet. You shall know it, and all our secrets, when you shall have taken your several degrees in our brotherhood."

"I will take none!" said Hurdis, with more emphasis than resolution.

"You do not say it!" was the cool reply of the emissary. "You dare not."

"How! not dare?"

"It's as much as your life is worth."

"You speak boldly."

"Because I am confident of strength, my brother," replied the emissary. "You will speak boldly too—more boldly than now—when you become one of us. You will feel your own strength, when you know ours. When you feel as I do, that there are friends for ever nigh, and watchful of your safety; making your enemies theirs; guarding your footsteps; fighting your battles; making a common cause of your interests, and standing elbow to elbow with you in all your dangers. Wherefore should I be bold enough to seek you here—two of you, both strong men—both, most probably armed—I, alone, having strength of person, not greater, perhaps, than either of you, and, possibly, not so well armed—but that I feel myself thus mighty in my connections? I know they have taken my footsteps—they know where I am at all seasons, as I know where to find others of our brotherhood, and if I could not call them at a given moment, to save me from a sudden blow, I am at least certain that they know where, and when to avenge me. But for this, brothers, both, I should not have ventured my **nose** into your very den, **as I** may call it, telling you **of** your tricks **upon** travellers, and **spurring** you into our ranks."

The audacious development **of the emissary absolutely con**founded the two criminals, before whom **he stood.** They looked **at** one another vacantly, without answer, **and the** emissary smiled to see in the ghastly starlight, their no **less** ghastly **counte**nances. He put his hand upon the arm of Hurdis who stood next to him.

"I see you are troubled, brother; but **what** reason have you to fear? The worst is over. Your secret is known to friends—to those only who can and will serve you."

"Friends! friends! God help me, what sort **of** friends!" was the bitter speech **of** Hurdis, as he listened **to** this humiliating sort of consolation. With increasing bitterness he continued. **"And what** do our friends **want** of **me? what** shall I do for **them—what give** them? Their friendship **must be paid** for, I suppose. You **want** money?"

"We do—**but none of yours.**"

"And why not mine **as well** as **others.** Is it **not quite as** good?"

"Quite, but not enough of it perhaps. **But we never take from** our friends—from those whom we are resolved **to** have in our brotherhood. You might give us money upon compulsion, but it would be scarce worth our while, to extort that, **when** your coöpera**tion** is necessary to our other purposes, and must result in getting us **a** great deal more."

"I must know how—I must know your other purposes, before I consent to unite with **you.** I will not league with those who are common robbers."

"Common robbers, brother," cried the emissary, with a contemptuous sneer, "are not, perhaps, such noble people as common murderers, but, I take it, they are **quite as virtuous. But** we are not common robbers, my brother; far from it. You do great injustice **to** the Mystic Brotherhood. Know from me that we are simply seekers of justice; and we only differ from all others having the same **object,** in the means which we take to bring it about. We **are** those **who** redress the wrongs and injuries of fortune, who protect the **poor** from the oppressor, who subdue the insolent, and humble the presumptuous and vain. Perhaps we are, in truth, the most moral community under the sun; since our policy keeps us from harming the poor, and, if we wrong anybody, it is only those who do. We take life but seldom, and then only with the countenance of our social laws, and by the will of the majority, except in individual cases, when the fundamental law of self-protection makes the exception to other laws which are specified. Does your courthouse in Marengo do better than that—more wisely, more justly? I know to the contrary, my brother, and so do you."

"But we are content with our laws," said Hurdis.

"Ah, indeed! are you willing to be tried by them? Shall I go to the attorney, and tell him what I know? shall I point to your agent beside you, and say he shot down a tall fellow without any notice, and would have robbed him of his money if he could, and all on your account?"

"You could not say that!" said Hurdis in trembling haste, "his robbery was not our object."

"His death was."

"Ay, but he was an enemy—a hateful, malignant enemy—one who trampled on his elder and his brother—"

"Was he your brother?" exclaimed the emissary, starting back at the words, and looking upon the criminal in undisguised astonishment.

The silence of Hurdis answered the question sufficiently.

"Your own brother—the child of the same mother! Well, it must have been a cruel wrong that he did to you."

"It was!" stammered out Hurdis in reply.

"It must have been," said the other—"it must have been. I would take a great deal from a brother, if I had one, before I'd shoot him; and then, I tell you, if 'twas necessary to be done, my own hands should do it. I wouldn't send another man on the business. But, I've nothing to do with that. All that I've got to say is, that you're just the sort of man we want. You must be one of us, swear to stand by us, help us, and counsel with us, and in all respects obey the grand council, and be faithful."

"Anything but that. Tell me, my good fellow, is there no alternative? Will not money answer?—you shall have it."

"Money! why, what can you give, that we might not take! What are you worth that you talk so freely of money? We can take your life and money too. You only live by our indulgence. And why do we indulge you? Not because of any affection that we bear you, nor because of any admiration which we entertain of your abilities and valor, but simply because we lack assistants, here and there, throughout the whole Southwest, in order to facilitate the progress of certain great events which we have in preparation. But for this, we should compound with you, and take a portion of your wealth, in lieu of your life, which you have forfeited. This is what we do daily. Whenever we detect a criminal—a friend, as it were, ready made to our hands—we do not expose, but guard, his secret; and when he becomes one of us, his secret becomes ours, which it is then no less our policy than principle to preserve. No, no, my brother—we want you, not your money. Do you keep your money, but we will keep you."

"Great God!" muttered the miserable wretch, in self-rebuke, "into what a pit have I fallen! Better die—better perish at once, than submit to such a bondage as this."

"As you please, my friend; but to one or the other you must submit. You have heard my terms: you must decide quickly. I have not much time to waste—I have other members to secure for the confederacy, and must leave you in a day or so."

"What am I to do? what is it you require?"

"Your oath—your solemn oath to do what I shall enjoin upon you now, and whatever else may at times be enjoined upon you by the grand council."

"What may that be? what sort of duties do they enjoin?"

'I cannot answer you that. Our duties are various, and are accommodated to the several capacities and conditions of our members. You, for example, are a man of substance and family. From you the tasks exacted would seldom be of an arduous character. You will, perhaps, be required to furnish monthly reports of the conduct, wealth, principles, and pursuits, of your neighbors, particularly the most wealthy, active, and intelligent. It is the most important branch of our study to know all those who are able to serve or to annoy us. You must also communicate to us the names of all who intend emigrating from you.

parts; find out and let us know their destination, the route they take, the amount of money they have with them, their arms and resolution. I will give you an address which will enable you to communicate these things."

The enumeration of these degrading offices filled the measure of John Hurdis's humiliation. A sense of the most shameful servitude vexed his soul, and he absolutely moaned aloud, as in the extremity of his despair he demanded —

"May there be more than this ?"

"Hardly. You will, perhaps, be required to meet the brotherhood before long, in order to learn what further duties they may impose."

"Meet them! — where — where do they meet?"

"Everywhere — but where is not to be said at this time. You will be warned in season by one of our messengers, and possibly by myself, who will show you the sign, and whom you must follow. Let me show you the sign now, and administer the oath."

The victim submitted, as Pickett had already done, and the bonds of iniquity were sealed and signed between them. John Hurdis began to feel that there was no slavery so accursed, no tyranny so unscrupulous, no fate so awful, as that of guilt. He almost began to steel himself with the conviction that it would be an easier matter for him to give himself up at once to the executioner of the laws. With a feeling almost akin to despair, he beheld the cool emissary take out his pocket book, and in the uncertain light of the night record their names — nay, actually tax both himself and Pickett for the right orthography in doing so — with all the exemplary and courtly nicety of one " learned in the law."

CHAPTER XXXV.

DESPERATE MEASURES.

—— " It must be done:
There is no timely season in delay,
When life is waiting. I must take the sword,
Though my soul trembles. Would it were not so!"
Conspirator.

THE conference was over. The emissary did not seem willing to waste more words than were absolutely necessary. He was a man of business. But Hurdis, to whom the conference had been so terrible, he was disposed to linger.

"I must speak with you, Ben Pickett, before you go," said he hoarsely to his colleague. The emissary heard the words, and went aside, saying as he did so, with a good-humored smile of indifference upon his countenance —

"What! you would not that I should hear, though you know we are now of the same family. You will grow wiser one day."

"It's nothing," said Hurdis, "a small matter—a mere trifle," and his tones faltered in the utterance of the lie.

"It's of no account," said the emissary, "I do not care to know it;" and whistling as he went, he put aside the bushes which surrounded the group, and made his way toward the road.

"Ben Pickett," said Hurdis, when the emissary had got out of hearing, "I cannot bear this dreadful bondage; it will kill me if I suffer it a week. We must break from it; we must put an end to it in some way or other. I cannot stoop to do the dirty business of this confederacy — these grand rascals — and what is our security ? This scoundrel, or any one of the pack, may expose us at any moment, and, after toiling deeper in the mire, we shall be taken out of it at the cart's tail. It is not to be thought on — I can not bear it. Speak to me. Say, what are we to do ?"

"Well, 'squire, I can't, say; it's for you to speak. You know best."

"Nonsense, Ben Pickett ! this is no time for idle compliments. It is you who should know best. You are better taught in the tricks of these scoundrels than I am, and can give better counsel of what we are to do. Something must be done. Is there no easier way to get rid of this fellow than by ——— you know what I mean ? I would not that either of us should do any more of that business."

"I reckon not, 'squire. There's only one way to stop a wagging tongue, that I know of; and if you're willing to lend a hand, why, the sooner it's done the better. The chap stands by the end of the broken fence—"

The constitutional timidity of John Hurdis arrested the suggestion ere it was fully spoken.

"That's too great a risk, Ben ; besides, we have not come prepared."

"I don't know, 'squire : I've got a knife that's sharp enough, and I reckon you've got your pistols. 'Twould be easy enough as we walk along beside him. The night's clear enough to let you take good sight upon him—"

"But should the pistol miss fire, Ben—"

"Why, then, my knife," was the prompt reply.

"It might do, Ben, if he were not armed also. But you remember he told us that he was, and it is but reasonable to think that he must be, coming on such a business as this. He must not only be armed, but well armed. No, no—it will not do just now ; and there's another objection to our doing it here : it's too nigh home. Let him leave us first, Ben, and it's safest in every respect to give him long shot for his passport. That's our plan, Ben — I see no other."

"Just as you say, 'squire — just as you say ; but, to tell you the truth, I'm almost of the notion that it's best to come toe-to-toe, at the jump : take it now, in the starlight, and have it over. It's a monstrous cold business, now, that watching behind a bush with your rifle, till your enemy comes in sight ; it's a cold business."

"Yes, it may be, but it's the safest of all, and our safety is now the single object of both of us. That must be the way, Ben; and—"

"But who'll watch for him? You, I think—there's no other, for, as he sleeps at my house, I can't leave him, you know, to take a stand. You'll have to do it."

The suggestion was an astounding one; and for a few moments, Hurdis was puzzled and silent. To become himself a principal actor in such a business was no part of his desire. He was unprepared, as well by habit as constitution, to engage in deeds of violence, where he himself was the chief performer, though at no sort of personal risk. Not that he had any moral or human scruples in the matter. We have seen enough of him already to know the reverse. It was necessary, however, for him to say something; and he proposed a course to his confederate which was vacillating and indecisive, and could promise not even a probable advantage. He could not muster courage enough to recognize the necessity of doing all himself, and looking his task in the face.

"Well, but you could let him off, and follow him, as you followed Dick Hurdis."

"Yes, if I knew his course so well. But when he leaves the neighborhood road, who knows where he'll strike? All we know is, that he goes upward. We are sure of him then before he gets to the 'Crooked branch,' which is but ten miles off. There you could watch for him snugly enough, and be sure of him from the opposite hill for a good quarter of an hour. But it would be impossible for me to beat round him, so as to get in front, before he reaches that point; and, after that, who knows where he turns his bridle?"

"Well, Ben, but you must find that out. You can inquire as you go, and mark his hoofs."

The other shook his head.

"I'm dubious about that way, 'squire. If the fellow says true, that he has his friends all about him, I may be asking about his tracks from one of them, and then all's dicky with both of us. I think, 'squire, there's only that one way, which is the safe one. You'll have to take the bush at 'Crooked branch,' and do this business yourself."

"But I'm not a sure shot with the rifle, Ben; and to miss, were to knock everything in the head."

"Take your double barrel; you're a good shot with that. Put twenty buckshot in each barrel, and give him one after the other. He won't know the difference."

"If I should miss, Ben—"

"You can't miss—how can you? The path's clear—nothing to stop your sight. You're out of his reach; you're on the hill. You see him coming toward—going round by—you, and you see him for two hundred yards on a clear track after he's passed you. There's no chance of his getting off, 'squire; and—"

"Ha! what's that?" cried Hurdis, as the sound of a pistol-shot aroused all the sleeping echoes of the wood. The voice of the emissary followed, and he was heard approaching them through the bushes.

"Don't be frightened, brothers; but, believing you to have fallen asleep, I thought to arouse you up, for fear that you'd take cold. Are you most done, for I'm getting cold myself?"

They were taught by this—which the emissary probably desired—that he had fire-arms, and enough too, to render the loss of one load a matter of small consequence.

"The fellow's getting impatient," said Hurdis, in suppressed tones to Pickett. Then, crying aloud, "We will be with you directly," he hurried through the rest of his bloody arrangements for the ensuing day. When they were about to go forth, Pickett suddenly stopped his employer.

"I had almost forgot, 'squire, but do you know Bill Carrington's got back already. He gave me a mighty bad scare to-day, that I han't got over yet."

"How?" demanded Hurdis, with natural alarm.

"I saw him going from my house door. He hadn't been in it, so Betsy swore to me, though I could almost swear I saw him come out; and without stopping to say what he wanted, he took to the woods, like one more frightened than myself."   -

"Strange! He hadn't come home by dinner time to-day. Did you take after him?"

"Yes, after a little while I did; but I was too much scared at first to do anything quickly—not that I was so much scared by Bill Carrington, as by another that I saw just afore him."

"Who was that?"

"Dick Hurdis."

John Hurdis started back, and with jaws distended, and checks, whose pallid hue denoted the cowardly heart within him, almost gasped his words of astonishment.

"Ha!—you do not say—but—why ask? You had not killed him then!—and yet, if you had wounded him even, how could he be there?"

"He was not there," replied the other, in low and trembling accents—"it was his ghost!"

"Pshaw! I believe not in such things," was the answer of Hurdis; but his faltering tones contradicted the confidence of his language. "It was your imagination, Ben —nothing else."

And, speaking thus, he drew nigher to Pickett, and looked cautiously around him. The other, who had faith, had less fear than him who had none.

"Well, I can't say I don't believe in the things that I see. Call it imagination, or what you will, it gave me a mighty scare, 'squire. But, come, sir; let us go to the man; he is approaching us again—I hear his whistle."

"A moment," said Hurdis. Pickett hung back while the other hesitated to speak. It required an unusual effort to enable him to do so.

"I say, Ben, I'm ready to do this matter, but if you could contrive any way to take it off my hands, I should like it—"

"I don't see, 'squire, how I can," said the other.

"If a couple hundred, or even three, Ben—"

"I'd like to serve you, 'squire, but—"

"Say five, Ben."

"I reckon it's impossible, 'squire. I see no way; besides, to tell you the truth, I'd rather not. When I think that the blood on my hands, already, is got for fighting another man's battles, 'squire, I'm worse satisfied than ever with what I've done, and I'm clear for doing no more, hereafter, than is for my own safety."

"But this is for our own safety, Ben—we are in the same boat."

"Not so, 'squire; our boats are different—very different. You are in a fine large ship with mighty sails—I am in a poor dug-out. If I lose my dug-out, it's no great matter. But your ship, 'squire — if you lose that?"

"I lose more than you do, and yet we both lose all we have, Ben. You, your life — I, mine! It matters not much which of us is the most wealthy, since we both lose everything in losing life. Our loss is equal then, and it is your interest, quite as much as mine, to put this fellow out of the way."

"Well, 'squire, the truth is, I'm tired of scuffling for life. I've been scuffling for it all my life. I won't scuffle any more. I'll take the world as I find it. I'll take my chance with this fellow, and run the risk of his blabbing, sooner than squat down behind a bush and blow his brains out."

"And yet you expect me to do it, Ben?"

"No, I don't expect you. You ask me how to put this fellow out of your way, and I tell you. I know no other way, unless you'll come to the scratch at once, and have it out with him now, while the stars are shining."

"What! just when you've heard his pistol too, and know that he's well provided in arms! That would be madness."

"I know no other way, 'squire," was the indifferent reply.

"Ah, Ben, don't desert me!" was the pitiful appeal of the imbecile villain. "Don't fly from me at the very first sight of danger!"

"I don't, 'squire! I'm ready to jump now, this minute, into its throat, though you know, as well as I do, that it's full of teeth!"

"That we must not do! We should both perish, perhaps — certainly, if my pistol should miss fire!"

"But it would be a warm scuffle for it, 'squire; and that's better than waiting in a cold bush."

"We must not think of such a plan. It would be folly. The first is the best after all — the safest. I must do it, then, myself. I will! why should I fear? All rests on it, and he — what is he? The deed were a benefit to society, not less than to ourselves."

A sudden fit of courage and morality grew at once prominent together in the spirit of the dastard. Driven to the necessity, he, at length, seemed to embrace it with the resolution of the man; and, thus resolved, he went forth to meet the person whom, the next day, he had decreed for the sacrifice.

CHAPTER XXXVI.

THE HEART FAILS.

> " Like dastard curres, that having at abay
> The savage beast embost in wearie chace,
> Dare not adventure on the stubborn prey,
> Ne byte before, but rome from place to place,
> To get a snatch, when turned is his face."
>
> *Faery Queen.*

THE emissary of the mystic confederacy had been well chosen for the business upon which he came. He discriminated at a glance between the characters of John Hurdis and his agent. The imbecility of the one had been the chief occasion of his vices; the destitution of the other had originated his. A proper education, alone, with due reference to their several deficiencies, could have saved them; and, under strict guidance and just guardianship, they had, doubtlessly, been both good men. They were not, however; and the task of the emissary was to make the particular deficiencies of each, the agent for securing the required degree of influence over them. To Pickett, when Hurdis left them, he had that to say, which, though it did not entirely answer the intended purpose of securing his hearty coöperation, had, at least, the effect of confounding him. Though the agent of Hurdis could not be immediately changed into an enemy, he was effectually prevented from appearing forever after in the attitude of an active friend. The words were few which effected this object.

"That is a poor creature for whom you risked your life. If he dared, he would even now have you risk it again for him. There is no need to risk it for yourself. He would pay you well to murder me ! The fool ! as if I, only, am in possession of his secret — as if I were utterly unguarded in coming down

Into his jaws, or stood in any sort of danger of their closing upon me! I'll tell you what, brother—when you stab or shoot, let it be on your own account. If you do it for another, let it be for one who is not too great a coward to do it for himself. Here's a wretch would kill his enemy—that's nothing—if his own arm held the weapon! Has the feeling which makes him hate—the malignity which prompts him to revenge—yet lacks the very quality which alone can make hate honorable, and malignity manly. By the seal of the grand council, if 'twere with me, I'd compound with the fellow for his life—take his money, as much as he could give—and let him off from the confederacy. I despise such sneaks, and would trust them with nothing. And yet, they have their uses. To save his own throat, he can tell us where others are to be found, and do the business of a spy, if he lacks the boldness to take the weapon of the soldier. The scoundrel, too, to strike his own brother; there's no trusting such a chap, Pickett, and it's fortunate for you that another has him on the skirts as well as yourself. If ever this business had come out, you would have suffered all; he'd have made you the scapegoat, and would have lacked the will, as well as the courage, to have helped you, by a proper effort, out of the halter. He is planning something now—I know it—something against me; but he must be a keener hunter of blood than I think him, to find me napping. By mid-day to-morrow, I'll put another hound upon his track, so that he shall take no step without the council knowing it."

Thus speaking, the emissary led the way back to the hovel of Pickett, with a manner of the utmost unconcern. The latter was too much bewildered by what he heard—by his own peculiar situation, and the position in which his former coadjutor was likely to be placed—to think of anything calmly, or to make any answer. He began, with that easy pliability to vice and its suggestions, which had always marked his character, to feel that there was no need for him to struggle against a power that almost seemed like a fate; and if he had any reflections at all, they were those of one, who, buffeting much with the world's troubles, had, at last, learned to make something of the worst of them. His mind began to address itself to the advantages which might result from this new association, and it was not an emissary, so faithful to his trust as the one before us, who would suffer these to go unmustered into notice. Before Pickett slept that night, he had come to the conclusion that he might as well take his share in the business of the mystic confederacy, which promised so magnificently, and paid so well.

But, meanwhile, what of **John Hurdis** ? What were his thoughts —his dreams—that night ? Anything but pleasant and promising. The hopes of Pickett, springing from his poverty and destitution, were nothing to him. He was rich—a man of family and substance. Standing fair in the world's esteem—seeking the regards and the affections of the virtuous and the beautiful—what were his reflections in the position in which he·now found himself ? His felony brought home to his doors, and only withheld from public exposure—at the mercy of a band of professed felons—and then, only, by his timely compliance with their laws and exactions—by his becoming one with them—forced into their crimes—forced·into all their thousand responsibilities. What a mesh of dangers gathered about him! What a fecund crime was that which he had committed! The teeth of his malignity were already sprouting from the ground, and under his own feet. Well might he tremble at every step he was about to take, and bitterly curse the folly, not ·less than the wickedness, of the deed which he had commissioned Pickett to perform. And Pickett, too, had deserted him—that was a blow not less severe than the rest. Could he have thrust upon the hands of his agent the other deed yet to be done, he had been comparatively easy, not so much because of the service itself, but because he would not then have·been taught so terribly to feel the awful solitude of crime. The desertion of the confederate is, perhaps, the first-felt warning which a just fate despatches to the vicious.

"Fool! miserable fool that I was!" raved the miserable Hurdis, when he found himself alone. "Where am I? What have I done? Where do I stand? The earth opens before me! Would it hide me? I have labored wildly, and without profit. I am no nearer to Mary Easterby than ever !—nay, farther off than ever! and the blood of a brother, shed that I might clear the way to her, is upon my hands in vain! She rejects me, and I have gained nothing but misery and danger. I am at the

mercy of the worst—the most desperate of mankind—with no
ties to bind them in my service and to secrecy! The very
wealth, which I believed capable to do everything, rejected at
my hands! There is but one hope —but one chance for freedom! It must be done, and—double misery!—my hand alone
must do it! I must not shrink—I must not falter now! On
the word of this desperado my life hangs! I must risk life that
he should not speak that word! He must be silenced! Better that I should do so now, than wait till the sheriff knocks at
the door! It can not be worse—it may save all!"

His terror did not deprive him of his cautions, nor operate
to defeat his deliberate thoughts upon the course which he resolved to take. On the contrary, it rather contributed to increase his acuteness, and make his caution more deliberate than
ever. Nature, which denied him courage, seemed to have provided him, in his strait, with a double share of cunning; and one
little incident will sufficiently serve to show his own providence
in making his arrangements. He had to take his gun from his
chamber, after he had carefully loaded both barrels with buck-
shot, and, lest he might be met while descending the stairs, by
any of the family or servants, he lowered it from his window by
means of a string—thus obviating any danger of being seen
armed at an unusual hour of the night. Before the day had
dawned, he had made his way to the place designed for his concealment; and with the patience, if not the indifference of the
professed outlaw, he waited for the approach of one.

He had to wait for some hours, for Pickett's hospitality
toward his new associate, would not suffer him to depart till
after breakfast. The same consideration was not sufficient,
however, to induce the former to acquaint the emissary with
the ambush which he well-knew had been set for him. His
regards had not yet been warmed to such a degree. His policy
may be comprised in a few words.

"If," thought he, "John Hurdis kills him, well and good—
I've nothing to do with it—I can lose nothing by it, but will
most probably escape from a connection, which is decidedly
dangerous. But whether I escape from the connection or not,
at least I am safe from any charges of having done this deed,
I am certainly untroubled with the consciousness of it. Should

he not **kill** him, still **well and good**—we stand **where we are**
I am **neither worse nor better.** The confederacy, if it **has its**
dangers, **has its rewards also**—and **what am** I, and what are my
prospects **in the world, that** I should heed the former, when the
latter **are to me, so important a consideration.** Live or die, my
brother"—**here he** adopted the affectionate language of the
emissary—"live or die, my brother, it's all one to me."

And with these thoughts, though unexpressed, he sent the
emissary forward on his path of danger. As was **inevitable**
he took the road upward according **to the** opinion of Pickett.
and, it may be added, his course was directly over the ground
which he had already travelled. **The** distance was small.
however, **from** the house of Pickett, to the **spot** where Hurdis
awaited him; and the fellow took no long time **in** approaching
it. Meanwhile, **what** were the emotions of the felonious watcher.
We may **imagine—I can** not describe them. Life **and death**
depended upon **his resolve—so he** thought, at least—yet was
he still **irresolute. He had chosen,** with the judgment of one
experienced in such matters, **the very spot** which, for all others,
afforded him the best opportunity **of putting his** design in execution. Approaching or departing from **him, his** victim was at
his mercy for a full hundred yards **on either hand.** The bushes
around effectually concealed him—his aim was unobstructed—
the path was not often travelled—not liable to frequent interruption—the day was dark—there was not a breath stirring
Yet **the** hand of the assassin trembled, **and** the tremor at his
heart **was even** greater than that **of his** hand. Nature had not
designed him for a bold villain. **He might have** made a cun
ning shopkeeper, **and succeeded,** perhaps, in doing a far better
business, though not a **more** moral **one, in vending** bad wares,
and spurious money, **than by** crying, "stand" **to a true** man
His nerves **were not of the iron order, and** painfully, indeed,
was **he** made conscious of **this** defect, as he beheld his enemy
approach. No opportunity could have been better. The road
by the branch, above which he lay in waiting, was almost under
him; and for **a** good three minutes, **the** movement of the travel-
ler was in a direct line with his first appearance. Hurdis got
his gun in readiness, and when **the victim** came within its reach
he raised it to his shoulder. But it sank again a moment after

The muzzle veered to and fro, as a leaf in the wind. He could not bring the sight to rest upon the traveller. Keen was the anguish which he felt when he brought it down to the earth: and it was in desperate resolve that he again lifted it.

"It must be done," he said to himself—"there is no hope else. My life or his—shall I hesitate? I must do it—I can not miss him now."

Again the instrument of death was uplifted in his unwilling hands, and this time he rested it upon a limb of the tree, which rose directly before his person.

"I have him now. It is but fifty yards. There he is beside the poplar! Ha! what is this—where is he—I can not see him—a mist is before my eyes."

A mist had indeed, overspread his sight. His straining eyes were full of water, and he drew back from the tube, and looked over it upon the road. Still, his enemy was there. Why had he not seen him before? He would have resumed his aim, but just then he saw the eyes of the emissary turned upward upon the very spot where he stood. Had he been seen through the bushes? The doubt was a palsying one, and he shrunk back in terror, and listened with a beating heart that shook in his very throat, to hear the steps of the enemy in pursuit of him up the hill. But he heard nothing and was emboldened to look again. He had lost one chance. The emissary had rounded the branch, and was now upon the other end of the trace and going from him. But his back was now turned to the assassin, and his base spirit derived strength from this circumstance. He felt that he could not have drawn a trigger upon his foe, while he looked upon his face. He now did not doubt of his being able to execute the deed. His arms were rigid—he felt that he was resolved. There was not the slightest quiver in limb or pulse; and with the confidence of assured strength, and a tried courage, he once more lifted the weapon. Never did man take better aim upon his foe. The entire back of the slow moving stranger was toward him. The distance was small, for, in rounding the branch, the traveller had approached, rather than receded from, the point where the murderer lay in waiting. Cautiously, but firmly, did he cock the weapon. The slight click upon his own ears, was startling, and before he could recover from the start which it had occasioned him, and while he was about to throw his eyes along the barrel, his marrowless purpose was again defeated, by one of the simplest incidents in the world. A flock of partridges, startled by the tread of the horse, flew up from the road-side, at the very feet of the traveller. The moment had passed. The victim was out of reach before his wretched enemy could recover his resolution. Desperate and wild, John Hurdis rushed out of his covert, and half-way down the hill. He would have cried aloud to the retreating emissary. He would have defied him to an equal, mortal struggle. But the soul was wanting, if not the will. The sound died away in his husky throat. The voice stuck — the tongue was palsied. The imbecile dropped his weapon, and sinking down upon the grass beside it, thrust his fingers into the earth, and moaned aloud. It is a dreadful misery to feel that we can confide in no friend — that we can trust no neighbor; but this sorrow is nothing to that last humiliating conviction, which tells us that we can not trust ourselves. That our muscles will fail us in the trying moment — that, when we most need resolution, we shall find none within our hearts. That our nerves shall be unstrung when their tension is our safety — that our tongue shall refuse its office, when its challenge is necessary to warm our own hearts, and alarm those of our enemies. Conscious imbecility next to conscious guilt, is the most crushing of all mental maladies. To look upon that poor, base criminal now, as he lies upon the grass — his fingers stuck into the sod and fixed there — his jaws wide, and the frothing tongue lolling out and motionless — big drops upon his forehead — bigger drops in his red and glassy eyes — his hair soaked by the sweat of his mental agony, and all his limbs without life — and we should no longer hate, but pity — we should almost forget his crime in the paralyzing punishment which followed it. But this was not the limit of his afflictions, though, to the noble mind, it must appear the worst. There were yet other terrors in store for him. He was yet to learn, even in this narrow life, that "the wages of sin is death."

CHAPTER XXXVII.

NAMELESS TERRORS.

"Why stand you thus amazed! Methinks your eyes
    Are fixed in meditation; and all here
    Seem like so many senseless statues;
    As if your souls had suffered an eclipse
    Betwixt your judgment and affections."—*Woman Hater.*

HOURS elapsed before John Hurdis arose from the earth upon which he had thrown himself, overcome by the mortification of his conscious imbecility. When he did arise he was like one bewildered. But he went forward. Stunned and staggering, he went forward—the stains of the soil upon his face and hands—his gun and clothes marked also with the proofs of his humiliation. But whither should he go? His mind, for a brief space, took no heed of this question. He wandered on without direction from his thought; but, with an old habit, he wandered toward the dwelling of his coadjutor, Pickett. He was partially awakened from his stupor, by the sounds of a voice—the merry voice of unheeding childhood. The sounds were familiar—they half recalled him to himself—they reminded him where he was, while fully impressing upon him his forlorn condition. They were those of the idiot girl, and she now came bounding toward him with an old feeling of confidence But ere she drew nigh, she remembered the interview with John Hurdis, in which her mother unexpectedly became a party Without knowing why, she yet well enough understood that her mother found fault with her conduct on that occasion, and the remembrance served to arrest her forward footsteps. She hung back when but a few feet from the criminal; and a faint cry escaped her. She shrunk from his altered appearance. There is no form of idiocy, which brings with it an utter insensibility to wo; and never was wo more terribly depicted upon human countenance, than it was then on that of John Hurdis. The involuntary exclamation and spontaneous speech of the girl, taught the miserable criminal, who had hitherto regarded his inner man only, to give a moment's consideration to his outer appearance; and he smiled, with a sick and ghastly smile, to behold the clay-stains upon his garments.

"Oh, Mr. John, what's the matter—what have you been doing to yourself? Look at your clothes. You've tumbled in the ditch, I reckon."

"Yes, Jane, yes; I've had a fall, Jane—a bad fall. But how do you, Jane? I haven't seen you for a very long time."

"'Most a week, Mr. John; and I've been wanting to see you too, Mr. John, to tell ·ou all about the strange man and dad; and how mother was frightened so. But you're hurt, Mr. John —you've got a bad hurt, I'm sure, or you wouldn't look so."

John Hurdis thought only of his hurts of mind, and his moral fall, in replying to the idiot in the affirmative—a reply which she received in a purely literal sense. She would have run on in a strain of childish condolence, but he listened to her impatiently, and, at length, with an air that mortified the child to whom he had always looked indulgence only, he interrupted her prattle, and bade her go to the hovel and send her father to him. She prepared to comply, but her steps were slow, and, looking back with an expression of mournful dissatisfaction on her countenance, awakened Hurdis to a more considerate feeling. Changing his tone of voice, and employing a few kind words, she bounded to him with a sudden impulse, caught his hand, kissed it, and then, like a nimble deer, bounded away in the direction of the hovel. An age seemed to pass away, in the mind of the criminal, ere Pickett came in obedience to his summons. When he beheld him coming, he retired into the wood, to which the other followed him, eagerly asking, as he drew nigh—

"Well, 'squire, how is't?—all safe—all done?"

"Nothing's done!" was the reply. "All's lost—all! Oh, Pickett! I am the most miserable, the most worthless wretch alive. My heart failed me at the very moment. My hand refused its office—my eyes, my limbs—all denied their aid to

rescue me from this accursed bondage. I knew it would be so
I feared it. I would that you had done it! I am—pity me,
Ben Pickett, that I must say the words myself—I am a coward
—a poor, despicable coward. I can not avenge my own wrong,
I can not defend my own life. I can not lift my arm, though
the enemy stands threatening before me. I must only submit
and die."

The look which accompanied these words—the looks of
mingled frenzy and despair, of feebleness and passion—would
beggar all attempt at description. The cheeks of the wretched
imbecile were white—whiter than the marble; his eyes glassy,
almost glazed with the glaze of death; his mouth was open, and
remained so during the greater part of their conference; and a
stupid stare which he fixed upon his companion while the latter
spoke in reply, was far from attesting that attention which his
ear nevertheless gave to his utterance. The inferior yet better-
nerved villain absolutely pitied, and, after his own humble fashion, endeavored to console him under his afflictions. But words
are idle to him who has need of deeds which he dares not to
perform himself, and can not purchase from another. It was a
bitter mockery to Hurdis, in his situation, to hear the commonplaces of hope administered by one whom guilt and ignorance
alike made hopeless as a teacher of others, as he must have
been in his own case hopeless. After hearing all that Pickett
could say, Hurdis was only conscious of increased feebleness.

"Go home with me, Ben—I feel so weak—I don't think I
can find the way myself. I am very weak and wretched. Let
me take your arm."

Pickett complied, and relieving him from the gun, the weight
of which was oppressive to him under his general mental and
physical prostration, conducted him through by-paths to his
home. Ere they reached the avenue, he gave him up the gun;
and finding that he was unable to confer further, though willing, upon their mutual situation and necessities, he left him,
with a cold exhortation to cheer up and make the most of his
misfortune. The other heard him with little head or heed, and
in the solitude of his own chamber endeavored to conceal the
marks of that misery which he was only now beginning to discover it was beyond his art to subdue.

But, to return to my own progress while these events were passing. It will be remembered that, stunned by the murder of my friend, I was for three days almost incapable of thought or action. I lingered during that time with Colonel Grafton, whose own kindness and that of his happy family ministered unremittingly to the sorrows which they did not hope to stay. After that time, I felt the necessity of action. The stunning sensations occasioned by the first blow were now over, and I began to look about me and to think.

I set forward on my way homeward, burdened with the cruel story, which I did not know how to relate. Nothing but a penknife and plain gold ring of William Carrington had been left untouched by his robbers. They had stripped him of everything in the shape of arms and money. The knife was in a vest-pocket, and was probably too insignificant for appropriation; the ring—one given him by Emmeline—was upon a little finger, and probably escaped their notice, or was too tight for instant removal. These I bore with me back—sad tokens of what I could not bring. His horse they had taken in their flight from the hovel, and probably sold the next day in the Choctaw nation. Mine was preserved to me; as, when William fell, and he felt himself freed from all restraint, he naturally made his way back to Colonel Grafton's, where he had been well provided for the night before. I had, indeed, lost nothing but that which I could not replace. My money was untouched in my saddle-bags, and even that which I had about my person had been left undisturbed. It is true I had concealed it in a secret pocket of my coat, but they had not even offered at a search. The flight of Carrington had too completely occupied their minds at first, and the large sum which they found upon his person had subsequently too fully answered their expectations to render it important, in their hurry, that they should waste time in examining me. Perhaps, too, they may have regarded William as the purse-bearer for both. Whatever may have been the cause of their neglect, I was certainly no loser of anything with which I had at first set out. And yet how dreadful was the loss which I had to relate! how could I relate it? how name to the poor girl, looking for her lover, any one of the cruel words which must teach her that she looked for him in vain? This was my continual thought as I travelled homeward. I had no other. It haunted me with a continual questioning, and the difficulty of speech seemed to increase with the delay to answer it, and, before I had answered it, I reached home.

The very first person I encountered was John Hurdis. I approached him unawares. He was walking from me, and toward the house. I had dismissed from my bosom all feeling of hostility; for, since the murder of William, it seemed to me that all my old hates and prejudices were feeble. They were all swallowed up and forgotten in that greater sorrow. So completely had this become the case that, though, at leaving him but a week before, I should have only spoken to him in curses, I now spoke to him in kindness. My speech seemed to confound him, no less than his conduct, on hearing it, confounded me. As I have said, he was walking from me in the road leading up to the avenue. He had nearly reached the entrance, and was so completely absorbed in his own thoughts, that the head of my horse provoked none of his attention. I called to him, and I am sure that my voice could not have been made more studiously unoffending.

"Well, John, how are you—how are all?"

"John—John!" he exclaimed, turning round, and staring at me with a face full of unspeakable agitation. "Who's that? what do you mean? what do you want with me? ha!"

"Why, what's the matter with you, John?" I cried; "what frightens you?—don't you know me?"

"Know you? yes, yes—I know you;" and his face and movements both indicated a strong disposition on his part to fly from me, but that his trembling limbs refused to assist him.

"Why do you shrink from me?" I asked, thinking that all his agitation arose from our previous quarrel, and the fear that I was seeking some opportunity of personal collision with him. "Why do you shrink from me, John Hurdis? I am not angry with you now; I do not seek to harm you. Be yourself, brother, for God's sake, and tell me how the old folks are: how's mother?"

He saw me alight from my horse, which I did at this moment, and approach him, without being able to give me any answer.

When, however, I had got alongside of him, he enforced himself to speech, but without replying to my question.

"And what brings you back? How did you—I mean, you have come back safely?"

"Ay, I am safe," was my answer; "but, truth to say, brother John, you do not seem to know exactly what you mean. What! you are still angry about the old business? but you are wrong. It is for me to be angry, if anybody; but I am not angry—I have forgiven you. Tell me, then, are the old people well?"

"They are!" was his only and brief answer; and I got nothing from him but plain yes and no, while we moved along together to the house. He was evidently overcome with astonishment and fear. I knew him to be timid; but, at that time, ignorant as I was then of the history which has been already related, I found it difficult to account for his imbecility. It was easily understood afterward. But even then I looked on him with pity, mixed with scorn, as, shrinking and silent, he moved along beside me. Guilty or not, I would not have had in my bosom such a soul as his for all creation.

CHAPTER XXXVIII.

THE BROKEN HEART.

"Hold! Hold!
Oh, stop that speedy messenger of death,
Oh, let him not run down that narrow path,
Which leads unto thy heart."—SATIRO MASTIX.

MY unexpected return, of course, brought the family together. John Hurdis could not well be absent, and he was a pale and silent listener to my melancholy narrative. The story was soon told, and a dumb horror seized upon all. I saw that he was palsied—that he shivered—that a spasmodic emotion had fastened upon all his limbs, but, even had he not been guilty, such emotion, at such a narrative, would have been natural enough. He rose to leave the room, but staggered in such a manner that he was forced once more to take his seat. My account of the murder had confirmed the story of the emissary. He had a vain, vague hope before, that the clan—the mystic confederacy—was a fable of the stranger, got up for purposes yet unexplained, or, if true, that its purposes and power had been alike exaggerated. The history of my seizure, and of the pursuit of William Carrington, however, was attended with so many circumstances of bold atrocity, that he could deceive himself no longer as to the strength and audacity of the clan. Still, his guilty soul could draw some consolation, even from a fate so dreadful. He breathed with more freedom, when he found that I unhesitatingly ascribed the murder of my friend to the robbers, and had no suspicion in any other quarter. His own common sense sufficiently taught him that such a belief was the most reasonable and natural to one who did not know the truth; and with a consciousness of increased security, from this quarter at least, he did not afflict himself much with the

reflection that he had been the murderer of one unoffending
person, and the cruel destroyer of another's dearest hopes. So
long as he was himself safe, these considerations were of small
importance. And, yet let us not suppose that they did not
trouble him. He had not slept in peace from the moment that
he despatched Pickett on his bloody mission. He was doomed
never to sleep in peace again—no, nor to wake in peace.
Forms of threatening followed his footsteps by day, and images
of terror haunted his dreams by night. He might escape from
human justice, but he soon felt how idle was any hope to escape
from that worst presence of all—the constant consciousness of
crime.

But I must not forget my own troubles in surveying those of
John Hurdis. Of his woes I had no thought at this moment.
My only thought was of that fearful interview with Emmeline.
What would I not have given could I have escaped it. But
such wishes were foolish enough. I had undertaken the task,
regarding it as a solemn duty, as well to the dead as to the
living, and, sooner or later, the task was to be executed. Delay was proof of weakness; and that afternoon I set out for the
house of the poor maiden, widowed ere a wife. During the
solitary ride, I thought in vain of the words which I should use
in telling her the story. How should I break its abruptness—
how soften the severity of the stroke. The more I thought of
this—as is most usually the case in such matters with most
persons—the more difficult and impracticable did the labor seem
and, but for the shame of such a movement, I could have turned
my bridle, and trusted to a letter to do that, which I felt it impossible that my lips should do well. I had seen preachers,
otherwise sagacious enough, undertake to console the afflicted,
by trite maxims which taught them—strangely enough—to
forbear grief for the very reason which makes them grieve—
namely, because their loss is irreparable. "Your tears are
vain," says the bookman. "Therefore I weep," replies the
man. How to avoid such wanton folly was the question with
me, yet it was a question not so easy to answer. The mind
runs upon commonplaces in the matter of human consolation,
and we prate of resignation to the end of the chapter to those
who never hear us. This, of course, assumes the grief to be

sincere. There is a conventional sort of sorrow which is relieved by conventional language; and the heir finds obedience to the will of Providence a very natural lesson. But the love of Emmeline Walker seemed to me a thing all earnestness. I had seen enough of her to know that she could freely have risked life for William Carrington—to tell her that no risk of life could save him now, I felt convinced would almost be at the peril of hers. Yet the irksome labor must be taken—the risk must be met. I had that sort of pride which always sent me forward when the trial appeared a great one; and the very extremity of the necessity, awakened in me an intensity of feeling, which enabled me to effect my object. And I did effect it—how, it will be seen hereafter. Enough, that I shared deeply in the suffering I was unavoidably compelled to inflict.

It was quite dark when I reached her dwelling. My progress toward it had been slow, yet I felt it too fast for my feelings. I entered the house with the desperate haste of one who distrusts his own resolution, and leaps forward in order that it may not leave him. My task was increased in difficulty by the manner in which Emmeline met me. The happy heart, confident in its hope, shone out in her kindling eye, and in the buoyant tones of her voice.

"Ah, Mr. Hurdis, back so soon! I did not look for you for a whole month. What brought you—but why do I ask, when I can guess so readily? Have you seen Mary yet?"

While she spoke, her eyes peered behind me as if seeking for another; and the pleasant and arch smile which accompanied her words, was mingled with a look of fondest expectation I could not answer her—I could not look upon her when I beheld this glance. I went forward to a chair, and sank down within it.

She arose and came hurriedly toward me.

"What is the matter—are you sick, Mr. Hurdis?"

And, though approaching me, her eyes reverted to the entrance as if still seeking another. Involuntarily, I shook my head as if in denial. She saw the movement and seemed to comprehend it. Quick as lightning, she demanded—

"You come alone?—Where's William—where's Mr. Carrington?"

"He did not come with me, Emmeline. He could not."

"Ha! could not—could not! Tell me why he could not
come, Mr. Hurdis. He is sick!—where did you leave him?
He is ill, perhaps—dangerously ill. Tell me—speak, Richard
Hurdis—your looks frighten me."

"They should, Emmeline."

I could not then speak more. My face was averted from
her. Trembling with half-suppressed emotion, she hastened to
confront me. Her **voice** grew thick and hoarse as she **again**
spoke.

"You have come for me, Richard. You have come for **me**
to go to him. He **must** be ill, indeed, when he sends for **me**.
I **will go to** him at once—let us set out instantly. **Where did**
you leave him? Is it far?"

I availed myself **of the** assistance which she thus furnished
me, and replied—

"Near Tuscalocca—a two days' journey."

"Then the less time have we to spare, Richard. Let **us go**
at once. I fear **not to** travel by night—I have done **it** before
But tell me, Mr. Hurdis, what is **his sickness.** From **what does**
he suffer?"

"An accident—a **hurt.**"

"Ha! a hurt—"

"A wound!"

"**God** be merciful—a wound—a wound. Out with it, Rich-
ard Hurdis, and tell me all, if you be a man. I am a woman,
it is true, but I can **bear the** worst, rather **than the doubt**
which apprehends **it.** How came he by a **wound—how was**
he hurt—what accident?"

"He was shot!"

"Shot! shot! **By what**—by **whom?** Tell me, Richard,
dear Richard—his friend—**my** friend—tell me not that he is
hurt dangerously—that he **will recover**—that there are hopes.
Tell me, tell me, if you love me **and** would have me live."

I shook my head mournfully. **Her** hand grasped my arm,
and her gripe though trembling, **was** firm as steel.

"You do not say it—you can not tell me, Richard—that his
wound is mortal. That William—**I can** not think **it—I** dare
not, though you may tell **me so**—that he will **die!**"

"Be calm, awhile, dear Emmeline, and hear me." I answered retreatingly, while I took her hand, with which she still continued to grasp my arm, in my own. She released her hold instantly.

"There! I am calm. I am patient. I listen. Speak now, Richard—fear not for me, but tell me what I must hear, and what, if my apprehensions be true, I shall never be better prepared to hear than now. William Carrington is hurt—by an accident you say. He sends for me. Well—I will go to him —go this instant. But you have not told me that there is hope —that he is not dangerously—not mortally hurt. Tell me that. It is for that I wait."

Wonderful woman! She had recovered her stature—her firmness—her voice—all, in a single instant. And never had she looked so beautiful as now, when her eyes were shining with a fearful light—when doubt and apprehension had imparted to their natural fire, an expression of wildness, such as the moon shows when mocked on her march, by clouds, that flit over her disk, yet leave no impresssion on its surface— when her small and rosy mouth, the lips slightly parted, and occasionally quivering, exhibited the emotion, which she was only able to subdue by assuming one of a higher character, and putting on the aspect of command. Full, finely formed in person, with a carriage in which grace and dignity seemed twins, neither taking precedence of the other, but both harmoniously co-operating, the one to win, the other to sway; she seemed, indeed, intended by nature to command. And she did command. Seeing that I hesitated, she repeated her injunction to me to proceed; but with a voice and words that evidently proved her to have lost some of her most sanguine hopes, by reason of my reluctant and hesiating manner.

"Tell me one thing, only—tell me that I am in time to see him! That he will not be utterly lost—that I may again hear his voice—that he may hear mine—that I may tell him I come to be with him to the last—if need be, to die with him. Say, Richard—say, my brother, for he called you his—say that I will be in time for this."

My answer was spoken almost without my own consciousness, and it seemed as instantaneously, to deprive her of all hers.

" You will *not !*"

With one wild, piercing shriek, she rent the air, while tossing her arms above her head, she rushed out of the room and into the passage. Then I heard a dead, heavy fall; and, rushing after her, I found her prostrate at the foot of the stairs, as utterly lifeless as if a cleaving bolt had been driven through her heart.

CHAPTER XXXIX.

THE MANIAC.

"What! thou hast fled his side in time of danger,
That clung to him in fortune!
Oh! cruel treachery; he had not done thee
So foul a wrong as this. Away, and leave me."—*The Paragon.*

I FOLLOWED her with all haste and raised her from the floor
My cries brought her mother to her assistance—a venerable
and worthy dame, whom years and disease had driven almost
entirely to her chamber. She received her daughter at my
hands in an almost lifeless condition. I assisted in bearing the
poor maiden to her room; and after giving the mother a brief
account of what had taken place—for the circumstances of the
scene would admit of no more—I left her for my father's habitation. I shall not undertake to describe my misery that night.
The thought, that, in my want of resolution, my haste, my imperfect judgment, I had given a death-stroke to the poor heart
that I had seen so paralyzed in a single instant before my eyes,
was little less than horrible to me. It was a constant and stalk-
ing terror in my eyes. In my dreams, I beheld the bloody
body of William Carrington, and the lifeless form of Emmeline
beside it, stretched out in the same damp, cold bed of death.
If I awakened, my active fancy represented a thousand similar
objects—familiar forms lying and gasping in all the agonies of
dissolution, or crouching in terror, as if beneath some sudden
bolt or blow. In all these visions I never lost sight of the
living and real scene of misery through which I had so recently
gone. At first, the smiling, hopeful face of Emmeline rose
before me; and I could distinguish the devoted love in the look
that asked after her betrothed, when her lips refused all question. Then rose the wonder why he came not—then the doubt

—then the **fear**—the terror next; and, lastly, the appalling and thunder-riving blow, which hurled her to the ground in a stupor scarcely less **felt and** freezing **than** was that which **had** stricken down her lover, **and from which** he could **never more** awake. Was it better that she **should awake?** Could the light of returning life, **be** grateful **to her eyes? Impossible!** The heart which had been so suddenly overthrown, **was never** destined to know any other than the consciousness of sorrow. There was no light in life for her. **The eyes** might kindle, and the lips might wear **a** smile, **in after** days, even as the tree which the wanton axe of the woodman **has** wounded, will some-**times** put forth **a** few sickly buds and imperfect branches. But these do not speak **for** life always. The life of **the** soul is wanting—carried off **by** untimely sap. The heart is eaten out and gone, and when **the** tree falls, which it does when the night is at the stillest, men **wonder** of what disease it perished. The natural world **abounds in** similitudes for humanity, which it is our misfortune, **perhaps, too** unfrequently to regard.

The next day, **to my surprise,** I was sent for, by Emmeline. I had not thought **it** possible she should recover in so short a time—she was, it seems, resolved, to hear all the dreadful particulars of my narrative; and strove, with wonderful energy, to listen to them calmly. Her **words** were subdued almost to a whisper, and uttered as if measured by the stopwatch. I could **see** that the tension of her mind was doing her but little good. That she was overtasking herself, and exhausting the hoarded strength of years, to meet the emergency of a moment. I implored her to wait but a day, before she required the intelligence she wished. I pleaded my own mental suffering in excuse; but to this, she simply answered, by touching her head with her finger, and smiling in such **a** sort, as if to rebuke me for arrogating to myself a greater degree of feeling and suffering than was hers. I could not refuse, and yet, I trembled to comply with **her** demand. I shuddered as I thought upon the probable—nay, the almost certain—consequences of evil which must follow to her life, from **the recital.** Her features denoted a latent war in the mind, **which my details, like the spark to** the combustible, I felt sure, must bring **about an explosion no** less terrible than sudden. Her eyes were **bloodshot and dry—**

without a sign of moisture. Had they been wet, I should have been more free to speak. Her cheeks were singularly pale; but in the very centre of her forehead, there was a small spot of livid red—an almost purple spot—that seemed like a warning beacon, fired of a sudden in sign of an approaching danger. I took her hand in mine, as I sat down by the couch on which she lay, and found it cold and dry. There was little, if any, pulse, at that moment. It was not long after, however, when it bounded hotly beneath my finger, like a blazing arrow, sent suddenly from the bended bow.

"And now," she said, "now that I am calm, Richard—I can hear all that you have to say—you need not be afraid to speak to me now, since the worst is known."

"You have heard, then, from your mother?" I asked affirmatively.

"Yes, I have heard all—I have heard that he is —" here she interrupted the sentence by a sudden pause, which was followed by a long parenthesis. "You will now see how strong I have become, when you hear the words that I can calmly speak—know then, that you can tell me nothing worse than I already know. I know that he is dead, to whom I had given myself, and whom—I repeat it to you, Richard, as his friend—and whom, as heaven is my witness, I most truly loved."

"I believe it—I know it, Emmeline; and he knew it too."

"Did he?—are you sure he knew it?" she asked, putting her hand upon my arm, as she spoke these words in a tone of appealing softness. "Ah, Richard, could I know that he felt this conviction to the last—could I have been by to have heard him avow it—to have laid bare my heart before him—to have listened to the last words in which he received and returned my affections! Oh, those last words! those last words! Let me hear them? What were they? It is for this I sent for you to come. It is those words that I would hear! Tell me, then, Richard, and set my heart at rest—give peace to my mind, and relieve me from this anxiety! What said he at the last— what said he?"

"Will it relieve you? I fear not, Emmeline—I fear it would only do you harm to listen to such matters now. You could not bear it now."

"Not bear it! Have I not heard all—have I not borne the worst? What more can you have to say to distress me? I tell you, I know that he is dead! I know that I shall speak to him no more—that I can never hear his voice in answer to mine! For him, I might as well be dumb as he! You see now, that I can speak the words which yesterday you could not speak! What, then, have you to fear? Nothing—nothing! Begin then, Richard—begin, my brother, and tell me the particulars of this cruel story. It will be a consolation, though a sad one, to know the history of the sorrow that afflicts me."

"Sad consolation, indeed, Emmeline, if any, but I will not believe that it can be a consolation now. Some time hence, when you have learned calmly to look upon your loss, and become reconciled to your privation, I doubt not that you will receive a melancholy satisfaction from a knowledge of the truth. But I do not think that it will benefit you now. On the contrary, I fear that it will do you infinite harm. You are not well—there is a flushed spot upon your brow which shows your blood to be in commotion; to-morrow, perhaps—"

"No to-morrow, Richard! all days are alike to me now! I am already in the morrow—the present is not mine—I live in the past, or in the future, or I live not at all! Let me, then, hear from you now—let me know all at once—now, while the cup is at the fullest, let me drink to the bottom, and not take successive and hourly draughts of the same bitter potion! I must hear it from you now, Richard, without delay or evasion, or, I tell you, I can not sleep again! If I do, it will only be to dream a thousand things, and conjure up a thousand fancies, much more terrible than any you can bring me now! Come, then! why should you fear to tell me, when I already know the worst? I know that he perished by the sudden stroke of the murderer, having no time given him for prayer and preparation! Can your story tell me worse than this? No, no! you have no words of darker meaning in my ears, than those which my own lips have spoken!"

"Emmeline, dear Emmiline, let me have time for this. Let me put it off for a while. Already the blood is rising impetuously in your veins. Your pulse beneath my finger is shooting wildly—"

"I am calm—you mistake, dear Richard—you are no doctor, clearly. I was never more calm—never more composed in all my life. My pulse, indeed!"

The impatient and irritable manner of this speech, was its sufficient refutation. I replied—

"Your will is calm and resolute, Emmeline; I doubt not your strength of mind and purpose; but I doubt your command of nerve, Emmeline, and your blood. You are very feverish."

She interrupted me almost petulantly.

"You are only too considerate, Richard. Perhaps, had you been half so considerate, when a fellow-traveller with the man you called your friend, and who certainly was yours, he had not perished!"

"Emmeline!"

"Ay! I speak what I think, Richard—what I feel! You are a grave physician when with me. You talk sagely and shake your head. But with him—with William Carrington! —were you grave, and wise, and considerate? You persuaded him to this journey; you knew that he was hasty and thoughtless; did you shake your head in warning, and lift your finger when you saw him running wide from prudence—from safety?"

"Emmeline, my child," exclaimed the mother, "you are unkind—you do Richard injustice!"

"Let him show me that I do him injustice, mother. That is what I wish him, and pray him, to do. I do not desire to do him injustice." Her tone and manner, which were almost violent before, now changed even into softness here; and, turning to me, she continued: "You know I do not wish to do you injustice; but why will you not oblige me? Why not tell me what I claim to know—what I have a right to know?"

I could see that the blood was mounting in torrents to her brain. Her pulse was momently quickening; and the little speck of red, so small and unimposing at first, had overspread her face, even as the little cloud, that dots the western heavens at morning, spreads by noon until it covers with storm and thunder the whole bosom of the earth. It was more than ever my policy to withhold a narrative so full of details, which, though they could unfold no circumstance worse in substance

than that which she already knew, were yet almost certain to
harrow up her feelings by the gradual accumulation of events
before her imagination, to a pitch almost unendurable. I resorted to every argument, plea, suggestion—everything which
might move her to forego her wish—at least, for the present.
But my efforts were unavailing.

"You entirely mistake me," she would say, "I am earnest—
not excited. My earnestness always shows itself in this manner. I assure you that my blood is quite as temperate as it
would be under the most ordinary affliction."

And this she said in words that were uttered with spasmodic
effort. Her mother called me aside for a moment.

"You will have to tell her," she said; "the very opposition
to her desire makes her worse. Tell her all, Richard, as she
demands it, and God send, that it be for the best!"

Thinking it probable that such might be the case, though
still reluctant, I waived my objections, and determined to comply. When I resumed my seat by the bedside, and avowed
this determination, as if to confirm the words of the mother, a
sudden change came over her. Her respiration, which had
been impeded and violent before, became easier; and, closing
her eyes, she leaned back upon the pillow, from which, during
the greater part of the previous conference, her head had been
uplifted, and thus prepared herself to listen. It was a strong
effort which she made to be, or seem, composed, and it was
only successful for a time. My confidence in it soon began to
waver, as I found, when fairly in my narrative, that her eyes
were re-opened, and with a fearful resumption of light—her
head once more raised from the pillow—and her unconscious
hand, when I reached that part of my narrative which detailed
the first assault upon us at the hovel of Webber, suddenly ex
tended and grasping my arm which lay on the bed beside her

"Stop—stop awhile—a moment—I am not ready yet to hear
you—not yet—not yet!"

I paused at her direction, and she sank back upon the pillow,
and closed her eyes with a rigid pressure of her fingers upon
their lids, as if to shut out from sight some horrible vision. In
this state she remained for a space of several seconds; and I
could perceive, when she resumed her attitude of attention.

and bade me proceed with my narrative, that though she might have succeeded in expelling the phantom from her sight, the very effort requisite in doing so, had accelerated the action of her blood. I proceeded, however, striving to avoid every word, phrase, or unnecessary incident, which might have the effect of increasing the vividness of an event, already too terribly impressive; but with all my caution I could perceive the constant flow and gathering of excitement in her brain. Her words became thick, yet more frequent. She started constantly from the pillow, to which she as constantly and immediately sank back, as if conscious of departing from the tacit pledge which she had given me, but which I had never relied on, to be calm and collected while I spoke. At length, when I told of the flight of Carrington, of his pursuit by the ruffians, of the long interval, in which, bound to the floor, I lay at their mercy, and after they had gone, before the arrival of Grafton to my relief; and how I looked for my friend in vain among those who rescued me; her emotion grew utterly beyond constraint, and she cried out aloud, and gasped with such effort between her cries, that I dreaded lest suffocation should follow from her fruitless endeavors at speech. But she contrived to speak.

"Yes! yes! they came—they loosed you—they set you free —but what did they for him—what did you, who called yourself his friend? What did you for him, who was yours? Tell me that—that!"

These were words of madness—certainly there was madness in the wild and roving expression of her fire-darting eye. I would even then have paused, if I could; but she would not suffer it. Resuming a look of calmness—such a look as mocked itself by its inadequacy to effect her object—when she saw me hesitate, she begged me to continue.

"I am calm again, Richard—it was for a moment only. Forgive me, I pray you, Richard—forgive me, and go on. Let me hear the rest. I will not cry out again."

I hastened to close the painful narrative, but she did not hear me to the end. She was no longer capable of knowing what she did or said; but leaping from the couch, in defiance of all my own and her mother's efforts—short of absolute violence—to restrain her, she strode across the chamber, as if with a leading purpose in view. Then, suddenly turning, she confronted me, with a face in which, if a face might ever be said to blaze with fire, and yet maintain its natural expression. hers did. She gazed on me for a few seconds with all the intensity of an expression which was neither hate nor anger, but blind ferocity, and destructive judgment; and then she spoke, in accents which would have been bitter enough to my heart, had I not well enough understood the maddening bitterness in hers.

"And so he was murdered—and you led him on this expedition to be murdered! You were his friend—and while they pursued him for the accursed money—you lay quietly—without effort—having bonds, which a child—a woman—which I—weak and feeble as I am—which I would have broken at such a time—which you might have broken, had you been warmed with a proper spirit to help your friend! And he thought you a brave man, too—he told me you were so, and I believed it—I gave him in charge to you, and you suffered your villains to murder him! Tell me nothing, I say, Richard Hurdis—they were your villains, else how should you, a brave man, submit, as you did, to be bound and laughed at, while he could break from his bonds and escape from the very snare to which you so tamely submitted! I will not hear you—they were your villains—else how should you, a brave man, submit and do nothing! Would he—would William have submitted thus? Would he have left his friend to perish?—or, if he could not save his life, would he have come sneaking home with the tidings of his friend's murder and his own base cowardice? No, Richard Hurdis!—I tell you—I answer for the dead—he would have pursued these murderers to the ends of the earth! He would have dragged them to justice, or slain them with his own hands! He never would have slept in his bed till he had taken this vengeance! Day and night would have been to him the same! Day and night, he had pursued them—through the forests—through the swamps, in all haunts, in all disguises, till he had revenged the murder of his friend—till, for the holy blood of friendship, he had drained the hearts of all having any hand in his murder! But you—what have you done? Ha! ha! ha! Bravely—bravely, Richard Hurdis! William thought you had courage—he did—and he relied on it! He relied too much. You have shed no blood, though he is murdered! You have neither shed the blood of his murderers, nor your own! Show me a finger-scratch, if you can! You are—ha! ha! ha! this is courage, is it?—and he thought you brave! Well, the wisest may be mistaken—the wisest—the very wisest!"

She went on much further, but her ravings grew incoherent, and at length, from imperfect thoughts, her strength being nigh exhausted, she only articulated in broken words and sentences. On a sudden, she stopped; her eye grew fixed while gazing upon me, and her lower jaw became paralyzed, ere the halting word was uttered. I saw that a crisis was at hand, and rushed toward her at the fortunate moment. I caught her as she fell; and she lay paralyzed and senseless, like the very marble, in my arms.

CHAPTER XL.

DEATH!

"Are they both dead?   I did not think
To find thee in this pale society
Of ghosts so soon!"— *The Brothers*

THOUGH little of a physician, I yet saw that something must
be done for her relief instantly, in this almost complete suspen-
sion of her powers, or she must perish; and procuring a lancet,
which was fortunately in the house, made an opening in one of
her arms.   The results were hardly satisfactory.   A few drops
of jellied and almost black blood oozed from the opening, and
had no visible effect upon her situation.   I opened a vein in
the other arm, but with little better success.   Warm fomenta-
tation and friction were next resorted to, but to no advantage;
and, leaving the patient to the charge of the mother, I mounted
my horse, and rode with all speed to the nearest physician—a
man named Hodges, an ignorant, stupid fellow, but the best
which at this time our neighborhood could afford.   He was one
of those accommodating asses who have the one merit at least,
if they are fools in all other respects, of being an unpretending
one; and gladly, at all times, would he prefer taking the opinion
of another to the task of making, or the responsibility of giving,
one of his own.   I have heard him ask an old lady if she had
jalap and calomel in the house; and when she replied that she
had not, but she "had some cream of tartar," answer, "That
will do, ma'am," and give the one medicine in lieu of the other.
There was little to be looked for at the hands of such a creature; but what were we to do?   I had already exhausted all

Dr. Hodges came, and did nothing. He reopened the veins without advantage, repeated the warm-water fomentations, took an extra chew of tobacco, shook his empty head, and remained silent. I ventured a suggestion, of the merits of which I had only a partial guess.

"Would not a blister to the head help her, doctor?"

"I think it would, Mr. Hurdis—I think you had better try it."

Cursing the oaf in the bitterness of my heart, I went to work, with the help of the old lady, and we prepared a blister. When it was ready, we proceeded to cut away the voluminous masses of her raven hair, the glistening loveliness of which we could not but admire, even while we consigned it to destruction. But we were not suffered to proceed in this work. Ere the scissors had swept away one shred, the unhappy maiden awakened from her stupor; but she awakened not to any mental consciousness. She was mad—raving mad; and with the strength of madness she rushed from the couch where she was lying, and flew at her mother like a tigress. I was fortunately nigh enough to interfere, and save the old lady from her assaults, or the effects might have been seriously hurtful. I clasped her in my arms, and held her, though with some difficulty. Her strength was prodigious under the terrible excitement which raged in her bosom; and, though rather a strong man, I found that I dared not relax for a single instant in my hold, or she became free. Yet she complained not that I held her. She uttered no word whatsoever. She knew nothing; she spoke to none. Sometimes a slight moaning sound escaped her lips, but she had no other form of language. Her eyes were fixed and fiery; yet they never seemed to look upon any one of us. I observed that they seemed instinctively to avoid the light, and that they shone with a less angry lustre when turned toward the darker sections of the apartment, and from the windows. Seeing this, I directed the mother to double her curtains, and exclude as much of the light as possible: this done, it seemed to relieve the intensity of her stare and action. But she was as little disposed to be quiet as before. The moment I yielded in my grasp, that moment did she make new exertions to escape; and when she failed in her object, that same slight moaning, per-

haps, once or twice repeated, was all the acknowledgment given
by her lips to the annoyance which the constraint evidently
put upon her.

In the meantime, what a terrible loveliness shone in her
countenance and form! The pythoness, swelling with the voluminous fires of the god, were but a poor comparison to the
divinity of desolation, such as she appeared at that moment to
my eyes. Her long, black tresses, which we had let loose in
order to cut, were thrown all around her own neck, and partially over my shoulders as I held her. Her eyes were shooting out from their spheres — the whites barely perceptible, as
the dilating orbs seemed to occupy entirely the dry and fiery
cells from which they yet threatened momently to dart. Purple lines and blotches gleamed out upon and as suddenly disappeared from her face — the consequence, probably, of her restraint, and the violent exertions which she made to get herself
free from it; and her teeth and lips were set as resolutely as if
death's last spasm had been already undergone. If they had
opened at all, it was only when she uttered that heart-piercing
moan — so faint, so low, yet so thrilling, that it seemed to indicate at every utterance the breaking of some vital string.

In this way she continued full two hours, without intermitting
her struggles. My arms had grown weary of the rigid grasp
which I had been compelled to keep upon her, and sheer exhaustion must have soon compelled me to relax my hold. But
by this time she, too, had become exhausted; her efforts grew
fainter, though the insane direction of her mind was not a whit
changed. Gradually, I felt her weight increase upon me, and
her own exertions almost entirely cease; and I thought at
length that I might safely return her to the couch. It was with
some difficulty that I did so, for her poor mother — miserable
and infirm, not to say terrified — could give me no help; and
the doctor, no less terrified than she, had hurried off, on the first
exhibition of the maiden's fury, to procure her, as he promised,
some medicine which was to be potential for everything. But
the doctor knew not the disease of his patient. With all his
"parmaceti" he could do nothing for that 'inward bruise"
which was mortifying at her heart.

When fairly placed in the bed, I found it still somewhat dif ficult to keep her there; and, in order to avoid giving her pain, which the grasp of my hand might do, I contrived to fold the bedclothes in such a manner about her as not only to retard her movements, but to enable us, by sitting upon either side, to keep her down. An old negro-servant was called in to assist in this duty, and with the mother's aid I was partially relieved. With a few struggles more, her eyes gradually closed, and her limbs seemed to relax in sleep. An occasional moan from her lips alone told us that she suffered still; and a sudden opening and flashing of her eye at other moments still served to convince us that her show of sleep was deceptive. She slept not, and we were compelled to be watchful still.

While she remained in this situation, our doctor returned, to my great surprise, bringing with him a score of bottles, with one nostrum or another. He seemed a little more confident now in what he should do, having most probably, during his absence, consulted some book of authority in the circle of his limited reading. Thus prepared, he compounded a dose from some two or three bottles, one of which, asafœtida, soon declared its quality to our nostrils, and left no hope to Dr. Hodges of making a medical mystery — a practice so common among small practitioners — of the agent by which he was to work the salvation of the patient. I had no great hope of the potion which he brought, for I had no great faith in the doctor; but I readily took the wineglass in which he compounded it, and addressed myself to the arduous task of forcing it down the throat of the poor sufferer. It was an arduous task indeed! Her teeth were riveted together, and she seemed to have just sense enough to close them more tenaciously in defiance to our prayer that she might open them. Here was a difficulty; but, as Hodges insisted upon the vital importance of the dose, cruel as the operation seemed, I determined to do all that I could to make her take it. In our efforts we were at length forced to pry her teeth apart with our fingers, and to force the glass between them. It was an error to have used the wineglass in such a situation; and the reflection of a single instant would have taught us to transfer the medicine to a spoon. We were taught this lesson by an incident of startling terror; for no sooner had we put the edge of the glass between her divided teeth, than they closed upon it, crunching it into the minutest fragments. Fortunately, I was prompt enough to prevent the worst consequences of this act. I dropped the fragment of the glass which remained in my hands, and grasped her instantly by the throat. I grasped her almost as tightly as I should have done a mortal foe. It was a desperate resort for a desperate situation. I nearly strangled her, but it was the only thing that could have saved her from swallowing the broken particles. With my fingers, while the jaws were stretched apart, I drew out the bits of glass, which were numerous, though not without cutting her mouth and gums in a shocking manner. The blood ran from her mouth, and over the side of her pallid face, staining its purity; and her tongue, bleeding also the while, hung over the lips. And yet she seemed to feel none of the pain: no cry escaped her; no struggle was made; and the occasional moan which now and then continued to escape her was the acknowledgment of a greater agony than any for which we labored to provide remedies.

Dr. Hodges persevered in his physic, but we might as well have spared the poor girl the pain of forcing it down her throat, for it did no good. Her madness, it is true, was no longer hysterical; but this change was probably quite as much the result of exhaustion as of the medicine we gave her. She seemed conscious of none of our labors; yet she studiously kept her eyes from the spectator, and fixed them upon the darkest part of the wall of her chamber. Her grief was speechless in all other respects; she seemed not to hear, and she answered none of our inquiries. In hope to arouse and provoke her consciousness, I even ventured to speak to her of her lover, and the cruel fate which had befallen him. I named to her the bitter words of death which I had shrunk before to utter. But the ear seemed utterly obtuse. She moved neither limb nor muscle, and the stupor of complete mental indifference was gradually overcoming all her faculties. Thus she continued throughout that day.

Night came on, and yet there was no change. It was a dismal night to me. I sat up with her and watched her with a degree of nervous irritation and anxiety which led me to fear, at moments, that I might fall into some condition of insanity like that I witnessed. The poor old mother strove to sleep, but she could not subdue the nature within her; and that raised her every moment to look into the face of her child, whose unconscious eyes were yet bright and unblessed by sleep. Besides these, there were no interruptions to the general silence of the night, unless that slight and now scarcely sensible moan, which continued at intervals to escape the lips of the sufferer, might be called one. Day dawned upon us, and found her still in the same condition. We gave her the prescribed physic; but I felt, while pouring it down her throat, that our labors were as cruel as they were idle. We administered the little nourishment which she took, in the same manner, by violence. She craved nothing — she asked for nothing; and what we gave her brought no nourishment in consequence.

The day and night passed in the same manner with the preceding. I snatched a few hours' sleep during the day, and this enabled me again to sit up with her the night following. But there were other watchers besides myself around her bed; and, amid all my agonizing thought of the terrible picture of affliction present in my eyes, there were other thoughts and feelings of a far different character mingling among them and operating upon my mind. Mary Easterby sat by the bedside of the invalid, and our eyes and hands met more than once during the night, which to me, though not less painful, was far less wearisome, than that which I had passed before. Such is the nature of man. We foster our petty affections even at the grave of our friend's sweetest hopes. Our plans and promises for self desert us nowhere; they mingle in with our holiest emotions; they pile the dust of earth upon the very altars of heaven! Perhaps it is only right that such should be the case. Our nature while on earth must be, to a certain extent, earthy. It may be, too, that our pride undergoes some restraint when it discovers that base necessities and narrow aims clog the loftiest wing, and dazzle the most eagle-eyed of the soaring spirits among men.

But why linger upon a painful narrative like this? why record throbs and agonies? I will hasten to a conclusion which the reader may readily anticipate. Emmeline Walker died. In three days more she was silent for ever! Her hopes, her fears, her pangs — all were silent, all buried. Five days did she live in this state of suspended consciousness—taking no nourishment save that which we poured down her throat by main force; and every added hour proved her less able to oppose us in our labors of doubtful kindness. She sank just after that last paroxysm in which she crushed the brittle glass between her teeth. Our man of art had exhausted his slender resources of skill, and, with a modesty that did not shake a confident head of power to the last moment, he soon declared his inability to help her more. But we needed not his words to give us painful assurance to this effect. We saw it with our own eyes, while looking into the fast-glazing orbs of hers. We knew, from every symptom, that she must die. Perhaps it was as well— what should she live for?

It was on the sixth day after her attack, when her powers had been so far exhausted that it became somewhat doubtful at moments whether she breathed or not—and when, up to that time, she had given no sort of heed to any of the circumstances going on around her—that she suddenly started, as if out of a deep sleep, and turned her sad but still bright eyes, now full of divine intelligence, upon me. There was "speculation" in their orbs once more. The consecrating mind had returned to its dwelling, though it were only to set all in order, and then dispose of it for ever. I bent forward as I saw the glance which she gave me, and breathlessly asked her how she felt.

"Quite well," she answered, in a scarcely-perceptible whisper—"quite well, Richard; but it is so dark! Do put aside that curtain, if you please. Mother has shut everything up. I don't know whether it's daylight or not."

I rose and put aside the curtain; and the waiting sunlight— the broken but bright beams that he sprinkled through the leaves—came gliding into the chamber. Her eyes brightened, as if with a natural sympathy, when she beheld them She made an effort to raise herself in the bed, but sunk back with an expression of pain, which slightly impressed itself upon her countenance, even as a breath passes over the mirror, giving a momentary stain to its purity. It was one breath of the approaching tyrant—to her the consoler. Seeing that she desired to be raised, I lifted and sustained her head upon my bosom. Her mother asked her if she felt better.

"Well, quite well," was her answer. A minute did not elapse after that, when I felt a slight shiver pass over her frame, which then remained motionless. Her breathing was suspended. I let her head sink back gradually upon the pillow, and, looking in her face, I saw that her pure yet troubled spirit had departed for ever. My watching was ended.

CHAPTER XLI.

LOVE AND REVENGE.

"I shall find time;
When you have took some comfort, I'll begin
To mourn his death and scourge the murderer."

T. HEYWOOD, 1655.

THE ending and beginning I had seen—the whole of this catastrophe. We buried the poor maiden in a grove near the dwelling in which her feet had often rambled with him whose grave should have been beside her. There was nothing more for me to do—there was no reason why I should linger in Marengo; and I resolved once more to leave it. - As yet, my error remained uncorrected in regard to Mary Easterby. I still deemed her the affianced wife of John Hurdis; and—sometimes wondering why he came not with her to the dwelling of Emmeline Walker, and sometimes doubting their alliance, from little signs and circumstances, which now and then occurred to my observation,—I was still impressed with the conviction that there was no more hope for me. I escorted her home after the burial of Emmeline, and sad and sweet was our conference by the way. We rode together, side by side on horseback, and we soon left the animals to their own motion, which was gratefully sluggish to me. I will not say whether I thought it so to her, but, at least, she gave no symptoms of impatience, nor made any effort to accelerate the movements of her steed. It will not, perhaps, be assuming too much, to suppose that, in some large respects, our thoughts and feelings ran together in satisfied companionship. We were both deeply affected and subdued by the cruel events to which we had been witnesses. There was a dreadful warning to hope, and love, and youth, in the sad history which has been written, and which we were forced to read in every stage of its performance. Never could morality teach more terribly to youth its own uncertainties, and the mutations hanging around that deity whose altar of love it is most apt to seek in worship. How evanescent to our eyes seemed then all our images of delight. The sunlight, which was bright and beautiful around us—making a " bridal of earth and sky,"—we looked upon with doubt and apprehension as a delusion which must only woo to vanish. We spoke together of these things; and what, it may be asked, was the conclusion of all this sombrous reflection? Did it make either of us forswear the world and hope? Did it make either of us more doubtful and desponding than before? No! Its effects were softening and subduing, not overthrowing—not destructive of any of those altars, to which love brings wreaths that wither, and offers vows that are rejected or forgotten. We lost not one hope or dream of youth. We gave freedom to none of our anticipations. Even the lessons taught us by the death of those who, loving in life so fondly, in death were not divided, were lessons of love. The odor of the sacrifice made amends for the consumption by fire of the rich offerings which were upon the altar; and love lost none of his loveliness either in her eyes or mine, because, in this instance, as in a thousand others, it had failed to rescue its votaries from the grasp of a more certain, if not a greater power. The lesson which was taught us by the fate of Emmeline Walker, made us esteem still more highly the sacred influence, which could consecrate so sweet and pure a spirit to immortality, and lead it, without struggle or reluctance, into the brazen jaws of death. What a triumph to youth, to fancy, to reflection, was the thought which portrayed a power so wonderful—so valuable to those who more than love already.

"I will see you before I leave Marengo, Mary," was my promise on leaving her that evening.

"What! you mean to leave us, again, Richard?" was her involuntary and very earnest demand. "Oh! do not, Richard —wherefore would you go? Why would you encounter such cruel risks as befell poor William? Stay with us —leave us not again."

With an utterance and movement, equally involuntary, I took her hand and replied:—

"And would you have me stay, Mary? **Wherefore? What
reward can you give?** what is there now in **your power to give**
that could bribe me **to compliance?"**

I paused just at the time when I should have spoken freely.
To what I had **said, she could make no** answer; yet **she** had
her answer ready to what **I might have said.** But I said nothing, and she made no reply. **Yet, could I have** seen it!—had
I not been still the blind and **besotted slave** and victim **to** my
own jaundicing and jealous apprehensions, the blush upon her
cheek, the tremor upon her lip, **the downcast** and shaded eye,
the faltering accent—all these **would have conveyed an** answer, which might have made me happy **then. And yet these**
persuasive signs **did not** utterly **escape my sight. I felt them,**
and wondered at them—and was almost tempted, in the new
warmth of heart which **they brought me, to declare my** affections, **but for the thought that it would be unseemly to** do so,
at a moment **when we had just** left the chamber of death, and
beheld the last **gleam of life pass** from the eyes of loveliness
and youth. **Fool that I was, as if love** did not plant his roses
even on the grave of his worshipper, **and find his most** flourish-
ing soil in the heart **of the beloved one.**

That night my mother **drew me aside, and asked me** with
some significance, what had **passed between Mary and** myself.

"Nothing."

"**What! have you not spoken?"**

"**Of what?"**

"**Of your love!—"**

"**No!** Why should you think it, mother? **What reason?**
Is she not engaged to John? is that matter **broken off?"**

"I think it is—he has not been to see her for a week."

"Indeed!"

"**And have you not** seen, my son, how sad she looks? she
has looked so ever since you went away."

"That may **be** only because **he has** not been to see her,
mother; or, it may be, **because of the** affliction which she has
been compelled to witness."

"Well, Richard, **I won't say that it is not,** and yet, my son,
I'm somehow inclined **to think that you could** have her for the
asking."

"Do you think so, mother, and yet—even if it were so mother, I would not ask. The woman who has once accepted the hand of John Hurdis, though she afterward rejects him, is not the woman for me."

"But, Richard, I'm not so sure now, that she ever did accept him. There was that poor woman, Mrs. Pickett, only a few days ago came here, and she took particular pains to let me know that Mary and John were never half so near together, to use her own words, as Mary and yourself."

"How could she know anything about it?" was my reply.

"Well, I don't know; but I can tell you, she's a very knowing woman —"

"She would scarcely be the confidant of Mary, nevertheless."

"But you will see Mary, Richard—you will try?"

"If I thought, mother, that she and John had never been engaged—if I knew that. But I will see her."

The promise satisfied both my mother and myself for the time; and I now gave myself up to reflection in solitude, as a new task had been forced upon me, by the circumstances of the few past days. I had suffered more in mind from beholding the misery and madness of Emmeline Walker, than it would be manly to avow; and there was one portion of this tragedy which more than any other, impressed itself upon me. I was haunted by the continual presence of the lovely maniac, as she appeared at the moment when she denounced me as deserting my friend, exposing and leaving him to peril, and finally, suffering his murder to go unavenged. The more I thought upon this last passage of her angry speech, the more impressively did it take the shape of moral requisition. I strove seriously to examine it as a question of duty, whether I was bound to go upon this errand of retribution or not, and the answers of my mind were invariably and inevitably the same. 'Shall the murderer go unpunished—shall so heinous a crime remain unavenged? Are there no claims of friendship—of manhood upon you? The blood of the innocent calls upon you. The indignities which you yourself have undergone—these call upon you. But a louder call upon you than all, is the demand of Society. She calls upon you to ferret out these lurkers upon the highway—to bring them to justice that the innocent travel-

ler may not be shot down from the thicket, in the sunshine, in
the warm morning of youth, and hope, and confidence. True
—the laws of man do not summon you forth on this mission;
but is there no stronger voice in your heart inciting you to the
sacred work? The brave man waits not for his country's summons to take the field against the foreign enemy—shall he need
her call when his friend is slain almost by his side; and when
sworn foes to friendship, and truth, and love, and all the social
virtues, lurk in bands around their several homes to prey upon
them as they unconsciously come forth? Can you doubt that it
is your duty to seek and exterminate these wretches? You say
that is the duty of others no less than of yourself; but does
the neglect of others to perform their duties, render yours
unnecessary or release you? On the contrary, does it not
make it more incumbent upon you to do more than would be
your duty under other circumstances, and to supply, as much as
lies in your power, their deficiencies?' Such was the reasoning
of my own mind on this subject; and it forced conviction upon
me. In the woods where I had meditated the matter, I made
my vow to the avenging deities.

"I will seek the murderers, so help me Heaven! I wil
suffer not one of them to escape, if it be within the scope of
my capacity and arm, to bring them to justice." And, ever
upon the ground where I had made this resolution, I kneeled
and prayed for the requisite strength and encouragement from
Heaven in the execution of my desperate vow.

This resolution induced another, and endued me with a courage
which before I had not felt. Conceiving myself a destined man,
I overleaped, at a moment, all the little boundaries of false delicacy, morbid sensibility, and mere custom, which before, had,
perhaps, somewhat taken from my natural hue of resolution—
and the next day I rode over to the house of Mary Easterby.
A complete change by this time had taken place in my feelings
in one respect. I was no longer apprehensive of what I said
in speaking to Mary. I now proceeded as if in compliance
with a prescribed law; and asking her to walk with me, I led
her directly to the favorite walk which, in our childhood, our
own feet chiefly had beaten out in the forests. I conducted her
lmost in silence to the huge fallen tree which had formed the

boundary of our previous rambles, and seated her upon it, and myself beside her, as I had done a thousand times before.

"And now, Mary," I said, taking her hand, "I have a serious question to ask you, and beg that you will answer it with the same unhesitating directness with which I ask it. Your answer will nearly affect my future happiness."

I paused, but she was silent — evidently through emotion — and I continued thus :—

"You know me too well to suppose that I would say or do anything to offend you, and certainly you will believe me when I assure you that it is no idle curiosity which prompts me to ask the question which I will now propose."

A slight pressure of her fingers upon my wrist, her hand being clasped the while in mine, was my sufficient and encouraging answer, and I then boldly asked if she was or had been engaged to John Hurdis? Her answer, as the reader must anticpate, was unequivocally in the negative. In the next moment she was in my arms — she was mine! Then followed explanations which did away, as by a breath, with a hundred little circumstances of my own jaundiced judgment, and of my brother's evil instigation, which for months I had looked upon as insuperable barriers. For the part which John Hurdis had in raising them, I was at that moment quite too happy not to forgive him. I now proceeded to tell Mary of my contemplated journey, but not of its objects. This I kept from the knowledge of all around me, for its successful prosecution, I had already well conceived, could only result from the secrecy with which I pursued it. Nor did I suffer her to know the direction of country in which I proposed to travel; this caution was due to my general plan, and called for, at the same time, by her natural apprehensions, which would have been greatly alarmed to know that I was about to go into a region where my friend had been so inhumanly murdered. I need not say that she urged every argument to keep me in Marengo. She pleaded her own attachment, which, having once avowed, she now delighted in; and urged every consideration which might be supposed available among the thoughts of a young maiden unwilling to let her lover go. But my resolve had been too seriously and solemnly taken. "I had an oath in heaven !" and no ties, even such, so dear ones, as those which I had just formed, could make me desire escape from it if I could. She was compelled to yield the contest, since I assured her that my resolution was no less imperative than my engagements; but I promised to return soon, and our marriage was finally arranged for that period. What an hour of bliss was that, in those deep groves, under that prevailing silence! What an Elysium had suddenly grown up around me! How potent was the magician which could make us forget the graves upon which we stood, and the blood still flowing around us, dreaming only of those raptures which, in the fortunes of two other fond creatures like ourselves, had so suddenly been defeated! In that hour, I thought not of the dangers I was about to undergo, and she — the dear girl hanging on my bosom, and shedding tears of pleasure — she seemed to forget that earth ever contained a tomb!

Next morning, after we had taken breakfast, I strolled down the avenue to the entrance, and was suddenly accosted by a man whom I had never seen before. He rode up with an air of confidence, and asked me if I was Mr. Hurdis — Mr. John Hurdis? I replied in the negative, but offered to show him the way to the house, where he would find the person whom he sought. We met John coming forth.

"That is your man, sir," said I to the stranger. He thanked me, and instantly advanced to my brother. I could not help being a spectator, for I was compelled to pass them in order to enter the house; and my attention was doubly fixed by the singular manner in which the stranger offered John Hurdis his hand. The manner of the thing seemed also to provoke the astonishment of John, himself, who looked at me with surprise amounting to consternation. I was almost disposed to laugh out at the idiot stare with which he transferred his gaze from me to the stranger, and to me again, for the expression seemed absolutely ludicrous; but I was on terms of too much civility with my brother to exhibit any such unnecessary familiarity; and, passing into the house, I left the two together. Their business seemed of a private nature, for they went into the neighboring woods to finish it; and John Hurdis did not return from the interview, until I had set forth a second time on my travels. The meaning of this conference, and the cause of that singular approach of the stranger, which awakened so much seeming astonishment in the face of John Hurdis, will be sufficiently explained hereafter. Little did I then imagine the nature of that business which I had undertaken, and of the mysterious developments of crime to which my inquiries would lead me.

CHAPTER XLII.

DESPAIR OF THE VICTIMS.

"**What!** thou dost quit me then—
In the first blush of my necessity,
The danger yet at distance."—*Captive.*

IT was, perhaps, an earnest of success in the pursuit which I had undertaken, that I did not underrate, to myself, its many difficulties. I felt that I would have to contend with experienced cunning and probably superior strength—that nothing but the utmost adroitness and self-control could possibly enable me to effect my purposes. My first object was to alter my personal appearance, so as to defeat all chance of recognition by any of the villains with whom I had previously come in collision. This was a work calling for much careful consideration. To go down to Mobile, change my clothes, and adopt such fashions as would more completely disguise me, were my immediate designs; and I pushed my way to this, my first post, with all speed, and without any interruption. My first care, in Mobile, was to sell my horse, which I did, for one hundred and eighty dollars. I had now nearly five hundred dollars in possession—a small part in silver, the rest in United States bank, Alabama, and Louisiana notes, all of which were equally current. I soon procured a couple of entire suits, as utterly different from anything I had previously worn as possible. Then, having a proper regard to the usual decoration of the professed gamblers of our country, I entered a jeweller's establishment, and bought sundry bunches of seals, a tawdry watch, a huge chain of doubtful, but sold as virgin, gold; and some breast-pins and shirt-buttons of saucer size. To those who had personally known me before, I was well assured that no disguise would have been more perfect than that afforded by these trinkets; but, when, in addition to these and the other changes in my habit, of which I have spoken, I state that my beard was suffered to grow goat-like, after the most approved models of dandyism, under the chin, in curling masses, and my whiskers, in rival magnificence, were permitted to overrun my cheeks — I trust that I shall be believed, when I aver that after a few weeks space, I scarcely knew myself. I had usually been rather fastidious in keeping a smooth cheek and chin, and I doubt very much, whether my own father ever beheld a two days' beard upon me, from the day that I found myself man enough to shave at all, to the present. The more I contemplated my own appearance, the more sanguine I became of success; and I lingered in Mobile a little time longer, in order to give beard and whiskers a fair opportunity to overrun a territory which before had never shown its stubble. When this time was elapsed, my visage was quite Siberian; a thick cap of otter-skin, which I now procured, fully completed my northern disguises, and, exchanging my pistols at a hardware establishment, for others not so good, but for which I had to give some considerable boot, I felt myself fairly ready for my perilous adventure. It called for some resolution to go forward when the time came for my departure, and when I thought of the dangers before me; but, when, in the next instant, I thought of the murder of my friend, and of the sad fate of his betrothed, my resolution of vengeance was renewed. I felt that I had an oath in Heaven — sworn — registered; — and I repeated it on earth!

Let me now return, for an instant, to the condition of my worthy brother, and relate some passages, in their proper place in this narrative, which, however, did not come to my knowledge for some time after. The reader will remember my meeting with the stranger at the entrance of the avenue leading to my father's house, who asked for John Hurdis, and to whom I introduced him. It will also be remembered that I remarked the surprise, nay almost consternation, which his appearance and address seemed to produce in my brother's countenance. There was a reason for all this, though I dreamed not of it then. John Hurdis had good cause for the terrors, which, at that time, I found rather ludicrous, and was almost disposed to laugh at. They went together into the woods, and, as I left the plantation for Mobile, an hour after, I saw no more of either of them on that occasion. The business of the stranger may best be told in John Hurdis's own words. That very afternoon he went to the cottage of Pickett, whom he summoned forth, as was his custom, by a signal agreed upon between them. When together, in a voice of great agitation, John began the dialogue as follows:—

"I am ruined, Pickett—ruined, undone for ever! Who do you think has come to me—presented himself at the very house, and demanded to see me?"

Pickett looked up, but exhibited no sort of surprise at this speech, as he replied by a simple inquiry: "Who?"

"A messenger from this d—d confederacy. A fellow with his cursed signs—and a summons to meet the members at some place to which he is to give me directions at a future time. I am required to be in readiness to go Heaven knows where, and to meet with Heaven knows who—to do Heaven knows what!"

Pickett answered coolly enough, and with an air of resignation to his fate, which confounded Hurdis:—

"He has been to me too, and given me the same notice."

"Ha! and what did you tell him—what answer—what answer?"

"That I would come—that I was always ready. I suppose you told him so, likewise?"

"Ay—you may well suppose it—what else, in the name of all the fiends, could I tell him. I have no help—I must submit—I am at their mercy—thanks to your bungling, Ben Pickett—you have drawn us both into a bog which is closing upon us like a gulf. I told him as you told him, though it was in the gall of bitterness that I felt myself forced to say so much, that I would obey the summons and be ready when the time came to meet the 'mystic confederacy.' Hell's curses upon their confederates and mystery — that I was at their disposal as I was at their mercy, to go as they bid me, and do as they commanded—I was their servant—their slave, their ox, their ass, their anything. Death! death! that I should move my tongue to such admission, and feel my feet bound in obedience with my tongue."

"It's mighty hard, 'squire, but it's no use getting into a passion about it. We're in, and, like the horse in the mire, we mustn't think to bolt, till we're out of it."

"It's mighty hard, and no use getting in a passion," said Hurdis ironically, and with bitterness repeating the words of his companion. "Well, I know not, Ben Pickett, what situation would authorize a man in becoming angry and passionate if this does not. You seem to take it coolly, however. You're more of a philosopher, I see, than I can ever hope to make myself."

"Well, 'squire, it's my notion," said the other, "that what's not to be helped by grumbling, will hurt the grumbler. I've found it so always; and now that I think of it, 'squire, there's less reason for you to grumble and complain than anybody I know; and as it's just as well to speak the truth first as last, I may say now once for all, that it was you that bungled, not me, or we shouldn't have got into this bog; or we might have got out of it."

"Indeed! I bungle, and how, I pray you, Mr. Pickett? Wasn't it you that was caught in your own ambush?"

"Yes — but who sent me? I was doing your business, 'squire, as well as I could; and if you didn't like my ability, why did you trust it? Why didn't you go yourself? I didn't want to kill Richard Hurdis — I wasn't his brother."

"And then to mistake your man too — that was another specimen of your bungling."

"Look you, 'squire, the less you say about that matter, the better for both of us. The bungling is but a small part of that business that I'm sorry for. I'm sorry for the whole of it, and if sorrow could put back the life in Bill Carrington's heart, and be security for Dick Hurdis's hereafter, they'd both live for ever for me. But if I was such a bungler at first, 'squire, there's one thing I may tell you, and tell you plainly. I was never afraid to pull trigger, when everything depended on it. The cure for all my bungling was in your own hands. When the man first talked with us in these same woods, under them willows, what did I say to you? Didn't I offer to close with him, if you'd only agree to use your pistol? And wasn't you afraid?"

"I was not afraid — it was prudence only that made me put it off," said Hurdis hastily.

"And what made you put it off when you waylaid him in

Ten-Mile Branch? No, 'squire, as you confessed yourself, it was because you were afraid to shoot, though everything hung on that one fire. Had you tumbled that fellow, we hadn't seen this; and if it had been convenient for me to have done it, as God's my judge, I'd much rather have put the bullet through a dozen fellows like that, than through one clever chap like Bill Carrington. That's a business troubles me, 'squire; and more than once since he's been covered, I've seen him walk over my path, leaving a cold chill all along the track behind him."

"Pshaw, Ben, at your ghosts again."

"No, 'squire, they're at me. But let's talk no more about it. What can't be undone, may as well be let alone. We must work out our troubles as we can; and the worst trouble to our thoughts is, that we have worked ourselves into them. We have nobody but ourselves to blame."

The manner of Pickett had become somewhat dogged and inflexible, and it warned Hurdis, who was prompt in observing the changes of temper in his neighbor, to be more considerate in his remarks, and more conciliating in his tone of utterance.

"Well, but Ben, what is to be done? What are we to do about this summons? How shall we get over it? how avoid it?"

"Avoid it! I don't think to avoid it, 'squire."

"What! you intend to go when they call you?"

"Certainly — what can I do? Don't you intend to go? Did you not promise obedience?"

"Yes, but I never thought of going. My hope was, that something might turn up between this and then, that would interpose for my safety. Indeed I never thought of anything at the moment, but how best to get rid of the emissary."

"That's the smallest matter of all," said Pickett.

"Now it is," replied Hurdis, "but it was not then, for I dreaded lest some one should ask his business. Besides, he was brought up to me by Richard, and his keen eyes seem always to look through me when he speaks. As you say, to get rid of him is in truth a small business, to getting rid of his gang. How can that be done is the question? I had hope when I came to you—"

The other interrupted him hastily.

"Don't come to me for hope, 'squire; I should bungle, per

hap., in what I advise you to do, or in what I di for you my self. Let us each paddle our canoes apart. I'm a poor man that can't hope to manage well the business of a rich one; and as I've done so badly for you before, it won't be wise in you to employ me again. Indeed, for that matter, I won't be employed by you again. It's hard enough to do evil for another, and much harder, to get no thanks for it."

"Pshaw, Ben, you're in your sulks now—think better of it, my friend. Don't mind a harsh word—a hasty word—uttered when I was angry, and without meaning."

"I don't mind that, 'squire—I wish it was as easy to forget all the rest, as to forgive that. But the blood, 'squire—the blood that is on my hands—blood that I didn't mean to spill, 'squire—'tis that makes me angry and sulky—so that I don't care what comes up. It's all one to me what happens now."

"But this fellow, Ben. You say you have resolved to comply with the summons, and to go when they call for you?"

"Yes."

"And what am I to do?"

"The same, I suppose. I'm ready to go now; and I give you the last counsel, 'squire, which I think I ever will give you, and that is to make the best of a bad situation—do with a good grace what you can't help doing, and it will go the better with you. They can't have any good reason to expose a man of family to shame, and they will keep your secret so long as you obey their laws."

"But suppose they command me to commit crime—to rob, to murder?"

"Well then you must ask yourself which you'd prefer—to obey or to swing. It's an easy question."

"On all sides—the pit—the fire—the doom!" was the pitiable and despairing exclamation of Hurdis, as he clasped his forehead with his hands, and closed his eyes against the terrors which his imagination brought before them. Suddenly recurring, he asked—

"But why, Ben, do you say this is the last counsel which you will give me? You do not mean to suffer a hasty and foolish word, for which I have already uttered my regrets, to operate in your mind against me—"

“No, 'Squire Hurdis, I don't mind the words of contempt that you rich men utter for the poor; if I did, I should be miserable enough myself, and make many others more so. That's gone out of my mind, and, as I tell you, I forget it all when I think of those worse matters which I can't so well forget.”

“Why, then, say you will counsel me no more?”

“Because I'm about to leave Marengo for ever.”

“Ha! remove! where—when?”

“In three days, 'squire, I'll be off, bag and baggage, for the ‘nation.’ My wife's ripe for it; she's been at me a long time to be off from a place where nobody knows any good of me. And I have heard a good deal about the ‘nation.’ ”

“And what will you do there for a livelihood?”

“Well, just what I can; try, at least, to live a little more honestly than I did here—or more respectably, which is not often the same thing.”

“But do you expect, when there, to evade this confederacy? ’ Hurdis eagerly demanded.

“No—I have no such hope.”

“How, then, can you hope to live more honestly?”

“More respectably, I may.”

“They will summon you to do their crimes.”

“I will do them.”

“What! shed more blood at a time when you are troubled for what's already done?”

“Yes—I will obey where I can not escape; but I will do no crime of that sort again on my own account—nothing which I am not forced to do. But if they say, ‘Strike,’ I will do so as readily as if it was the best action which they commanded. I will cut the throat of my best friend at their bidding; for you see, 'squire, I have been so long knocked about in the world—now to one side, now to another, like a clumsy log going downstream—that I'm now quite indifferent, I may say, to all the chances of the current, and I'll just go wherever it may drive me. This ‘confederacy’ can't make me worse than I have been—than I am—and it increases my security and strength. It gives me more certain means and greater power; and, if I am to be forced, I will make what use I can of the power that forces me.

"But, Ben, such a resolution will make you a willing and active member of this clan."

"Surely!" said the other indifferently.

"All your old interests and friendships, Ben, would be forsaken, rooted up—"

"Ay, 'squire, and my old friends just as liable to my bullet and knife as my enemies, if the command of the confederacy required me to use them. You yourself, 'squire—though we have worked together for a long time—even you I would not spare, if they required me to shed your blood; and you will see from this that there is no hope for you unless you comply with the summons, and heartily give yourself up to the interests of the whole fraternity."

Hurdis was stricken dumb by this frank avowal of his associate. He had no more to say; and, with a better understanding of each other than either had ever possessed before, there was now a wall between them, over which neither at the present moment seemed willing to look.

In three days more, Pickett with all his family was on his way toward the "nation," where, it may be added in this place, he had already made arrangements with the emissary for a more active co-operation with the members of the "Mystic Confederacy." His destiny, which forced him into the bosom of this clan, seemed thoroughly to yield to his desire. The buffeting of the world, of which he had spoken, had only made him the more indifferent to the loveliness of virtue—more reckless of the risk, and less averse to the natural repulsiveness, of vice.

CHAPTER XLIII

AMONG THE ENEMY.

————— "He seemed
For dignity composed, and high **exploit;**
But all was false and hollow."— Milton.

Were it proper for me to pause in my narrative for the purpose **of** moral reflection, how naturally would the destitute condition **of the criminal, as instanced in** the case of John Hurdis,
present **itself for comment!** Perhaps the greatest penalty which
vice ever suffers is its isolation—its isolation from friends and
fellowship—from **warm trust, from yielding** confidence. Its
only resources are in the mutual interests of other and perhaps
greater criminals, **and what is there in life so unstable as the**
interests of the vicious? How they fluctuate with the approach
of danger, or the division of the spoil, or the drunkenness of
heart and habit which their very destitution in all social respects
must necessarily originate! When John Hurdis separated
from his late colleague, who had taught him that they were no
longer bound to each other by mutual necessities, he felt as if
the last stay, in the moment of extremity, was suddenly taken
from him. A sickness of soul came over him, and that despair
of the spirit which the falling wretch endures in the brief instant when, catching at the impending limb, he finds it yielding
the moment that his hold is sure upon it, and, in its decay, be-
traying utterly the last fond hope which had promised him
security and life.

But, enough of this: **my journey is begun.** I entered a
steamboat one fair morning, and, with promising auspices, so
far as **our** voyage is considered, we went forward swimmingly
enough. But our boat **was an old one**—a wretched hulk, which
having worked out its term of responsible service in the Missis

sippi, had been sent round to Mobile, at the instance of cupidity, to beguile unwitting passengers like myself to their ruin. She was a piece of patchwork throughout, owned by a professional gambler, a little Israelite, who took the command without knowing anything about it, and, by dint of good fortune, carried us safely to our journey's end. Not that we had not some little stoppages and troubles by the way. Some portion of the machinery got out of order, and we landed at Demopolis. built a fire, erected a sort of forge, and in the space of half a day and night repaired the accident. This incident would not be worth relating, but that it exhibits the readiness with which our wildest and least scientific people can find remedies for disasters which would seem to call for great skill and most extensive preparations.

On the eleventh day we reached Columbus; but, in the meantime, practising my new resolves, I made an acquaintance on board the boat. This was an old gentleman, a puritan of the bluest complexion, whom nobody would have suspected of being a rogue. Setting out to seek for and meet with none but rogues, he yet nearly deceived me by his sanctity; and had I not maintained my watchfulness a little longer than I deemed necessary myself, I should have taken it for granted that he was a saint of the most accepted order, and, if I had not committed my secret to his keeping, I should at least have so far involved its importance as to make my labor unavailing. Fortunately, as I said, having put on the dress common to the gamblers of the great Mississippi valley, as much of their easy impudence of demeanor as I could readily assume, I succeeded as effectually in convincing my puritan that I was a rogue, as he did in persuading me at the beginning that he was an honest man. It was my good fortune to find out his secret first, and to keep my own. It so happened that there were several passengers, like myself, bound for Columbus, on the Tombeckbe, to which place our boat was destined. As customary at that time, we had no sooner got fairly under way, before cards were produced, and one fellow, whose lungs and audacity were greater than the rest, was heard throughout the cabin, calling upon all persons, who were disposed to "take a hand," to come forward. With my new policy in view, I was one of the first to answer this challenge. I had provided myself in Mobile with several packs, and, taking a couple of them in hand, I went forward to the table, which meanwhile had been drawn out in the cabin, and coolly surveyed my companions. Our puritan came forward at the same moment, and in the gravest terms and tones protested against our playing.

"My young friends," he cried, "let me beg you not to engage in this wicked amusement. Cards are—as it has been often and well said—cards are the prayer-books of the devil. It is by these that he wins souls daily to his gloomy kingdom. Night and day he is busy in these arts to entrap the unwary, whom he blinds and beguiles, until, when they open their eyes at last, they open them in dwellings of damnation. Oh, my dear children, do not venture to follow him so far! Cast the temptation from you—defy the tempter; and, in place of these dangerous instruments of sin, hearken, I pray you, to the goodly outpourings of a divine spirit. If you will but suffer me to choose for you a text from this blessed volume—"

Here he took a small pocket-bible from his bosom, and was about to turn the leaves, when a cry from all around me silenced him in his homily, which promised to be sufficiently unctuous and edifying:—

"No text, no text!" was the general voice; "none of the parson, none of the parson!"

"Nay, my beloved children—" the preacher began, but a tall, good-humored looking fellow—a Georgian, with the full face, lively eyes, and clear skin, of that state—came up to him, and laid his broad hand over his mouth.

"Shut up, parson, it's no use. You can't be heard now, for you see it's only civility to let the devil have the floor, seeing he was up first. If, now, you had been quick· enough with your prayer-book, and got the whip-hand of him, d—n my eyes, but you should have sung out your song to the end of the verses; but you've been slow, parson—you've been sleeping at your stand, and the deer's got round you. You'll get smoked by the old one, yourself, if you don't mind, for neglecting your duty."

"Peace, vain young man!—"

He was about to begin a furious denunciation, but was allowed to proceed no further. The clamor was unanimous around him; and one tall fellow, somewhat dandyishly accoutred, like myself, coming forward, made a show of seizing upon the exhorter. Here I interposed.

"No violence, gentlemen; it's enough that we have silenced the man—let him not be hurt."

"Ay, if he will keep quiet," said the fellow, still threatening.

"Oh, quiet or not," said the Georgian, "we mustn't hurt the parson. 'Dang it, he shan't be hurt! I'll stand up for him. Parson, I'll stand up for you; but, by the hokey, old black, you must keep your oven close!"

I joined in promising that he would be quiet, and offer no further interruption; and he so far seemed to warrant our assurance as, without promising himself, to take a seat, after a few half-suppressed groans, on a bench near the table on which we were about to play. I was first struck with suspicion of the fellow by this fact. If the matter were so painful to his spirit, why did he linger in our neighborhood when there were so many parts of the boat to which he might have retreated? The suspicion grew stronger when I found him, after a little while, as watchfully attentive to the progress of the game as any of the players.

Favorably impressed with the frankness of the Georgian, I proposed that we should play against the other two persons who were prepared to sit down to the table, and my offer was closed with instantly. We bet, on each hand, on the highest trump, and on the game with each of our opponents, a dollar being the amount of each bet, so that we had a good many dollars staked on the general result of the game. I know that I lost nine dollars before the cards had been thrice dealt. I now proceeded to try some of the tricks which I had seen others perform, and in particular that in which the dealer, by a peculiar mode of shuffling, divides the trumps between his partner and himself. My object was, to fix the attention of one of my opponents, whom I suspected from the first to be no better than he should be, simply because he wore a habit not unlike my own, and was covered with trinkets in the same manner. But I lacked experience: there was still a trick wanting, which no sleight-of-hand of mine could remedy. Though I shuffled the cards as I had seen them **shuffled, by drawing** them alternately from top **to bottom together,** I found **neither mine nor my** partner's hand **any better than before; and looking up, with some** affected chagrin in my **countenance, I caught sight of what** seemed to be an understanding **smile between the opponent in** question and the parson, **who, sitting a little on one side of me,** was able to **look,** if he **desired it, into my hand. This** discovery — as I thought it — **gave me no little pleasure. I was** resolved to test it, and ascertain how far **I was correct** in my suspicions. I flattered myself that **I** was in a fair way to fall **upon** the clue **which might conduct** me into the very midst of the **gamblers, who** are all supposed to be connected more or less on the **western** waters, and yield me possession of **their secrets.** Accordingly, **I** displayed certain **of** my cards ostentatiously before the eyes of the **preacher,** and had occasion to observe, **an** instant after, **that the play of my** opponent **seemed to be regulated** by **a certain knowledge of** my hand. He finessed constantly upon **my lead, and with** an adroitness which compelled the continual expression **of** wonder and dissatisfaction from the lips of my partner. I was satisfied, **so** far, with the result of my experiment, and began to think **of** pausing before I **proceeded further; when** my **Georgian** dashed **down his cards as** the game was ended against us, and **cried out to me, with a** countenance which, though flushed, **was yet full of most excellent** feeling : —

"**Look you,** stranger, suppose we **change. We don't seem to have luck** together, and there's **no fun in being all the time** on the losing **side.** The bad luck **may be with me, or it may** be with you, **I don't say, but** it can do no harm **to shift** it to other shoulders, whoever **has it.** I've been **diddled out** of twenty-six **hard** dollars in mighty short order."

"Diddled!" **exclaimed my brother** dandy, with an **air of** ineffable heroism, turning **to my partner.** Without **discomposure** the other replied :—

" I don't mean any **harm when** I say diddled, **stranger, so** don't be uneasy. **I call it** diddling when I lose my money, fight as hard **for it as** I can. **That is** the worst **sort** of diddling **I** know."

The other looked fierce for **a moment, but** he probably soon discovered that the Georgian had replied without heeding his air of valor, and there was something about his composed manner which rendered it at least a doubtful point whether anything in the shape of an insult would not set his bulky frame into overpowering exercise. The disposition to bully, however slightly it was suffered to appear, added another item to my suspicions of the character before me. The proposition of my partner to change places with one of the other two, produced a different suggestion from one of them, which seemed to please us all. It was that we should play *vingt-un*.

"Every man fights on his own hook in that, and his bad luck, if he has any, hurts nobody but himself."

I had begun to reproach myself with a course which, however useful in forwarding my own objects, had evidently contributed to the loss by my partner of his money. If free to throw away my own, I had no right to try experiments on his purse, and I readily gave my assent to the proposition. Our bets were more moderate than before, but I soon found the game a losing one still. The preacher still sat at my elbow, and my brother dandy was the banker; and in more than one instance when I have stood on "twenty" he has drawn from the pack, though having "eighteen" and "nineteen,"—upon which good players will always be content, unless assured that better hands are in the possession of their opponents, when, by "drawing," they can not lose. This knowledge could only be received from our devoted preacher, and when I ceased to play —which, through sheer weariness I did—I did so with the most thorough persuasion, that the two were in correspondence —they were birds of the same brood.

Moody and thoughtful, for I was now persuaded that my own more important game was beginning to open before me, I went to the stern of the boat, and seated myself upon one of the bulks, giving way to the bitter musings of which my mind was sufficiently full. While I sat thus, I was startled on a sudden to find the preacher beside me.

"Ah, my young friend, I have watched you during your sinful play, against which I warned you, with a painful sort of curiosity. Did I not counsel you against those devilish instruments—you scorned my counsel, and what has been your fortune. You have lost money, my son, money—a goodly sum, which might have blessed the poor widow, and the portionless orphan—which might have sent the blessings of the word into strange lands among the benighted heathen—which might have helped on in his labors some wayfaring teacher of the word—which might be most needful to yourself, my son; which, indeed, I see it in your looks—which you could very ill spare for such purposes, and which even now it is your bitter suffering that you have lost."

Admiring the hypocrisy of the old reprobate, I was yet, in obedience to my policy, prepared to respect it. I availed myself of his own suggestion, and thus answered him.

"You speak truly, sir; I bitterly regret having lost my money, which, as you say, I could ill spare, and which it has nearly emptied my pockets to have lost. But suppose I had been fortunate—if I was punished by my losses for having played, he who won, I suppose, is punished by his winnings for the same offence. How does your reason answer when it cuts both ways?"

"Even as a two-edged sword it doth, my friend; though in the blindness of earth you may not so readily see or believe it. Truly may it be said that you are both equally punished by your fortunes. You suffer from your losses—who shall say that he will suffer less from his gains. Will it not encourage him in his career of sin—will it not promote his licentiousness —his indulgence of many vices which will bring him to disease, want, and possibly—which Heaven avert—to an untimely end. Verily, my friend, I do think him even more unfortunate than thyself; for, of a truth, it may be said, that the right use of money is the most difficult and dangerous of all; and few ever use it rightly but such as gain it through great toil, or have the divine instinct of Heaven, which is wisdom, to employ it to its rightful purposes."

Excellent hypocrite! How admirably did he preach? How adroitly did he escape what had otherwise been his dilemma. He almost deceived me a second time.

"In your heart, now, my friend, you bitterly repent that you heeded not my counsel."

"Not a whit!" was my reply; "if I were sure I could win, I would stick by the card table for ever."

"What! so profligate and so young. Oh! my friend, think upon your end—think of eternity."

"Rather let me think of my beginning, reverend sir, if you please. The business of time requires present attention, and to a man that is starving your talk of future provision is a mere mockery. Give me to know how I am to get the bread of life in this life before you talk to me of bread for the next."

"How should you get it, my friend, but by painstaking and labor, and worthy conduct. The world esteems not those who play at cards —"

"And I esteem not the world. What matters it to me, my good sir, what are the opinions of those to whom I am unknown, and for whom I care nothing. Give me but money enough, and I will make them love me, and honor me, and force truth and honesty into all shapes, that they may not offend my principles or practice."

"But, my son, you would not surely forget the laws of honesty in the acquisition of wealth?"

This was said inquisitively, and with a prying glance of the eye, which sufficiently betokened the deep interest which the hypocrite felt in my answer. But that I was now persuaded of his hypocrisy, I should have never avowed myself so boldly.

"What are they? what are these laws of honesty of which you speak? I can not, all at once, say that I know them."

"Not know them!"

"No!"

"Well," he continued, "to say truth, they are rather frequently revoked among mankind, and have others wholly opposite in character substituted in their place; but you can not mistake me, my young friend—you know that there are such laws."

"Ay, laws for me—for the poor—to crush the weak—made by the strong for their own protection—for the protection of the wealth of the cunning. These are not laws calculated to win the respect or regard of the destitute—of those who are desperate enough, if they did not lack the strength, to pull down society with a fearless hand, though perhaps, they pulled it in ruin upon themselves."

"But you, my friend, you are not thus desperate—this is not your situation."

"What! you would extort a confession from me, first of my poverty, then of my desperation—you would drag me to the county court, would you, that you might have the proud satis-faction of exhorting the criminal in his last moments, in the presence of twenty thousand admiring fellow-creatures, who come to see a brother launched out of life and into hell. This is your practice and creed is it?"

"No, my friend," he replied, in a lower tone of voice, which was, perhaps, intended to restrain the emphatic utterance of mine. "Know me better, my friend—I would save you—such is my heart—from so dreadful a situation—yes, I would even defeat the purposes of justice, though I felt persuaded you would sin again in the same fashion. Be not rash—be not hasty in your judgment of me, my friend. I like you, and will say something to you which you will, perhaps, be pleased to hear. But not now—one of these vicious reprobates ap-proaches us, and what I say must be kept only for your own ears. To-night, perhaps—to-night."

He left me with an uplifted finger, and a look—such a look as Satan may be supposed to have fixed on Adam in Paradise

CHAPTER XLIV.

DEEPER IN THE PLOT.

> " 'Twill be a bargain and sale,
> I see, by their close working of their heads,
> And running them together so in counsel."—Ben Jonson.

The old hypocrite sought me out again that night. So far,
it appears that my part had been acted with tolerable success.
My impetuosity, which had been feigned, of course, and the
vehemence with which I denounced mankind in declaring my
own destitution, were natural enough to a youth who had lost
his money, and had no other resources; and I was marked out
by the tempter as one so utterly hopeless of the world's favors,
as to be utterly heedless of its regards. Of such, it is well-
known, the best materials for villany are usually compounded,
and our puritan, at a glance, seems to have singled me out as
his own. We had stopped to repair some accident to the
machinery, and while the passengers were generally making
merry on land, I strolled into the woods that immediately bor-
dered upon the river, taking care that my reverend fox, whose
eye I well knew was upon me, should see the course I took. I
was also careful not to move so rapidly as to make it a difficult
work to overtake me. As I conjectured would be the case, he
followed and found me out. It was night, but the stars were
bright enough, and the fires which had been kindled by the
boat-hands, gave sufficient light for all ordinary objects of sight.
I sat down upon the bluff of the river, screened entirely by the
overhanging branches which sometimes almost met across the
stream, where it was narrow, from the opposite banks. I had
not been here many minutes before the tempter was beside me.

"You are sad, my friend—your losses trouble you. But
distrust not Providence, which takes care of us all, though,

perhaps, we see not the hand that feeds us, and fancy all the while that it is our own. You will be provided when you least look for it; and to convince you of the truth of what I say, let me tell you that it is not in goodly counsel alone that I would serve you, I will help you in other matters—I can help you to the means of life—nay, of wealth. Ha! do you start? Do you wonder at what I say? Wonder not—be not surprised— be not rash—refuse not your belief, for of a truth, and by the blessing of God, will I do for you all that I promise, if so be that I can find you pliant and willing to strive for the goodly benefits which I shall put before you."

"What! you would make me a preacher, would you? You would have me increase the host of solemn beggars that infest the country with stolen or silly exhortations, stuffed with abused words, and full of oaths and blasphemy. But you are mistaken in your man. I would sooner rob a fellow on the highway, than pilfer from his pockets while I preach. None of your long talks for me—tell me now of some bold plan for taking Mexico, which, one day or other, the southwest will have to take, and I am your man. I care not how bold your scheme— there is no one so perfectly indifferent to the danger as he who can not suffer the loss of a single sixpence by rope or bullet."

"You do not say, my friend, that you would willingly do such violence as this you speak of, for the lucre of gain. Sure- ly, you would not willingly slay your brother for the sake of his gold?"

"Ask me no questions, reverend sir," I replied, moodily. "I am not in the humor to be catechized."

"And yet, my friend," he continued, "I much fear me that your conscience is scarcely what it should be. This was my surmise to-day, as I beheld you with those unholy cards in your hands. Did I not see you, while giving them that sort of dis- tribution which is sinfully styled shuffling—did I not see you practising an art which is commonly held to be unfair among men of play? Ha! my son—am I not right? have I not smit- ten you under the fifth rib?"

"And what should you, a preacher of the gospel, as you call yourself, what should you know about shuffling?"

"Preacher of the gospel I am, my friend," was his cool reply.

"I am an expounder of the Holy Scriptures, though it may be an unworthy one. I have my license from the Alabama conference, for the year 18—, which, at a convenient season, I am not unwilling that you should see. Yet, though I am a preacher of the blessed word, I have not, and to my shame be it spoken, been always thus. In my youth, I am sad to say, I was much given to carnal indulgence, and many were the evil practices of my body, and many the evil devices of my heart. In this time of my ignorance and sin, I was a great lover of these deadly instruments of evil; and, among my fellows, I was accounted a proficient, able to teach in all the arts of play. It was thus that I acquired the knowledge—knowledge which hurts—to see when thou designedst a trick in which thou didst yet fail, to win the money of thy fellow. I will show thee that trick, my friend, that thou mayst know I tell thee nothing but the truth."

Here was a proposition from a parson. I closed with him instantly.

"You will do me a great service, I assure you."

"But, my friend, you would not make use of thy knowledge to despoil thy fellow of his money?"

"Would I not? For what else would I know the art?"

"But, if I could teach thee other and greater arts than these—if I could show thee how to make thy brother's purse thine own, at once, and without the toil of doling it out dollar by dollar—I fear me, my friend, that thou wouldst apply this knowledge also to purposes of evil—that thou wouldst not regard the sinfulness of such performances, in the strong desire of lucre which I see is in thy heart—that thou wouldst seek an early chance to put in practice the information which I give thee."

"And wherefore give it me, then? Of a certainty I would employ it, as you see, to increase my means of life."

"Alas! my friend, but thy necessity must be great, else would I look upon thee with misgivings and much horror."

"Great, indeed! I tell you, reverend sir, but that for your coming, it is ten to one I had sent a bullet through my own head, or buried myself in the waters of the Bigby."

"Thou surely didst not meditate an act so heinous."

"Look here!" and I showed him my pistol as I spoke. He

coolly took it into his hands, threw up the pan, and, with his finger, assured himself that it was primed. His tone was altered instantly. He dropped the drawling manner of the exhorting; and, though his conversation was still sprinkled with the canting slang of the itinerant preacher, which long use had probably made habitual, yet he evidently ceased to think it necessary to play the hypocrite with me any longer.

"You are too bold a fellow," he said, "to throw away your life in such a manner, and that, too, because of the want of money. You shall have money—as much as you wish of it; and, I take it, you would infinitely prefer shooting him who has it rather than yourself—"

"Nay, nay, not that neither, reverend sir. There's some danger of being hung for such a matter."

"Not if you have money. You forget, my friend, your own principles. You said, and said truly, that money was the power which made virtue and opinion take all shapes among men; and, when this is the case, justice becomes equally accommodating. You shall have this money—you shall compel this opinion as you please, so that you may do what you please, and be safe—only let me know that you wish this knowledge."

I grasped his hand violently.

"Ask the wretch at the gallows if he wishes life, and the question is no less idle than that which you put to me."

"Come farther back from the river—some of these boatmen may be pulling about; and such matters as I have to reveal, need no bright blaze like that which gleams upon us from yon forge. That wood looks dismal enough behind us—let us go there."

Thither we went; and, having buried ourselves sufficiently among the thick undergrowth to be free of any danger of discovery or interruption, he began the narrative which follows; and which, together with much additional but unnecessary matter, I have abridged to my own limits :—

"There was a boy," said he, "a poor boy of West Tennessee, who knew no parents, and had no friends—who worked for his bread and education, such as it was, at the same moment—and, in spite of all his labors, found, at the end of every year, after casting up his accounts, that he had gained during its passage many more kicks than coppers."

"No uncommon fortune in a country like ours."

"So he thought it," continued the parson, availing himself of my interruption—"so he thought it. He wasted no time and feeling in idle regrets of a condition which he found was rather more general than grateful to mankind, and one day he asked himself how many years he was willing to expend in trying to get a living in an honest way?"

"Well, a reasonable question. What answer?"

"A reasonable one—like the question. Life is short even if we have money, said he to himself; but we have no life at all without it. Following a plough gives me none—I must follow something else."

"Well?"

"He resolved on being honest no longer."

"Indeed! But how could he put his resolution into effect in a country like ours, where we are inundated with so much professional virtue?"

"He put on a professional cloak."

"Excellent."

"But, though commencing a new, and, as it proved, a profitable business, he was not so selfish as to desire a monopoly of it; on the contrary, a little reflection suggested to him a grand idea, which was evolved by the very natural reflection which you made just now."

"What was that?"

"Simply, that his condition was not that of an individual, but of thousands."

"Well, that is a truism. What could he make of that?"

"A brotherhood."

"How?"

"He conceived that, if there were thousands in his condition, there were thousands governed by his feelings and opinions. We all have a family likeness in our hearts, however disguised by habits, manners, education; but when habits, manners, education, are agreed, and to these is added a prevailing necessity, then the likeness becomes identity, and the boy who, on reaching manhood, resolved to be no longer despicably honest, felt assured that his resolve could be made the resolves of all who are governed by his necessities.

"A natural reflection enough—none more so."

"Accordingly, his chief labor was that of founding an order—a brotherhood of those who have learned to see, in the principles which ostensibly govern society, a nice system of cobwebs, set with a double object, as snares to catch and enslave the feeble and confiding, and defences for the protection of the more cunning reptiles that sit in the centre, and prey at ease upon the marrow and fat of the toiling insects they entangle."

"Such is certainly a true picture of our social condition. Man is the prey of man—the weak of the strong—the unwary of the cunning. The more black, the more bloated, the spider, the closer his web, and the greater the number and variety of victims. He sits at ease, and they plunge incontinently into his snare."

Such were some of the reflections with which I regaled my companion. He proceeded with increasing earnestness.

"He travelled through all the slave states making proselytes to his doctrine. With the cassock of a sanctified profession, which we no more dare assail now than we did four hundred years ago, he made his way not only at little or no expense, but with great profit. On all hands he found friends and followers—men ready to do his bidding—to follow him in all risks—to undertake all sorts of offences, and in every respect to be the instruments of his will, as docile and dependent as those of any Oriental despot known in story. His followers soon grew numerous, and having them scattered through all the slave states, and some of the free, he could enumerate more than fifteen hundred men ready at his summons and sworn to his allegiance."

I was positively astounded.

"But you are not serious?"

"As much so as at a camp-meeting. There is not an atom of the best certified texts of scripture more true than what I tell you."

"What! fifteen hundred men—fifteen hundred in these southern states professing roguery!"

"Nay, not professing roguery; there you are harsh in your

epithet. Professing religion, law, physic, planting, shopkeeping—anything, everything, but roguery. They practise roguery, and roguery of all kinds, I grant you, but no professions could be more immaculate than theirs."

"Is it possible?" My wonder could not be concealed, but I contrived to mingle in some delight with my tones of astonishment, and my words were cautiously adapted to second my affectation of delight.

"Yes," he continued, "by the overruling influence of this boy, as I may call him, though now a full-grown man, such has become the spread of his principles, and such is the power which he wields. Yet, in all his labors, mark me, he himself commits no act of injustice with his own hand. He manages, he directs others; he sets the spring in motion, and counsels the achievement, yet no blow is struck by his hand. He is above the petty details of his own plans, and leaves to other and minor spirits the task of executing the little offices by which the grand design is carried out, and the work effected."

"Why, this man is a genius."

My unaffected expression of admiration warmed my companion, and he soon convinced me not only that he had all the while spoken of himself, but that he was remarkably sensitive on the subject of his own greatness. Discovering this weakness, I plied him by oblique flatteries of the wonderful person whom he had described to me, and he became seemingly almost entirely unreserved in his communications. He related at large the history of the clan—the Mystic Confederacy, as it was termed—as it has already been partially narrated to the reader; and my horror and wonder were alike increased at every step in his progress. I could no longer doubt that the fellows who murdered William Carrington were a portion of the same lawless fraternity; and while the developments of my new acquaintance gave me fresh hope of being soon able to encounter with those murderers, they opened my eyes to a greater field of danger and difficulties than had appeared to them before. But I did not suffer myself to indulge in apprehensive musings, and pressed him for an increase of knowledge; taking care, at my each solicitation, to lard my inquiries thick with oily eulogies upon the great genius who had planned, and so far executed, his enterprises.

"How has this **wonderful man** contrived to evade detection, or suspicion **at least?** It is **not easy to** have **a secret** kept, which is **so numerously confided.**"

"That **is one of the** beauties of his scheme, that he confides little **or nothing which** affects himself, **and he secures the** alliance and obedience **of** those **only who have secrets of their** own much more detrimental to them if made public **than could** be any which they have of his. His art consisted simply in seeking out those who had secrets of **a** dangerous nature. In finding these he found followers. But, though he has not always escaped suspicion — he has been able always to defy it. Societies have been formed, schemes **laid,** companies raised, and juries prompted, to catch him in the act, but all in vain. It is not easy **to** entrap a man who has an emissary in every section **of the country.** The **most** active secretaries of the societies were **his** creatures — the schemes have been reported him as soon as laid, and **one of** his own right-hand men **has** more than once been **an officer of** the company sworn to keep watch over him in secret."

"Wonderful man! — and what does he design with all **this** power? To rob merely — to procure **money** from travellers upon the highway — would not seem to call for such an extensive association."

"Perhaps not! — but he has other purposes; and the time **will** come, I doubt not, when his performances will, in no respect, **fall** short of the **power** which he will employ to effect them. When I tell **you** of **such** a man, you see at once that he is no common robber. Why should he confine himself to the deeds of one — be assured he will not. You will see — you will hear yet of his performances, and I tell you they will be such that the country will ring with them again."

"He **must** be a man of great ambition — he should be, to correspond with the genius which he evidently has for great achievements. I should like to know — by my soul, but I could love such a man as that."

"You shall know him in season — he is not unwilling to be **known** where he himself knows **the** seeker, but—"

He paused, and I determined upon giving my hypocrisy a crowning virtue, if possible, by utterly overmastering his. I

put my hand upon his shoulder suddenly, and looked him in
the face, saying deliberately at the same time :—

"You are the man himself—I'll swear it."

"How!" he exclaimed, in some alarm; and I could see that
he fumbled in his bosom as if for a weapon. "How! you mean
not to betray me?"

"Betray you, no. I honor you—I love you. You have
opened a road to me—you have given me light. An hour ago
and I was the most hopeless, benighted wretch under heaven
—without money, without the means of getting it, and fully
resolved on putting a bullet through my head. You have saved
my life—you have saved me."

He seized my hand with warmth.

"I will be the making of you," he replied. "I have the
whole southwest in a string, and have only to pull it to secure
a golden draught. You shall be with me at the pulling."

What more he said is unnecessary to my narrative, though
he thought it all important to his. In brief, he told me that he
had concocted his present schemes for a space of more than
twenty years—from the time that he was fifteen years of age,
and he was now full thirty-five; showing by this, a commendable perseverance of purpose, which, in a good work is seldom
shown, and which, in a good work must have insured to any
individual a most triumphant greatness. We did not separate
that night until he had sworn me a member of the "Mystic
Confederacy," and given me a dozen signs by which to know
my brethren, make myself known, send tidings and command
assistance—acquisitions which I shuddered to possess, and the
consequences of which, I well knew, would task all my skill
and resolution to escape and evade.

CHAPTER XLV.

THE TOO CONSCIENTIOUS BROTHER.

"I protest,
Maugre thy strength, youth, place and eminence,
Despight thy victor sword, and fire new fortune,
Thy valor and thy heart — thou art a traitor."— King Lear.

MY thoughts, in my berth that night, were oppressive enough. I had involved myself in the meshes of a formidable conspiracy, and was now liable to all its dangers. It mattered not to the public how pure were my real purposes, so long as the knowledge of them was confined only to myself. The consciousness of virtue may be a sufficient strengthener of one's resolve, but I doubt whether it most usually produces a perfect feeling of mental quiet. I know all was turmoil in my brain that night. I tossed and tumbled, and could not sleep. Thought was busy, as, indeed she had need be. I had now full occasion for the exercise of all my wits. To entrap the black and bloated spiders in their own web was now my task — to escape from it myself, my difficulty. But I had sworn to avenge William Carrington; and now, with a less selfish feeling, I registered another oath in heaven.

In my next conversation with the parson, who gave me, as his name, Clement Foster, though I doubt not — indeed I afterward discovered — that he had twenty other names; I endeavored, with all my art, to find out if he knew anything of Webber and his associates. To do this without provoking suspicion, was a task requiring the utmost caution. To a certain extent I succeeded. I found that Webber was one of his men, but I also discovered that he let me know nothing in particular — nothing, the development of which might materially affect his future plans, or lead to the discovery of his past projects. I was evidently regarded as one, who, however well estimated, was yet to undergo those trials which always precede the confidence of the wicked. I was yet required to commit myself, before I could be recognised in a fellowship of risk and profits with them. Foster gave me to know, that there was a test to which I would be subjected—a test depending on circumstances—not arbitrary—and my full and entire admission to the fraternity, would depend on the manner in which I executed my task.

"You will have to take a mail-bag, or shoot an obstinate fellow, who has more money than brains, through the head. Our tasks are all adapted to the particular characters of our men. Gentlemen bred, and of good education and fine feelings, will be required to do some bold action : our common rogues and underlings are made to run a negro from his master, or pick a pocket at a muster, or pass forged notes, or some small matter of that sort. You, however, will be subjected to no such mean performances. I will see to that."

Here was consolation with a vengeance! I felt my cheek burn, and my heart bound within me ; but I was on the plank, and the stern necessity schooled me so, that I was able to conceal all my emotion. But I soon found that there were other tests for me, and that my friendly parson was not yet so satisfied that my virtue was of the desirable complexion. My brother-dandy sought me out one day before we reached Columbus :—

"I see," said he, confidentially, "that parson talking with you very frequently ; and, as you seem to listen to him very respectfully, I think it only an act of friendship to put you on your guard against him. Between us, he's a great rascal, I'm more than certain. I know him to be a hypocrite ; and while I was last in Orleans, there was a man advertised for passing forged notes, and the description given of the rogue answers to a letter the appearance of this fellow."

I thanked him for his kindness, but told him that I really thought the parson a very good man, and could not believe that he would be guilty of such an act as that ascribed to him.

"You're mistaken," said he ; "you're only too confiding, and I'll convince you, if you'll only back me in what I do. Stand

by me, and I'll charge him with it before the captain; and, if
so, we'll have the reward. I'll lay my life his pocket is full of
forged bills at this very moment."

I answered him with some coolness, and more indifference:

"I'm no informer, sir, and do not agree with you in your
ill opinion of the poor man. At least, I have seen nothing in
his conduct, and witnessed nothing in his deportment, to warrant me in forming any such suspicions. He may have forged
notes or not, for me; I'll not trouble him."

The fellow went off, no wise discomfited, and I heard nothing more of his accusation. That night I related the circumstance to Foster, who smiled without surprise, and then said to
me in reply—

"You see how well our agents work for us. Haller [that
was the dandy's name] is one of our men. He knew from me of
what we had spoken, and proposed to try you. It is no small
pleasure to find you so faithful to your engagements."

In this way, and by the practice of the most unrelaxing cunning, I fully persuaded Foster of my integrity—if I may use
that word in such relation. Hour after hour gave me new revelations touching the grand fraternity—the "Mystic Brotherhood"—into the bosom of which I was now to be received;
and of the doings and the capacities of which Foster spoke at
large and with all the zest of the truest paternity. After repeated conferences had seemed to assure him of my fidelity, he
proceeded to reveal a matter which, in the end, proved of more
importance to my pursuit than all the rest of his revelations.

"We have quarterly and occasional meetings of our choice
spirits, who are few in number, and one of these meetings is at
hand. We meet in the neighborhood of the Sipsy swamp, on
the road from Columbus to Tuscaloosa, where we have a famous
hiding-place, which has heard, and kept too, many a pretty
secret. We have a conference to which twenty or more will
be admitted, who will report their proceedings in western Alabama. There will be several new members, like yourself, who
are yet in their noviciate; but none, I am persuaded, who will
go through their trial half so well as yourself."

"What! the stopping the mail, or shooting the traveller?"

"Yes—'tis that I mean. You will do your duty, I doubt not

There is another business which we have on hand, which is of some importance to our interests. It is hinted that one of our leading confederates—a fine young fellow, who committed an error, and joined us in consequence a year ago—is about to play the traitor, or at least fly the track."

"Ah, indeed! and how do you punish such an offence?"

"How, but by death? Our very existence as a society, and safety as men, depend upon the severity which we visit upon the head of the traitor. He must die—that is, if the offence be proved against him."

"What! you give him a trial, then?"

"Yes, but not by jury: no such folly for us! We put on the track of the offender some two or three of our most trusty confederates, who take note of all his actions, and are empowered with authority to put the law in force without further reference to us. I will try and get you upon this commission, as your first trial before we invest you with our orders. Haller will most probably be your associate in this business. He brings the report of the suspected treason, and it is our custom to employ in such a business those persons who have the clue already in their hands. Haller has some prejudice against Eberly; there have been words between them, and Eberly, who is a fellow of high spirit, got the better of him, and treats him with some contempt."

"Will there not be some danger of Haller's abusing the trust you give him, then, and making its powers subservient to his feelings of personal hostility?"

"Possibly; but Haller knows our penalty for that offence, and will scarcely venture to incur it. Besides, I fear there is some ground for his charges: I have heard some matters about Eberly myself which were suspicious."

"Eberly!" said I, "where did I hear that name before? I have surely heard it somewhere."

"Not unlikely: I know several Eberlys in Georgia and Alaabama; it's not a very uncommon name, though still not a common one."

The consciousness of the next instant made my cheek burn. I remembered hearing the name of Eberly uttered by one of the banditti, while I lay bound in the hovel of Matthew Web-

ber; and then it appeared to me in language which was dispar-
aging. Things were beginning to fit themselves strangely to
gether before my eyes; and when the parson left me, to retire
to his berth, I was soon lost in a wilderness of musing.

We soon reached and landed at Columbus—a wild-looking
and scattered settlement, at that time, of some thirty families,
within a mile of the Tombeckbe. We proceeded boldly to the
tavern—our parson leading the way; and never was prayer
more earnest and seemingly unaffected than that which he put
up at the supper-table that night. He paid amply for his bacon
and greens by his eloquence. He tendered no other form of
pay—nor, indeed, did any seem to be desired.

The next morning it was arranged between us that we should
all meet at a spot a little above the ford at Coal-Fire creek—
a distance of some thirty miles from Columbus, and on the direct route to Tuscaloosa. But here a difficulty lay in my way
which had been a source of annoyance to me for the three days
past. I had no horse, and had declared to Foster my almost
absolute want of money. To proceed on my mission, it was
necessary to procure one, and, if possible, a good one; and how
to do this while Foster stayed, was a disquieting consideration.
But he was too intent upon securing his new associate, and not
less intent upon his old business, to suffer this to remain a difficulty long.

"You must buy a horse in Columbus, Williams (that was the
name I had set out with from Mobile); you can not get on without one. As you have no money, I must help you, and you can
repay me after you have struck your first successful blow. Here
are a couple of hundred dollars—bills of the bank of Mobile—
counterfeit, it is true, but good here as the bank itself. There's
an old fellow here—old General Cocke—that has several nags;
you can possibly get one from him that will do you good service, and not cost you so much, neither. Go to him at once and
get your creature: you'll find me to-morrow noon at the creek,
just as I tell you. Set up a psalm-tune, if you can, even as you
reach the creek, and you'll hear some psalmody in return that
will do your heart good."

He left me, followed by Haller, and I took a short mode for
getting rid of the counterfeit bills he gave me. I destroyed

them in my fire that night, and, taking the necessary sum from my own treasury, I proceeded to procure my horse, which I found no difficulty in doing, and at a moderate price, though General Cocke had none to sell. I bought from another person, whom I did not know.

Being so far ready, I took a careful examination of my pistols, procured me an **extra** knife of large size in Columbus, and commending myself to Providence with a prayer mentally uttered, as earnest as any which I ever made either before or since, I set off for the place of meeting, which I reached about sunset. Though nothing of a psalm-singer, I yet endeavored to avail myself of the suggestion of Foster, and accordingly set up a monotonous stave, after the whining fashion of the methodists of that region; and was answered with a full burst of the same sort of melody, of unsurpassable **volume, proving the lungs of** the faithful whom I **sought to be of the most undiseased** complexion. I was immediately joined by Foster and three other persons, among whom I felt a spontaneous **movement of pleasure** in my bosom as I recognised the features of Matthew Webber. But it was the pleasure of the hunter, who, having his **rifle** lifted, discovers the wolf at the entrance **of the den.** It relieved me from many apprehensions to find that Webber, though looking at me with some attention, did so without seeming to recognise me. This was an earnest of success in my pursuit which cheered me not a little in my onward progress.

We entered their hiding-place together, where, in a leafy cover that might have been used by innumerable tribes of bears and foxes before, we found our supper and a tolerable lodgment for the night. There we slept, though not till some hours had been spent in conversation touching a thousand plans of villany, which astounded me to hear, but to which I was compelled not only to give heed, but satisfaction. But little of their dialogue interested me in my pursuit. To some parts of it, however, I lent an ear of excited attention. Webber spoke of Eberly; and though I could not understand much of the matter he referred to, yet there was an instinct in my mind that made me nervous while the discussion continued, and melancholy long after it was over. To me was the task to be assigned of pursuing this young man, of spying into his conduct, and reporting

and punishing his **return** to the paths of virtue. **Not** to do this
work faithfully to **those who** sent me, **was to incur** his risk; and
this was **a position into** which, with **my eyes open,** I had **gone**
of my **own head.**

It was no small addition to **my** annoyance, **that, in** prosecu-
ting the search into Eberly's conduct, I was ministering to the
mean malice of Haller and the open hate of Matthew Webber.
But there was no room for hesitation now. I was to go forward, or fall. My hope, as well as purpose, was for the best;
my resolution to do nothing **wrong.** My task was to steer wide
of injury to others, and of risk to myself—no easy task, with
so many villains around **me.** A sentence or two of the dialogue
which so interested me may be well enough repeated here. It
will be supposed that what was said must have had the effect of
lifting **the destined youth in** my consideration : it certainly
placed **him in a more favorable** light than could well be claimed
for one found **in** such a **connection.**

"He is become **too melancholy** for any business at all," said
Webber, "and least of all for such a business as ours. Set **him**
to watch for a traveller, and he plays with **the** leaves, twists
the vines round his finger, writes in **the sand, and sighs all the**
while **as if** his heart were breaking."

"Why, he has suffered himself really **to fall in love with the**
girl!" exclaimed Foster. "What an **ass!**"

"So he is; and that is perhaps his chief offence, since a man
who is an ass can never **be a** good knave—certainly never a
successful one," **was** the reply of Webber.

"True enough, Matthew," **said** Foster, "but this is the poor
fellow's misfortune. **In** this condition he can do nothing for
himself any more than for **us.** Will he marry **the girl?**"

"If he can."

"And **can** he not?"

"Yes, I think **he may**—he might if he could keep his secret.
But it is my fear **that he can** not keep his secret. His heart
has got the better of his head—his conscience of his necessities; and these gloomy fits which he has now so constantly not
only make him neglectful of **our** interests and his duties, but
will, I am dubious, precipitate **him** into some folly which will be
the undoing of all of us. You know the laws, Clement Foster :

don't you think he could get clear of justice, by telling all he knows about us ?"

"Pshaw! what does he know ? and who would believe him, unless he gave us up to justice—unless he brought the hounds to our cover ?—and even that would do little, unless he could point out and prove particular acts. What does he know of me, or you ? We could prove him a liar by a cloud of witnesses whom he never saw, who could go into court and swear everything."

"True enough; but that we should get clear does not do away with his offence, should he endeavor to involve us."

"By no means—but wherefore should he seek to do so ?— what could be his object ? His own exposure follows, or, indeed, precedes ours; and for a man to prove himself a knave, merely to show that his neighbor is just as bad, is thrice-sodden folly."

"Well, such is always your conscientious fool."

"But Eberly is a fool of love, Mat, and not of conscience."

"And fools of love, Foster, are very apt to be fools of conscience."

"By no means: they are the greatest knaves in the wide world, and worse hypocrites than a pork-eating parson ! They lie or do anything to get the woman; for passion was never yet a moralist."

"Well—I don't know—but Eberly has done nothing for some time past. He has let several matters slip through his fingers. There was an affair—only two weeks ago—that nearly swamped us all, from his not coming according to promise."

"What affair ? something I have not heard of ?"

"Yes. There were two larks that were hitched at my house, or rather that we tried to hitch. One of them got out of the noose, and thumped Breton over his mazzard so that the bridge of his nose is broken down for ever. He got off as far as the 'Day Blind,' and there was tumbled by a stranger—a fellow that we sent after, and made sure of. I told you something already of the matter."

Here was something to confound me. Webber evidently alluded to the affair of William and myself; yet he spoke of my

friend being killed by a stranger. I was confused and bewildered by the new position of events, but was quite too awk-
wardly placed to venture any questions on so dangerous a topic.
They proceeded in their dialogue :—

"All this comes of his passion for the girl. When they are
once married, you'll see that he'll recover."

"If I thought so, by God, it would please me the best of all
things. It would do my heart good to sing it in the ears of her
insolent father, that his daughter was the wife of a public robber—a thief of the highway !"

"So, so, Mat! Don't, I pray you, disparage our profession !
Tenderly, tenderly — no nicknaming — and have done with your
malice. Malice is a base, bad quality, and I heartily despise
your fellows who treasure up inveterate prejudices. They are
always a yellow-souled, snakish set, that poison themselves
with the secretions of their own venom. Now, for my part, I
have no hates, no prejudices: if I have anything to thank
Heaven for, it is possessions of a better sort than this. My
chickens lay better eggs, and hatch no vipers."

A pretty sentiment enough for a rogue and hypocrite ! But
of what strange contradictions are we compounded ! The dialogue was soon brought to a close :—

"It is understood, then," said Foster, "that Haller and Williams" (meaning me) "are to watch his motions, and see that
he keeps in traces. Are these two enough, or shall we put a
third with them ?"

"Quite enough to follow and to punish, though it is well that
we should all note his movements, and watch him when we can.
Does Mr. Williams know the extent of his power ?" demanded
Webber, turning to me.

"Ay," was the reply of Foster; "he knows that he has
power to adjudge, and execute even to death; but I would beg
him to recollect that he must award with great caution against
a confederate. An unjust punishment incurs similar judgment ;
and we are prompt to avenge an injury done to one of our comrades. I would not have him too precipitate with Eberly : he
is a fellow of good qualities; he is bold as a lion—generous
to the last sixpence—"

"And a little too conscientious, you should add," was the in-

terruption of Weboer—"a little too conscientious. We were
a few thousand dollars the richer, but for that."

"Ah, you mistake, Matthew; he was busy making love, and
had holyday. Let him but become a husband, and you'll
then see how constant he will be—in his absence from home."

Here the conversation ended for the night.

CHAPTER XLVI.

DESPAIR OF THE WEAK BROTHER.

'The drunkard after all his lavish cups
Is dry, and then is sober; so, at length,
When you awake from the lascivious dream
Repentance then will follow, like the sting
Placed in the adder's tail."— *White Devil.*

THE next morning, before it was yet dawn, Foster aroused me where I was sleeping beneath my green-wood tree.

"We must be stirring, Williams; I have tidings from some of our friends in Tuscaloosa, who appoint to meet me to-morrow noon, at the Sipsy. We have a snug place in the River Swamp, more secure and comfortable even than this; and we shall no doubt meet many of our friends. There, too, you must keep a bright look out, for you will there see Eberly, and your watch must begin from the moment you encounter him."

I arose with no very comfortable feelings at this assurance. I was to begin the labors of the spy. Well! my hand was in for it, and it was no time to look back. I must on, with what feeling it mattered little to those around me; and, having gone so far, perhaps but little to myself. I strove, as well as I might, to shake off my sombre feelings—certainly to conceal their expression. Foster did not seem to heed my taciturnity. If he did, he did not suffer me to see that he remarked it; but playfully and even wittily remarking upon the sluggish movements of our companions, Webber included, to whom early rising seemed an annoyance, he led the way, and we were all soon mounted and on our journey. It was near noon when we reached our place of destination, and such a place! Imagine for yourself, a thousand sluices over a low boggy ground running into one, which, in time, overflowing its channels sluices all the country round it, and you have some faint idea of the borders of the Sipsy River. Nothing could we see but a turbid yellow water, that ran in among the roots of the trees, spread itself all around for miles, forming a hundred little currents, some of which were quite as rapid as a mill-race. The road was lost in the inundation; and but that our men were well acquainted with the region, we should have been drowned— our horses at least—in the numerous bays and bogs which lay everywhere before us. Even among our party a guide was necessary—and one who understood the route better than the rest was singled out to lead the way. For a time we seemed utterly lost in the accumulating pits and ponds, crossing currents and quagmires in which our path was soon involved, and I could easily conjecture the anxiety of our company from the general silence which they kept. But our guide was equal to the task, and we soon found ourselves upon a high dry island, within a few yards of the opposite shore, which, when we reached, Foster throwing himself with an air of satisfaction from his horse, proclaimed it our present resting-place. Here we were joined by a man whom I had not seen before, who had been awaiting us, and who brought letters to Foster. Some of these, from Mobile, New Orleans, Montgomery, and Tuscaloosa, he was pleased to show me; and their contents contributed not a little to confound me, as they developed the large extent of the singular confederacy, of which I was held a member. Some of the plans contained in these letters were of no less startling character. One, which was dwelt on with some earnestness by two of the writers was a simultaneous robbery of all the banks.

"A good proposition enough," was the quiet remark of Foster, passing his finger over the paragraphs—"had they in money but one-tenth part of the amount which they have in paper. But to empty vaults which have no specie, is little to my taste. I should soon put a stop to specie payments, without rendering necessary an act of Congress. Here now, is something infinitely more profitable, but far more dangerous. We shall consider this."

He pointed out to me another suggestion of the writer which seemed to have been debated upon before—the atrociousness

of which curdled my blood to read. I could scarcely propose
the question.

"But you will hardly act upon this—it is too —"

I was about to say horrible—it was well I did not. Foster
fortunately finished the sentence for me in a different manner.

"Too dangerous you would say ! It would be to a blunderer.
But we should be off the moment it was over. Having made
use of the torch, we should only stay long enough to take what
was valuable from the house, and not wait until it had tumbled
upon us. But this matter is not yet ready. We have business,
scarcely less profitable, to be seen to, and three days more may
give us a noble haul. See to this. Here I am advised by a
sure friend at Washington, that a large amount of government
money is on its way for the Choctaws—it will not be my fault
if they get it. That is worth some pains-taking—but—"

He paused and folded up his papers. The tramp of steeds
was heard plashing through the mire and approaching the
island. Webber was next heard in conversation with the new-
comers, whose voices now reached us distinctly. Foster addressed me as he heard them in suppressed tones and with a
graver manner.

"That's Eberly's voice," he said—"you must look to him,
Williams. From this moment do not lose him from your sight
till you can report on his conduct decisively. Here is Haller
coming toward us. He has heard of Eberly's approach and
like yourself will be on the watch. Let me say to you that
Haller will report of you as narrowly as he does of Eberly.
He does not know you yet, and has no such confidence in you
as I have. I know that you will fear nothing that he can
report; and yet, that my judgment may not suffer in the estimation of our people, I should be better pleased if you could
outwatch your comrade."

I made out to say—"Trust me—you have no need of apprehension. I will do my best at least."

"Enough," said he,—"he comes. Poor fellow, he looks sick
—unhappy !"

This was said in an under-tone, as if in soliloquy, and the
next moment, the person spoken of, emerging from the shade of
a bush which stood between himself and me, came full in my

sight. What was my astonishment and misery to behold in him, the young man Clifton, introduced to me by Colonel Grafton, and, as I feared, the accepted lover of his daughter. I was rooted to the spot with surprise and horror, and could scarcely recover myself in time to meet his approach. A desperate resolve enabled me to do this, and when he drew nigh, I was introduced to him as "one of us" by Foster. Clifton, or as I shall continue to call him Eberly, scarcely gave me a look. His eyes never once met either Foster's or my own. He was pale and looked care-worn. With a haggard smile, he listened to the kind yet hypocritical compliments of Foster, but uttered nothing in reply. Other· persons now began momentarily to arrive, and by night our number was increased to twenty-five or thirty. I underwent the fraternal hug, with all the old villains, and some five noviciates like myself; and, in a varied discussion of such topics as burglary, horse and negro stealing, forging, mail-robbing and various other similarly innocent employments, we contrived to pass over the hours without discord or monotony until the coming on of night put our proprietors in mind of supper. I need not dwell upon any of the plans and purposes of crime, in particular, which underwent discussion on that occasion, since none of them will affect very materially my own narrative. It is enough for me to affirm that among these members of the Mystic Brotherhood, crime of all sorts and complexions, seemed reduced to a perfect system, and the hands which ministered seemed to move rather like those of automata than of thinking and resolving men. At supper I sat opposite to Eberly—my eye was fixed upon him all the while, and my recognition of him, as the lover of the poor Julia, fully reconciled me to the task I had undertaken, of convicting him of treason to his associates. His treason to beauty —to innocence—to hospitality, and confiding friendship— made my otherwise odious duty a grateful one; and I felt a malignant sort of pleasure, as I watched my victim, to think that his punishment lay in my own hands. And yet, while I looked upon him, I felt at moments, my heart sink and sicken within me. I somehow began to doubt how far he could be guilty —how far he could be guilty with these—how far guilty to her? He ate nothing, and looked very pale and wretched

His spirit seemed anywhere but with his associates—and though his eye acknowledged every address, and his tongue replied to every demand, yet it was evident enough that there was a lack of mental consciousness—an abstractedness of mood and thought, which left it doubtful when he spoke whether he was altogether assured of the words he uttered, or of those he heard.

After supper our chief rogues renewed the discussion of sundry of their plans, and for a while the curiosity which I felt at the strangeness of some of their propositions, and the stories of their several achievements, half reconciled me to listen to their heinousness. But there was quite too much of it in the end—a still-beginning, never-ending repetition of the same business, only varied by the acting persons, place, and time; and, following the lead of Webber and one or two others, I went aside to the fire which Haller had kindled up, and under a tent of bark, I housed myself for the night. I did not hope for sleep, for my mind was full of troublesome thoughts, yet I was surprised by the feather-footed visitant, and slept soundly for a space of two hours. I was awakened by some one shaking me by the shoulder, and, starting to my feet, found my comrade Haller standing beside me.

"Get up," he said, "it's time to look after Eberly. He has gone out into the bushes, having left Webber whom he slept with. He thought Mat was asleep, and stole off. We must get on his trail and see what he's after."

I obeyed and we went together with great caution to the rude tent in which Webber slept. He gave us some directions, and following them we soon found our man. He had gone to the place where Foster slept alone—a bushy dell of the woods scooped out sufficiently to enable one, by crawling through a narrow mouth to secure an easy, though perhaps confined, couch within. The greater apertures made by torn branches or fallen leaves were supplied by sapplings hewn from neighboring places, and twisted in with the native growth of the spot; and with the aid of some rushes, a blanket, and a good warm watch-coat, Foster had a tenement which art could scarcely have made warmer, though in social respects, it certainly might have undergone considerable improvement.

We reached a spot within hearing distance of this, in sufficient time to note the first approaches of Eberly to its inmate. Foster came forth at his summons, and as my eye turned upon the course which they took together, Haller touched my arm. When I turned, I beheld Webber also standing beside us, who, taking Haller with him, proceeded cautiously to an opposite point, where it seems they expected the two to go, Webber giving me instructions to follow them cautiously from where I stood; by which division of our force, he seemed resolute that one of us should succeed in our espionage. The several fires of the party were nearly extinguished. But there was still light enough to enable me to discern the outlines of their persons as they moved from me. I crept and crawled upon my mission of baseness, with all pains-taking circumspectness, but every moment increased the space between me and the men I pursued, until I had nearly lost sight of them altogether, when, on a sudden, they turned about and came again toward me. It is probable that they may have been disturbed by the too eager progress of the two spies on the other side, who thus drove them back upon me. Whatever may have been the cause of their return, I had barely time to shrink back into the shade of a large tree as they approached it; and the spot being sufficiently dense and dark prompted them to make it the scene of their conference. Foster was the first to speak. Stopping short as he reached a cluster of saplings, only a few paces removed from the place where I stood in shadow, he said:—

"Here now, Eberly, we are safe. Everything is still here, and there is no more danger of interruption. Unfold yourself now. What secret have you—why do you bring me forth at an hour when I assure you a quiet snooze would be more agreeable to me than the finest plot which you could fancy for robbing the largest portmanteau in Alabama?"

"Do not jest with me, Foster—I can not jest; it is a matter of life and death to me which makes me disturb you, else I should not do it. My life hangs upon your hands—more than life; I can not sleep myself; forgive me that I have taken you from yours."

Never were the tones of a man more piteously imploring than

those of the speaker. I could well believe him when he said he could not sleep.

"Your life and **death!**" said **Foster;** "why, what mean you, man? **Don't stop to apologize for breaking my** sleep, when such is the danger! Speak—speak out, **and let us** know from what quarter the storm is coming. **Who is the** enemy you fear?"

"You!" was the emphatic reply. "**You are my enemy!**"

"**Me!**"

"**You,** your fellows, and mine—myself! These are my enemies, **Foster!** It is from these that my apprehensions come—it is these that I fear; my life **is in** their hands! **More than** life—much, much more!"

"**Ha! what is** all this?"

"**You wonder.** Hear **me, Foster. I will tell** you the truth —nothing but the truth! **I** must leave the fraternity! I am not fitted for its membership. I can not do the work it requires at my hands. I dare **not**—my soul sickens at its duties, and I can not perform **them! I** lack the will—the nerve!"

"You know not what you say, Eberly," was the grave reply of Foster. "You surely **do not forget the** penalties which follow **such an** avowal as this?"

"**No!** would I could forget **them! Have I not said that my** life and death are in your hands?"

"Wherefore have you awakened me then?" was the cold and inauspicious reply. "I could tell you **no more** than you already **know.**"

"Yes, **you can save me!** I come to you for pity! I implore you to save **me, which you can! A** word from you will do it."

"Can I—should **I speak that word?** It would ruin me—it would ruin us all!"

"No; it would not. **You could** lose nothing by letting **me go** free—nothing! **for I** can do nothing for you. I can not commit crime! **I can** neither lie, nor rob, nor slay! I can not obey you; and, **sooner or** later, you must execute your judgment upon me for neglect or **perversion of my** pledges!"

"This is certainly a very sudden attack of virtue, Mr. Eberly. You can neither lie, nor steal, nor slay. You have become too pure for these duties; but I remember the time, and that too, no very distant time, when you were guilty of one or more of these dreadful sins from which your soul now shrinks.”

“Ay, and I remember it too, Foster.　I did not need that you should remind me; would I could forget it!—hence came my bondage.　You discovered my unhappy secret, and forged my shackles!　It is to you that I come to break them!”

“You deny it not that you were guilty of the robbery of old Harbers then?”

“I deny it not; and yet I know not, Foster, if it was an offence of which I have so much reason to be ashamed.　Thank God! I took not his money for myself; the wants of a dying mother, the presence of a cruel necessity, was my extenuation, if not excuse, for that hapless act—an act which has been the heavy millstone around my neck in each succeeding moment of my life!　Bitterly have I repented—”

“You can not repent—you shall not repent!” was the sudden speech of Foster.　“You have not the right to repent—you are sworn to us against it, and can not repent without our permission.”

“It is for that permission, Foster, that I come to implore you now.　I know that you are superior to the cold and cruel people whom you lead.　You will, you must, feel for my situation. I am of no use to you,　I can not rob the traveller, nor forge a note, nor inveigle a negro from his master—still less can I stab or shoot the unoffending man who opposes my unlawful attempts upon his property.　I am, indeed, only an incumbrance upon you—”

“You have our secrets.”

“I will keep them—I swear to you, Foster, by all that is sacred that I will keep them!”

“You can not, to be honest—to go back to the paths of virtue.　You must reveal our secrets; and not to do so is a half virtue which looks monstrously like hypocrisy.　It is a compromise with vice, to say the least of it, which puts the blush upon your late returning innocence.　No, Eberly, we must keep our secrets ourselves by keeping bound those who know them.　Say that you are unable to serve us by any of the acts you mention—you are not less able to serve us in other respects, equally sinful yet not so obnoxious to public censure or

punishment. **As a strong man it might** be my lot to depend on
your friendly sympathy **to save me** from a halter."

"I would **do it,** Foster, **believe me."**

"**We must make you do it. We must keep our reins upor.**
you. **But of** what avail **would be a** permission to **you which**
could **not** annihilate the **proofs which we** have against **you?**
Whether we suffered **you to go free, and** held **you to be no**
longer one of us **or not;** the offence **which we could prove**
against you, would still make you liable to **the law. Our mere**
permission to depart would be nothing—"

"Yes—everything! It would free me from a bondage **that**
now crushes me to the earth, and defeats **all my** meditated action in other respects! For the wrong I **have** done to Harbers,
I **would make atonement—"**

"**Repay him the money from the robberies** of others," replied Foster, **with a sneer.**

"No, **Foster," said the young** man patiently, "**not a cent**
would **I bear from your treasury.** I would go forth as unencumbered with your **booty as I** hope to **be** unencumbered with
the sin and shame of **the** connection."

"You use tender words in speaking **of your comrades and**
their occupations, Eberly."

"**Without** meaning **to offend, Foster. But hear me out. I**
should **not merely repay Harbers, but** I would confess to him
the crime **of which I** had been guilty."

"Ha! **and the** subsequent sinful connections which you have
formed with **us, and our precious** doings together. This is your
precious plan, **is it?"**

"Not so! Though **resolved to** declare my **own crimes and**
errors, I am not bound **to betray** the confidence **of others."**

"**This is** your resolution **now;** how long will it remain so, and
what **will be our** security **when** the chance happens—which
may happen—when, at one full swoop, you may take us all
like a flock of partridges, and **deliver us up as** an atonement
for your own youthful sins, to the hands, **so** called, of Justice?
Eberly—Eberly, you are speaking like a child. Do you think
we can hearken to a prayer, such as that you **make?** Why
every white-livered boy of our band, **who happened** to fancy a
pair of blue eyes, and a dimity petticoat, would be seized with

a fit of virtue toward us, in precise degree with his hot lust after the wench he fancied—"

"Stay, Foster; I see that you are aware of my intimacy with Miss Grafton."

"Surely. You have never taken a step that I am not acquainted with. And now let me ask, did you feel our bondage so oppressive till you became acquainted with this girl?"

"I did not; my knowledge of her first impressed upon me, with a more just sense of their worth, the value of those rewards which follow virtuous practice."

"Pshaw, man, how is the getting of this girl a reward of virtue. Can't you get her now, while you are a trusted member of the confederacy? To the point, man, and speak out the truth, have you not spoken to her, and has she not consented to be yours?"

"She has."

"What more! Marry her—we do not hinder you. We object not to the new bonds which you propose to put on yourself, though grumbling so much at ours. Be sure, we shall none of us forbid the banns. Marry her, and settle down in quiet; our laws will give you no trouble; your duties shall be accommodated to the new change in your condition, and, as a justice of the peace, a juror, member of the assembly, or of Congress, you can be as eminently useful to us as, nay, more useful than, a striker along the woods, or a passer of counterfeit notes. These are small matters which any bull-head among us can perform; you have talents which can better serve us in higher stations."

The youth shook his head, as he replied sadly—

"If I did not love Julia Grafton, or if I loved her less, it might be easy to be satisfied with what you say. But I neither can nor will fetter myself or her in a bondage such as you mention. In truth, Foster, I can serve you no more—I can serve the confederacy no more. I make this declaration to you, though I die for it! On your mercy I throw myself—on your kindness often professed, and tried on more occasions than one! Be my friend, Foster—on my knees I pray you to save me in this respect—save me—let me go free—I will leave the country—I will go into a distant state, where you can be in no danger from anything that I can do or say! You can have no rea son to refuse me, since you can have no interest in keeping me to pledges which yield you no interest, and only bring me suffering! Feeling as I do now, and situated as I am, I can do nothing for you! Command me to strike here or there, and I can not obey you! From this day forth I must withhold my service, though you do not cancel my bonds!"

Foster seemed touched while the young man spoke, but this, perhaps, was only a part of his cool and ready hypocrisy. He interrupted Eberly when he had said the last sentence.

"Your refusal to serve us, would, you know, be the signal for your death."

"I know it; and if you send forth the decree, I must meet my doom, and, I trust, will meet it like a man. But I would escape this doom; and to you, and you only, I refer, to extricate me from it, to effect my object, and get my release from the secret council. There is but one man whose refusal I fear, and with him you would have some difficulty, I doubt not; but even that I know you could overcome. Webber hates Grafton the father of Julia, and hates me, because I love her honorably. It was he who brought her to my notice, and prompted me to the scheme by which I became an intimate in the family; a scheme projected for a dishonorable and foul purpose, which has resulted so far, in one of which I have no reason to be ashamed. I would spare her the shame, Foster, of having consented to share the name and affections of one, who may be outlawed the very moment that he confers upon her his name."

I have said enough to exhibit the nature of this conference, which was continued twice as long. In its progress, the youth exhibited a degree of remorse and sorrow on the score of his own offences, and an honorable and delicate consideration in reference to Julia Grafton, which turned all my feelings of hostility into feelings of pity. Nor was this sentiment confined to my own bosom. I conscientiously believe, that Foster sympathized with his grief, and inly determined, so far as the power in him lay, to help him to the desired remedy. The conference was ended by the latter saying to him, as he led the way back to his place of rest:—

"I must think on this matter, Eberly. I will do what I can for you, but I can promise nothing. I deny not that I have influence, but my influence depends, as you well know, upon such an exercise of it as will best accord with the views and wishes of those whom I control. I am sorry for you."

The youth stood a moment when the other had gone. Then throwing his arms up to Heaven, as he turned away, he exclaimed : —

"At the worst I can but perish. But she ! she, at least, shall suffer nothing, either from my weakness or my love. She, at least, shall never be wedded to my accursed secret. Sooner than that, let the bullet or the knife do its work. Thank God, amidst all my infirmities, I have no dastard fear of death ; — and yet, I would live. Sweet glimpses of joy in life, such as I have never known till now, make it a thing of value. Oh ! that I had sooner beheld them — I had not then been so profli gate of honor — so ready to yield to the base suggestions of this wretched clan."

CHAPTER XLVII.

FLIGHT OF THE WEAK BROTHER.

'I'll note you in my book of memory,
   To scourge you for this reprehension;
   Look to it well, and say you are well warned."—SHAKSPERE.

THE unhappy youth had scarcely gone from sight when Mat Webber and my colleague Haller emerged from a bush opposite, not ten paces off, in which they had, equally with myself, listened to the whole dialogue as I have already narrated it.

"So!" was the exclamation of Webber, shaking his slow finger after the departing form of the youth—"So! It is as I expected; and your doom is written, Master Eberly. Foster can save you, can he? We will see to that! It would be a difficult matter for him to save himself, were he to try it. It is well you have no hopes from me—well! I hate your girl, do I, because she is the daughter of Grafton, and I ate you because you love her honorably? Well? there is truth in the notion, however your dull brains happened to hit upon it. I do hate both of you for that very reason. Had the fool used his pleasure with the girl, by G—d, I had forgiven him—he had had my consent to go where he pleased, and swear off from us at any moment, for he has done nothing since he has been a member —he was never of much use, and will be of still less now. But to love where I hate, is an offence I can not so readily forgive. No, Haller, the bullet and the knife for him. He shall keep our secrets, and his own too, if you and Williams do your duty. Ha!—who's that?"

"Williams himself," was my answer, as I came out of my hiding-place, and joined them.

"Well!—you have heard him—he avows his treason, and

you know his doom. What need of delay! Go after him alone—you will not have a better place for the blow if you waited a month. Go alone, and despatch the business."

I was not prepared for so sudden a requisition, and the sanguinary and stern command at once confounded me. Yet Webber had only repeated the words of Foster. In our hands lay the award and the execution of justice. We had been instructed to punish, the moment we resolved that the penalty had been incurred; and there was no reasonable pretext for doubt. What to do or say, I knew not—to think of committing the cruel deed was, of course, entirely out of the question. Fortunately, the answer of my colleague, Haller, relieved me.

"We had better wait and hear what Foster has to say. He may not be pleased that we should proceed so suddenly, particularly when we knew that he had promised to take the affair into consideration."

"And what can his consideration come to? What can he have to say? He can not alter the laws—he can not acquit an offender whom we condemn—he has no power for that."

"No! He has no power for that; and, so far as my voice goes, we shall give him no such power in this instance," was the reply of Haller. "Yet, as a matter of civility only, it will be better that we should not proceed in this business till we have heard what Foster has to say. He might look upon it, that we slighted his opinions, and his wishes, at the least; and there's no necessity for our seeming to do that. Besides, we can not lose by the delay. We can execute to-morrow just as well as to-day—Eberly can not escape us."

"True—that's true," was the reply of Webber; "though, to speak plainly, I don't like this undertaking to interfere on the part of Clem Foster. He can't certainly hope to persuade us to reverse our judgment, and let this boy loose, unmuzzled, to confuse and convict us in some of their dirty courts of justice!—"

"No! As you heard him say, that's a matter more easy to think upon than to do. All that Eberly could say in a court-house could not prove against one of us, and we might hang him whenever we choose."

"Yes, but we don't want to get into a court of justice at all,"

said Webber; "and there's little need for it, when we have
laws, and courts, and executioners, of our own. I tell you,
Haller, that I shall regard as an enemy any man who attempts
to get this chap off from punishment. He shall die, by the
Eternal!"

"So he may, for what I care," said Haller. "So, indeed,
he shall, under our own certainty of what he deserves, and the
power which has been entrusted to us. Be at rest, Mat Webber—I have as little reason to let Edward Eberly escape as
you have. I hate him—from my heart I hate him! He has
scorned and insulted me before our men; and it will go hard
with me if I don't avenge the insult with sevenfold vengeance."

"I'm satisfied that you will keep your word, Haller; but
Foster's a smooth-spoken fellow, and he may have some kink
in his head for saving this chap. He used to be very fond of
keeping company with him, and they were always spouting
verses and such stuff together. I know, too, for all Foster
speaks so promptly of punishing him, that, in his secret heart,
he had much rather let Eberly go clear from punishment, though
he risked the safety of the whole company by it."

"No danger of his doing it, whatever may be his wish," said
Haller; "you have my oath upon it, Mat. Whatever Foster
may say or do in the business, he can't say or do anything to
alter my determination. So make yourself easy. To-morrow,
or the next day, at farthest, will wind up the traitor."

"You must keep watch meanwhile upon him."

"Yes!—go about it now, Williams; look to Eberly for the
space of an hour, and I will come and relieve you. I must go
with Webber, to see what Foster has to say in the business—
and hearken to his interference, even if we do not mind it. But
I don't think he'll interfere, Mat. The spouting poetry might
please his ears well enough, but I'm convinced he could slit the
pipe of the spouter the moment he was done."

"Perhaps so," was the reply of Webber; "but, at all
events—"

They were leaving me now, and Haller interrupted the
speaker to counsel me before he went.

"I showed you, Williams, the place where Eberly sleeps:
do you think you can find it?"

"Yes — I doubt not."

"Then go to it at once, and note well who goes in to him, and who comes out. If he comes out slyly, and seems disposed to make off, do not stop to consider, but give him your bullet. Be sure to do this if you find him with his horse."

These were the instructions of Webber. The other merely said —

"Don't fear that he will try to make off He knows such efforts can not give him security, though he should, for the present, escape us. No — he thinks Foster's influence can save him, and he will remain quiet in reliance upon it."

"Be not now too sure, Williams," were the parting words of Webber; "watch closely, or the fellow may escape you yet. Remember you are on trial now : your promotion depends upon your zeal and success."

Nothing but the purposes which influenced me could have enabled me to tolerate, with patience, such language from such a wretch. I felt my heart burn, and my blood rise, and my lip quiver, with an anger which it required all my strength of resolution to repress, every moment which I spent in my connection with this herd of rogues. They left me, and, obeying their instructions, I proceeded to the place among the bushes — a leafy house — where Eberly slept; and, taking a position which enabled me to observe all the movements of its inmates, I prepared, with a thoughtful and sleepless mind, to pass away my hour of watch.

Haller afterward related to me what took place in their interview with Foster. As he had predicted, the latter made but a feeble effort to excuse the unfortunate Eberly.

"We first tried to find out," said Haller, "if Foster was disposed to have any concealment from us; and, pretending that we knew nothing of the interview between Eberly and himself, we spoke of other matters entirely. But he volunteered, and told us all pretty nearly as we ourselves heard, except he may have suppressed some of those parts where Eberly spoke scornfully of Mat Webber. These he did not speak. He then asked us what we thought of the application; and when we told him that now there was no doubt that Eberly ought to die and must die, he agreed with us entirely. Indeed, even if he had not agreed with us, he must have seen, from the resolved manner in which we spoke, that it would not have been wisdom in him to express his disagreement; and his death is therefore resolved upon. We are instructed to do the business at once— better now than never. You say he is still in his house?"

This conversation took place where I had been watching in front of the bushy dwelling in which Eberly slept; but my answer to the con luding question of my comrade was a falsehood:—

"Yes, he is still there. No one has gone in or out since I have been here."

Nothing but the lie could save me, and I had no scruples whatsoever in telling it. I had seen persons go in and out. Scarcely had I got to my place of watch, indeed, when I saw Foster enter the dingle. I crawled closely up behind it, and heard enough to convince me that Foster was a greater hypocrite than I had thought him, yet not so bad a man.

"Eberly!" he said quickly. The youth started from the ground where I could see he was kneeling. He started and drew a pistol in the same moment. The click of the cock warned Foster to speak again. He did so, and announced his name.

"I come to warn you that you can stay here no longer. I can not save you, Eberly. I wish I could. But that is impossible. My lips must denounce you, to keep myself unsuspected. There is a conspiracy against me, which I must foil. To seek to save you, I would only sacrifice myself, and do you no service. I can do nothing, therefore, but counsel you to fly. The sooner you are off the better. Indeed, I risk not a little in coming to you now. Breton, the trusty fellow, advises me that Webber, Haller, and Williams, are even now denouncing me in the woods, where it seems they overheard all our conference. It was well that I suspected them, and scrupulously addressed my words rather to their ears than yours. This will excuse to you my seeming harshness. But I can say no more. In a short time they will seek me. Take that time to be off. Fly where you can. Put the Ohio between us as soon as possible, for no residence in the Southwest will save you."

But few words were uttered by the visiter, but these were

enough to prompt the immediate exertions of the youth. Hith
erto he had appeared to me in an attitude rather feeble and
unmanly; there was something puny and effeminate in the
manner of his appeal to Foster in their previous interview;
but this he seemed to discard in the moment which called for
resolute execution. He drew forth and reprimed his pistols,
set his dirk-knife in readiness, and was ready in two minutes
to depart.

"Fortunately, I left my horse on the very edge of the island,"
was his self-congratulating remark. "Foster, God bless you, as
I do! Would that I could persuade you to fly with me!"

The other shook his head.

"Go! go! that is impossible. You fly—because you have
hopes to fly to. I have none. You love, Eberly—may your
love be more fortunate than mine has been—than I am disposed to think human affections generally are. It is because I
too have loved, that I sympathize with you, and am willing to
assist you in your flight. I know not that I am serving you,
Eberly, in this, yet it is my will to serve you. Take the will
for the deed, and be gone with all haste. You have not a moment—adieu!"

Foster left him, and, in an instant after, Eberly emerged from
the dingle. It was in my power to have obeyed to the very
letter the instructions which had been given me, and to have
shot him down without difficulty. My extended arm, at one
moment, as he passed from the copse, could have touched his
shoulder. But my weapon was unlifted; and I felt a sudden
satisfaction as I found it in my power to second the intentions
of Foster. This personage had placed himself also in a more
favorable light before my eyes during the brief interview which
I have narrated. It gave me pleasure to see that, amid brutal
comrades, and wild, lawless, and foul pursuits, he yet cherished
in his bosom some lingering sentiments of humanity. There
was something yet in his heart which partook of the holy nature of a childhood which, we may suppose, was even blessed
with hopes and kindred, and which, however perverted now to
the lessons and performances of hate, once knew what it was to
do homage at the altar of confiding love. Foster, as may already have appeared to the reader, was not deficient in those

requisitions of education which refine the taste and sentiment, however much they may fail to impress themselves for good on a corrupt and insensible spirit.

To return. I denied to Haller, as already stated, that any one had gone in or out from the place where Eberly slept. In the unequivocal lie was my only hope, and I had no scruple to utter it. My comrade then spoke as follows:—

"We have agreed among ourselves that he must be wound up Foster makes no objections, and Webber insists that it be done immediately. To you it is intrusted to give the blow; and this concludes your trial. I will go in and entice him out to you. Do you creep forward as you see me enter. Stand behind yon tree to the left, and I will bring him under it on the other side. Have your pistol cocked, and use it. But take care not to mistake your man. If you notice his white hat, you can't blunder. Keep quiet, now, while I go in."

He left me, and I paused where I was. Musing on the un-anticipated disappointment of the ruffian, a sudden whisper at my side aroused me to a recollection of myself. The voice was Webber's. He had crawled up to me with the stealthy pace of the wild-cat, and my involuntary start, as he spoke, attested my wonder at the ease and dexterity of his approach.

"Why do you stand?" he said in stern accents; "were you not told what to do—where to go? You have no time to waste —go forward!"

Not to seem remiss, I answered promptly :—

"I wished him first to get there. Both of us moving at the same time, might alarm him."

"More likely to do so moving one at a time; but move now —you are slow. You will win no favor in the club if you are not more prompt."

I could have driven my fist into his teeth as he spoke thus authoritatively; but prudence stifled my anger. As it was, however, I gave a sharp reply, which had in it a latent threat:

"You will find me prompt enough when the time comes, Mr. Webber."

"I hope so, I hope so," he said coolly. I went forward, and reached my station but a single instant before Haller re-emerged from the copse.

" He is gone — the bird is off ! " he cried out as he approached.

" Ha ! how is this ? " exclaimed Webber, putting his hand upon my shoulder with a firm grip. " You have let him escape, Williams ! You have slept on your post, man ; or you have connived —"

He paused ; but his language, tone, and manner, were so irresistibly provoking, that I shook his grasp from my shoulder, and, facing him boldly, replied :—

" It's false, whoever says it ! I have done neither, sir — neither connived with him, nor seen him fly. Recall your words, or, by Heavens, I strike you in the mouth ! "

" And if you did, young 'un, you'd get little profit from it — you'd get quite as good as you sent. But this is no time to vapor. It's very likely you're right, and I'm wrong, and that must satisfy you at present. How is it, Haller ? — wherefore should he fly ? Did you not understand that he would wait to hear Foster's decision ? "

" No, I did not understand, but I inferred it. It seemed to me, from the confidence which he expressed in Foster's ability to save him, that he would scarce think it policy to fly ; since flight, as it indicated distrust of us, would at once provoke our distrust of him, and lead to a denial of his prayer. I would have sworn that we should find him there."

" He has thought better of it, and taken to his heels. But he has not gone far. He will not go far. He's to marry Grafton's daughter ; I know that they're engaged, and the affair is to take place very soon. I shouldn't be at all surprised, from his agitation and hasty reference to Foster — not to speak of his flight now — if it is fixed for to-morrow or the next night."

There was much in this speech to confound and afflict me. " That marriage must be prevented," I inly declared to myself. " I must risk everything to prevent its consummation. The poor girl must not be sacrificed to such a connection. However much I may pity him " — and circumstances really began to impress me favorably toward Clifton — " I must yet save her."

While the two confederates debated the matter, I formed my own plans.

" Mr. Webber," I said, " you have ascribed the flight of this man to my neglect, or, which is worse, my connivance ; and your apology, if it may be called such, is scarcely satisfactory to me. But I leave my personal atonement over, and waive my own claims to the interests of our confederacy. I claim to pursue this man Eberly — to pursue and put him to death. The privilege is mine, for several reasons : the principal are enough. I will establish my claim to the confidence of the confederacy ; and, as the death of Eberly seems now essential to our secret, secure that. Instruct me where to seek for him. I will pursue him to Grafton's, and put a stop to this wedding in the most effectual manner. Give me the necessary directions, and you shall see that I am neither a sleeper nor a traitor. You will also see whether I am bold enough to strike either in our common cause or in defence of my own honor."

"Shrewdly crowed, young chicken, and to the purpose," was the chuckling response of Webber. "Now, that's what I like — that's coming out like a man ; and if you succeed in doing what you promise, you will undoubtedly have an equal claim on me and the confederacy. But don't misunderstand me, Williams. I never had any doubt of your honor, and, if I had, your offer now sufficiently proves me to have been wrong. I spoke from the haste and disappointment of the moment ; and I have not the slightest question that Eberly took off the moment after leaving Foster. He took the alarm at something or other — and men who have in them a consciousness of wrong, find cause of alarm in everything ; or it may be that he meditated flight from the first — for, now I think of it, I observed, when he first came, that he fastened his horse on the edge of the swamp, by ' Pigeon-Roost branch,' which you know, Haller, is scarce a stone's throw from the main road ; though that would be a stranger plan than all, since, if he meditated flight, he need not have come ; he only incurred useless risk by doing so."

"He's half mad — that's it," said Haller. "But let us look if his horse is gone. That will settle our doubts. It may be that he is still on the island somewhere."

To ascertain this fact did not take many minutes, and the absence of the horse confirmed the flight of the fugitive. I now demanded of Webber if my proffer was accepted. To go upon a mission of this kind, which would enable me to seek out and confer with Colonel Grafton, was now the dearest desire of my heart. To save his daughter was a sufficient motive for this desire ; to wreak the measure of my great revenge upon the damnable fraternity with which I had herded for this single object, was no less great, if not, in a public point of view, much greater. I had a stomach for the lives of all—all. The memory of my murdered friend took all mercy from my heart.

To my question, Webber answered :—

"We must see what Foster says. We will go to him at once. I'm willing that you should go about this business, and will help you to all information ; but I'm scarcely in a hurry about it now. I've been thinking it would please me better to let him marry the girl before we kill him. Then, if it so happened that I could ever lay my foot on Grafton's throat, as I hope to do before long, I could howl it in his ears, till it hurt him worse than my bullet or my knife, that his sweet Julia, his darling, of whom he is so fond and proud and boastful, was the wife of a common robber — a thief of the highway — a rogue to all the world, and worse than a rogue to his own comrades! That would be a triumph, Haller; and Grafton, if I know the man rightly, would go out of the world with a howl when I cried it in his ear !"

Sickening at the fiendish thought, I turned with revulsion from the fiend, and felt humbled and sad as I was constrained to follow such a ruffian in silence, and without any show of that natural resentment which I felt. But I conquered my impatience as I reflected that, by delay, I hoped to obtain at once a complete and certain satisfaction. An image of my sanguinary revenge rose before my eyes as I then went forward; and, in fancy, I beheld streaming wounds, and I felt my feet plashing in rivulets of stagnating blood!—and a strange but shuddering pleasure went through my bosom at the fancy.

CHAPTER XLVIII.

THE AFFAIR GROWS MORE INTRICATE.

> ————"The land wants such
> As dare with vigor execute the laws;
> Her festered members must be lanced and tented:
> He's a bad surgeon that for pity spares
> The part corrupted, till the gangrene spreads,
> And all the body perish: He that's merciful
> Unto the bad is cruel to the good."—RANDOLPH.

Foster received the tidings of Eberly's flight with well-affected astonishment. Putting on the sternest expression of countenance, he looked on me with suspicion.

"And you were set to watch him, Williams. How is this? I fear you have been neglectful — you have slept upon your watch — I can not think that you have had any intelligence with Eberly."

In answering the speaker, I strove to throw into my eyes a counselling expression, which it was my hope to make him comprehend. My answer, shaped to this object, had the desired effect.

"I have not slept, and you do me only justice, when you think that I have had no intelligence with the fugitive. But I have volunteered to pursue him, and will execute your judg ments upon him, if I can; even though *he should put the Ohio between us.*"

The reader will remember, that the phrase here italicised was employed by Foster himself, in giving his parting counsels to Eberly. Foster readily remembered it, and I could detect — so I fancied — in the tone of voice with which he adressed me in reply, a conviction that I was privy to his own partial and perhaps, pardonable treachery to his comrades. In every other respect he seemed unmoved, and his reply was instantaneous.

"And we accept your offer, Williams — you shall have the opportunity you seek to prove your fidelity, and secure the confidence of the club. We are agreed, Webber, are we not, that Williams shall take the track of Eberly?"

"Ay — to-morrow, though I care not that he should strike till the day following, if it be that I conjecture rightly on one matter."

"What matter? What is it that your conjecture?" demanded Foster, suspiciously.

"Why, that Eberly is about to marry Julia Grafton. It would not surprise me much if the affair takes place in a day or two. I think it must be so, from his present anxiety."

"He would be a fool, indeed, to think of such a thing, without our permission," replied Foster; "but even if such be the case, wherefore would you defer execution upon him till the day following, supposing that Williams should get a chance to strike as we blow."

"I would have the marriage completed," was the answer. "I would have Grafton's pride humbled by his daughter's union with one whom we should be able, not only to destroy, but dishonor. By all that is devilish in my heart, Foster, I could risk my life freely, to tell Grafton all his story, with my own lips the day after his daughter's nuptials."

"Well, you hate fervently enough," said Foster; "and, perhaps, where one's hand's in, he may as well thrust away with his whole soul. But this helps not our purpose. It is agreed, you say, that Williams goes upon this business?"

"Yes."

"Then his course must take him at once to Grafton's neighborhood."

"Yes — that is our course too. We meet to-morrow, you recollect, with Dillon and others, at the 'Blind.' Our beginners must be examined there."

"But Williams must start before us."

"No — it needs not," said Webber. "We need be in no hurry now, since there can be no doubt that we shall be able to find Eberly at any moment within the three next days

Williams knows that he must find him in that time, and if he does not, send Dillon and Haller on his track, and they find him, I'll bet my life, though they hid him in the closet scuttle-hole of Natchy swamp. Let us all go together to the meeting of the 'Blind,' and not alarm the traitor by pressing the pursuit upon him in the very moment of his flight. Let him have a little time — let him marry away, and be happy, if he can, for a night or two. It will not diminish his punishment that he has a taste only of wedlock. Julia Grafton is a sweet girl enough — I could have taken her myself, and, perhaps, been an honest overseer of her father's plantation all my life — bowing respectfully to his high mightiness, and kissing the rod of his rebuke — had he only looked a willingness to let me have her. But, as it is — let the game go! It matters not much who has what we can't have; and yet I hate Grafton so cursedly, that it gives me pleasure to think that she is to be the wife of one so completely in our power as Edward Eberly — or Clifton, as we should call him in Grafton Lodge. Let him swing freely on his gate awhile; and Williams may take his time. He cannot escape all of us, though he may escape him."

"You will instruct Williams, then, when he shall go, and where," said Foster.

"Yes — that shall be my look-out. In the meantime, let us go to sleep. We have to start early, and the small hours are beginning — I can tell from the increasing darkness and the cold. Let us wrap up, and sleep fast, for we must be stirring early. Williams, I'll wake you in the morning."

"The sooner the better," was my reply; "for, between us, I don't like this putting off. If I am to go after Eberly, I'd rather start at daylight, and strike as soon as I get a chance. I hate, when I have such a business on hand, to risk its justice by my own delay; particularly when delay can be avoided. Besides, I'm thinking that if Eberly marries this girl, he will be cunning enough to leave the country. Ten to one, he's made all his arrangements for an early start, and will be off on fast horses soon after the event."

"That's true," said the ruffian; "I did not think of that — you shall start as soon as possible after we have met our men at the 'Blind' to-morrow. We must meet them there first, for

I have business of importance with one of them that must be seen to; and you'll have to wait till I can show you the way to Grafton's, and some few of our hiding-places, thereabouts.

In my eagerness, I had almost told him that I knew the place well enough, and could find it without him. My anxiety to be in season to prevent the nuptials, had near'y blinded me to the great risk of detection, to which such an avowal must have subjected me. But I met the inquiring glance of Foster's eye at this moment, and that brought me to my senses. It taught me that I was playing a part of triple treachery, and warned me to be duly cautious of what I uttered. Without further question or reply, we broke up for the night; and it seemed to me that I had scarcely got snugly into my place of rest, and closed my eyes for an instant, before I was awakened by Webber, with a summons to set forward. However wanting in proper rest, for my partial slumbers of the night had given me no refreshment, I had too greatly at heart the peace of Grafton's family, and the safety of the poor girl Julia, not to leap with alacrity at the summons. Ten minutes sufficed to set us all in motion, and as the bright blaze of the sun opened upon us, we were speeding on at full gallop, some seven of us, at least, to our place of meeting at the "Blind." There had been, at different periods of the night, full thirty men in our bivouac in the Sipsy, but they came and went at all hours, and none remained but those who had something of the general management of the rest. Five of these were my companions now. The other two were Haller and myself. Haller, it seems, was not so much a counsellor as a trusted underling or orderly — a fellow sufficiently cunning to seem wise, and so much of the rogue as to deserve, even if lacking wisdom, a conspicuous place among those whose sole aim was dishonesty. But our business is not with him.

A smart ride of a few hours brought us to our resting-place, a nest of hills huddled together confusedly, and forming, with the valley already described, called the "Day Blind," a hundred natural hiding-places of like form and character. Here I was within a few miles of Col. Grafton's residence. I had passed the dwelling of Matthew Webber, already so well known to the reader, and who should be my companion, side of the mountain, threatened in their flow to break down all barriers,

by side with me as I passed it, but Webber himself. I watched him closely when we came in sight of it, and though I could see that he regarded it with wistful attention, yet he was as silent as the grave even on the subject of his own late proprietorship; and my position was too nice and ticklish to make any reference to it, advisable on my part.

When we got to the place of rest, which was about noon, we found several of the brotherhood already assembled, most of whom were instantly taken aside by Foster, Webber, and one or two others, who ruled with them, and underwent an examination as to what they had done or were in preparation to do. For my part I had nothing to do but saunter about like many others—lie down on the sunny knolls, and tumble among the yellow leaves, lacking employment. This was no pleasurable exercise for one who had in his heart such an unappeasable anxiety as was then pervading mine, and which I could scarce keep from exhibition. Meantime, I could see men coming and going on every side; the persons seeming quite as multiformed and particolored as the business was diverse in character in which they were engaged. While I gazed upon them without particular interest, my eyes were drawn to a group of three persons who now approached the valley from a pass through the two hills that rose before me. At the distance where I lay, I could not distinguish features, but there was an air and manner about them, which, in two of the party, compelled my closest attention. The horses which they rode seemed also to be familiar; and with more earnestness of feeling than I can now describe, or could then account for, I continued to gaze upon them, as, without approaching much nigher to where I lay, they continued their progress forward to where Foster and Webber were in the habit of receiving their followers. But, at length, overcome by strange surmises, I sprang to my feet, and shading my eyes with my hands, endeavored to made out the parties. The next moment they disappeared behind the knoll, and, with my anxiety still unsubdued, I threw myself again upon the ground, and strove with my impatience as well as I could. Perhaps a full hour elapsed when I saw the three re-emerge from behind the knoll, and come out into the valley. They were followed by Foster, who conducted them a little aside the four seated themselves together for a while, on the side of the hills; after a brief space, Foster left them and came toward me. He threw himself down beside me, with an air of weariness.

"Well, Williams, you seem to take the world easily. Here you lie, stretched at length upon the ground, as if it had no insects, and looking up to the skies as if they were never shadowed by a cloud. For my part I see nothing but insects and worms along the earth, and nothing but clouds in heaven. This comes from the nature of our pursuits, and to speak a truth, I sometimes see a beauty in virtue which I have never been able to see in man. I almost think, if circumstances would let me, that I would steal away, like poor Eberly, from our comrades, and try to do a safer and an humbler sort of business, among better reptiles than we now work with."

This speech, if meant to deceive, did not deceive me.

"You would soon long to return, Foster, to your present companions and occupations, or I greatly mistake your temper," was my reply. "Your ambition is your prevailing principle— to sway, your leading object—to be great, to have distinction, is the predominating passion of your heart."

My reply was intended merely to flatter him, and it had its effect. He paused for an instant, then said, with a smile:—

"And you would add, Williams, that, like Milton's devil, I am not at all scrupulous as to the sort of greatness which I aim at, or the quality of the instruments with which I wrought."

"And, if I did, Foster, I do not see that the imputation would do you any discredit. Men are pretty much alike wherever we find them, and there are virtuous monsters no less than vicious ones. Circumstances, after all, make the chief differences in the characters of mankind; and many a saint in white, born in my condition, would have cut many more throats than it's my hope ever to do. To rule man is to rule man—any inquiry as to the moral differences between those you rule and those you rule by, is a waste of thought, since the times, and the seasons, the winds and the weather, or a thousand differences which seem equally unreal and shadowy, are the true causes of the vices of one class and the virtues of another. A planter pays his debts, and is liberal if he makes a good crop—he fails in both respects if his crop fails; and the creditor denounces him

as a rogue, and sells his property under the hammer of a sheriff, while the church frowns upon him from the moment he
ceases to drop his Mexican in the charity hat. Saints and
devils are pretty much the same people, if the weather prevails
with equal force in their favor; but when the wind changes
and blights the crop of the one, and ripens that of the other, ten
to one, the first grows to be a general benefactor and is blessed
by all, while the other is driven from society as a miserable
skunk, whom it is mere charity to kick out of existence. You
should not bother your head in wishing for better followers or
a dominion less questionable. If you have fifteen hundred
men willing to fight and die for you, and not minding the laws
on the subject, you are a better and a greater man than the
governor of Mississippi, who, do his best, can not command
fifteen hundred votes. To my mind, it is clear that yours is the
greater distinction."

"That is true; and yet, Williams, what is distinction, indeed,
but a sort of solitude—a dreary eminence, which, though we
may behold many laboring at all seasons to scramble up its
side, how few do we see able to occupy it, how much more few
the number to keep it. My eminence, imposing as it may seem
to you, is at best very insecure. I have rivals—some who seek
to restrain me and to crush my power, by lopping off my best
friends at every opportunity, and on the slightest pretences.
These I am bound to save, yet I do so at great peril to myself.
I risk my own rule, nor my rule only—I risk my life daily, in
this connection, by seeking to save, as I am resolute always to
do, the friend, however wanting in other respects, who has
proved true to my desires and cause."

I saw which way these remarks tended; and resolved, at
once, to put a satisfactory conclusion to the apprehensions
which I saw prevailed in the mind of my companion. He was
obliquely seeking to justify himself for his course in regard to
Eberly, which he saw that I knew—and, probably, he was
aiming to discover in how far I might be relied on in sustain-
ing him in any partisan conflict with the rivals of whom he
spoke. My answer was not without its art; and it fully answered its intended purpose.

"You do no more than you should," was my reply. "You

are bound to succor your friends even against the laws of your comrades, since they risk the peril of these laws in serving you. I understand your difficulty. Indeed, it did not need that you should declare it to me, in order to make me know it. I had not been au hour in your camp on the Sipsy before I saw the secret strife which was going on; and, I may say, Foster, once for all, you may count upon me to sustain you against any rival that may be raised up in opposition to your just rule from among the confederates. Count on me, I say, to support you against Webber and his clan, for it strikes me that he is the fellow you have most to fear."

"You are right!" he said, grasping my hand nervously— 'you are quite right, and I admire your keenness of observation, only less than the warmth of your personal regard for me. Webber is, indeed, the person who is now plotting secretly against me. There will be a trial of strength between us in the council of twelve to-morrow—and I shall defeat him there, though by so small a vote that it will tend to stimulate him to still greater exertions, and to make him more inveterate in his hostility, which he has still grace enough to seek to hide."

He would probably have gone on much further in the development of the miserable strife that followed hard upon his state, but that a movement of my own interrupted him. My eyes had been for some time turned watchfully upon the group of three persons to which I have already called the reader's attention. They had left the little knoll on which they seated themselves when Foster first emerged with them from the place of conference, and had advanced somewhat further into the valley, and consequently rather nearer to my place of repose, which was half way down one of the hills out of which it was scooped. This approach enabled me to observe them better; and, as they moved about among another party, who were pitching quoits, my eyes gradually distinguished their persons first, and at length their features. This discovery led to my interruption of Foster's developments. What was my consternation and wonder to recognise John Hurdis in one, and Ben Pickett in another of this group. With difficulty I kept myself from leaping upright—my finger was involuntarily extended toward them

"What see you?" demanded Foster, looking in the same direction. His demand was a sufficient warning for me to be cautious, and yet, for the life of me, I could not forbear the question in reply.

"Who are those?"

"What, the pitchers?"

"Yes! yes! and their companions — the lookers-on."

"One of the pitchers is a fellow named Hatfield — a close friend of Webber, and one of our most adroit spies; he is the fellow in green; the other two are common *strikers*, who will set out on an expedition to-night. They are exceedingly expert horse-stealers, and the people near Columbus will hear of them before they are two days older — the tallest one is named Jones, the other Baker."

"And how do they incline — toward you or Webber?" was an indifferent question, almost too indifferently put to answer the purpose of a disguise to my real curiosity, for which it was intended. I heard his answer impatiently, and then, with lips that trembled, I demanded —

"And who are the three lookers-on? I have not seen them before! They were not with us on the Sipsy last night?"

"No; they have just come from down the river. The smaller fellow is one of our keenest emissaries, and, perhaps, one of our bravest men. He has just brought up the two men who are with him—"

"What! as prisoners?" I exclaimed, in my impatience.

"Prisoners, indeed! No. What should we do with prisoners? They belong to us. They are our men."

"Why, then, do you say he brought them up?"

"This is the affair. I have just finished their examination. It appears that the large, fat fellow, is rather a rich young planter somewhere in Marengo. He had a brother with whom he had a quarrel. This brother set off with a companion some weeks ago for the 'nation,' where they proposed to enter lands The elder brother avails himself of this opportunity to revenge himself for some indignities put upon him by the younger, and despatches after him the fellow in homespun, whom you see beside him, his hands in his breeches pockets. Webber, it appears, about the same time. laid a trap for the two travellers, one of whom fell into it very nicely — the other broke off and got away. They pursued him, but they must have lost him, but for the timely aid of the chap in homespun, who, lying in wait, shot down the fugitive, and then made off to his employer. According to our general plan, an emissary was sent after the murderer, and, in securing him, the secret of the brother was discovered. In this way, both have been secured, and are now numbered among our followers."

I have abridged Foster's narrative, in order to avoid telling a story twice. Here was a dreadful discovery. My stupid amazement can not be described. I was literally overcome. Foster saw my astonishment, and inquired into its cause. My reply was, perhaps, a sufficient reason for my astonishment, though it effectually concealed the true one.

"Great God! can this be possible? His own brother?"

"Even so. Neither you nor I would have done such a thing, bad as we may be held by well-ordered society. The fellow seems but a poor creature after all, and could hardly stand during our examination. Of such creatures, however, we make the most useful, if not the most daring members. We will let him go back to Marengo after to-morrow, and be a pillar of the church, which, I think it not improbable, he will instantly join, if, indeed, he be not already a member. The other fellow, who is called Pickett, takes to us with a relish, and Webber has found him a place to squat somewhere on the banks of the Big Warrior. But, a truce to this. Here Webber approaches. Do not forget, Williams — and, I am your friend. We must act together for mutual benefit. Mum, now."

Webber drew nigh, bringing with him the emissary who had gone after Pickett and John Hurdis. They remained with the pitchers, among whom, I may add, Pickett was, at this time, incorporated, and working away as lustily as the most expert. But I had no time allowed me to note either his, or the labors of John Hurdis. My attention was instantly challenged by Webber, who, unless angry, was not a man of many words.

"Get yourself in readiness, Williams; I will set you on the track in an hour, and show you a part of the route."

I proceeded to obey, and it was not long, as may be conjectured, before I was properly mounted for that journey which

was to eventuate in the rescue of my friend's child from the
cruel sacrifice which was at hand.   Webber and myself set off
together.   Foster shook my hand at parting, and his last phrase
was one, which, between us, had a meaning beyond that which
met the ear.

"I trust you will find your man, Williams, though he even
puts the Ohio between us.   Let us see you back soon."

I was annoyed by the searching stare of the keen-eyed emissary.   His eyes were never once taken from my countenance,
from the moment of my introduction to him; and, I am sure,
that he had some indistinct remembrance of me, though, fortunately, not of a sufficiently strong character to do more than
confuse him.   I dreaded discovery every moment, but, though
watching me keenly to the last, with a most unpleasant pertinacity of stare, he suffered me to ride away without the utterance of those suspicions which I looked momently to hear
spoken.

CHAPTER XLIX.

TROUBLES AT GRAFTON LODGE.

"Cold tidings, sir,
I bring you, of new sorrows. You have need
To make division of your wide estate,
And parcel out your stores. Take counsel, sir,
How you will part from life; for 'tis my fear
That you must part from hope, which life more needs,
Than the dull fare it feeds on."—*Knight Errant.*

WE did not delay, having now put ourselves in readiness, but, after a few brief words of parting, we left Foster and the emissary, whose searching eyes I was truly anxious to escape from. That fellow's stare gave me more uneasiness, and a greater idea of the danger that I ran, than any other one circumstance since my connection with the ruffians. Foster did not let me leave him without giving me some expressive glances. I could see that he was desirous of saying something to me, which, I fancied, must concern Eberly; but we had no opportunity for a private word after Webber joined us, and to make an opportunity was wishing far more than I desired or Foster was prepared for. Off we went at full gallop, and we were soon out of sight of the encampment, and rough hills were momently rising between us. In the course of a quarter of an hour, I found myself going once more over the very spot where we found the body of William Carrington. I shuddered involuntarily as my eyes rested upon it; the next moment I saw the glance of Webber fixed curiously on the same spot, and a slight smile played upon his lips, as he caught my look of inquiry.

"A tall fellow was tumbled here only the other day," he said, with an air of indifference that vexed me "who might have been alive and kicking now, if his heels had been less

I now drew nigher, and pretended a curiosity to hear the story, but he baffled my desire as he replied—

"Not now: another time, when we are more at leisure, I'll tell you stories of what I've seen and know, to make you open your eyes much wider than you do now. But here we reach the road, the 'Day-Blind' as they call it, for it's so deep and narrow that there's always a shade over it. This road taking the left-hand fork, when you get on a mile farther, takes you direct to Grafton's. You'll see the avenue leading to the lodge, to the right, and a pretty place enough it is. You can lie to-night at a house which you'll see two miles after you pass Grafton's, where you'll find two of our people. Give them the first two signs, and they'll know who you are, and provide you with any help you may call for. But the places which you must watch in particular are the two avenues to the lodge—the front and rear. There is a thick wood before the back avenue, where we've got one of our men watching now. You must relieve him and send him to me instantly. He will not need you to urge him to full speed if you will only remember to tell him that 'the saddle wants nothing but the stirrups.' He'll understand that, and come."

"But what does that mean?" I demanded.

"Oh, nothing much—it's a little matter between us, that doesn't at all concern the fraternity."

"What! have you secrets which the club is not permitted to share?"

"Yes, when they do not conflict with our laws. An affair with a petticoat is a matter of this sort."

"And yet such is Eberly's affair."

"True; but Eberly would sacrifice all to the petticoat, and for that we punish him. He might go after a dozen women if he pleased, and have a seraglio like the Grand Turk, and none of us would say him nay, if he did not allow them to play Delilah with him, and get his secret. But listen, now, while I give you the necessary information."

Here we stopped a while, and he led me into the woods where he gave a brief account of Grafton family and lodge, informed me of one or two hiding-places of Eberly, and even told me at what hour I might look to see him arriving at the avenue.

So keen had been his watch, and that of his creatures, upon the
doomed fugitive, that, as I afterward discovered, he was not only
correct to the very letter in what he told me, but he also knew every
movement which his victim made; and there had not been a day, for
the three months preceding, in which he had not been able at any
time to lay hands upon him. Indeed, had the directions of Webber
been followed while in the Sipsy swamp, Eberly could not by any
possibility have escaped, unless through my evasion of the murderous task which had been then assigned me. I need not add
that such would have been the case. Regarding the unhappy youth
as not undeserving of punishment, I had yet no desire to become his executioner. I had taken enough of this duty on my
hands already ; and my late discovery, touching John Hurdis,
had increased the solemnity of the task to a degree which put the
intensity of my excitement beyond all my powers of description.
I could now only reflect that I had sworn in the chamber of
death, and in the presence of the dead, to execute the eternal sentence of justice upon the person of my own brother. When
Webber left me in that wood, I renewed the terrible oath before
Heaven.

But to my present task. I rode forward as I had been counselled, and soon came in sight of the well-known lodge, which,
whatever might be my wish, I did not dare to enter, until I
had first got out of the way of the spy whom Webber kept
upon it, and whom he requested me to send to him. Avoiding
the entrance accordingly, I fell into a by-path, which ran round
the estate, and whistling a prescribed tune, as I approached the
back avenue, I had the satisfaction to hear the responsive note
from the wood opposite. Who should present himself at my
summons, but my ancient foe, the Tuscaloosa gambler whom
they called George? I felt the strongest disposition to take
the scoundrel by the throat, in a mood betwixt merriment and
anger ; but there was a stake of too much importance yet to be
played for, and with praiseworthy patience I forebore. Subduing my voice, and restraining my mood to the proper pitch, I
introduced myself to him in the prescribed form. I showed him
the first two signs of the club—the sign of the *striker*, and the
sign of the *feeder* —the first being that of the common horse-
thief or mail robber ; the other that which empowers a member

to probe the nature of the man he meets, and secure him, if he thinks he can, to the uses of the brotherhood. I gave him my assumed name, and the history of my membership, and then sent him on his way—happy to get him out of mine—to the brothers in the encampment. I waited with impatience till he had gone fairly out of sight; then, with a full heart, and a bosom bounding once more with freedom, I entered the avenue, and hurried forward to the dwelling of my friend.

My disguise was quite as complete in concealing me from Colonel Grafton as it had been in hiding me from my foes. It was with difficulty I persuaded him to know me. His first words, after he became convinced of my identity, were—

"And the poor girl Emmeline? How did she stand your tidings?"

"She is dead." I told him all the particulars; and accounted for the disguise in which I appeared, by telling what were the novel duties which I had undertaken.

"You are a bold man—a very bold man, Mr. Hurdis. And how far have you been successful?"

Briefly, I related to him my meeting with Foster; the success of my plans; his revelations to me; and the progress of events until I came to the encampment in the Sipsy swamp. These he listened to with an intense interest, and frequently interrupted me to relate little incidents within his own knowledge, which, strange and unaccountable before, found an easy solution when coupled with such as I related. When I had told him thus far, I came to an uneasy halt. He had evidently no apprehension that he could be interested further in such a narrative than as a good citizen and a public magistrate. Finding me at a pause, he thus spoke:—

"And you left these rascals in the Sipsy; you have come now for assistance, have you not?"

"You are right, colonel: I have come to get what assistance I can to bring them to punishment. But I left them not in the Sipsy; they are nigher than you think for, and much more conveniently situated for a surprise."

"Ha! in the 'Day-Blind'—is it so? That has long been a suspicious place; and, if my conjecture is right, I will do my best to ferret them out, and clear it for good and all."

·"They are near it, if not in it," was my reply. I proceeded to describe the place, which he very well knew.

"In three days more, Hurdis, I shall be ready for the hunt. We can not conveniently have it sooner, since a little domestic matter will, for the next day or two, take up all my attention; and I must forget the magistrate for a brief period in the father. You are come in season, my friend, for our family festivities. My daughter, you must know—

"Let me stop you, Colonel Grafton—I do know; and I trust you will not regard the bearer of ill tidings as responsible for the sorrow which he brings. Your daughter, you would tell me, is to be married to Mr. Clifton."

"Yes—it is that. But what ill tidings?"

·Mr. Clifton is with these ruffians; I saw him in the Sipsy swamp."

"What! a prisoner?"

I shook my head.

"Nothing worse, I trust. They have not murdered him, Mr. Hurdis? He lives?"

"He lives, but is no prisoner, Colonel Grafton. It is my sorrow to be compelled to say that he was with them voluntarily when I saw him."

"How! I really do not understand you."

I hurried over the painful recital, which he heard in speechless consternation. The strong man failed before me. He leaned with a convulsive shudder against the mantel-place, and covered his face with his hands. While he stood thus, his daughter entered the room, with a timid and sweet smile upon her lips, but shrunk back the moment that she saw me. As yet, none of the family but Colonel Grafton himself knew who I was. The father turned as he heard her voice.

"Julia," he said, "my daughter—go to your chamber—remain there till I send for you. Do not leave it."

His voice was mournful and husky, though he strove to hide his emotion. She saw it, and prepared to obey. He led her by the hand to the door, looking back at me the while; and, when there, she whispered something in his ears. He strove to smile as he heard it, but the effort was a feeble and ineffectual one.

"Go to your mother, my child : tell her that it matters nothing. And do you keep your chamber. Do not come down stairs till I call you."

The girl looked at him with some surprise, but she did not utter the question which her eyes sufficiently spoke. Silently she left the room, and he returned to me instantly.

"Hurdis, you have given me a dreadful blow ; and I can not doubt that what you told me you believe to be the truth. But may you not be deceived? It is everything to me and my child, if you can think so; it is more important, if you are not, that I should be certified of the truth. You saw Clifton in the swamp with these villains : that I doubt not. It may be, too, that you heard them claim him as a colleague. This they might do — such villains would do anything; they might claim me as well as you; for the horse-thief and the murderer would not scruple to rob the good name from virtue, and murder the fair reputation of the best of us. They have sought to destroy me thus already. Tell me, then, on what you ground your belief; give me the particulars. It may be, too, that Clifton, if he leagues with them at all, does so for some purpose like your own."

How easy would it have been to deceive the father — to persuade him to believe anything which might have favored his desires, though against the very face of reason and reflection!

"I would I could answer you according to your wish, but I can not. I have told you nothing but the truth — what I know to be the truth — if the confessions of Clifton himself, in my hearing, and to the leader of this banditti, can be received in evidence."

His own confessions? Great God! can it be possible? — But I hear you. Go on, Mr. Hurdis — tell me all. But take a chair, I pray you ; be seated, if you please, for I must."

He strode over the floor toward a seat, with a slowness of movement which evidently proceeded from a desire to conceal the feebleness of body which he certainly felt, and to a certain extent exhibited. He sunk into the chair, his hands clasped, and drooping between his knees, while his head was bent forward, in painful earnestness, as I proceeded in my story. I related, step by step, all the subsequent particulars in my own narrative, suppressing those only which did not concern Clifton. He heard me patiently, and without interruption, to the end. A single groan only escaped him as I concluded; and one brief exclamation declared for whose sake only, all his suffering was felt—

"My poor, poor Julia!"

Well might this be his exclamation; and as it came from his lips, while his eyes were closed, and his head fell forward upon his breast, I could see the cherished hopes of a life vanishing with the breath of a single moment. That daughter was the pride of his noble heart. Nobly had he taught—dearly had he cherished her; with a fond hand he had led her along the pleasant paths of life, securing her from harm, and toiling with equal care, for her happiness. And all for what? My heart joined with his, as I thought over these things, and it was with difficulty I could keep my lips from saying after his own—"Poor, poor Julia!"

At this moment a servant entered the apartment.

"Mr. Clifton, sir!"

"Ha! comes he then!" was the sudden exclamation of the father, starting from his chair, and, in a single instant, throwing aside the utter prostration of soul which appeared in his features, and which now gave place to a degree of energy and resolution, which fully spoke for the intense fire which had been kindled in his heart.

"Show him in!"

The servant disappeared.

"This night, Mr. Hurdis, this man was to have married my daughter. You have saved us just in time. You speak of his repentance—you have almost striven to excuse him—but it will not answer. I thank you—thank you from my heart—that you have saved us from such connection. Step now into this chamber. You shall hear what he will say—whether he will seek to carry out his game of deception; and, to the last, endeavor to consummate by villany, what his villany had so successfully begun. It is but right that you should hear his answers to my accusation. He may escape the vengeance of his brother scoundrels—but me he shall not escape. He comes —into that chamber, Mr Hurdis. I must beg you to retire—

bear with me if I seem rude in hurrying you thus. My misery
must excuse me, if I am less heedful than I should be of ordinary politeness."

Thus, with that nice consideration of character which made
him somewhat a precisian in manners, he strove to forget his
own feelings in his effort to avoid offending mine. At that moment I could have forgiven him a far greater display of rudeness than that for which he apologized. When I looked upon
the face of that father, solicitous to the last degree for the wel-
fare of the beloved child of whom such care had been taken,
and thought upon the defeat of all his hopes, and possibly all
of hers, which had followed my narration, I could not but wonder at the iron strength of soul which could enable him to bear
his disappointment so bravely.

He conducted me into the little room, to which for the present he had consigned me, and taking from it a small mahogany
box, which I readily conceived to be a case of pistols, he returned instantly to the apartment which I left, where, a moment
after, he was joined by Clifton.

CHAPTER L.

CAPTIVITY.

> "To what gulfs
> A single deviation from the track
> Of human duties, leads ever those who claim
> The homage of mankind."—*Sardanapalus.*

" COLONEL GRAFTON."

"Mr. Clifton," were the simple forms of address employed by the two on first encountering.

" You are surprised to see me so soon, Colonel Grafton," was the somewhat abrupt speech of Clifton the next minute.

"Surprised! not a whit, sir," was the quick reply. "You were looked for."

"Looked for, sir! Ah! yes, of course, I was expected to come, but not yet, sir—not for some hours. You looked for me, indeed, but you scarcely looked for the person who now seeks you; and when you know the business which brings me, Colonel Grafton, you will not, I am afraid, hold me so welcome as before."

"Why should you be afraid, Mr. Clifton? Believe me, you were never more welcome than at this very moment—never!" was the grave and emphatic reply. "You seem surprised, sir, that I should say so, but wherefore? Are you surprised that I should promptly welcome the man who seeks to do so much honor to my family as to become one of it? Why do you look on me so doubtingly, Mr. Clifton? Is there anything so strange in what I say?"

" No, sir, nothing, unless it be in the manner of your saying it. If you speak, Colonel Grafton, in sincerity, you add to the weight of that humility which already presses me to the earth

—if in derision—if with a foreknowledge of what I come to say—then, I must only acknowledge the justice of your scorn and submit myself to your indignation."

"Of what you came to say, Mr. Clifton?" slowly replied the half-hesitating listener. "Speak it out then, sir, I pray you—let me hear what you came to speak. And in your revelations do not give me credit for too great a foreknowledge, or you may make your story too costive for the truth. Proceed, sir—I listen."

"You seem already to have heard something to my disadvantage, Colonel Grafton. It is my misfortune that you have not heard all that you might have heard—all that you must hear. It is my misery that my lips alone must tell it."

The unfortunate young man paused for an instant, as if under the pressure of emotions too painful for speech. He then resumed:—

"I come, sir, to make a painful confession; to tell you that I have imposed upon you, Colonel Grafton—dreadfully imposed upon you—in more respects than one."

"Go on, sir."

"My name, sir, in the first place, is not Clifton, but—"

"No matter, sir, what it is! Enough, on that point, that it is not what you call it. But the letters, sir—what of them? How came you by letters of credit and introduction from my known and tried friends in Virginia?"

"They were forged, sir."

"Well, I might have known that without asking. The one imposition fairly implies the other."

"But not by me, Colonel Grafton."

"They were used by you, and you knew them to be forged, sir. If your new code of morality can find a difference between the guilt of making the lie, and that of employing it when made, I shall be informed, sir, if not pleased. Go on with your story, which seems to concern me; and, considering the manner of its beginning, the sooner you bring it to an end the better. What, may I ask, did you propose to yourself to gain by this imposition?"

"At first, sir, nothing. I was the creature—the base instrument of the baser malice of another. Without any object my

self, at first, I was weak enough to labor thus criminally for
the unworthy objects of another."

"Ha! indeed! For another. This is well—this is better
and better, sir; but go on—go on."

"But when my imposition, sir, had proved so far successful
as to bring me to the knowledge and the confidence of your
family—when I came to know the treasure you possessed in
the person of your lovely daughter—"

"Stay, sir—not a word of her. Her name must not pass
your lips in my hearing, unless you would have me strike you
to my feet, for your profanity and presumption. It is wonderful to me, now, how I can forbear."

"Your blow, though it crushed me into the earth, could not
humble me more, Colonel Grafton, than my own conscience has
already done. I am not unwilling that you should strike. I
came here this day to submit, without complaint or prayer,
to any punishment which you might deem it due to your
injured honor to inflict. But, as a part of the reparation which
I propose to make to you, it is my earnest desire that you
should hear me out."

"Reparation, sir—reparation! Do you talk to me of reparation—you that have stolen into my bosom, like an insidious
serpent, and tainted the happiness, and poisoned all the springs
of joy which I had there. Tell your story, sir —say all that
you deem essential to make your villany seem less, but do not
dare to speak of reparation for wrongs that you can not repair
—wounds that no art of yours, artful though you have proved
yourself, can ever heal."

"I do not hope to repair—I feel that it is beyond my power
to heal them. I do not come for that. I come simply to declare the truth—to acknowledge the falsehood—and, in forbearing to continue a course of evil, and in professing amend-
ment for the future, to do what I can for the atonement of what
is evil in the past. To repair my wrongs to you and yours,
Colonel Grafton, is not within my hope. If it were, sir, my
humility would be less than it is, and, perhaps, your indulgence
greater."

"Do not trust to that, sir—do not trust to that. But we will
spare unnecessary words. Your professions for the future are

wise and well enough; it is to be hoped that you will be suffered to perform them. At present, however, our business is with what is past, of evil, not with what is to come, of good. You say that you were set on by another to seek my confidence —that another prepared the lies by which you effected your object. Who was that other? Who was that master-spirit to which your own yielded such sovereign control over truth and reason, and all honesty? Answer me that, if you would prove your contrition."

"Pardon me, sir, but I may not tell you that. I may not betray the confidence of another, even though I secured your pardon by it."

"Indeed! But your principles are late and reluctant. This is what is called 'honor among thieves.' You could betray my honor, and the confidence of a man of honor, but you can not betray the confidence of a brother rogue."

"My wrong to you, Colonel Grafton, I repent too deeply to suffer myself to commit a like wrong against another, however unworthy he may be. Let me accuse myself, sir; let me, I pray you, declare all my own offences, and yield myself up to your justice, but do not require me to betray the secrets of another."

"What! though that other be a criminal—though that other be the outlaw from morals, which you should be from society, and trains his vipers up to sting the hands that take them into the habitations of the unwary and the confiding! Your sense of moral justice seems to be strangely confounded, sir."

"It may be—I feel it is, Colonel Grafton, but I am bound to keep this secret, and will not reveal it. It is enough that I am ready to suffer for the offence to which I have weakly and basely suffered myself to be instigated."

"You shall suffer, sir; by the God of Heaven you shall suffer, if it be left in this old arm to inflict due punishment for your treachery. You shall not escape me. The sufferings of my child shall determine yours. Every pang which she endures shall drive the steel deeper into your vitals! But proceed, sir, you have more to say. You have other offences to narrate—I will hear you."

"I feel that you will not heed my repentance. I know

too, why your indulgence should be beyond my hope. I do not ask forgiveness, which I know it to be impossible that you should grant; I only pray that you will now believe me, Colonel Grafton, for before Heaven I will tell you nothing but the truth."

"Go, on, sir, tell your story; your exhortation is of little use, for the truth needs no prayer for its prop. It must stand without one or it is not truth. As for my belief, that can not effect it. Truth is as certainly secure from my doubts, as I am sorry to think she has been foreign to your heart for a long season. If you have got her back there, you are fortunate, thrice fortunate. You will do well if you can persuade her to remain. Go on, go on, sir."

"Your unmeasured scorn, Colonel Grafton, helps to strengthen me. It is true, it can not lessen my offence to you and yours, but it is no small part of the penalty which should follow them; and holding it such, my punishments grow lighter with every moment which I endure them."

"Trust not that. I tell you, William Clifton, or whatever else may be your true name—for which I care not—that I have that tooth of fire gnawing in my heart, which nothing, perhaps, short of all the blood which is in yours can quench or satisfy. Think not that I give up my hope of revenge as I consent to hear you. The delay but whets the appetite. I but seek in thought for the sort of punishment which would seem most fitting to your offence."

"I will say nothing, Colonel Grafton, to arrest or qualify it —let your revenge be full. The blood will not flow more freely from my heart, when your hand shall knock for it, than does my present will, in resignation, to your demand for vengeance. Let me only, I pray you, say a few words, which it seems to me will do you no offence to hear, and which I feel certain it will be a great relief to me to speak. Will you hear me, sir?"

The humility of the guilty youth seemed not without its effect on the heated, but noble old man, who replied promptly :

"Surely, sir—God forbid that I should refuse to hear the criminal. Go on—speak."

"I am come of good family, Colonel Grafton —" began the youth

"Certainly—I doubt not that. Never rogue yet that did not."

A pause ensued. The voice of the youth was half stifled, as with conflicting emotions, when he endeavored to speak again. But he succeeded.

"I am an only son—a mother—a feeble, infirm mother—looked to me for assistance and support. A moment of dreadful necessity pressed upon us, and in the despair and apprehension which the emergency brought with it to my mind, I committed an error—a crime, Colonel Grafton—I appropriated the money of another!"

"A fit beginning to so active a life—but go on."

"Not to my use, Colonel Grafton—not to my use, nor for any pleasure or appetite of my own, did I apply that ill-got spoil. It was to save from suffering and a worse evil, the mother which had borne me."

"I believe, Mr. Clifton, in no such necessity," was the stern reply. "In a country like ours, no man need steal, nor lie, nor cheat. The bread of life is procured with no difficulty by any man having his proportion of limbs and sinews, and not too lazy and vicious for honest employment. You could surely have relieved your parent without a resort to the offence you speak of."

"True, sir—I might. But I did not know it then—I was a youth without knowledge of the world or its resources. Brought up in seclusion, and overcome by the sudden terror of debt, and the law —"

"Which, it seems, has kept you in no such wholesome fear to the end of the chapter. Pity for both our sakes that it had not. But to make a long story short, Mr. Clifton, and to relieve you from the pleasure or the pain of telling it, know, sir, that I am acquainted with all, and, perhaps, much more than you are willing to relate."

"Indeed, sir—but how—how came you by this knowledge?"

"That is of no importance, or but little. Not an hour before you made your appearance, I received an account of your true character and associates—thank Heaven! in sufficient time to be saved from the fatal connection into which my child had so nearly fallen."

"She should not have fallen, Colonel Grafton," said Clifton solemnly. "I came on purpose to declare the truth, sir."

"So I believe. Mr. Clifton; and it is well for you, and, perhaps, well for me, that you were so prompt to declare the truth when you made your appearance. Had you but paused for five minutes—had you lingered in your self-exposure —I had put a bullet through your head with as little remorse, as I should have shot the wolf which aimed to prey upon my little ones. I had put my pistols in readiness for that purpose. They are this instant beneath my hands. Nothing but your timely development could have saved you from death, and even that would not have availed, but that you have shown a degree of contrition during your confession, to which I could not shut my eyes. Know, sir, that I not only knew of the deception practised upon me, but of your connection with the daring outlaws who overrun the country; and from whom, by the way, you have much more at this moment to fear, than you can ever have reason to fear from me. Their emissaries are even now in pursuit of you, thirsting for your blood."

"Colonel Grafton, tell me—I pray you tell me—how know you all this."

"Is it not true?"

"Ay!—ay! true as gospel, though my lips, though I perished for denying, should never have revealed it."

"What! you would still have kept bond with these outlaws?"

"No, sir; but I would not have revealed their secrets."

"But you shall, sir—you shall do more. You shall guide me and others to the place where they keep. You shall help to deliver them into the hands of justice."

"Never, sir! never!" was the quick reply.

"Then you perish by the common hangman, Mr. Clifton," said Colonel Grafton. "Either you deliver them up to punishment, or you die for your share in their past offences."

"Be it so—I can perish, you will find, without fear, though I may have lived without honor. Let me leave you now, Colonel Grafton—let me pass."

"You pass not here, while I have strength to keep you, sir," said Grafton; and as these words reached my ears, I heard a rushing sound, and then a struggle. With this movement, I opened the door, and entered the apartment. They were closely grappled as they met my sight, and though it was evident enough that Eberly studiously avoided the application of his whole force in violence to Grafton, it was not the less obvious that he was using it all in the endeavor to elude him, and break away. I did not pause a moment to behold the strife, but making forward, I grasped the fugitive around the body, and lifting him from the floor, laid him, in another instant, at full length upon it. This done, I put my knee upon his breast, and presenting my dirk-knife to his throat I exacted from him a constrained and sullen submission.

CHAPTER LI.

STRATAGEMS.

> "The sun has set;
> A grateful evening doth descend upon us,
> And brings on the long night."—SCHILLER.

To DISPOSE of him now was a next consideration, and one of some little difficulty. It was no wish of mine, and certainly still less a wish with Colonel Grafton, to hold the unfortunate and misguided youth in bondage for trial by the laws. This was tacitly understood between us. By the statements of his associates, it was clear enough that he had been a profitless comrade, doing nothing to earn the applause, or even approval of the criminal; and as little, if we except the mere fact of his being connected with such a fraternity, to merit the punishment of the laws. His hands had never been stained by blood; and, setting aside his first offence against virtue, and that which brought him into such perilous companionship with vice, we knew nothing against him of vicious performance. Apart from this, the near approximation which he had made toward a union with the family of Colonel Grafton, however mortifying such an event may have become to his pride, was calculated to produce a desire in his mind that as little notoriety as possible should be given to the circumstances, and even had Eberly been more guilty than he was, I, for one, would rather infinitely have suffered him to escape, than to subject the poor girl, whose affections he had won, to the constant pain which she must have felt by the publication of the proceedings against him. Even as it was, her trial was painful enough, as well to those who witnessed her sufferings as to the poor heart that was compelled to bear them. Enough of this at present.

But it was essential at this moment, when it was our design

to entrap the heads of the Mystic Brotherhood, that Eberly,
though we refrained to prosecute him before the proper tribu-
nal, should not be suffered to escape our custody. By his reluctance to accuse, or to act against these outlaws, he evidently
held for them a degree of regard, which might prompt him, if
permitted, to apprize them of their danger, even though he may
have held himself aloof, as he had promised, from all future connection with them. But how and where to secure him was another difficulty for which an answer was not so readily provided.
To imprison him in the dwelling, in which that very day he was
to have found his bride, and in which, as yet uninformed of the
melancholy truth, that unconscious and full-hearted maiden was
even then preparing to become so, was a necessity of awkward
complexion; and yet to that necessity we were compelled to
come. After deliberating upon the matter, with an earnestness
which left no solitary suggestion unconsidered, the resolution
was adopted to secure the prisoner in the attic, until our pursuit
of his comrades was fairly over. This, it was our confident
hope, would be the case by the close of the day following, and
only until that time did we resolve that he should be a prisoner.
His comrades once secured, and his way of flight, it was intended, should be free. How our determination on this subject was
evaded and rendered unavailing, the following pages will show.

His course once resolved upon, and the measures of Colonel
Grafton were prompt and decisive.

"Keep watch upon him here, Hurdis; let him not stir, while
I prepare Mrs. Grafton with a knowlege of this unhappy business. My daughter, too, must know it soon or late, and better
this hour than the next, since the strife will be the sooner over.
They must be out of the way when we take him up the stair
—out of hearing as out of sight. Once there, I have a favorite
fellow who will guard him as rigidly as I should myself."

He left me, and was gone, perhaps, an hour—it was a tedious hour to me, in the painful watch that I was compelled to
keep over the unhappy prisoner. In this time he had commu-
nicated the discovery to both his wife and Julia; and a single
shriek, that faintly reached our ears, and the hurried pace of
many feet going to and fro in the adjacent chambers, apprized
us of the very moment when the soul of the poor maiden was

anguish-stricken by the first intelligence of her hapless situation. My eye was fixed intently upon the face of Eberly, and when that shriek reached us, I could see a smile, which had in it something of triumph, overspread his cheek, and, though it did not rest there a single moment it vexed me to behold it.

"Do you exult," I demanded, " that you have made a victim of one so lovely and so young? Do you rejoice, sir, in the pang that you inflict?"

"No! God forbid!" was his immediate answer. "If it were with me now, she should instantly forget not only her present, but all sorrows—she should forget that she had ever known so miserable a wretch as myself! But is it wonderful that I should feel a sentiment of pleasure, to find myself an object of regard in the eyes of one so pure—so superior? Is it strange that I should rejoice to find that I am not an outcast from all affections, as I am from all hopes—that there is one angelic spirit, who may yet intercede for me at the bar of Heaven, and pray for, and command mercy, though she may not even hope for it on earth?"

Grafton now returned, and the flush of anger was heightened on his face, though I could see a tear even then glistening in his eye.

"Mr. Clifton," he said calmly, but peremptorily, "we must secure your person for the night."

"My life is at your service, Colonel Grafton—I tender it freely. As I have no hopes in life now, I do not care to live. But I will not promise to remain bound, if I can break from my prison. I came to you of my own free will, without any impulse beside; and, though I thought it not unlikely when I came and revealed my story, that you would take my life, I had no fear that you would constitute yourself my jailer. I am not prepared for bonds."

"Make what distinctions you please," was the cold reply; "you hear my resolution. It will be my fault if you escape, until I myself declare your freedom. I trust that you will not render it necessary that we should use force to place you in the chamber assigned for you."

"Force!" he exclaimed fiercely, and there was a keen momentary flashing of the youth's eye, as he heard these words,

that proved him a person to resent as quickly as he felt but
the emotion soon gave way to another of more controlling influence. His tone changed to mildness, as he proceeded :—

"No, sir; no force shall be necessary. Lead me where you
please. Do with me as you please. I know not whether it
would not be better and wiser for me, henceforward, to forego
my own will and wishes altogether. God knows it had been
far better and wiser, had I distrusted them half as much hitherto as I now distrust them. I had now—but, lead on, sir; conduct me as you will, and where you will. I will not trouble
you longer—even with my despondency. It is base enough to
be humbled as I am now—I will not further debase myself by
the idle language of regret. I have put down a boy's stake in
he foolish game which I have played—I will bear with its
loss as a man. I will go before you, sir, or follow even as you
desire. It shall not be necessary to employ violence. I am
ready."

We could not help pitying the youth, as we conducted him
up stairs into the small garret-room, which had been prepared
for him. He was evidently of noble stuff at first—naturally
well fashioned in mind and moral—with instincts, which, but
for circumstances, would have carried him right—and feelings
gentle and noble enough to have wrought excellence within
him, could it have been that he had been blessed with a better
education, and less doubtful associates, than it was his fortune
to have found. He certainly rose greatly in my esteem within
the last two hours, simply by the propriety of his manners, and
the degree of correct feeling with which he had, without any
ostentation, coupled their exhibition. Securing the windows
as well as we could, and placing a sturdy and confidential servant at the door of the chamber, which was double-locked upon
him, we descended to the lower apartment, where we immediately proceeded to confer upon the other toils before us.

"There is some public good," said Colonel Grafton, with a
degree of composure, which spoke admirably for the control
which his mind had over his feelings—"there is some public
good coming from the personal evil which has fallen to my lot
The proposed festival, which was this night to have taken place,
brings together the very friends, as guests, whom I should have

sought in our proposed adventure to-morrow, and whom it would have taken me some time to have hunted up, and got in readiness. Our party was to have been large, and I trust that it will be, though the occasion now is so much less loving and attractive than was expected."

This was said with some bitterness, and a pause ensued, in which Grafton turned away from me and proceeded to the window. When he returned, he had succeeded quite in obliterating the traces of that grief which he was evidently unwilling that his face should show. He continued :—

"We shall certainly have some fifteen able-bodied and fearless men, not including ourselves; there may be more. Some of them will, I am sure, bring their weapons; they have done so usually; and, for the rest, I can make out to supply them, I think. You shall see I have a tolerable armory, which though anything but uniform, can be made to do mischief in the hands of men able and willing enough when occasion serves to use it. There is a rifle or two, an old musket, two excellent double-barrelled guns, and a few pistols, all of which can be made use of. You, I believe, are already well provided."

I showed him my state of preparation, and he then proceeded :—

"I know the region where these fellows harbor, much better than you do, and, perhaps, much more intimately than they imagine. My plan is to surprise them by daybreak. If we can do this, our fifteen or twenty men will be more than a match for their thirty And then, I trust, we have no less an advantage in the sort of men we bring to the conflict; men of high character, and among the most resolute of the surrounding country. I have no doubt that we shall be able to destroy at least one half of them, and disperse the rest. We must strike at your master-spirits—your Foster and your Webber—though the former, according to your account, seems not without his good qualities. The latter is a tough villain, but he fears me, deny it as he may. If he did not, having such a feeling toward me as he has so openly avowed, he would have drawn trigger on me before now. I must endeavor, this time, to wipe out old scores, and balance all my accounts with him. These two, and one or two more provided for, and we may be content with the dispersion of the rest. I care nothing for the pitiful rascals that follow — let them go."

But such was not my thought. There was one of these pitiful rascals whom it brought the scarlet to my cheek to think on. Brother though he was, he was the murderer of William Carrington, and I had sworn, and neither he nor Pickett could escape, according to my oath. But of this I said nothing to Colonel Grafton. I was resolved that John Hurdis should perish, but that he should perish namelessly. There was a family pride still working in my breast, that counselled me to be silent in respect to him. We proceeded in our arrangements.

"There are two fellows, belonging to this clan," said Grafton; "that lodge, if I recollect rightly what you said, some two miles below me."

"Yes, at a place called 'the Trap-Hole,' if you know such a spot. It was described to me so that I could find it easily, but I know nothing of it."

"I know it well — it's an old hiding-place ; but I had not thought the hovel was inhabited. These fellows must be secured to-night at an early hour. They are spies upon us, I doubt not, and will report everything that happens, if they see anything unusual. Certainly, it is our policy to clear our own course as well and speedily as possible ; and as soon as our men come, which will be by dark or before, we will set forth as secretly as we may to take them into custody. This, as you have the signs which they acknowledge, can be done without risk. You shall go before, and set them at rest, while we surround the house and take them suddenly. They will hardly lift weapon when they see our force ; and, once in our possession, we will take a lesson from the book of Master Webber, and rope them down in the woods, with a handful of moss in their mouths to keep them from unnecessary revelations."

Such, so far, was our contemplated plan. It was the most direct of any, and, indeed, we hardly had a choice of expedients. To come upon our enemy by surprise, or in force, was all that we could do, having so little time allowed us for preparation of any sort. It was fortunate that we had a man like Grafton to manage — a man so well esteemed by the friends he led, and so worthy in all respects of the confidence they put in him. As the hour drew nigh, and the looked-for guests began to assemble, he rose superior to the paternal situation in which he stood, and seemed to suppress the father in the man and citizen. He revealed separately to each of his guests the affair as it now stood, upon which they had been summoned together, then submitted the new requisition which he made upon their services, as a friend and magistrate alike. With one voice they proclaimed themselves ready to go forth against the common enemy, and with difficulty were restrained from precipitating the assault; changing the hour to midnight from the dawn. This rashness was fortunately overruled—though it could scarcely have been thought rashness, if all the men had possessed an equal knowledge with Colonel Grafton, of the place in which the outlaws harbored. To quiet the more impetuous among his guests, he led them out after dark, in obedience to our previous resolve, to take the two fellows at "the Trap-Hole," and, I may say, in brief, that we succeeded to a tittle in making them prisoners just as we had arranged it. Surprise was never more complete. We roped them to saplings in a thicket of the woods, filled their mouths with green moss, and the arms of which we despoiled them, enabled us the better to meet their comrades.

CHAPTER LII.

ANOTHER VICTIM.

> "Had we never loved so kindly,
> Had we never loved so blindly—
> Never met or never parted,
> We had ne'er been broken-hearted!"—BURNS.

WE completed our preparations at an early hour, and by midnight were ready to depart on our work of peril. We had so arranged it as not to go forth *en masse;* it was feared that, if seen, our array would occasion apprehension, and possibly lead to a detection and defeat of all our plans. By twos and threes, therefore, our men set forth, at different periods, with the understanding that, taking different routes, we were all to rendezvous at the "Day-Blind," by one o'clock, or two, at farthest. The onslaught we proposed to make with the first blush of the morning. I remained, with two others, behind with Colonel Grafton, until the designated hour drew nigh; then, with emotions exciting in the last degree, and greatly conflicting with each other, I mounted my steed, and we took our departure for the place agreed on.

Let us now return, for a few moments, to the unhappy maiden, whose bridal-night was so suddenly changed to gloom from festivity. We were permitted to see nothing of her sorrows. When first stricken by the intelligence which her father gave of her felon-lover, her grief had shown itself in a single, sudden shriek, a fainting-fit, and, for some time after, a complete prostration of all her physical powers. Restorative medicines were given her, and it was only when she was believed to be in a deep and refreshing slumber, that her mother retired to her own apartment.

But the maiden did not sleep. The medicines had failed to work for her that oblivion, that momentary blindness and forgetfulness, which they were charitably intended to occasion. The desire to relieve her mother's anxiety, which she witnessed led her to an undoubted effort at composure, and she subdued her sorrows so far as to put on the aspect of a quiet, apathetic condition, which she was very far from enjoying. She seemed to sleep, and, as the hour was late, her mother, availing herself of the opportunity, retired for the night, leaving her daughter in charge of a favorite nurse, who remained in the apartment.

Julia who was no less watchful than suffering, soon discovered that her companion slept. She rose gently, and hurried on her clothes. Her very sorrows strengthened her for an effort totally inconsistent with her prostration but a little while before; and the strange and perilous circumstances in which Eberly stood prompted her to a degree of artfulness which was alike foreign to her nature and education. The seeming necessity of the case could alone furnish its excuse. She believed that the life of the youth was jeoparded by his position. In the first feeling of anger, her father had declared him to be liable to the last punishments of the law, and, in the same breath, avowed himself, as an honest magistrate, bound to inflict them. She was resolved, if possible, to defeat this resolution, and to save the unhappy youth, whom, if she might no longer look upon with respect, she, at least, was still compelled to love. Without impugning the judgment of her father, she felt the thought to be unendurable which told her momently of the extreme peril of the criminal; and, under its impulse, she was nerved to a degree of boldness and strength quite unlike the submissive gentleness which usually formed the most conspicuous feature in her character and deportment.

We have already seen that it was no part of Grafton's desire, whatever might be the obnoxiousness of Eberly to the laws, to bring him to trial. Though evidently connected with the banditti that infested the country, and, strictly speaking, liable to all the consequences of their crimes, yet the evidence had been conclusive to Grafton that the unhappy youth had shared in none of their performances. Could he have proved specifically any one offence against him, Grafton must have brought him to punishment, and would have done so, though his heart writhed at its own resolution; but it was with a feeling of relief, if not

of pleasure, that he found no such evidence, and felt himself
morally if not legally freed from the necessity of prosecution.
which such a knowledge must have brought with it. To secure
Eberly until his late associates were dispersed or destroyed
was the simple object of his detention ; for, to speak frankly, it
was Grafton's fear that, if suffered to go forth, he might still be
carried back, by the desperate force of circumstances, to the
unholy connections from which he had voluntarily withdrawn
himself. He had no confidence in the avowed resolutions of
the youth, and deemed it not improbable that, as his repentance seemed originally to have been the result of his attachment to Julia, the legitimate consequence of her rejection would
be to throw him back upon his old principles and associates.
But this doubt did injustice to the youth. The evil aspects of
crime had disgusted him enough, even if the loveliness of vir
tue had failed to persuade him. His resolution was fixed ; and,
considering his moral claims alone, without reference to the
exactions of society, it may be safely said that never was Eberly more worthy of the love of Julia Grafton than at the very
moment when it was lost to him for ever.

With cautious hands she undid the fastening of her apartment, and, trembling at every step, but still resolute, she as-
cended the stairs which led up to the garret-chambers. In one
of these Eberly was confined. From this—as there was but a
single window, to leap from which would have been certain
death—there was no escape, save by the door, and this was
securely fastened on the outside, and the key in the possession
of a faithful negro, to whom Colonel Grafton had given particular instructions for the safe-keeping of the prisoner. But the
guardian slept on his post, and it was not difficult for Julia to
detach the key from where it hung, upon the fore-finger of his
outstretched hand : this she did without disturbing him in the
slightest degree. In another moment she unclosed the door,
and fearlessly entered the chamber.

"Julia !" was the exclamation of the prisoner, as, with a fresh
sentiment of joy and love, he beheld her standing before him.
"Julia, dear Julia, do I indeed behold you? You have not
then forgotten—you do not then scorn the wretch who is an
outcast from all beside?"

He approached her. Her finger waved him back, while she replied, in melancholy accents:—

"Clifton, you must fly! You are in danger — your very life is endangered, if you linger here."

"My life?" cried the criminal, in tones of melancholy despair,—"my life? Let them take it! If I must leave you, Julia, I care not to live. Go to your father — let him bring the executioner — you will see that I will not shrink from the defiling halter and the cruel death — nay, that I will smile at their approach, when I am once assured that I can not live for you."

"And you cannot!" said the maiden, in sad but firm accents. "You must forget that thought, Clifton — that wish — if, indeed, it be your wish. You must forget me, as it shall now be the chief task of my life to forget you."

"And can you, Julia — can you forget me, after those hours of joy — those dear walks, and the sweet delights of so many precious and never-to-be-forgotten meetings? Can you forget them, Julia? Nay, can you desire to forget them? If you can — if such be, indeed, your desire — then death shall be doubly welcome — death in any form. But I can not believe it, Julia — I will not. I remember — but no! I will not remind you — I will not seek to remind you, when you declare your desire to forget. Why have you sought me here, Julia? Know you not what I am? have you not been told what the world calls me — what the malice of my cruel fortune has compelled me to become? Have you not heard? must I tell you that I am —"

"Hush!" she exclaimed, in faltering and expostulating accents; "say it not, Clifton — say it not. If, indeed, it be true, as they told me —"

"They have told you, then, Julia? your father has told you? and, oh, joy of my heart! you ask of me if what they have said to you can be true. You doubt — you can not believe it of me. You shall not believe it —"

"Then it is not true, Clifton?" cried the maiden eagerly, advancing as she spoke, while the tear which glistened in her eyes took from her whole features the glow of that joy and hope which had sprung up so suddenly in her bosom. "They

have slandered you when they pronounced you the associate
of these outlaws; it is a wanton, a malicious falsehood, which
you can easily disprove? I knew it—I thought it from the
first, Clifton; and yet, when my father told me, and told me
with such assurances, with such solemn looks and words, and
upon such evidence—ah! Edward, forgive me, when I confess
to you I could not doubt what I yet dreaded and trembled to
believe. But you deny it, Edward; you will prove it to my
father's conviction to be false; you will cleanse yourself from
this polluting stigma, and I feel, I hope, we shall be happy yet
My father—"

The chilling accents of her lover's voice recalled her from the
hopeful dream which her young heart began to fancy. He
dashed the goblet of delight from the parting lips which were
just about to quaff from its golden circle.

"Alas, Julia, it is only too true! your father has told you
but the truth. Bitter is the necessity that makes me say so
much;· but, I will not deceive you; indeed. if he told you all,
he must have told you tha ' came of my own free will to un-
deceive him. My own lips pronounced to him my own fault,
and, humbling as its consciousness is to me, I must declare that,
in avowing my connection with these wretched associates, I
have avowed the extent of my errors, though not of my sufferings. Thank God! I have taken part in none of their crimes;
I have shared in none of their spoils; my hands are free from
any stain save that which they have received from grasping
theirs in fellowship. This, I well know, is a stain too much,
and the contact of my hands would only defile the purity of
yours. Yet, could I tell you the story of wo and suffering which
drove me to this miserable extremity, you would pity me, Julia,
if you could not altogether forgive. But wherefore should I
tell you this?"

"Wherefore!" was the moaning exclamation of the maiden,
as the youth briefly paused in his speech, "wherefore?—it
avails us nothing! Yet, I will believe you, Clifton; I must believe that you have been driven to this dreadful communion, if
I would not sink under the shame of my own consciousness. I
believe you, Edward—I believe you, and I pity you—from
my very soul I pity you. But I can no more: let us part now

Leave me — fly, while there is yet time ! My father returns in the morning, and I fear that his former regard for you will not be sufficient to save you from the punishment which he thinks due to your offences. Indeed, he will even be more strict and severe because of the imposition which he thinks you have practised upon him—"

"And upon you, Julia: you say nothing of that."

"Nothing ! because it should weigh nothing with me at such a moment. I feel not the scorn which you have put upon me, Edward, in the loss which follows it."

"Blessed, beloved spirit ! and I, too, must feel the loss; and such a loss ! Oh, blind, base fool that I was, to suffer the pang and the apprehension of a moment to baffle the hopes and the happiness of a life ! Ah, Julia, how can I fly ? how can I leave you, knowing what you are, and not forgetting that you have loved me, worthless as I am ?"

"No more of this, Edward," replied the maiden, quickly withdrawing her hand from the grasp which his own had passionately taken upon it—"no more of this; it will be your policy, as it shall be my duty, to forget all this. We must strive to forget — *we must* forget each other. It will be my first prayer always to be able to forget what it must only be my constant shame and sorrow to remember."

"And why your shame and sorrow, Julia ? I tell you that, in connecting myself most unhappily with these wretched people, I have abstained from their offences. If they have robbed the traveller, I have taken none of their spoils; if they have murdered their victim, his blood is not upon my hands. I have been their victim, indeed, rather than their ally. They forced me — a dire necessity forced me — into their communion, in which I have been a witness rather than a partaker."

"Alas ! Edward, I am afraid the difference is but too slight to be made use of in your defence. Did you witness to condemn and disapprove ? did you seek to prevent or repair ? did you stay the uplifted hand which struck down the traveller ? did you place yourself on his side to sustain and help him in the moment of his deadly and last peril ? My father would have taken this part—his lessons have always taught me that such was the part always of the brave and honorable gentleman. If

you have taken this part, Edward; if you can prove to him
that you have taken this part—"

She paused. The criminal shrunk from her while she spoke,
and covered his face with his hands, while he murmured hoarsely, and in bitter, broken accents—

"I have not. I have seen him robbed of his little wealth
I have seen him stricken down by the unexpected blow; and 1
have not lifted voice or weapon in his defence. Basely have I
witnessed the deeds of baseness, and fittingly base should be
my punishment. And yet, Julia, I could say that—will you
hear me?" he demanded, seeing that she turned away.

"Speak, speak," she murmured faintly.

"Yes, Julia, I have that to say which would go far to make
you forget and forgive my weakness—my crime."

"Alas! Edward, I fear not. There is nothing—"

"Nothing! nay, Julia, you care not to hear my defence!
you are indifferent whether I live or die—whether they prove
me guilty or innocent of crime!" said he, with a bitter manner
of reproach. She answered with a heart-touching meekness:

"And yet I come even now to save your life. I throw aside
the fears and delicacy of my sex—I seek you at midnight,
Edward—I seek you but to save. Does this argue indifference?"

"To save my life! Oh, Julia, bethink you for a moment
what a precious boon this is to one of whom you rob everything
which made life dear, at the very moment when you profess to
save it. This is a mockery—a sad, a cruel mockery! Let
them take the life, if they will: you will see how that boon is
valued by me, to which you offer to prove that you are not indifferent. You will see how readily I can surrender the life
which the withdrawal of your love has beggared—which the
denial of your esteem has embittered for ever!"

"Ah, Edward, speak not thus! Wherefore would you force
me to say that my love is not to be denied nor my esteem withheld, by a will, or in an instant?"

"And you do still love—you will promise, Julia, to esteem
me yet—"

"No! I will promise nothing, Edward—nothing. I will
strive only to forget you; and though I promise not myself to

be successful in the effort, duty requires that it should yet be made. Go, now. Let us part, and for ever! My father and his guests are all gone; there is none to interrupt you in your flight. Fly — fly far, Edward, I pray you. Let us not meet again, since nothing but pain could come from such a meeting."

"But, Julia, will you not promise me that if I can acquit myself worthily, you will once more receive me?"

"I can not. My father's will must determine mine, Edward, since it is to his judgment only that I can refer, to determine what is worthy in the sight of men and what is not. Were I to yield to my affections this decision, I should, perhaps, care nothing for your offences; I should deem you no offender; and Love would blindly worship at an altar from which Truth would turn away in sorrow and reproach. Urge me not further, Edward, on this painful subject. Solemnly I declare to you, that, under no circumstances henceforward, can I know you, unless by permission of my father."

Eberly strode away, with a spasmodic effort, to another part of the chamber. His emotions left him speechless for a while. When he returned to her, his articulation was still imperfect and it was only by great resolution that he made himself intelligible at last : —

"I will vex you no more. I will be to you, Julia, nothing — even as you wish. I will leave you; and when next you hear of me, you will weep, bitterly weep; not, perhaps, that you have sent me from you in scorn, but that I was not wholly worthy of that love which you were once happy to bestow upon me."

He passed her as he spoke these words, and, before she could fix any one of the flitting and confused fancies in her mind, he had left the apartment, and her ear could readily distinguish his footsteps, as, without any of the precautions of the fugitive, trembling for his life, he deliberately descended the stairs. She grasped the post of the door, and hung on it for support. Her strength, which had sustained her throughout the interview, was about to leave her. When she ceased to hear his retreating steps, she recovered herself sufficiently to reach her chamber; where, after locking carefully her door, she threw herself, almost without life, upon her bed, and gave vent to those emotions which now, from long restraint, like the accumulated torrent

and overwhelm the region which they were meant to invigorate and refresh. One bitter sentence of hopelessness alone escaped her lips; and the unsyllabled moaning which followed it attested the depth of these sorrows which she had so long and nobly kept in check : —

"He leaves me — I have seen him for the last time — I have heard his departing footsteps — departing for ever! Hark! it is the tread of a horse. It is his. He flies — he is safe from harm. He will be free, he will be happy, and I — O my father — I am desolate!"

CHAPTER LIII.

CONCLUSION.

"——— If thou couldst redeem me
With anything but death, I think I should
Consent to live."—*The Traitor.*

MEANWHILE, we sped toward our place of rendezvous. We reached it, as we had calculated, in sufficient season. The whole party was assembled at the "Blind," according to arrangement, and within the limited hour; and for a brief period after our reunion, nothing was to be heard but the hum of preparation for the anticipated strife. Our weapons, as before stated, were of a motley description. But they were all effective; at least we resolved that they should be made so. Leaving as little to accident as possible, we reloaded and reprimed our firearms, put in new flints, where we could do so, and girded ourselves up for the contest with the cool considerateness of men who are not disposed to shrink back from the good work to which they have so far put their hands. Encouraged by the feeling and energy of Colonel Grafton, who was very much beloved among them, there was not one of the party who did not throw as much personal interest into the motives for his valor as entered either into Grafton's bosom or mine.

When we were all ready, we divided ourselves into three bodies, providing thus an assailing force for the three known outlets of the outlaws' retreat. One of these bodies was led by Grafton, and, under his lead, and by his side, I rode. To two sturdy farmers of the neighborhood, who were supposed to be more conversant with the place than the rest, the other divisions were given; and it was arranged that our attack upon the three designated points should be as nearly simultaneous as possible. The darkness of the forest—the difficulty of deter-

mining and equalizing the several distances—the necessity of
proceeding slowly and heedfully, in order to avoid giving alarm
—and other considerations and difficulties of like nature and
equal moment—rendered our advance tedious and protracted;
and, though we had not more than two miles to cover after sep-
arating at the "Blind," yet the gray streaks of the early dawn
were beginning to vein the hazy summits in the east before we
reached the point of entrance which had been assigned us.

The morning was cold and cloudy, and through the misty
air sounds were borne rapidly and far. We were forced to continue our caution as we proceeded. When we reached the valley, the porch, as it were, to the home among the hills where
the robbers had found their refuge, we came to a dead halt.
There were slight noises from within the enclosure which annoyed us, and we paused to listen. They were only momentary, however, and we rode slowly forward, until the greater
number of our little party were fairly between the two hills.
In my anxiety, I had advanced a horse's length beyond Colonel
Grafton, by whose side I had before ridden. We were just about
to emerge from the passage into the area, when the indistinct
figure of a man started up, as it were, from beneath the very
hoofs of my horse. I had nearly ridden over him, for the day
was yet too imperfect to enable us to distinguish between objects not in motion. He had been asleep, and was, most probably, a sentinel. As he ran, he screamed at the loudest pitch
of his voice; the probability is, that in his surprise he had left
his weapon where he had lain, and had no other means of
alarming his comrades, and saving them from the consequences
of his neglectful watch. In the midst of his clamors, I silenced
him. I shot him through the back as he ran, not five steps in
front of my horse, seeking to ascend the hill to the right of us.
He tumbled forward, and lay writhing before our path, but
without a word or moan. At this moment, the thought possessed me, that it was John Hurdis whom I had shot. I shivered involuntarily with the conviction, and in my mind I felt a
busy voice of reproach, that reminded me of our poor mother.
I strove to sustain myself, by referring to his baseness, and to
his deserts, yet I felt sick at heart the while. I had the stran-
est curiosity to look into the face of the victim, but for worlds

I would not then have done so. It was proposed that we should examine the body by one of the men behind me. It was a voice of desperation with which I shouted in reply :—

"No—no examination! We have no time for that!"

"True!" said Grafton, taking up the words. "We must think of living, not dead enemies. This shot will put the gang in motion. We must rush on them at once, if we hope to do anything, and the sooner we go forward the better."

He gave the word at this moment, which I seconded with a fierce shout, which was half-intended to overcome and scare away my own obtrusive fancies.

"Better," I said to myself—"better that I should believe John Hurdis to be already slain, than that I should think the duty yet to be done. He must perish, and I feel that it will be an easier deed to slay him while he is unknown, regarding him merely as one of the common enemy."

These self-communings—indeed, the whole events which had occasioned them—were all the work of a moment. I had fired the pistol under the impulse which seemed to follow the movement of the victim, as closely as if it had been a certain consequence of it. In another instant we rushed headlong into the valley, just as sounds of fright and confusion reached us from one of the opposite entrances, which had been assigned the other parties. There was now no time for unnecessary reflections— the moment for thought and hesitation had gone by, and the blood was boiling and bounding in my veins, with all the ardor and enthusiasm of boyhood. Wild cries of apprehension and encouragement reached us from various quarters, and we could see sudden forms rushing out of the bushes, and from between the hollows where they had slept; and with the sight of them, our men dashed off in various directions, and divided in pursuit. Colonel Grafton and myself advanced in like manner toward a group consisting of three persons, who seemed disposed to seek, rather than fly, from us. A few bounds brought us near enough to discover in one of these, the person of Matthew Webber.

The two deadly enemies were now within a few steps of each other; and, resolving to spare Colonel Grafton the encounter with a man who had professed such utter malice toward him

and such a blood-thirsty and unrelenting hate, I put spurs to my
horse, and, with earnest efforts, endeavored to put myself between
them; but my object was defeated, and I was soon taught to
know that I required all my address to manage my own particular
opponent.

This was the man whom we have before seen as the emissary
of the brotherhood, at the habitation of Pickett, and, subsequently,
when I left the encampment, ostensibly as the spy upon
Eberly. This fellow seemed to understand my object for he
put himself directly in my way, and, when not three steps distant, discharged his pistol at my head. How he came to miss
me, I know not. It would appear impossible that a man, resolved and deliberate as he certainly showed himself then and
elsewhere to be, should have failed to shoot me at so small a
distance. But he did; and, without troubling myself at that
moment to demand how or why, I was resolved not to miss him.
I did not.

But my bullet, though more direct than his, was not fatal. I
hit him in the shoulder of the right arm, from the hand of which
he dropped the knife which he had taken from his bosom, the
moment after firing his pistol. My horse was upon him in another instant; but, as if insensible to his wound, he grasped the
bridle with his remaining hand, and, by extending his arm to its
utmost stretch, he baffled me, for a brief space, in the effort
which I was making to take a second shot. It was but a moment only, however, that he did so. I suffered him to turn the
head of the horse, and deliberately took a second pistol from my
bosom.

He sunk under the breast of the animal as he beheld it, still
grasping him by the bridle, by swinging from which he was enabled to avoid the tramplings of his feet. But I was not to be
defeated. I threw myself from the animal, and shot the outlaw
dead, before he could extricate himself from the position into which
he had thrown himself.

This affair took less time to act than I now employ to narrate
it. Meanwhile, the strife between Colonel Grafton and Webber had proceeded to a fatal issue. I had beheld its progress
with painful apprehensions, beholding the danger of the noble
gentleman, without the ability to serve or succor him. On

their **first encounter, the** deliberate ruffian calmly awaited the bold assault **of his foe, and, perhaps,** feeling some doubt **of his** weapon in aiming at the **smaller object, or, resolved** to make sure of him, though **slow, he** directed his pistol muzzle at the advancing steed, and put the bullet into **his breast. The animal** tumbled forward, and Webber, nimbly **leaping to one** side, **avoided** his crushing carcass, which fell over upon the very spot where the outlaw had taken his station.

In the fall of the beast, as Webber had anticipated, Grafton **became** entangled. **One of** his legs was fastened **under** the animal, **and he lay prostrate and immovable for an** instant, from **the stunning effect of the fall. With a grim** smile of triumph, Webber **approached him, and when not three paces** distant from his enemy, **drew his pistol, but before he could fix** the sight upon him, **a fierce wild scream rang through the** area, **and in the** next instant, **when nothing beside could** have saved Grafton, **and when looking fearlessly at his advancing enemy,** he momently expected **the death which he felt himself unable to avoid,** he beheld, **with no less satisfaction and surprise, the** figure **of** the doubly fugitive **Clifton bounding** between them, **to arrest** the threatened shot. **He came too late** for this, **yet** he baffled **the vengeance of the murderer. The** bullet took effect **in his own** bosom, **and he fell down between Grafton and** Webber, expiating **his errors and offenses, whatever may have been their** nature and extent, **by freely yielding up his life to save that of** one, who **just before, as he imagined to the last, had sat in** inflexible **and hostile judgment upon his own. A faint smile** illuminated his **countenance a moment before his** death, **and** he seemed desirous **to turn his eyes where** Grafton **lay,** but **to this** task he was unequal. **Once or twice he** made an effort at speech, **but** his voice sunk away **into a gurgling** sound, and, at length, terminated in the choking rattle **of** death.

Webber, **while yet the breath** fluttered upon the lips **of his** victim, **strode forward, with one foot upon his** body, to repeat the assault **upon Grafton, which had been baffled thus, but** before he **could do** this, **he fell by an unseen hand. He** was levelled to the earth **by a stroke from the butt of a** rifle from behind, and despatched, in the heat **of the moment, by a second** blow **from** the hands of the sturdy **forester who wielded it.**

We extricated Grafton from a situation which had been productive to him of so much peril, and addressed ourselves to a pursuit of the surviving outlaws, who were scattered and flying on all hands. In this pursuit it fell to my lot to inflict death, without recognizing my victim at the time, upon the actual murderer of William Carrington. I saw a fellow skulk behind a bush, and shot him through it. That was Pickett. I only knew it when, in the afternoon of the day, we encountered his wife, with countenance seemingly unmoved, and wearing its general expression of rigid gravity, directing the burial of her miserable husband, whom a couple of negroes were preparing to deposit in a grave dug near the spot where he had fallen.

But our toils were not ended. Seven of the outlaws had been killed outright, or so fatally wounded as to die very soon after. Two only were made prisoners; and we had started at least eight or ten more. These had taken flight in as many different directions, rendering it necessary that we should disperse ourselves in their pursuit. My blood had been heated by the affray to such a degree that I ceased to think. To go forward, to act, to shout, and strike, seemed now all that I could do; and these were performances through which my heart appeared to carry me with an ungovernable sensation of delight—a sensation cooled only when I reflected that the body of John Hurdis had not yet been found — that we were in pursuit of the survivors, and that I had sworn by the grave of the hapless Emmeline Walker, to give no mercy to the murderers of my friend. My oath was there to impel me forward, even should my heart fail me, and forward I went in the bloody chase; we urged, having a distant and imperfect view of two wretches, both mounted, and fleeing backward upon the Big Warrior. They had gone through the "Blind," and for a mile farther I kept them both in sight. At length, one disappeared, but I gained upon the other. Every moment brought the outlines of his person more clearly to my eye, and, at length, I could no longer resist the conviction that the fates had brought me to my victim. John Hurdis was before me.

What would I not then have given to have found another enemy. How gladly would I then have unsworn myself, and, could it be so, have given up the task of punishment to other persons.

There was a sound of horsemen behind me, and at one moment, I almost resolved to turn aside and leave to my comrades the solemn duty which now seemed so especially to devolve itself upon me. But there was a dread in my mind that such a movement might be misconstrued, and the feeling be taken for fear, which was in strict truth the creature of conscience. The conviction grew inevitable that the bloody duty of the executioner was mine. The horse of my brother stumbled; the fates had delivered him into my hands—he lay on the earth before me; and, with a bursting heart, but a resolved spirit, I leaped down on the earth beside him. He had weapons, but he had no power to use them. I would have given worlds had he been able to do so. Could he have shown fight—I could have slain him without scruple; but when, at my approach, he raised his hands appealingly, and shrieked out a prayer of mercy, I felt ashamed of the duty I had undertaken. I felt the brutal blood-thirstiness of taking life under such circumstances—the victim but a few paces off—using no weapons, and pleading with a shrieking desperate voice for that life, which seemed at the same time too despicable to demand or deserve a care.

And yet, when I reflected that to grant his prayer and take him alive, was not to save his life, but to subject him to a death, in the ignominy of which I too must share, I felt that he could not live. I rushed upon him with the extended pistol, but was prevented from using it by a singular vision, in the sudden appearance of the poor idiot daughter of Pickett. She came from the door of a little cottage by the road-side, which I had not before seen, and to which, it is more than probable, that John Hurdis was bending his steps, as to a place of refuge. To my horror and surprise she called me by name, and thus gave my brother the first intimation which he had of the person to whom he prayed. How this idiot came to discover that which nobody besides had suspected, was wonder enough to me; and while I stood, astounded for the instant, she ran forward like a thoughtless child, crying as she came :—

"Oh, Mr. Richard, don't you shoot—it's Master John—it's your own dear brother—don't you shoot—don't."

"Brother!" cried the miserable wretch, with hoarse and husky tones, followed by a chuckle of laughter, which indicated the latent hope which had begun to kindle in his breast at this discovery.

"Away—I know you not, villain," was my cry as I recoiled from him, and again lifted the pistol in deadly aim. The idiot girl rushed between us, and rising on tiptoe, sought to grasp the extended hand, which I was compelled to raise above her reach.

"Run, Master John, run for dear life," was her cry, as she clung upon my shoulders. "Run to the bushes, while I hold Mr. Richard—I'll hold him tight—he can't get away from me. I'll hold him tight enough while you run."

The miserable dastard obeyed her counsel; and while clinging, now to my arms, and now to my legs, she baffled my movements, and really gave him an opportunity, which a cool, brave fellow would have turned to account, and most probably saved himself. He, in his alarm, actually rushed into the woods, in the very direction of the pursuit. Had he possessed the spirit of a man, he would have leaped upon his horse, or upon mine, and trusted to the chase a second time. Hardly a minute had elapsed from his disappearance in the woods, and when I had just extricated myself from the clutches of the girl, which I did with as little violence as possible, when I heard one shot and then another. I resumed my horse and hurried to the spot whence the sounds came. One of our party, who had taken the same route with me, had overtaken the fugitive, and had fired twice upon him as he fled. My voice trembled when I asked the trooper, as he emerged from the bush, if the outlaw was dead.

"As a door-nail!" was the reply. I stopped for no more, but turning the head of my horse again, I renewed the pursuit of the second fugitive, whom I had first followed. My companion kept with me, and we went forward at full speed. As we rode we heard the faint accents of the idiot girl crying in the woods for "Master John;" as, here and there, she wound her way through its recesses, seeking for him who could no longer answer to her call. The sounds were painful to me, and I was glad to get out of hearing of them. I had now none of those scruples in the pursuit which had beset me before. My trial was over; and fervently in my heart did I thank God, and the stout fellow who rode beside me, that my hand had not stricken the cruel blow which was yet demanded by justice. I urged my horse to the utmost and soon left my companion behind. I felt that I must gain upon the footsteps of the fugitive. There were few horses in the country of better bottom, and more unrelaxing speed than mine. He proved himself on this occasion. Through bog and branch, he sped; over hill, through dale, until the road opened in double breadth upon us. The trees grew more sparsely—the undergrowth was more dense in patches, and it was evident that we had nearly reached the river. In another moment I caught a glimpse, not of it only, but of the man I pursued; and he was Foster. He looked round once; and I fancied I could detect a smile playing on his lips. I felt loth to trouble this strange fellow. He was a generous outlaw, and possessed many good qualities. He had given me freely of his money, though counterfeit, and had shown me a degree of kindness and consideration, which made me hesitate, now that I had brought him to the post. I concluded it to be impossible that he should escape me, and I summoned him with loud tones to surrender, under a promise which I made him, of using all my efforts and influence to save him from the consequences of the laws. But he laughed aloud, and pointed to the river.

"He will not venture to swim it surely," was my thought on the instant. A few moments satisfied my doubts. There was a pile of cotton, consisting of ten or fifteen bags, lying on the brink of the river, and ready for transportation to market whenever the boats came by. He threw himself from his horse as he reached the bags, and tumbling one of them from the pile into the stream, he leaped boldly upon it, and when I reached the same spot, the current had already carried him full forty yards on his way, down the stream.* I discharged my pistol at him but without any hope of touching him at that distance. He laughed good-naturedly in return, and cried out—

"Ah, Williams, you are a sad dog, and something more of a hypocrite than the parson. I am afraid you will come to no good, if you keep on after this fashion; but should you ever

---

* This is a fact; such a mode of escape would not readily suggest itself to a romancer's invention, but it did to that of a very great rogue.

get into a difficulty like this of mine, I am still sufficiently your friend to hope that you may find as good a float. You can say to the owner of this cotton—a man named Baxter, who, I suppose, is one of your party this morning—that he will find it some five miles below; I shall not want it much farther. Should he lose it, however, it's as little as a good patriot—as it is said he is—should be ready at any time to lose for his country. Farewell—though it be for a season only. We shall meet some day in Arkansas, where I shall build a church in the absence of better business, and perhaps make you a convert. Farewell."

Colonel Grafton came up in time to hear the last of this discourse; and to wonder and laugh at the complacent impudence and ready thoughts of the outlaw. Foster pulled his hat, with a polite gesture, when he had finished speaking, and turned his eyes from us in the direction which his strange craft was taking.

"Shall I give him a shot, colonel?" demanded one of the foresters, who had come up with Grafton, lifting his rifle as he spoke.

"No, no!" was the reply—"let him go. He is a clever scoundrel and may one day become an honest man. We have done enough of this sort of business this morning, to keep the whole neighborhood honest for some years. Let us now return, my friends, and bury those miserable creatures out of sight. Hurdis!" He took me suddenly aside from the rest, and said:

"Hurdis, there is a girl back here, who says that you have killed your own brother. She affirms it positively."

"She speaks falsely, Colonel Grafton," was my reply; "I am not guilty of a brother's blood; and yet I may say to you that she has spoken a portion of the truth. A brother of mine has been killed among the outlaws. Guilty or not guilty of their offences, he pays the penalty of bad company. If you please we will speak of him no more."

I had been married to Mary Easterby about three years, when one day who should pay us a visit but Colonel Grafton and the lovely Julia, the latter far more lovely than ever. Her sorrows had sublimed her beauty, and seemed to give elevation to all her thoughts and actions. The worm was gnawing at her heart, and its ravages were extending to her frame; but her cheek, though pale, was exquisitely transparent, and her eye, though always sad, was sometimes enlivened with the fires of an intense spirituality which seemed to indicate the approximation of her thoughts to the spheres and offices of a loftier home than ours. She lived but a year after this visit, and died in a sweet sleep, which lasted for several hours, without being disturbed by pain, and from which she only awakened in another world. May we hope that the loves were happy there which had been so unblessed on earth.

THE END.